PRAISE FOR THE DEAD OF NIGHT

Jean Rabe always manages to surprise and never fails to deliver the goods! THE DEAD OF NIGHT has plenty of twists and turns. Highly recommended!

—Jonathan Maberry, *New York Times* bestselling author of *Dogs of War* and *Mars One*

Jean Rabe writes the perfect mystery! I was kept guessing about *everything* to the very last word. Great characters. The girl can write!

—*New York Times* bestselling author Faith Hunter, writing as Gwen Hunter

In THE DEAD OF NIGHT, Jean Rabe gives us another compelling Piper Blackwell mystery. After a clandestine meeting with a grizzled WWII veteran "Mark the Shark," also known as "Mr. Conspiracy," Piper stumbles, literally, over the bones of a child. Rabe weaves Piper's investigations of this long-cold case and the high-tech theft of an old man's earnings into a thoroughly satisfying and complex novel with deeply realized characters and beautifully vivid writing.

—Jaden Terrell, Shamus Award nominee and internationally published author of the Jared McKean Mysteries

THE DEAD OF NIGHT was my first introduction to Piper Blackwell's world, and based on this one, I'm looking forward to seeing more. The story of two different crimes, set many years apart—one against the very young and one the very old—pulled me in until I had to finish the last section in one sitting so I could find out "whodunit." Rabe keeps the reader on the edge of their seat, but also includes a lot of terrific character building, especially Piper, her father, and the quirky "Mark the Shark." The characters were engaging and very real

—I care about what happened to them, which for me is one of the most important things in any kind of story. A great read!

—Amazon bestselling author R.L. King, author of the Alastair Stone Chronicles

## PRAISE FOR THE DEAD OF WINTER

Mystery just got a little less cozy in THE DEAD OF WINTER.
*New York Times* and *USA Today* bestselling author Steven Savile

Jean Rabe delivers a suspenseful morsel that not only celebrates the Yuletide season, but also keeps you up at night with a well-crafted mystery. THE DEAD OF WINTER is chilling indeed!
Raymond Benson, author of The Black Stiletto series, *New York Times* bestselling author of James Bond novels

For years I've admired Jean Rabe's work in the science fiction and fantasy genres, and now, with THE DEAD OF WINTER, she's applying her considerable talents to the field of mysteries. The first in a very promising series with an attractive main character, Piper Blackwell, a female county sheriff who faces obstacles both on and off the job while investigating a puzzling homicide. Very much recommended.
Multiple award-winning and three-time Edgar nominee author Brendan DuBois

THE DEAD OF WINTER was a blast—lots of fun to read! Jean Rabe's characters come to life through the written word, and it takes a real writing talent to accomplish this feat.
Denise Dietz, *USA Today* bestselling author

# THE DEAD OF NIGHT

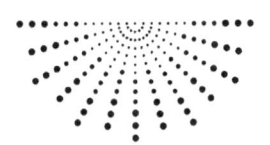

# THE DEAD OF NIGHT

## A PIPER BLACKWELL MYSTERY

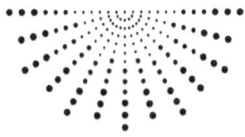

## JEAN RABE

Boone Street Press

*For Bill Gilsdorf and Robert Scales*
*who taught Piper how to be a good sheriff*

Boone Street Press

Name: Rabe, Jean, author

Title: The Dead of Night / Jean Rabe

First Edition Imajin Books: September 2017

Boone Street Press: June 2018

Identifiers: ISBN-13: 978-1-7320036-9-9/ 10: 1-7320036-9-6

LCCN: 2018905558

Printed in the United States of America

❀ Created with Vellum

# ONE

## MONDAY, APRIL 30TH

T he old man sat in the middle of a bench under a big oak, his shoulders hunched and back curved, reminding Piper of a turtle. Hard to make out more details from where she stood under the streetlight.

The light didn't quite reach his perch, and she suspected he'd picked the spot for that reason; there were closer benches. The clouds hindered, a dense gray dome that coupled with the hour had turned the stretch along the bluff into a mass of twisting shadows. Lights in the houses at the edge of the park were flickering dots, will-o-the-wisps, she mused, more fitting for Halloween than spring.

She started toward him as threads of lightning flashed. Maybe the rain would hold off for a little while. Despite the frequent storms of the past several days, Piper hadn't brought an umbrella. The ground felt spongy, comfortable to walk on. She quickened her step.

Maybe this wouldn't take long and she could go home and crawl into bed with the latest Harry Bosch book.

He scooted over, making room for her. She guessed him to be in his early eighties. Twin canes were hooked over the top slat, and he wore a bulky jacket. The dispatcher had mentioned he was a geezer

—"a whack-job paranoid geezer likely visited by aliens" were the exact words—and said that he claimed it was urgent and he would only speak to the sheriff... and only at this time and place.

"Evening, Mr. Thresher," Piper said as she sat, keeping a good foot between them. He was redolent of old-man smells—warring liniments and too much aftershave. She swiveled to face him, took off her hat and rested it on her knees.

"Mark, Sheriff Blackwell."

"Evening, Mark," she said.

"Mark the Shark."

"Interesting nickname," Piper said.

"Had it a long time. Had it since the war."

His voice was gritty like sheets of sandpaper rubbing together, a smoker's voice, though she didn't detect a hint of nicotine. She tipped her head and found the scent of the nearby river and the headiness of the sodden ground. More lightning speared the clouds, looking like metallic threads embroidered on a garment.

"You were in a war of sorts yourself," Mark the Shark continued. "Read it in the newspaper last fall. That was a few weeks before the election. Read all about you."

"Two tours in Iran. Downrange assignments mostly."

"That's why I voted for you. I like folks with military experience, serving the country and all. Patriotic. Didn't matter to me that you were what—"

"Twenty-three." She still was. Her birthday was five months away.

"Yeah, didn't matter that you were a pup. The article said you were Military Police. I figured that'd make you an excellent sheriff... just like your dad. Good man, Paul Blackwell. Good sheriff." A pause. "Despite his politics."

The wind gusted and the branches above gently clacked. Piper grabbed her hat to keep it from blowing away, and with her free hand pushed the annoying curls out of her eyes, a reminder of the haircut appointment tomorrow. She watched Mark the Shark fold in on himself and wrap his jacket tighter. The temperature in the mid-fifties, her windbreaker sufficed. But she knew some elderly people chilled easily. He'd mentioned the war. Korea probably.

"I helped liberate the Philippines," he said. Leaning forward with his elbows on his knees, he looked around, nervous, and then focused on the streetlight.

She corrected herself. WWII. He had to be ninety-something.

"Signed up in forty, saw a recruiting poster 'Man the Guns, Join the Navy.' Got my pop to sign permission 'cause I was seventeen. Way at the end, Luzon in forty-five, that's when I got my nickname." He rubbed at his chin and coughed, his shoulders bouncing. "Before we left the islands, one very early morning, me and some mates went fishing. We jury-rigged poles and tackle, used shiny fish we'd scooped out of the surf with a bucket. Went out on a sandbar and cast into the shallows. Figured we might catch something 'cause we saw lots o' life in the shoals. I still remember how good the water felt, and how salty the air tasted."

She forced down her impatience. Whatever matter he'd called the department about obviously wasn't urgent after all.

"Out in them shoals, I hooked something with size to it and it broke. The sky was lightening, all pale and pretty like a Kinkade painting, and so we saw it clear the surface. 'Bout shit my pants, I did. Excuse the language, ma'am. Easy a dozen feet long, maybe longer, probably longer, half of it tail. It snapped the line and we got the hell out of there. It was a goddamned big shark. My mate Gerald, he'd been studying to be a marine biologist before the war. He said it was my namesake, a thresher shark. We looked it up in a book when we got back to the ship. Threshers are a mackerel shark, you know, nocturnal with big eyes to help them see in the dark. Like deep water they do, but they come into the shallows early in the morning to feed, use their tails to sweep the little fish together so they can eat 'em easier. There's not as many of 'em anymore, them threshers. Sharks declining all over, hunted for their fins and meat. Pity, don't you think?"

Piper nodded as if she was interested. More lightning flashed, a broad stroke that illuminated his face. Horsey, fitted with a long nose, white whiskers peppering his jawline, skin wrinkled and ruddy like a farmer's or someone who spent a lot of hours outdoors. Couldn't tell the color of his eyes behind the thick lenses of his boxy-framed glasses, and a hood covered his head, adding to the turtle image. His clothes were a mix of dark blue and gray, everything rumpled and worn. Old man attire. He nervously scanned the park again and cocked his head, listening. After a moment, he lowered his voice.

"I'm being hunted, too."

Piper sat straight. Now he had her interest. "Hunted, Mr. Thresher?"

"Mark," he countered.

"Mark," she said.

"Mark the Shark. Guys on the ship... that fishing story I just told you spread. They started calling me Mark the Shark. Thresher for a Thresher. Mark the Shark stayed with me all through my Navy days, and I kept it afterward, liking the sound of it. Put in thirty years in the Navy before I retired, bought a big piece of property along the north line of the county with the military pay I'd saved up. Started farming that year. I was forty-seven then. A second career."

"Hunted?"

"I'm getting to it. Don't you go hurrying an old man. Never ever should you hurry an old man."

Piper did the math. Mark the Shark was probably ninety-four. Who would hunt a nonagenarian in a sleepy little county?

"You told my dispatcher it was urgent," Piper pressed. "What did you—"

He interrupted with a tsk-tsking sound. "You don't know where Malapascua is, do you? Being Army and all. Airborne. You were with the Screaming Eagles, right? I remember that from the news article, the 101st out of Fort Campbell."

"I don't know where Malapascua is," Piper admitted. She was going to repeat her question, but he cut her off with a wag of his long-fingered hand.

"Don't you hurry me."

"Sorry."

"It's a sunken island in the Philippines. I went there years and years ago, right after I bought my farm. A tropical vacation with the girl I'd just married—a late start at that for both of us, eh? Way the hell too late for kids. Wanted to show her where the war had been... part of the war. A history teacher, she was interested in where I'd been stationed. She's been dead three years now." He shook his head. "Anyway, we did some diving. I used to dive, you know. I was certified for open ocean. The Monad Shoal is near Malapascua, and the sides of that island, they drop off to the real inky depths. Thresher sharks hunt there, and though we weren't looking for them, we saw a couple on our early dive. Beautiful creatures. Cleaning wrasse, those are small fish that live on the dead skin from the shark—its gills, inside its mouth—the wrasse were hanging on them threshers. A symbiotic relationship, and—"

Thunder boomed, and Piper felt the tremor ripple through the ground beneath her three-day-old Nikes. Ozone mingled with the river scent and Mark the Shark's old man smells.

"Gonna rain," Mark said.

"Yeah."

"I like the rain. Good for the ground. Good for the early beans and peas the farmers put in. I'd have had carrots and cukes in by now, too. It's supposed to be sunny tomorrow and the rest of the week. I heard the forecast. But it looks like April's wanting to go out with a nice drenching."

"Yeah, looks like it," she said. "Listen, I—"

"Do you got a dog?"

"My father does, an old pug."

"Everyone should have a dog."

"Someday, when I'm not living in an apartment above a garage. When I have my own place with a yard." Why was she continuing a pointless conversation? "Listen, I—"

"My dog doesn't like the rain. But I do. April showers bring May flowers. May Day tomorrow. Maybe you'll get a bouquet from your feller. You probably got a feller, right?"

She let out a long breath. "You said this was urgent."

"It is. I suppose you want me to get to the point of this. Regretful to bring you out here so late, Sheriff, weather threatening and all."

Piper put her hat on when she felt the first big drop find its way through the branches. "I can handle rain." She couldn't handle an old man rambling about long-tailed sharks far removed from Spencer County, Indiana.

"I 'spect you can handle a lot of things, Sheriff. Medals and such… I read that in the article. About your medals, saving all the soldiers you were with." He glanced nervously around the park again, then leaned back against the bench, squared his shoulders, pulled his hood down farther over his forehead so all of his features disappeared. "I've been robbed, Sheriff Blackwell. Money taken from me, some of what I got from selling the last parcels of my farm to that real estate company. I got a stash at my house, hidden real good. That hidden money's safe. It's what I got in the bank… some of that is gone. Good money gone. Hunted for my money just like sharks are hunted for their meat."

"Mr. Thresher—"

"Mark."

"Mark—"

"Mark the Shark."

Piper stood. "Listen, Mark, you should come to the office, first thing in the morning and we'll fill out a report. Detail how much you think has been taken."

"A lot. A lot was taken."

"We'll call the bank, maybe go over there—"

"Not coming to your office. Too many eyes there. Eyes downtown. I done called the bank about it. Didn't get nowhere."

"We'll call the bank," she pressed, "see if there really has been a theft. See if it's just a records problem instead. Maybe you—"

He made fist and bumped it against his knee just as thunder boomed again. "I'm not some daft codger that can't remember shit, what he's done with his money! It's a conspiracy, Sheriff Blackwell, and that's why we're out here, away from any eavesdroppers, away from any gawkers... away from the government and—"

"Mark—"

"It's a good bit of money and you need to fix it. Get back for me what they took and keep them from taking the rest of it. A symbiotic relationship we can have, working together to catch the thieves. We'll be the hunters now."

Piper adjusted her belt and shifted from one foot to the other, turned, and directly faced the old man. "This isn't the place to—"

"It's the best place to talk about this. No one comes to the park this late."

"That's because the park is closed this late."

"My point," he cut back. "No one can see us, hear us. Somebody's spying on me, Sheriff Blackwell. And if you're caught with me, maybe they'll start spying on you."

"Who do you think is—"

"It's the Democrats. Probably. Spencer County's thick with Democrats. You know that. You ran as a Republican. So I know you understand. Your father ran as a Democrat, and he was good despite that. But a Republican, you'd understand."

Piper ran as a Republican solely to be unopposed in the primary. She personally didn't claim allegiance to any particular party.

"You *do* understand, don't you?" he pushed. "Don't you?"

She wanted to be angry at Mark the Shark, instead she was sad. Some form of dementia had no doubt hobbled his mind; her grandfather on her mother's side had died of Alzheimer's six years ago. She'd visited him, but he didn't know who she was. He just smiled at her and talked about the midnight bowling alley in the nursing home parking lot and the circus horses that paraded by his door in the middle of the afternoon. Her grandfather had been eighty; Mark had more than a decade on that.

"Can I give you a ride home, Mark?"

He shook his head and grumbled as the lighting and thunder stepped it up and the rain started to fall steady.

"I've got my old Chevy, parked it on the side street down that way.

Under a broken streetlight so's no one will notice it." He pointed to his right. This was a small park; Piper figured he probably had only a block or so walk to get to his car. "I'll be fine. And you need to wait a bit before you leave. Stick around, watch, just to make sure nobody's following, spying. Despite all my precautions, someone might have tailed me. I been looking, but I ain't seen anybody else in this park except me and you. Still, they might be clever and—"

"I'm sure we're the only ones—"

"But just in case, you stick around a bit."

"Mark—"

"Can't be too careful. Can't ever be too careful." He levered himself up and reached for his canes. "I gotta go now. So are you going to fix it, Sheriff Blackwell? Get my money back? All on the Q T?"

"How much money was stolen?" Piper should have asked that right away. "How much?" She played along... just like she'd told her grandfather the horses that paraded past his room were pretty, how fine their hooves sounded clacking against the hallway tile floor.

"One hundred and sixty thousand, more or less."

She whistled. "That's a good amount of money, Mark."

"I told you it was. Yeah. Well, it is and it isn't," he said. "If I have to go in one of them damn nursing homes it'll stretch about a year and a half. But they didn't take everything out of the bank, them robbers—not yet, and they didn't get the secret stash at my place. I got enough to pay for six or seven years, maybe eight, in one of them damn nursing homes if I have to before I would need to go on the county dole. And I don't want to do that. Damn Democrats." He coughed. "Maybe I won't live long enough to worry about that. Maybe nobody should live to be that old."

The rain came harder as he ambled a dozen feet away, paused, and called over his shoulder. "I voted for you. Are you going to fix it, Sheriff Blackwell? And keep it all hush-hush? No Democrats? No spies? Just you. Only you doing the looking. I got no family. I don't trust nobody else."

"Yeah, I'm going to fix it, Mark." She raised her voice so she was certain he could hear her. "I'll fix it. I promise." *Why the hell had she said that?* "I'll stop by to see you sometime tomorrow morning. I'll call and let you know when I'm coming. You have a good evening, Mark." *What was left of it.*

"Mark the Shark," he corrected. Then the night and the now-driving rain swallowed him.

2

# TWO

Piper hoped that Mark the Shark had been robbed.

As unfortunate a thing as having "one hundred and sixty thousand, more or less" stolen, it would mean the old man was not suffering from dementia. And it would be an intriguing case that would stretch her skills and definitely make her routine less ordinary.

Her skin tingled, not from the chill of the rain, but from the possibility of investigating what would be a Class C felony. That notion was almost enough to make her forget she was standing on the bluff in the middle of the night, getting soaked. But it wasn't quite enough to chase away her dispatcher's warning that Mark Thresher wasn't all there.

Maybe it was a clerical error on Mark's part... or wishful thinking he had that much money. She could almost hear the hooves of the horses clicking against the tile floor as they paraded past her grandfather's room. Or was that just the rain ticking against the patches of mud around her?

Were the spies imaginary, too? Or was someone really shadowing the old man?

"Who the hell would follow you, Mark the Shark?"

*And what the hell am I doing here?*

Not what was she doing in the park, praying that a lot of money had been taken from an elderly county resident. What was she doing here, as Sheriff of Spencer County?

It was a question she'd asked herself dozens of times since she'd chosen not to re-up at Fort Campbell. She'd come back a little more than a year ago because her father was ill—and only last month he was declared cancer free a second time. He'd encouraged her to run for sheriff—a post he'd held for a long while; campaigning had given them both something to do. She'd won in November, though not by much, using her family name to defeat the man who was her chief deputy, and who she believed was far more qualified for the job. As of today, she'd been sheriff for a whopping four months. Piper wondered what her life would have been like if she'd stayed in the Army. She'd fit in there. This whole sheriff thing… she was still growing into it.

*What the hell am I doing here? And why the hell did I promise that man I'd find his money?*

She reached into her waterlogged pocket and pulled out a flashlight, fingers slick and fumbling not to drop it. She turned it on and nothing happened.

"Crap." She shook it and felt the batteries move. "Stick around a bit," she repeated his words. To make sure he hadn't been followed. She jiggled the flashlight again and tightened the end. It finally came on. Piper waved the beam around, seeing tree trunks and benches, spreading puddles in the patches absent of grass, and watching the rain splash back up because it was driving so hard. The mud was ample and glistened in the light, evidence the parks department needed to do some serious reseeding. A thick stroke of lightning, a resounding *crack!* and the streetlights went out, as did the will-o-the-wisp lights in all the houses across from the park.

Power outage.

Awesome.

And all she had was the small flashlight.

She continued to scan where her beam reached. The dispatcher who'd taken Mark's call had encouraged Piper to ignore it, said the old man had a reputation for his "elevator not reaching the top floor," suggested she instead send one of the deputies on shift. Piper'd had a slow week and figured she could use a little distraction. This certainly was distracting. A tidy sum maybe stolen and conspiracies involving Democrats—not very likely. She didn't see a soul in the park.

*What the hell am I doing here? Looking for spies?* The more she thought about it, the more it became likely that Mark the Shark was missing a few of the fries from his Happy Meal. And how many fries was she short for staying out here?

Another sweep with the flashlight.

There was a break in the clouds near the bluff, the full moon poking through. She slogged toward the edge, around a clump of birch trees, intending to stare down at the river, take a brief sodden stroll before getting the interior of her department vehicle all wet. Make sure no one else was in the park. Harry Bosch could wait until tomorrow night.

Harry Bosch would never get a case like this one.

The river was a shiny black ribbon and reflected a piece of the moon. Normally she could hear it, perched even this high above, the sound of it sloshing against the bank, a comforting susurrus. But all she heard now was the angry tat-a-tat-a-tat of the rain.

As a teenager, Piper had loved the stretch along the river, picnicked on the bank with friends—the place called Lincoln Landing to commemorate the spot where Abraham Lincoln set off on a flatboat. This park above was known as Rockport City Bluff. She used to climb these rocks, watch the boats go by; great entertainment for a sparsely-populated county at the southern end of the state. The bluff and the landing below because there wasn't a single movie theater or shopping mall.

*What the hell am I doing here?*

She'd passed the Plainfield Sheriff's Academy fifteen days ago, meaning she could retain her office. She knew her chief deputy had hoped she'd fail. Had she, he would have been appointed to fill the vacancy. Piper had expected him to retire when she nailed a near-perfect score. Maybe he would retire... but he hadn't yet. And she wasn't ready to push him out. Oren's experience with the department, and with the Rockport police before that, was yin to her inexperienced yang.

But maybe she should have sent him to deal with Mark the Shark. To schlep around here and—

The lightning played erratically high above the river, nature's fireworks. In spaces between the growls of thunder, and accompanying the constant staccato rain, she heard the cry of some night bird, probably complaining about all the water the county had been blessed with. Farther away a horn honked repeatedly.

April showers indeed.

*Conspiracies, Democrats, and spies, oh my.*

It was a notch more interesting than the steady thread of DUIs—Spencer County's number one ticketed offense. Dealing with drunks and sifting through applications for a vacant deputy position had not stirred her imagination.

She'd delve into Mr. Thresher's complaint, see if there was truth to it or get him to realize his bookkeeping was off. She'd drive out to see him, get the name of his bank, and go there with him to iron everything out. Symbiotic-like. Not much else pressing in the office at the moment, she could help the old man.

Piper whipped around, deciding to call it a night and go home. A dozen steps to the minimal shelter of the birch clump and the toe of her Nikes connected with an exposed root. She flailed forward, lost her balance and her flashlight, and splatted stomach-first, her chin bouncing against the soggy ground.

"Shit," she sputtered, pushing herself up on her knees, spitting a gob of mud out of her mouth. *And two is four and four is eight,* she added. Piper felt the mud soak all the way through her clothes and to her skin. Her right shoe had been pulled off by the root, her sock soaked. The chill was no longer invigorating. It was awful.

*Shit. Shit. Shit.* She grabbed the narrowest trunk with both hands, pulled, and stood, stomped in frustration and brushed at the muck that was a frosting-like coating on the front of her pants and jacket. The department vehicle wasn't just going to get wet; it was going to get filthy. Too dark to see the roots and her absent shoe, but she saw her flashlight and went for it, snatched it up—that took two attempts because the handle was slick.

"Shit," she repeated turning and aiming the light toward the trunk and spotting the Nike, the toe wedged under a white birch root. Piper retrieved it and froze. It wasn't a root; it was a bone she'd tripped on. She'd seen enough bodies, pieces of bodies, skeletons from her time in Iraq. She was pretty sure it was human. "Holy shit."

She held the beam close, just to be sure, and then panned it back and forth around the trunks. All the rains—and before that the winter's record snow—had turned parts of the park into a slurry-like mix that had eroded. A good measure that had lacked grass cover had slipped away, revealing the roots and the bone.

And on closer inspection the top of a skull.

Piper had been looking for a distraction. But this wasn't what she'd had in mind.

# THREE

Teegan, the second shift dispatcher, had a pop up canopy. She'd found it on sale at the Walmart Supercenter in Owensboro a few weeks past and intended to sit under it at craft fairs when hawking her fused-glass jewelry. She'd mentioned her grand purchase to everyone in the department. Piper had remembered, traipsed back to her car, and called to borrow it.

They put the canopy up against the birch clump, using the roll down sides to help keep the rain off the bones and the already soggy ground.

"Thanks, Teegan," Piper said. "This will be a serious help."

"Not a problem. I wasn't gonna go out drinking tonight anyway. Power's out in most of Rockport. I'm not into warm beer by candlelight." Teegan chewed noisily on a wad of gum and held her umbrella so Piper could share it. Teegan was forty-something but dressed like a teenager and resembled Morticia Addams because of her pale complexion, straight black hair, and heavy eyeliner. She wore a clear plastic raincoat that crinkled with her every move and that seemed incongruous to the Goth attire underneath. Piper had inherited Teegan when she took over the department, and found her nosey but highly efficient.

"Was Mr. Conspiracy with you when you found the bones?" Teegan continued to *smack* her gum.

Piper shook her head. "He'd left. I just stuck around a while."

"To make sure he wasn't followed?" It appeared Teegan was familiar with Mark the Shark. "Did you talk about aliens?"

"Democrats."

Oren arrived with battery-powered lights he set up on tripods and aimed under the canopy.

"Want me to stick around, Sheriff?" Teegan asked. "I don't mind. I could use the overtime. This is interesting as all hell, a skeleton on the bluff. Wonder how long it's been rotting here? Who it could have—"

"We're fine," Piper cut back.

"Coroner's on her way," Oren announced. "Said she wants to be the one to pull the bones. Asked that we don't touch anything."

"What about Rockport cops?" Teegan blew a bubble. When Piper didn't answer, she sucked the bubble in with a *pop!* "Ah, you haven't called Rockport yet. You know it's technically their jurisdiction, right? The bluff is in—"

"Yeah, I know," Piper said. "The bluff's in the city."

"Well... okay. See ya tomorrow afternoon, then," Teegan said. "But if I have power in my house I'm gonna keep my scanner on in case you all have something interesting to say about Bonesy there. Oh, and Councilman Sampson called again. He wants you to consider his nephew for the open deputy position. I put a note on your desk. Says you should have the resume and application. And take care of my tent."

"I'll take care of your tent," Piper said. "If anything happens to it, I'll replace it."

"Cool beans." Teegan scurried away and Piper felt the rain tat-a-tat-tatting against her again. The lightning still danced.

"Handy thing, that tent." Chief Deputy Oren Rosenberg made Piper look tiny. He had a foot on her at six-four, and he was built like a linebacker, with curly steel-gray hair that had managed to stay dry under the wide brim of his hat. "I suppose you should think about getting a couple for the department."

Piper had already added it to her shopping list.

"So you found him, eh?"

Piper nodded.

"You didn't mention that when you called."

"Tripped on him, or her, actually."

"Out here in the park, in the dead of night, and in the rain." He waited a beat. "What were you doing out in the park so late?"

Piper gave him an abbreviated version of her meeting with Mark the Shark.

Oren whistled in response. "So if you hadn't come out to meet Mr. Conspiracy, these bones—"

"—would have been found by someone else," Piper said. "A jogger, dog walker, kids." She shivered at that last notion. "Or someone with the Rockport Police or parks department. Maybe tomorrow, or the day after. Somebody would have found him. Or her."

The ground shuddered with a drumming of thunder.

"That lightning hit close," Oren said. "The river pulls it down. Nasty electrical storm Mr. Conspiracy picked for your meeting. Ask your dad about the crop circle incident from two years back. Maybe it was three. Paul handled it."

The "a whack-job paranoid geezer likely visited by aliens" comment Teegan had made to Piper hours ago resurfaced.

Piper edged under the canopy. "All the rain, washing away the ground. That's why the skeleton appeared. Or at least parts of it. Wonder if it's all here?"

"The snow before that. A lot of snow we had." Oren joined her. "No grass under these trees, the earth didn't have a choice but to give up the dead. Whoever buried him—"

"—or her."

"Should've planted him—or her—deeper." Oren, apparently not satisfied with the pole lights, pulled a flashlight from his belt, turned it on, and aimed the beam at the trunks. "A dog walker, kids… anybody else discovered it they might have messed with this, poked around. Hell, if you hadn't found it when you did, this storm might have washed away the tiny bits. Finger bones and such." He squatted for a closer look and let out a sigh. "Skull's a little small to be an adult, I think."

Piper thought the same thing.

"But Annie'll tell us for sure," Oren continued. "Helluva thing, this. Who'd go and bury a kid in the park?"

"Maybe the soul who killed him. Or her. Has to be murder." Piper hunched over next to the skull, her shoulder against the thickest trunk. Water trickled down the papery bark where the canopy wasn't sufficient to form a seal. "A natural death, you'd bury the body in a cemetery or cremate it. Not a public park." She pointed to a curl of rusted metal. "A piece of cheap jewelry maybe."

Oren brought his light closer. "Barbed wire. I'd wait on Annie before you start pulling anything out. It would be bad if—"

"I'm not touching anything." Piper almost said, *Of course we'll wait for the coroner. I'm not an idiot.* But she kept the words in. She'd woken Oren, and he'd been good about coming out here on his day off without a grumble. Night off, she corrected. He'd dressed in his uniform, always everything proper. He had forty more years of law enforcement experience than she did, twenty with the Rockport police, twenty with the Spencer County Sheriff's Department. She'd called him not because she needed his experience here—though it would be useful—but because she knew he'd be pissed that something out of the ordinary had happened and he wasn't a part of it. She was making strides in getting along with him.

"Rockport might make a claim for this," Oren said, seemingly needing to cut the silence. "They have to be notified."

"Yeah. But I found him."

"Or her."

"I want this," Piper admitted. DUI reports, reading the resumes for the open deputy position, handling Mark the Shark's claim...a cold case would be more intriguing than all of that. "I found the bones," she repeated. "This is our case." She had stopped herself from saying *my case.*

"Chief Hugh might disagree with you, just to give you a hard time. It's in the city."

*Yeah, I know it's in the friggin' itty bitty city.*

Piper nearly argued that the sheriff held jurisdiction anywhere in the county. But she knew the default comes when a crime occurs in a city's limits and there is a city police department; then that department gets the case—unless it is not equipped to handle it. The Rockport Police Department was equipped. Or unless for whatever reason a police department decides to defer to the sheriff. Piper hoped for the "decides to defer."

"We handled the last body in Rockport. Hugh didn't want the roofer." Piper referred to one of the targets of the serial killer who'd slain and artfully posed his victims throughout the county around the holidays.

"That body was black and swollen," Oren said. "And it stunk so bad I had to toss my clothes. Couldn't get the smell out of them. Of course he didn't want that one. Nobody would've wanted that one. This? This is just bones."

"Of maybe a child."

Oren let out a hissing breath. "You want me to call Curtis, deal with jurisdiction issue? I've known him for—"

*—longer than I've been alive.*

"Yeah," Piper said. "I'd like you to call Chief Hugh." That was the main reason she'd summoned Oren, though she'd never admit it. All Oren's years with the city police, and the fact that he was boating buddies with Chief Curtis Hugh. Oren would have a much better chance at winning the jurisdiction issue. She *really* wanted this; something different to tackle.

"I'll invite him out here, have to do that. But I'll suggest the victim might have been killed outside the city. If that's barbed wire, the victim could have been tied up, killed elsewhere—"

"—has to be murder," Piper repeated flatly. "No other reason to bury a body on the bluff."

"—could have been killed elsewhere in the county and brought here. Maybe for the view. Maybe because the bluff meant something to the killer or the victim. That'd make it our jurisdiction if the murder took place outside the city. That this spot was just the disposal site; I'll bring that possibility up."

"Think he'll accept that?"

"We're friends." Oren shrugged. "It's eleven. I'm thinking Curtis will say it's ours, to keep him posted, and will roll over and go back to sleep. Besides, it's a cold case. A cold case? If it goes unsolved it won't be a good mark for Curtis. Could influence his personal review by the mayor and city council. I might mention that, too."

Piper tipped her head so Oren wouldn't see her smile.

"Wonder who'd go and bury a kid in the park," he mused again as he pulled out his cell phone. "I'll give Curtis a call now, then wait for Annie. A cold case. It's ours."

4

# FOUR

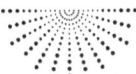

## TUESDAY, MAY 1ST

- a ten-inch section of rusted barbed wire
- four marbles
- two pieces of a thin black leather belt
- a curl of brown leather
- five copper rivets
- a handful of coins
- seven small black buttons
- three slightly larger brown buttons
- and a brass belt buckle

Those items had been culled from the bluff after the bones were removed and were now set out on a sheet of butcher block paper on a table in the department's all-purpose room.

Piper sat in front of them, staring.

JJ—Jeri Jones—the department's sole detective, stood across from her. Piper had promoted JJ three months past after the previous detective became a victim of the Christmas Card Killer, as the county's serial slayer had been dubbed.

"So?" Piper asked.

"Won't have the coroner's report for a while—" JJ began.

"I'm well aware. Oren left at seven for Evansville."

"—and so we don't know for certain how old he was."

"Or she," Piper said.

JJ shook her head, her curls shining in the fluorescent light. *"He.* And I can tell you that he probably died fifty to sixty-some years ago and wasn't from around here."

"Go on." JJ, known for being a thorough investigator, had been a good choice for detective. Piper hadn't needed to advertise outside the department, she'd simply "promoted from within," even though that had caused considerable hard feelings from the other in-house applicants.

"The four marbles. I found an online catalog of vintage marbles and matched them up. These three are common machine-made from the late forties, worth maybe three or four bucks each to a collector. The larger one." She whistled. "Agate lemonade with oxblood-red swirls from the late thirties. It'd go for several hundred. Maybe as much as seven."

*"Now* it would," Piper said. "Decades ago? Probably not so much."

"Marbles were more of a boy-thing back then. Part of the reason I say the victim was a boy."

"Maybe," Piper said. "Go on."

"The twist of barbed wire, no idea about that. Haven't really looked into that piece yet, or this strip of brown leather, other than to notice it has holes at each end. Maybe it was tied together or it connected something. I'll get digging into them next. It's the other stuff."

"Go on," Piper repeated.

"The coins." JJ pointed. "This is a farthing, British, dated 1940. This one's also dated 1940, twenty francs, *Liberte Egalite Fraternite* it says on the back. It means freedom, equality, and fraternity. The one with the hen and the chicks on it, the other side has a raised harp and reads Eire 1943. Despite being buried, those three coins are in remarkable condition and don't look like they were circulated, likely from someone's coin collection. The U.S. nickels and pennies—forty-eight cents worth—range in dates from 1942 to 1949 and are beat to hell, definitely circulated. Nothing more recent than 1949, so I'd say the bones have been there maybe six decades."

"Good work," Piper said.

"Took me half an hour on the coins. Google is my friend." JJ had long blonde hair reminiscent of Dolly Parton, was pencil thin, and had been with the department ten years. She was the only other woman in the ranks, and she and Piper had established a solid rapport. She pulled out a chair and sat.

"But coins, JJ? That's why you think the bones are from a boy based on—"

"Not based on the coins. But I had to mention them, the dates and such. If you pull coins out of your pocket, you'll find a mix of recent and old stuff. So I'm just guessing the 1949 coin might have been fairly recent at the time. The belt buckle is pretty convincing, too, on the 'boy' front. That took some digging, and I finally thought to look on eBay of all places. Should've started there. Two and a half inches by an inch and three-quarters is pretty small and would have worked with the belt. We got two pieces of the belt. The brass patina's long gone, but you can see the detail in the buckle, the 'Merit Award' at the top, 'The Arizona Republic' at the bottom. The boy in a suit delivering newspapers in the center, and on the newspaper bag it says 'busy boys…better boys' all in caps. The Arizona Republic still publishes, out of Phoenix, a Gannett paper now. Began in 1890, called The Arizona Republican then. Switched to the Republic in 1930. In 1952 they gave out these belt buckles to their carriers. In the fifties most carriers were boys. Oh, and the image on the belt buckle? That's based on the 1952 three-cent postage stamp called 'Newspaper Boys.' I suppose a newspaper girl could have been given the buckle, could have had all those coins and the marbles, still it's unlikely especially since—"

Piper raised an eyebrow and waited.

"It's the copper rivets that cements it for me. They're from blue jeans, and in the early fifties young girls weren't likely to wear them. Oh, some did, but most girls wore skirts, dresses, capris, slacks. So, the jeans coupled with the belt buckle—I'm saying the skeleton belongs to a boy. These two brown buttons? I emailed pictures to a big online vintage clothing collector in New York, and she got back to me in minutes. Says they're definitely from jeans. She sent me a few links with more information. Turns out that back in the day jeans had a button fly. Levi Strauss started using some zippers in 1947, and that was to appeal to women. Our boy easily could have been wearing hand-me-down jeans, and so they could have come from the 1940s, before the zippers. Clothes can last a long time. The little black buttons? They had to have come from a shirt, she says. And all the buttons are Bakelite, an early plastic, molded resin."

Piper whistled. "Nice. I agree, a boy. Maybe a teenager, at best, definitely not an adult." She rocked back in the chair, wishing she would have gone to the coroner's, as she was curious about the bones. But she could not be in two cities at the same time. Besides, Oren got on well with Dr. Annie Neufeld; they traced their friendship back to childhood. And Piper had Mark the Shark to deal with in a little while. A glance at the clock—9 a.m.—the banks should be open now. She'd call Mark and they'd go over to his—

"High school graduation is on the nineteenth," JJ said.

JJ didn't have kids, Piper knew. But maybe a niece or nephew was graduating.

"Are you scheduled that day and need off?" Piper would rather talk about the items in front of her than schedules.

"No." JJ pushed away from the table, stood, walked behind the chair, and wrapped her fingers around the top rail. "I— I know this isn't the best time for me to bring this up, but it's just you and me here, and I owe you for the promotion, for believing in me. I like working for you. A lot."

"What's going on JJ?" When Piper scooted back, her chair made a screeching sound across the tile; one of the legs was missing its rubber end cap. The department could use new furniture. "What's high school graduation got to do with—"

THE DEAD OF NIGHT

"You know my husband's the athletic director, right? He's been there a dozen years, and the past six basketball teams have been amazing. Took state in its division four of those, placed this year with no seniors on the squad. A few of his former players are in the NBA, and they credit him with getting them there." She shifted from one foot to the other. "I like working here. I like it a lot. But Andy's been offered a college position. He'd been casting a net every once in a while. And—and—he's taking this incredible job as head basketball coach at the University of North Carolina in Wilmington. They want him out there for the summer athletic program. That's why this is such a rush, our moving. I probably should have said something before now, that we'd been looking. We've just been thinking about living in a bigger place. And Wilmington alone has five times as many people as this whole county. It's on the coast, nice climate, and—"

"Shit," Piper whispered. *And two is four and four is eight.* The rest of JJ's one-sided conversation drifted to the back of her mind. Words like "beaches," "Riverwalk," and "historic places," trickled in.

Piper was supposed to have fourteen deputies—and one detective —to cover the county in three shifts, working four days on, two off, rotating schedules so no one was stuck on the night tour forever. She had thirteen deputies at the moment because one retired a few weeks ago, a fifty-three-year-old with twenty-five years in the department. And now she'd also be down her detective. The youngest deputy in the Spencer County Sheriff's Department was two years older than Piper, the oldest was Oren, three were in their fifties, and the *only* other woman—her detective—was leaving. One more shred of diversity gone, in this case to the east coast. All but one of Piper's deputies was white. Diego, the twenty-five-year old, just into his second year with the department, was a fair-skinned Hispanic with an associate degree in law enforcement. It all fit the demographics of the county. According to the latest census, only fifty or so of the county's whopping twenty-thousand people were Hispanic, and about one hundred were black. But it didn't sit right with Piper. And JJ leaving... that sat worse.

"I know I should have said something earlier, that he was looking, that we were thinking about going somewhere else. But he only got the offer last week, and we kept things quiet for a few days, then word leaked out at school. This county is one big game of telephone. You're going through that stack of applications now for the open deputy spot. Maybe there's someone in there good for detective. Maybe somebody else in the department could get promoted. Maybe—"

JJ clearly paused for Piper to say something. When she didn't, JJ finally continued. "So we're putting our place up for sale right away, signed papers with a realtor yesterday, and have been looking at houses online. There's this gorgeous two-story Andy's going to see when he's out on the weekend. Two hundred thousand is all, three beds, three baths, only twenty years old. I looked at all the pictures. It could be perfect. A whirlpool tub in the master bath, fenced backyard so we can get a dog or two. It doesn't have a basement. But he's going to look at others with basements, get it narrowed down before I go out and—"

"—and when are you going out? To look at houses?"

"Right after high school graduation. The day after. Andy and all the other teachers always go to graduation. So he wants to go. That night some of the guys are throwing us a farewell party. This is my notice. More than two weeks I'm giving you, less than three. My last day will be the eighteenth. But I figure you're already going through applications and—" JJ looked at Piper expectantly.

Piper crossed her arms and waited.

"—and I was wondering if you would give me a letter of recommendation because the New Hanover County Sheriff's Department has an opening in the detective division and the Wilmington Police Department has two vacancies. I figure I could land one of them. I've updated my resume and—"

"I'll get you a letter of recommendation by the end of today," Piper interrupted.

JJ let out a big breath. "Thanks, and—"

"—and I hope that you'll devote your full attention to this department while you're still here," Piper said, knowing that JJ would be distracted with the upcoming move.

"Oh, yeah. Yes. You bet I will. I'll holler as soon as I figure out something on the brown leather and the barbed wire." JJ sat again and let out another big breath. "And we want you to come to the going away party."

"I'm very happy for you," Piper lied.

"I'm very happy, too." JJ beamed. "Okay, back to all of this." She waved her hand across the items like a model displaying prizes on *The Price is Right.* Jake and Diego are still out at the bluff, combing through the mud like archeologists at a dig site. I called the parks department to go out and pull up the birch trees. But it looks like what we found last night is it. Just this stuff. The jeans would have been made of denim, cotton, the shirt probably cotton, too. And that disintegrates when a body does. It's the polyesters and leathers and stuff that sticks around a while. I'm thinking he wasn't from around here because of the buckle. Maybe got dumped here as the doer was driving through. I'll call out to Phoenix police, give them a head's up and mention the newspaper boy bit."

Piper leaned forward. "Wait on that. I want to get the coroner's report first. Confirm it was a boy, get a good estimate on age, a better guess on how long ago he was buried, and cause of death. Get a dental. Then we'll have more for the Phoenix police to go on. I want our records checked, too, missing persons forty to sixty-some years ago."

"That's not all on the computer, those records. A lot of the old stuff's still in boxes and files."

"I know." Piper had moved stacks of those boxes into her office, intending to go through all of them, looking for puzzle pieces to connect.

JJ nodded. "Strange thing, huh, bones on the bluff? I only got a couple hours sleep after we left the park. Kept thinking about who'd bury someone up there. Bothered me, you know."

"I know." It had dominated Piper's dreams, too.

"Does your dad got a clue who—"

"His house was dark when I pulled in the drive, and I left to come here at six. Saw his kitchen light come on—" And she almost stopped and went in for a cup of his good coffee, but she had this puzzle festering and didn't want to spare the minutes. "Haven't talked to him about it yet. *Can't* talk to him about it, actually. An open case and all. But I have looked through one of the boxes of old files, got a start on them. I found two kids, both twelve, initially reported as missing, but were later determined runaways who returned to their parents." Piper liked talking to JJ. She was really going to miss that.

"So you only got a couple hours of sleep, too?"

"Yeah." Piper unsuccessfully tried to stifle a yawn. "I'll be drinking coffee all day, JJ. Caffeine in my veins and—"

"Delivery, Sheriff!" Drew Farrar poked his head through the doorway. "I put it on your desk." He glanced at the table and visibly shuddered. Drew was the first-shift dispatcher, and he'd celebrated his thirty-seventh birthday at lunch Friday with Piper and half the department. An errant helium balloon from the festivities clung to the ceiling near where he stood, the curl of green ribbon hanging down. "Helluva thing, finding bones in the park. Any idea who—"

"No," Piper and JJ said in unison. "We're just starting," Piper added.

"Ummm, we picked up another complaint about the Mailbox Mauler over in Gentryville. The old bat took out three with her Buick. Are we going to arrest her this time? One of the maulees is seriously pissed and says we have to do something. Second time since the first of the year that she's whacked his mailbox. Said he'd spent sixty bucks on a fancy one."

Piper made a face. "Yeah. We're gonna arrest her this time. Send Diego pronto."

"Will do," Drew said. "But she's not going to like that. Diego being—"

"Yeah, Diego being," Piper said with a smile. "Diego will forgive me. I'll take him to lunch next week." *Send the lone minority... that'll frost her eighty-some-year-old prejudiced cookies. Serves her right for destroying property. Again.* "How many mailboxes does this make for her scorecard?"

"Eleven since the first of January, Sheriff. Last year, before you came on, she—"

"Lovely." To JJ, "I'll leave you to catalog all this, take more pictures. Put it back in the evidence bags when you're done. It's possible the coroner might want to look at this stuff, but she didn't say anything about it last night. Too bad we couldn't get any fingerprints, but that long underground—" A pause. "I'm happy for you. I know you'll love the coast." Was JJ a good enough detective to tell that Piper was lying?

5

# FIVE

The delivery was a big wicker basket decorated with a rosy satin bow and filled with goodies. Piper glanced at the contents—two packages of Eight O'clock Dark Italian Coffee, a jar of sea-salted cashews, box of chocolate-covered raisins, shimmery glass bottle of Avon Haiku cologne, a lottery ticket, pair of fuzzy socks with pug dogs printed on them, three large oranges, and a potted African violet in full bloom.

Next to the basket was a stack of memos from Drew. Leafing through them, she noted some were from Teegan from the night before. Commissioner Ayers. Councilman Sampson. Councilman Sampson. Councilman Sampson. Commissioner Ayers. Her father. Ayers and Sampson were no doubt promoting their "candidate" for the open deputy position. Good thing they hadn't yet discovered there was now also an opening for detective.

"Drew," she said. Piper knew the dispatcher desk was close enough; she could talk without needing to pick up the phone. "Set up two interviews for me tomorrow, all right?"

"You already have two interviews scheduled," he called back.

"Two more. Fill up my afternoon."

"Ah, need to get Sampson and Ayers off your back. Will do."

She'd talk to Sampson's nephew and Ayer's son-in-law—and keep an open mind about them despite being badgered. Get it out of the way so the phone calls and messages from the local politicians would stop. Ayer's son-in-law looked good enough she should consider him anyway. Sampson's nephew might also be worth a look. Mollifying the local politicians was important, as she wanted to cover some new items in her budget.

Piper stopped herself from diving into the raisins, sat at her desk, and opened the laptop. She started typing JJ's letter of recommendation. It wasn't the most pressing thing—the bones were, and Mark the Shark's claim. But she'd learned in the military to address the little things right away, knock 'em out fast and move on before they got buried under more tasks coming in. One page, short and sweet; she saved it and would give it a proof this afternoon before PDFing it and passing it along to her departing detective.

Then she called up monster.com, jobsgalor.com, policeone.com, and jobrapido.com. There were other sites she could use, but these would suffice for the first wave. She posted the same job advertisement on each—Sheriff's Department detective opening, asking for candidates who had experience with investigating and prosecuting drug crimes, as she really wanted to tackle the county's meth problem. She added the necessary requirements—must be twenty-one, high school diploma or GED, US citizen, valid driver's license, must complete a pre-employment drug screen, no felony convictions, good physical condition, must meet all state requirements for certification as an Officer to include: able to complete a timed agility test, full range of motion, able to operate firearms, eyesight 20/20 natural or correctable, night and peripheral vision certified by a physician, and must be able to read, write, and speak fluent English.

Hope to fill soon, she added.

*As soon as possible, actually.*

Then she included a few tidbits about Spencer County. Let the applicants know just how rural this place is. Let them know where they might be landing. This time she wouldn't promote from within. Not that she didn't have a few deputies that might be able to handle the detective job; she just didn't want to cause the same discord again. Hindsight—she should have advertised just like this before handing JJ the job. Piper hit ENTER on each job site and then called up the webpage for the local weekly newspaper and pasted the same notice. She also emailed the vacancy to the public affairs office at Fort Campbell, in case someone there knew a veteran leaving who might be a good fit. Hopefully someone from outside the county—with fresh, wide-open eyes—would answer the listing. Finally, she printed it out for the office bulletin board. She'd have to look at any locals—including her current deputies—who applied, but she wouldn't have to take them. She doubted anyone from around here would have the drug credentials.

Piper stretched for the box of chocolate-covered raisins and saw an envelope tucked underneath it. She pulled it out and opened it. *Happy May Day*, it read. *Dinner tonight at 6 in your father's kitchen. I will prepare Chả Lụa and Gà Nướng Xã, extra spicy just for him, and we'll have red velvet cake for desert. Call if this plan is not good. Nang.*

Piper grinned, reaching for the violet, and recalling what Mark the Shark said—"Maybe you'll get a bouquet from your feller. You probably got a feller, right?"

Piper enjoyed Nang's company, and they'd been dating since Valentine's Day—when he took her to Charlie's Mongolian Barbeque in Evansville. This basket was the first gift. She hoped it didn't signal that Nang was getting serious. She wasn't looking for serious, didn't want anything to threaten her notion of eventually returning to Fort Campbell. But a home-cooked Vietnamese dinner sounded like a good plan.

Job interviews and Mark the Shark and bones on the bluff. The Mailbox Mauler was icing on that proverbial cake. At least the workload had stopped being boring. And dinner tonight? Piper's stomach growled in anticipation. Things were looking up.

6

# SIX

The bones were displayed on a stainless steel table in the autopsy room. Oren was puzzled why he had to come here to see them laid out. There wasn't any flesh to autopsy, yet Dr. Annie Neufeld had insisted on toting the remains to the Vanderburgh County Coroner's facilities. Spencer County lacked such equipment, and so typically transported its dead either here to Evansville or across the border to Louisville, Kentucky, for examination. He thought they could have just as easily spread the bones out on a table at the sheriff's department and sent what they wanted to the state lab for testing. It would have saved them both a fifty-minute drive.

But maybe this was protocol. Despite all his decades in law enforcement, he'd never dealt with a skeleton—and he hadn't dealt with all that many bodies until the recent exception of the serial killer. Before that there had been only a few murders during his four-decade tenure, and those corpses had been intact, the cases easy to solve.

At least these remains didn't stink; all he picked up was the scent of cleaning antiseptic and his own musky aftershave.

The coroner stood on the other side of the table, staring at him. "You've lost some weight," she said. Dr. Neufeld wore scrubs and gloves, the mask pulled down and dangling around her neck. He didn't think she needed her official get-up, nothing she could catch from the bones, and there was nothing she could infect. But who was he to talk? He practically lived in his uniform. She had prominent dark circles and age creases at the edges of her eyes—to Oren she always looked tired, rarely bothering with makeup to smooth her features. She'd colored her hair though, a soft brown that looked good on her, the customary gray streaks gone. She'd retired as a pediatrician seven years ago, citing rising malpractice insurance costs, took a year or so off, then ran for coroner because she needed something important to do. She was his age, and in her second term. And she was one of his closest friends.

"Thirteen," he said. "Pounds down."

"Because—" The word hung as a question.

Oren growled softly. "I'm not sick, Annie, if that's what you're asking. I ate too much over the holidays, into January, first of February. Uniform got tight and so I bought this book, *Skinny Bastard*. Really, that's the name of it. *Skinny Bastard*. Found it on the sale table at the Barnes & Noble in Owensboro when I had a couple of gift certificates to spend. Hard to follow for me, this diet. It really pushes that vegan stuff. But it made me take a look at some of my not-so-healthy choices. Another dozen down and I'll call it done."

"You look good," she said. "But now your pants are a little baggy. Keep going and you'll have to take them in. Haven't seen you since—"

"Yeah, since then. I know. I know. We should've gotten together before now, and under better circumstances. My fault. Just been... busy." Oren knew Annie meant since winter and the end of the CCK as she'd dubbed it, the Christmas Card Killer who'd plagued Spencer County and had ranged down into Kentucky. She'd done most of the autopsies, and Oren, who'd been seriously wounded by the killer, had attended all but one. Annie had come with Oren's wife to visit him every day while he was in the hospital recovering from a gunshot wound. The three of them had talked about the "good old days" and whether it was time to retire.

"It's just bones, Annie. Why'd you bring them here?"

She made a tsk-tsking sound. "I don't do anything half-assed, Oren Rosenberg. You know that. We're doing a complete study."

He rolled his eyes. *Bones*, he mouthed.

"I've already had them X-rayed."

"It's not all there, the skeleton." Oren heard music start, probably coming from the adjacent office. It was modern-country, someone singing about girls drinking beer in the back of a pickup truck. It wasn't Annie's music. "We've still got people out at the bluff, but it doesn't look like we're going to find anything else. It looks like this is it. But we'll keep digging for a while, just to be sure."

The skull was at one end of the table, but was missing the lower jaw; extending down from it some vertebrae, the shoulder blades, clavicle, sternum, arms, eight ribs that he counted, only a few finger bones. The pelvis was there, along with one femur, one tibia, and pieces that Annie had set at the ends—ankle and toe bones, and definitely not all there.

"Enough of it is here. Quite a bit, actually," she said. "Animals probably got parts of it."

"A kid, right? The skeleton's a—"

"Sure. And I'll guess he—the pelvis suggests to me that it was a he —between ten and twelve. I'm basing that on the size of the skull and femur length. Thirty years in pediatrics, I'd say I have to be close." She took a step back. "But Dr. Abernathy will be more precise."

Oren cocked his head. "You? Call in another coroner? I'm surprised that—"

"Ha! You're right. I wouldn't call in another coroner. Dr. Ulysses Abernathy is a forensic anthropologist teaching here at USI. Sort of famous, actually. Your granddaughter goes to USI, doesn't she? Maybe she's been in one of his classes."

Oren growled again. His granddaughter was the same age as Piper Blackwell. Annie had just reminded him that he worked for a twenty-three-year-old. "Yeah, she graduates with a master's this coming Saturday. Got accepted to Maurer law school in Bloomington. She'll start there in August." Softer, "And I'll probably have to pony up for the tuition. Maybe I'll make that her graduation present. We haven't gotten her anything yet." Oren was going to have lunch with her before heading back to Spencer County.

"Congrats. She'll make a good lawyer."

"Wants to work in a district attorney's office somewhere. Maybe a big city—Chicago, New York. I hope not Indianapolis. Her mother lives in Indy."

Annie smiled warmly. "And you're proud of her."

Oren gave a nod. His three children had all married, but only his daughter—who had married twice and divorced twice—had a child. Oren had always been proud of his granddaughter.

"Dr. Abernathy should have been here by now. I've never met him, but the Vanderburgh Coroner consults with him regularly, especially on those bones they find at Angel Mounds."

"The Indian site."

"Native American site," she politically corrected. "Sometimes people find bones in the area and Dr. Abernathy comes in to confirm if they're prehistoric."

"These aren't that old. Found a belt buckle from the early fifties with them, some coins. We're guessing maybe the boy was buried forty to sixty years ago. I'm leaning toward sixty."

"And I wish you would have brought all of that stuff over here to help Dr. Abernathy date these bones."

Oren shrugged. "You didn't say anything about that last night on the bluff. You were there when we started pulling stuff."

"Honestly, I didn't think about it then. Never dealt with something like this before," Annie admitted. "Bet you haven't either. So, you going to wait for him?"

"Dr. Abernathy? Nothing else planned for the day. Besides lunch with my granddaughter." He looked to the door. "I'm gonna get some coffee. You want—"

"Black with two sugars. No. Just one sugar, you skinny bastard."

In the hallway outside the antiseptic smell wasn't as strong.

Oren leaned against the wall. The conversations they'd shared in his hospital room in January swirled. Should he retire? His wife had encouraged him to do just that; she'd been traumatized over his shooting. Admittedly, he'd come close to dying, to ending up on some table like the unknown boy's skeleton in the autopsy room. Annie had argued against the notion, saying, "Piper Blackwell is pleasant enough, but damn well not experienced enough to be sheriff." He'd memorized Annie's words. She said the department—and the county—needed Oren. He didn't want the extra time on his hands that retirement would bring—not yet. He was learning to tolerate Piper, doubted he would ever respect her because of her age. But he respected the sheriff's department and loved the work. Maybe he'd work until the day he ended up under Annie's knife. He shuddered at that thought and headed to the coffee machine.

On his way back down he met Dr. Ulysses Abernathy—who looked more the age of a college student than a college professor.

Oren had only managed three or four hours of sleep. But he doubted that was the reason he was feeling particularly old today.

---

D r. Ulysses Abernathy wore frameless oval glasses tinted blue-gray. Oren guessed he was five-eight or five-nine and was a little on the pudgy side. His ash brown hair was shaved on the sides and had a styled curly mound on top that likely had been doused with a liberal amount of hairspray or mousse; Oren swore he could smell it. His cheeks were dotted with freckles, standing out because his skin was so light. A dime-sized gold skull and crossbones hung from his pierced left ear, and his clothes were casual—jeans and an orange pocketless, oversized polo.

*Young*, Oren thought, and then corrected himself when he noticed the crinkles at the edges of Abernathy's eyes and lips. Young-*looking*, but probably late thirties, maybe even a touch over the forty-year mark. A little more scrutiny, and he spotted some gray in the buzzed sides. That made Oren feel a little better.

"Dr. Neufeld," Abernathy said with a nod. "Good to meet you."

"And I'm happy to meet—"

Abernathy took a position by the table and plowed ahead, interrupting Annie's pleasantries. "Interesting," he said. "See the dent on the right side of the skull here? Forceps were used during delivery. The bone was deformed. As a person grows, the bones thicken. The skull is normal on the inside. But the dent on the outside. Forceps. No lower teeth and jaw available for inspection. Would make it a little more challenging for a facial reconstruction. But the upper teeth on cursory examination suggest that your remains are that of an eight- to ten-year-old. The teeth are not permanent, they are deciduous—milk teeth, some call them." His voice was low-pitched and strong. Oren figured he would do well in front of a classroom.

"Because permanent teeth are in by age twelve," Annie said.

Abernathy hummed. He pulled a pair of gloves from his pocket, put them on, and picked up pieces of vertebrae. "T1 and T2, broken. Yet to determine if post mortem, but not likely." He looked up at Oren. "These are the first and second vertebra in the thoracic spine."

Replacing them, he slid farther down the table and picked up the femur. "Note the diaphysis." He pointed with his free hand. "And the epiphyses at each end? There is no fusion there, definitely a child. Look here." Abernathy replaced the bone and indicated the arm. "Not joined, no fusion, under the age of twelve." He made a clicking noise. "It's the ribs. Fortunately we have the desirable third, fourth, and fifth ribs. You were lucky with these bones, Dr. Neufeld. Count your stars providential. But I'm probably not telling you anything you don't know. I understand you were a pediatrician for many years. For the sheriff here—"

Oren did not correct him with *chief deputy sheriff*, though he noted Annie's raised eyebrow.

"—the ends of these ribs are rounded, and they'd be smooth to the touch. As a man ages the ribs display pitting, and the edges here and here—they'd be sharper. I want an MRI done. X-rays are good, but not sufficient. An MRI will give us the calcium density, and that's useful in a final determination of age. I suspect they'll reveal that your boy was eight or nine years old. The ribs tell me that, not the ten I first mentioned as a possibility. I'm very good at this. Eight or nine. Probably nine. I'll want to pull DNA, too, though it might not help because—" He looked to Annie. "You mentioned these remains might be forty to sixty years old."

"They found some coins."

"Sixty," Oren said. "I'm leaning toward sixty."

"That old, might be hard to trace to relatives. But you never know. MRI, DNA. Might not need to bother with facial recognition if there are dental records to compare with missing children reports. We'll see." Abernathy shifted his weight. "No evidence of carnivore scavenging on these bones, no rat bite marks. But the lack of some bones might indicate animals removed pieces. They've been subjected to repeated freezing and thawing cycles, and those reduced some of your finger and toe bones to fragments. Some evidence here and here of plant abrasion—roots growing across the body, probably into the flesh before it dissolved. Can't tell if these bones were moved. You didn't call me to the scene. You packed them up and brought them here." He paused and frowned. "Then you called me. You should have called me to the scene."

Abernathy stood a little taller and Oren figured the forensic anthropologist was thoroughly "full of himself." Nevertheless, Oren was impressed.

"Eight or nine, eh?" Oren said.

"Probably nine." Abernathy made the clicking sound again. "I'm always right to within a year to a year and a half. Always. But like I said, I want the MRI before I write a report. I see some evidence of nutritional deficiencies, but a further analysis will confirm that." He made a circle of the table, picked up the skull, turned it over in his hands and replaced it. Picked up a few vertebrae to study, and then put them back down. "This arm bone is thicker than the other. See? That was the boy's dominant side. So he was right handed. The right femur would be thicker than the left, dominant side. But we don't have a right femur. The radius of this arm bone, and the skull—it has a more distinct ridge here—say 'boy.' The pelvis is not, in my opinion, strong enough evidence given the young age. Still, it all suggests 'boy.' Caucasian. Right handed. Nine, eight on the outside. I think—"

"Excuse me, Dr. Abernathy," Oren cut in. "Okay, you know skeletons. Can you tell from the bones how he died?"

Ire flashed across Abernathy's figure, clearly not pleased with the interruption.

"I could give you an educated guess right now, but I won't. I want the MRI, and I want to take a closer look. Come back later this afternoon. After I've had a few hours with all of this. Can you do that? Some test results take days, weeks. But I'm pretty confident on this one already. After lunch. I'll give you a cause after lunch. But the official ruling has to come from your coroner here. Dr.—"

"Dr. Annie Neufeld," Annie supplied.

"And that won't come until all the test results are back," he finished.

Oren figured he could talk his granddaughter into a long lunch.

"Yeah, I can do that," Oren said. "I can come back after lunch."

Abernathy waggled his gloved fingers in a dismissive gesture.

Oren sincerely hoped his granddaughter had not been in one of Abernathy's classes.

# SEVEN

It was a big red Case tractor, double wheels on the back, hitch, with a raised disc harrow attachment used for cultivating the ground prior to planting—all of it caked with dried mud and in need of washing. Piper was stuck behind it on 66, on her way to Hatfield, an unincorporated dinkburg where Mark the Shark lived.

Piper figured this ten-mile endeavor would take her an hour away from her cold case—fourteen minutes to Mark's, fourteen minutes back, and a half hour at the bank or looking through his records to show him the bookkeeping error and ease his conspiracy fears.

But the tractor was fouling her time-frame.

It belched fumes; her windows rolled down, the stink wafted inside and made her eyes water. It was noisy, overwhelming the oldies station she'd had on and just now clicked off. It was slow, riding in the center of the road, impossible for her to pass on either side without risking the ditch. And it wasn't traveling straight, sometimes in the proper lane, sometimes veering into the left lane. Usually it held to roughly the middle.

She honked.

The driver raised his left hand and flipped his middle finger.

"Really?" Piper stuck her head out the window and hollered, "Pick a lane!" Then thinking he might not be able to hear over the racket the tractor was making, she used the PA in her car. "Pull over. Spencer County Sheriff. Pull over."

The tractor had no rearview mirrors that she could see, and the driver hadn't turned around to notice who was honking at him.

She honked again, this time laying on the horn. Piper really didn't want to further delay her visit to Mark Thresher's and subsequent return to the alluring skeleton case by citing the farmer for a simple traffic violation, but— She honked a third time, the driver took both hands off the wheel and gave her the dancing double middle fingers. The tractor, which according to the speedometer in Piper's Ford was going about twenty miles an hour, shimmied to the right. As she started to pass, and reached to turn on her flashing lights, it sped up, drifted back to the left, and nearly clipped her front fender. She pumped the brakes and eased behind it, matching its speed—twenty-five miles an hour now. A boxy station wagon pulled behind her, and another car was coming farther back. Fortunate no one was in the opposite lane at the moment.

The tractor wobbled farther right, then left, shuddered, and went faster still. Thirty miles an hour.

"What the hell?"

Then the driver tossed an empty whiskey bottle off to the side of the road.

"That's it."

She turned on the siren and called the dispatcher to report her impending traffic stop. No license plate on the tractor, so no identification to note. Fleeing to avoid arrest, failure to yield, she mentally started writing the charges. She couldn't yet add DUI—that would have to be proven.

It looked like the driver—she guessed him to be young to middle-aged, as he had a flowing mane of ink-black hair—was finally going to acquiesce. He slowed to twenty, then ten, and pulled to the right, one of the big back tires drifting to the berm. A car and a motorcycle appeared in the opposite lane and zipped past. Piper continued to follow the tractor, the station wagon still behind her. Then she cursed when he sped up again. *How fast could a farm tractor go?* It jinked left, the sudden motion causing the tractor's back right set of tires to come off the road. They dropped back down with a clatter and the disc harrow made an ominous clunking sound, came loose, and cut into the blacktop, leaving grooves like open wounds.

"This is just absolutely wonderful." Piper's lip curled as she tried to maneuver her Ford Explorer around it again. "Pull the hell over!" She pressed on the gas, was nearly even with it and could read the MX 240 model on the side, then it trundled left again and she slammed on the brakes to avoid being run off the road. "Sonofabitch!"

Wisely, the two cars behind her drifted back.

The tractor surged forward, weaving and now straddling the center line. She matched its speed. Forty miles an hour.

"Really? Tractors go that fast?" She almost called for backup. *Should call*, she told herself. But Piper was proud and stubborn. How would it look if a decorated Army veteran couldn't stop a drunk on a farm tractor? Her deputies would not respect a sheriff who could not manage a traffic stop. She used the PA again. "Pull over! Pull over now!"

A beer can sailed away into the ditch. The hand that threw it raised the middle finger again.

"I left the 101st for this," she hissed. Piper was a skilled driver, able to operate armored personnel carriers, combat support vehicles, light armored vehicles, and an assortment of heavy trucks. This Ford was easy, and she could use it—if she absolutely had to—to force the tractor off the road. But there wasn't much shoulder, and she worried the tractor would flip into the ditch and seriously injure, or possibly kill, the drunken driver. She slammed her hand against the steering wheel and looked at the speedometer. The tractor had slowed back to thirty. Then twenty.

"Now ten," she encouraged. "Ten."

A few moments later it did, but it hung to the middle. Piper laid on the horn again; that coupled with the siren causing a clamor she was certain this rural stretch of road wasn't used to. The tractor ambled to the right, just as a bright green SUV came down the opposite lane.

"Five," Piper said. "That's it. Stop. Please stop you double dumbass drunken idiot."

She spotted him working some kind of gear. The tractor stopped, and she braked the Ford and put it in park.

"Oh, thank God." She let out a breath, which turned into a shriek when he stomped on the gas pedal and ran the tractor and its disc harrow into reverse. It slammed into her Ford with enough power to jar her and cause the airbag to inflate. The pillowy mass pushed Piper back; it felt like she'd been punched in the face with a boxing glove. The bag started to auto-deflate in a handful of seconds.

When she cleared the empty bag away from the windshield, she saw the tractor was churning away, weaving across both lanes and listing so that the back left tire came up, and then slammed down, the disc harrow digging another gouge into the blacktop.

She was nearly at the outskirts to Hatfield when the tractor slowed again and shuddered to the right, made a coughing noise that told Piper it had run out of gas.

"A little more. Get over. Get the hell over," she said. There was no way the farmer could have heard her, but he pulled farther right nevertheless, the outside rear tire at the very edge of the ditch. Piper held her breath as the tractor stopped. She flipped off the siren, left the lights on, and jumped out. The two cars that had been trailing her slowly passed, drivers' heads craned in lookie loo fashion.

"Keys!" she shouted up to him. "Throw me the keys!" That was the first thing to take care of, making sure he didn't start the damn thing up again and run it on fumes. Another car approached from the opposite direction. It stopped several yards back as if the driver was unsure she could proceed. Piper motioned her forward, and she complied—slowly and with her window down so she could catch all the details. "Keys! Now!"

The farmer tossed a glittering mass of silver and hit Piper in the chest. She grabbed them with both hands, not willing to take her eyes off the drunk. There were at least a dozen keys on the ring. It didn't matter which went to the tractor, not at the moment anyway. The fob was a three-inch long plastic ear of corn that said DEKALB on it in green block letters, Schmidt scrawled in faded marker on the other.

"Are you Mr. Schmidt?" Piper called up to him.

He nodded, swaying on his perch.

"I need you to climb down, Mr. Schmidt. Do you need help?" She stuffed the mass of keys in her front pocket and reached out to him.

"Nope. No help." He shakily stood and climbed down, knocking an open beer can off. It splashed Piper on its way to the blacktop. "Oops. Not shorry." His laughter turned into a hiccup, and he gave her the dancing fingers again. "Gonna arresht me? I don't need a license to drive a tractor on—"

"Yeah, I'm gonna arresht you." She took one wrist and then the other. He struggled, but as drunk as he was and as pissed off as she was, he was no match. Piper half-carried him and nudged him toward her Ford, noting the heavy grille and bumper damage the disc harrow had caused.

"Oopsh," he said again, as he noted the damage too. "I'd say shorry, but that wash on purpose, me ramming into you. Not shorry. I done good."

"Glad you admitted that," she said. "You have the right to remain silent."

"Oh, now you're shounding like my wife, and she's—"

"Anything you say can and will be used against you in a court of law." Piper didn't need to read him his rights here, not until she requested him to take a breathalyzer test or started asking him questions. But she intended to do both of those. Maybe more than once. And she'd have the rights read to him again at the department. "You have the right to an attorney."

"Can't afford one," he hiccupped. "I gots to shave my money for a camper I wanna buy. I can't shpend it on no damn lawyer."

"If you cannot afford an attorney, one will be provided for you."

"That'sh nish." He belched and a noxious mix of booze and cigarette smoke assailed her.

"Do you understand the rights I have just stated to you?"

"I undershtand just ducky, little chickie."

"Not giving you a field sobriety test," she said. "You're falling down drunk and the road's uneven. Not safe." She wrangled him into the back seat, retrieved her breathalyzer, and leaned over him. Piper knew that this test on the side of the road would only be useful for probable cause. To get anything admitted during a trial, she'd need a more formal test, which they could do at the station. There would have to be a twenty-minute stretch where he was observed not drinking before that test was administered. It would provide more accurate—and admissible—results.

"Shit," he said, looking through the screen that divided the front and back seats and kicking at the floorboard. "Shit. Shit. And back again. Shit."

Piper heard what upset him. A groan and clatter of metal heralded the tractor and its disc harrow tumbling into the ditch. All the rain must have softened the edge of the bank just enough, and the tractor's weight did the rest. She withdrew from the Ford and saw the gaping section of embankment where the big tire had rested. A road warning sign would have to be posted ASAP. At least she didn't have to worry about getting the tractor gassed up and moved off the road. Just towed—and that would be on Mr. Schmidt.

"Do you have some identification on you?"

He looked dully at her.

"A driver's license?"

"Don't need a goddamned driver's licenshe to take a tractor out on the road. I don't have a driver's licenshe. That gotten taken the lasht time I was picked up. Why the hell do you think I was out on the trac-tor? Don't need no goddamned driver's licenshe to take a tractor out on the goddamned road." He said that much louder, as if she might not have heard him the first time. "Don't gotsh no goddamned wallet on me with ID. Don't gotsh no—"

"Got a first name?"

"Shandy."

"Sandy?"

"Yeah, Shandy."

"I'm going to give you a breathalyzer test. All right with you, Mr. Schmidt?"

"Fine and ducky, little chickie. I know how to do it. I'm good at it."

"Breathe into this, Mr. Schmidt." Piper held the device to his face. This close to him, she could see that his cheeks were pockmarked, like he'd had serious acne in his younger years. His eyes were a watery blue, puffy, his hair shoulder-length, and his face clean-shaven. He was wearing jeans and a short-sleeved sport shirt, both looking relatively new. He had a pair of bedroom slippers on his feet. She placed him at about thirty-five to forty.

"What ish it? Whatsh my reading?" He looked almost excited.

"Point two-eight-nine," she said.

"I'm shnot drunk enough. I've got pasht three before."

"Wow," Piper said. Mr. Schmidt was an alcoholic. She guessed he weighed about one-eighty, meaning he'd consumed the equivalent of at least ten drinks in the past hour or so. She was surprised he was awake. Only an alcoholic would be this coherent and conscious with a .289.

She got in and radioed the department.

"I'm charging him with DUI," Piper said.

Schmidt made a growling, gacking sound then spewed vomit all over his shirt and the back seat. "Oops," he said. "Not shorry."

"This early?" Drew came back. "You got a DUI this early in the day? It's not even eleven."

"And damage to public property." Piper's Ford. She wrinkled her nose at the stench coming through the partition. "And damage to state property." The roadway. "And assault with a deadly weapon." The tractor, as she was in the car—and Schmidt's act of ramming her was admittedly intentional. She suspected some of the charges would be reduced, AA part of the deal. And maybe some more would be added. It would tie Sandy Schmidt up in knots with worry and hopefully give him enough attorney fees to make him more cautious in the future. He'd get stuck with insurance claims, too. For her Ford and for the team that would be called to handle re-righting the tractor. "And littering."

Indiana Code Title 35. Piper had memorized it among many other passages when she took the test at the sheriff's academy. Criminal Law and Procedure Indiana Code Section 35-45-3-2. A person, in this case Sandy Schmidt, who recklessly and knowingly left refuse on another person's property—the tossed beer cans and whiskey bottle—commits littering, a Class B infraction.

"And littering," she repeated. She told Drew to contact the roads department and get signs and flashers out.

"Mary's fault," the drunk moaned as Piper turned the battered Ford around and headed back to Rockport. "My shweet wife. She made a big to-do 'bout that new camper I wanna buy. She drove me to drink."

"You're not going to have enough money to buy that camper," Piper grumbled. "And now I'm not going to meet Mark the Shark until sometime this afternoon."

"And my tractor. That'sh your fault. That'sh all your damn fault. If you hadn't pulled me over, it wouldn't be in the damn ditch."

"Ooops. Not shorry," Piper said.

# EIGHT

Oren Rosenberg met his granddaughter for lunch at the Taj Mahal buffet on Tutor Lane. He'd arrived a little early and started with a plate of appetizers—paneer pakora, consisting of cottage cheese and spices dipped in flour and fried, and aloo tiki, potato slices topped with onion, yogurt, and chutney. Oren loved the Indian restaurant and ate here anytime he was in Evansville between the hours of eleven and two.

"Pops!"

"Millie. I've already paid for both of us. Go get started."

She came back a few minutes later with a sampling of batter-fried vegetables.

"You've lost weight, Pops."

"A little."

"That'll put it back on."

"I'll work it back off."

She laughed merrily and started eating.

Oren smiled. Annie was right, he was so very proud of his granddaughter. He'd helped her pay for college and bought her a beater-of-a-VW. He'd wanted her in something more substantial, but she'd set her heart on the sky-blue, high-mileage Beetle. His daughter—Millie's mother—helped when she could. But nearly five years ago, she'd rear-ended a daycare van while visiting friends in the Chicago suburbs. A girl died, a little boy was left a quadriplegic, and she was still paying on the judgment against her—and probably would be for at least a dozen more years. She'd been distracted, arguing with her boyfriend on her cell phone. A Class 4 felony, she could have spent three years in prison, but a savvy lawyer got her off without jail time. Oren had refused to help his daughter financially; she'd killed a child, and the accident had been wholly her fault. He felt that helping her would have been accepting what she'd done.

But Millie? His granddaughter was another matter.

Oren often wondered if Millie was pursuing law school because of her mother's woes. He'd never asked, and certainly didn't intend to today. Her t-shirt read I Love the Smell of Torts in the Morning.

"Pops, this is soooooooooooo good!" Millie stuffed an appetizer in her mouth and tried to talk around bites. Oren waved her to finish chewing; he couldn't understand her. "I've been going to classes here five years and never been to this place. Why didn't you take me here before? How had I not heard of this?"

"You've always been too busy when I've been in the city at lunchtime. This is the best buffet, I swear."

"When I go out—rarely—it's Charlie's Mongolian Barbeque or the Acropolis. This is awesome, Pops. I gotta come back."

She continued to stuff her face. Oren finished the aloo tiki, savoring the flavors that had settled nicely on his tongue, and went in search of more ample fare. Tomorrow he'd go back to his diet book. He returned with pepper chicken and a bowl of lentil soup. There were desserts up there. Those cheese balls soaked in honey couldn't be that bad, right?

"*Skinny Bastard* the rest of the week."

"What'd you say, Pops?"

"Nothing." He sat and tucked in his napkin into the collar of his shirt. He knew it was a juvenile move, but he didn't want to risk spilling on his shirt.

"So what brings you to the city?" She kept eating and looked at him expectantly.

Oren told her about the bones and the forensic anthropologist. "I can't say more than that, nothing more than what's gone out over the scanner and was sent to other departments. Open case, you understand."

"Sure. I understand. But you working with Doc Natty. Awesome sauce," Millie pronounced. "I'll be right back, gotta get me a little more. Is that pepper chicken good?"

Oren nodded, his mouth full.

"I'll try that, too. I'm not going to want any dinner tonight."

"Think you'll be able to figure out who the bones were?" Millie asked when she came back with a heaping plate. "With Doc Natty's help? He's dope, you know. I know. I know. Can't say anything else. Open case. Can only talk about what's on the blotter or went over the scanner. What you sent to other states. You did send it to other states, right?"

Oren nodded and drew his lips into a line and swallowed a bite of chicken. He decided to add a take-out order for his wife. "Doc Natty. Hah. Seems to know his stuff, but he's a bit pretentious."

"Pretentious? He's a *zhlub*, insensitive, but brilliant. An ego the size of— Well, a very big ego. He's been a consultant at the original body farm down by Fort Knox, and an advisor on some TV mysteries. One of the CSI shows, I think. Or maybe it was NCIS."

"*Zhlub*. Throwing around the Yiddish. And I suppose you call me a *zeyde*."

"Never."

"Behind my back probably."

"Never."

"I am, you know."

"You're not *that* old."

"My boss is your age. I could collect Social Security. I am a *zeyde*."

"*Zeyde*?" She shook her head. "You're Pops to me. I suppose I should call you Chief Deputy Pops. Though it should have been Sheriff Pops. Maybe you should run at the next—"

"I'll be sixty-nine, then. No one is gonna vote—"

Millie waved a fork at him in a scolding manner. "We'll talk about it in three years, when you'd have to start printing campaign posters. So about the bones—"

"You're gonna drag it out of me?" Between bites, Oren gave in and chatted a little about Piper finding the bones on the bluff and the work ahead to search for an identity. He didn't mention any of the items found with the bones; that would be going well beyond the boundaries of proper.

"So Doc Natty says a boy dead sixty or more years." She paused. "But records back then—none of that is going to be on your department's computer."

"Tell me about it. And the boy might not have come from Spencer County. That'll make it, I dunno, easier if old records are on other departments' computers. Departments that have everything computerized."

"Harder if they're not. Computerized."

"Yeah. I called in 'Doc Natty's' first impressions right before I got here, and JJ sent it out to departments in Indiana, Kentucky, and Arizona, hoping we get a hit. Eight to ten-year-old boy, missing sixty to sixty-five years. White, right handed. Specific enough it might match something. Sent it to a national database, too. So long ago, though, if the records aren't computerized—" He let that thought hang.

"Sounds like a mystery that's wonderful and awful in one fell swoop." She smiled excitedly, and then looked serious. "At least you won't get shot with an old, cold case. Whoever killed that boy is long dead. Sad that there is no one to prosecute. A crime with a victim, but no justice for him. I think it would be tough to work. No satisfying end." Millie had come to visit Oren in the hospital, too, and they'd chatted about the serial killer who would be sent away for life. "But at least no bullets."

"There is that, not getting shot at. Hey, you want a graduation party? Should have asked you that before now, I guess. This weekend,

I know. Saturday. Probably not enough time to put something together. But the next weekend. We could do a party then."

"Hell no. No, no, no party. Me and some of my peeps from communications are going to Roppongi to celebrate."

He tipped his head.

"It's a Japanese steak and sushi place here in town."

"I don't like sushi."

"You're not invited. It's a last hurrah before going our separate ways. I'll let you take me out for my birthday next month, though."

"Great. Then you'll be older than my boss. At least you got college under you. Two degrees, and going to be a lawyer. Piper's only got a high school diploma." That was another sticking point he hadn't been able to let go of. A high school graduate, twenty-three-years-old, was his boss *and* made more money than he did. He had forty more years of experience on Piper. Forty! Where was the justice? "Your degrees are a hairy big deal, Millie."

Oren knew Millie had earned top honors with her bachelor of science in criminal justice, and this graduation was for her master's— in communications—a good combination for the jump into law school. He decided to talk about financial arrangements for law school later, when she came to the house on her move to— "Where are you going to stay before law school? You got, what, two and a half, three months before it starts?"

"I don't want to talk about more school. Not today. I've spent the past five years in classrooms. I want to talk about going out on your boat, and the latest Elizabeth Vaughan romance novel. I adore romance novels. I want to picnic at the lake. I want to—"

"Where are you going to stay?"

Millie scowled. "Not staying with mom, that's for certain. Not staying in Evansville. Don't worry. I already got it covered. I found this month-to-month on Washington in Rockport, a house that's a hundred and thirty-some years old. Needs some work, and maybe I'll work on it for something to do. Cheap rent, really, really, really cheap rent, especially for the size 'cause it needs work. But it's got four bedrooms, two baths. Good for having company stay over. They have to get the electric and plumbing working before I can move in, but that should be taken care of by Monday. That's what I'm shooting for. To move in Monday. I'll get to see more of you and grandma. Go out on your boat. And I'm gonna try to start paying you back for all the college money."

He didn't care if she paid him back. *Renting a house*, he mouthed. He hoped the rent really was cheap. Oren pushed his empty plate away and started on the soup. "Heard from your dad?"

Her scowl deepened. "Just the Hanukkah card. Only ever the Hanukkah card. But this one was postmarked Dutch Harbor. I did some Googling, and he's on a crab boat in Alaska, something he always wanted, mom says. I'll watch *The Deadliest Catch* when its new season rolls around and see if I can spot him on one of the big boats. Speaking of boats—"

"I took mine out last weekend. A tad chilly, but not too bad."

"Doc Natty's not too bad either, Pops. Give him a chance. I'm glad he's working with you. Just ignore the arrogant side of him."

"There's another side?" Oren got up to get himself too many cheese balls soaked in honey.

9

# NINE

Called Fair Fight when it was established in the eighteen hundreds, Hatfield was basically a "straight shot" over from Rockport and was one of the county's "suggestions of a town," as Piper referred to the tiny communities. Population a breath over eight hundred.

Mark the Shark's immaculate-looking Cape Cod was a single-story frame with a steep-pitched gabled roof, a thick central chimney, and displayed little ornamentation beyond its navy blue shutters. It sat on a corner lot well back from the road. Piper had pulled up county records before she'd headed over. He'd had it built new four and a half years ago, before he'd put his farm up for sale. Most people his age would be moving into a nursing home, not ordering new construction. But he'd been selling off parts of his land—he'd owned a lot of land—and was accumulating plenty of money. Might as well spend it on something, she mused.

Piper pulled into the gravel drive and approached the front door, noting motion-sensor lights, a camera, grates on the windows, an ADT post by the walk, and a BEWARE OF DOG sign at the stoop. A window air-conditioner was in a bracket, had a rust-dotted chain wrapped around it, and an impressive padlock. The satellite dish on the roof also had a chain and a padlock—these looking shiny new.

When she pushed the doorbell, a thunderous "woof" responded. Definitely a big dog. Piper waited, tapped her foot, and knocked. The woofing was louder and sounded vicious. Worried about Mark, she walked around the house, seeing more motion-sensor lights and more cameras, a second window air-conditioner, and a good-sized dog door—probably so the dog could go out as it pleased and terrify people trying to climb the fence. Said chain link fence that ringed the backyard was six feet high. Piper whistled when saw the barbed wire on top. She was pretty sure that was illegal and not intended to keep the dog in as much as intruders out. She made a mental note to check the regulations.

She walked the rest of the perimeter, seeing two more BEWARE OF DOG signs, then came to the extra-deep double-garage. It could easily hold four cars. Piper rose up on her toes and looked into a side window. One long bay was empty. The other had two old motorcycles and a vintage Franklin convertible that she guessed was from the early 1920s. Olive green, it looked mint—except it was on blocks, the wheels probably stored elsewhere to keep someone from driving it away. Mark the Shark's paranoia was evident everywhere. She noted an alarm rigged to the garage doors and more motion sensors.

"Not home, are you?" Piper growled. She figured the empty garage slot meant the old man had driven somewhere. Should he be driving at his age? She stopped at the side of the house, stood on a cement block planter and looked in between the bars of a window. The room beyond was a den. She saw an old recliner with the stuffing coming out of the arms, an orange tabby curled in the seat staring back at her. Craning her neck she saw a battered desk with a computer on it—big flat-panel monitor, ergonomic keyboard. She idly wondered if it was wireless. Next to it was a police scanner, and on the hutch above it a weather-band. A stand nearby held a ham radio.

"You're an interesting fellow, Mark. Why the hell aren't you home? I told you I was coming over." She amended that. Piper had told him she'd be over in the morning, in the neighborhood of ten-thirty. It was well into the afternoon. Dealing with the drunk, cleaning the vomit out of the back seat, filling out the arrest report—and starting the paperwork about damage to her Ford and getting pictures of it—took a big chunk of unintended time. He might have gotten tired of waiting for her.

The dog must have heard her. It came to the window, foam bubbling on the sides of its mouth. A golden retriever that, judging by its white muzzle, was a senior. It didn't look dangerous, and was clearly happily wagging its brushy tail as it started barking again.

Piper stepped down, returned to her car, and radioed Teegan, who had recently come on shift.

"Hey, Sheriff. Mr. Conspiracy called several minutes ago. I was trying to get you on the radio."

"I was walking his property."

"He's not home."

"Obviously," Piper returned.

"He's at the old fart's club."

Piper buckled in and started the Ford. It made a disturbing chugging sound before settling down. Maybe the tractor had caused more damage than she thought. She'd drop it at the garage—she had to at some point anyway to finish the accident report and get it repaired—and catch a ride home with someone. But she'd set aside time to delve more into the boxes of records in her office. The cold case was festering and she wanted to get back to it.

"Why aren't you asking me what the old fart's club is, Sheriff?"

"Because I figure you'll tell me eventually." Piper turned back toward Rockport and heard the chugging sound again. Then the engine quieted and ran smooth.

"The old fart's club. It's the genealogy club. They're meeting this afternoon in the community room at the library's Parker Branch, probably not more than a mile or so from where you are. They move from branch to branch each week, and it's always on a Wednesday to convenience the high school computer class that helps them. You lucked out with it being at Parker."

"Thanks, Teegan."

"Hey, Sheriff? The guys found a few more things on the bluff. JJ's cleaning them up. I haven't had a chance to go take a look. Swamped with paperwork. Oh, and Oren's back. He says the bones belong to a nine-year-old, right handed white boy who as a baby had been delivered with forceps. Some fancy forensic specialist who took a look claims that T-bone vertebrae, something like that, were broken, a broken hyoid. Those are all in the neck somewhere. Says the broken vertebrae means the boy was likely strangled to death, or his neck snapped. Won't have the official coroner's report for days, though, maybe weeks. They're still doing some tests. Not sure yet just how long the bones were in the park. The bone guy is going over late this afternoon to look at the site. I'm emailing you Oren's initial report." The radio made a crackling sound. "Who the hell would strangle a nine-year-old?"

*Someone evil*, Piper thought. "I'm stopping at the Parker Branch." After she plugged it into her Garmin. She'd never been there. "I won't be long." She hoped. "Then I'm coming back in." To see what else had been found in the park and to walk the park again. The Ford was sounding fine now. She'd take it to the garage for repairs tomorrow.

"I heard that you and your dad are getting a May Day dinner tonight?"

So nosey Teegan probably looked in her office, saw the basket, and read Nang's card. Great. If the woman wasn't so efficient, Piper would replace her.

"Home cooked Vietnamese, Sheriff?"

Piper didn't reply. If she hadn't told Nang yes, she'd be spending the entire evening in the office. Instead, she'd let the office come home with her—or at least one of those big old records boxes.

She'd found the bones. This was her case.

Piper used her phone to call up her department email, wanting to see Oren's notes. They were concise and nothing different than what Teegan had relayed. There was also another message, that had been sent around noon, with a sender address that was an odd series of numbers.

Stay away from Thresher
The air will be fresher
And U will B safer
Drop it bitch

She stared at the screen. Mark Thresher wasn't paranoid, she decided. Not about someone stealing from him. And that "someone" knew Piper was looking into the case.

Piper called the salon and cancelled her hair appointment. Maybe she'd just hack it off herself tonight—after she figured out who sent her the threatening note.

# TEN

Piper stood in the doorway of the small library branch's community room. It was packed, and she wouldn't call *all* of them "old farts," though the majority fit the category. Her father was in the group, and he was only fifty-five. There were teenagers, too, eight that she counted. Each hovered behind senior citizens at computers, pointing, talking, assisting with some task or other. After a few moments, the teenagers shifted to other targets and started pointing and talking again.

Her father was right inside the entrance at a table stacked with books. She knew he didn't need any lessons on surfing the Internet. Paul Blackwell was computer savvy, and he looked so absorbed in research that he didn't notice her. Actually, everyone in the room seemed engrossed. Only the teenager in a bright red shirt had nodded an acknowledgment to her.

"Dad?" Piper went to him first. She spoke in a polite hush. "I didn't know you were in this club."

"I joined last year. Needed another hobby. What are you doing here, Punkin?" Paul sat back. "Did you come here looking for me?"

"No, Dad, I—" Piper motioned toward Mark the Shark two tables over. He was being tutored by a short, round-faced teen with a side ponytail.

"Ah, Mr. Conspiracy." Paul's voice dropped so she could barely hear him. "Can't be crop circles. He sold the last piece of his farm three years ago after he thought aliens had visited him. Nothing left to cut circles in. What's he got going on?"

"I'll tell you about it later."

"Later? Like you'll tell me about the bones you tripped over in the park?"

*How had he heard?*

Paul kept his voice library-low. "Drew called me. Told me all about the bones and coins and the buckle and stuff. He likes to keep me up to date. How come I have to hear something like that from him when—"

Piper let out a hissing breath. She was going to have a long chat with all of her dispatchers about their nose and lips problems. "I've been busy, Dad. I—"

"Certainly don't answer to me, I know that. But I hate to hear stuff from somebody else, Punkin, and—"

Piper inwardly bristled. Yes, her father was with the sheriff's department for more years than she'd been alive, and he remained interested in the goings on. He'd won four terms as sheriff, the final one cut short by his cancer diagnosis. But this was her department now. She didn't answer to him. She answered to the county commissioners and council.

"Nang is fixing dinner for us—"

"—something fancy and foreign. I heard that from Drew, too. Six, right? Dinner is to be served in our kitchen at—"

So Drew had read the card in the basket, and he no doubt told Teegan. She headed toward Mark. He was discussing something with the cherubic teenager in a t-shirt that read, Music + Cats Make Life Worth Living. A spreadsheet was displayed on the screen in front of them, color-coded and filled with names and numbers. Mark Henry Thresher was at the bottom, all alone like the cap of an inverted pyramid. Piper focused on it while she stood behind the pair, courteously waiting for their conversation to end. The people at nearby tables looked up at her curiously, whispered among themselves, and then went back to their projects.

"They called her the monkey woman," Mark was telling the girl. His long index finger touched a name on the screen. "Because she had this box of stuffed animals, most of them monkeys. She had a big stuffed orangutan, her favorite, called it Clementine, and she would dress it in different outfits and bring it to breakfast and place it on the chair next to her. She always sat alone, and she'd lean close and talk to that stuffed orangutan and try to feed it. The nursing home staff was always miffed because they had to pick up Cheerios and bits of scrambled eggs off the floor. She was never so ill-mannered as the fellow that had dementia and sat a few tables over and would shout 'hello hello hello' anytime you walked by. Got on my nerves, I tell you, that hello fellow did. Then there was this big guy with a bib who—"

The teenager smiled as if she was interested, tapped the spreadsheet, and interrupted. "Mr. Thresher, this is how you can list all your ancestors, names, birthdates, this field here for important notes. I can email the file to you or put it on a jump drive or—" The girl's eyes got wide when she finally noticed Piper. "Oh! Sheriff! Sheriff Blackwell!" Her squeaky voice cut through the surrounding conversations and the room quieted.

Mark turned and looked up. "Why'd *you* come here?"

"Looking for you."

"Piss. I called your dispatcher, said I wasn't gonna wait for you any longer. I had my attorney appointment and then I had this club. Shouldn't've told her about the club." To the teenager, "Sheriff Piper Blackwell, she's here working on an important matter with me. We can't talk about it in public, you understand. All hush-hush." To Piper, "Sheriff Blackwell, this is Cassandra Cassidy Blossom Keaton."

"Just Cassidy," she said. "So nice to meet you. I would've voted for you, but I wasn't old enough then. I am now, though." The girl had a silver hoop in her pierced eyebrow and had a nametag on her shirt that read Cassandra K.

Piper nodded to her.

"Cassandra is teaching me how to put together Excel spreadsheets. They're tricky beasts. See that little square? Looks like it'll hold ten letters in small print. But you can keep typing in it. Fits a hundred or more, you just can't see 'em all unless you—"

"Maybe we could get together tomorrow, Mr. Thresher." Piper wanted to get back to the old records and the park—and the threatening email. She noticed that everyone was watching her, whatever projects they'd been working on put on hold. Whispered conversations reminded her of gnats buzzing.

Mark made a harrumphing sound and added, "You were supposed to come by my house this morning. Called and said you were on your way and—"

"Something came up." Piper was about to repeat her suggestion about tomorrow when Mark pushed back from his chair and stood, knocking his twin canes to the floor with a clatter.

"Was that 'something' the bones you found in the park last night?" He'd raised his voice, clearly intending for his comments to carry across the community room. "That skeleton?"

Piper glanced her father's way. Paul Blackwell immediately opened another book and avoided her stare. *A game of telephone*, she thought. From Drew to her father to the genealogy club—and no doubt from here to every suggestion of a town in the county. The bones would be discussed at every diner table.

*But maybe that wasn't a bad thing*, she thought. Maybe that might lead to their identification.

The man sitting next to Mark edged around. "We've been wondering about those bones, Sheriff, speculating a bit. Any idea who it is? Find any identification with it? A medical alert bracelet?" She noticed he had one of those medical alert bracelets. "A driver's license or—"

"Are you going to call in the FBI?" This came from one of the teenagers, a broad-shouldered boy in a blue t-shirt with the slogan NOSOCIALLIFE on it. He had a cell phone in his hand and was texting on it.

"What about the Rockport cops?" A librarian standing in the

doorway posed this question. "Are you helping Chief Hugh with the case?"

"I listened to the scanner at lunch—not a word about them bones with the Rockport Police." This came from an elderly woman with a blue tint to her tightly-curled hair. She tapped a finger on her computer monitor. "Nothing on Facebook either, and I've been looking ever since Paul Blackwell told us."

"Haven't found anything about it on the blasted Internet. Maybe I'm not looking at the right sites." The man wore a US Navy Veteran ball cap backwards. "I emailed the fellow at the VFW and he didn't know nothing."

"Seems like a tough case for you to handle," the librarian said. Piper guessed her to be fifty, stern-looking, and with dark eyes that seemed too small for her wide face. "You've been sheriff, what, five months?"

"Four," Piper idly corrected.

"I read true crime," the librarian continued. "Cold cases are hard to solve."

*Coming here to find Mark had been a bad idea, even if this was only a mile from his house.*

Piper looked toward the exit. She didn't like that her visit here had turned into a community forum.

*This had been a very bad idea.*

"That serial killer—she solved that one." The man in the Navy hat.

"But she had Gretchen arrested!" The blue-haired woman. "Shame on her. Paul Blackwell would never have arrested Gretchen. Putting an old woman in jail just 'cause she runs into—"

*Ah, Gretchen the Mailbox Mauler. Word had spread about that, too. Never again show up at the old fart's club.*

"She pinched Sandy Schmidt today, too." The white-bearded man. "I feel sorry for him. Having trouble with his wife."

"Heard that on the scanner about Sandy." This from a reed-thin woman wearing a stocking cap. Her eyes looked sunken and Piper wondered if she was undergoing chemotherapy. "Pulled his drunken ass down off his brother-in-law's tractor and then pushed the tractor into the ditch for good measure. Bet the brother-in-law sues Sheriff Blackwell. Tractors are damn expensive."

*Oh. Dear. God.*

Piper felt her stomach twist.

*This wasn't the old fart's club. This was the Busybodies of Spencer County Club.*

She watched some of the members pull out cell phones and text. What the hell was she doing here? She saw her father lean closer to the pages.

"The bones, Sheriff Blackwell. What about the bones?" This from Cassidy. The teenager locked her wide eyes with Piper. "Tell us about the bones! It's exciting!"

"Yeah, Sheriff. What do you know? You tripped over the skull, right?" This from NOSOCIALLIFE. He'd put his phone away.

"How many bones?" Cassidy.

NOSOCIALLIFE. "Did the skull have a bullet hole in it?"

"It was an accident, finding the bones?" Blue-haired. "Really? An accident?"

"Wasn't no accident," Mark said. "God was responsible. God tripped her."

"What did you do with the bones?" NOSOCIALLIFE.

"Enough!" Piper felt a headache blossoming and swore she could hear her heart. Her stomach twisted tighter still. She would never seek a second term. She would never ever revisit the old fart's club. Fort Campbell was looking like an oasis in the sea of sharp wagging tongues.

"It's big news, a skeleton on the bluff," the librarian put in. "Hard not to talk about it."

"All right." Piper decided to give in and provide a little information —which might, *maybe*, stop wild, incorrect stories from spreading throughout the entire county. Maybe she could turn this to her advantage. Maybe, with luck, it might indeed help identify the skeleton. "All right. Let's talk about the bones."

The sudden resulting silence was eerie in comparison to the minutes before.

"I found the bones late last night when I walked through the park. I'd been near the edge, looking down on the river. I turned and—"

"Paul already told us that part." The white-bearded man.

"What were you doing in the park so late? Out in the rain?" This from the old man next to Mark. He had a name tag—Gary Frank. She realized most of the people in the room had name tags. But not her father. But then everyone knew Paul Blackwell. "What were you doing on the bluff—"

That beautiful eerie silence felt so far away.

Piper blew out a long breath and held up her hands as if in surrender. "I like the park. I like to walk in the park. I'm going back to the park when I leave here. I was in the park last night and found the bones."

"So, them bones, Sheriff?" The blue-haired woman again. Her name tag read Sylvia D. "Just *how* did you find them? Did you *really* trip on the skull? Or were you *digging* for—"

"I wasn't digging for anything. I found them by accident. The power went out in town while I was going for a walk—"

"In the rain?" Gary Frank.

"I like to walk in the rain."

"So do I." Sylvia D. "But I don't buy you walking in the rain late at night. From what your dad said, the park was closed."

"The department often patrols parks after hours." That was true. It contributed to the alcohol-related arrests made. "I couldn't see well," Piper went on. That was also true. "I was headed back to my car when I tripped. I thought it was a root I'd caught my foot on. It turned out to be a bone. All the rain had washed away enough dirt to expose them. We got a crew out and started working."

"Wow. Just like an episode of *Law & Order*," said Cassidy.

"Where are you going to bury them?" Gary Frank. "You're going to, right?"

"Where are the bones now, Sheriff?" NOSOCIALLIFE. His nametag read Zeke the Geek.

"The skeleton is in Evansville, with the coroner. We're running tests to—"

"—determine cause of death," Sylvia D supplied. "I used to dispatch for Rockport police. I know stuff. That's what they're doing right? Gotta be a murder."

"Of course its murder," a doughy-faced man in a flannel shirt said. "They found a gun under the bones. Paul told us about the gun."

"What gun?" Gary Frank. "I must not have been paying attention."

Piper felt dizzy and turned back to her father—where her father had been sitting. He was gone. Teegan had mentioned a few more things had been found, but the Goth dispatcher said she hadn't yet looked at them. If Teegan had known about a gun, she would have told Piper. That meant Drew again. Drew had told her father a gun was found before she'd been told. She took a deep breath.

"Maybe they're really, really, really old bones, Sheriff," Cassidy speculated. "I read in local history class about land grabbers purchasing plots a few hundred years ago. Daniel Grass was the first in 1807. He was a justice of the peace who built a cabin near Hanging Rock. That might be right near where the bones were on the bluff, I'd bet. I wrote an essay about him. And William Berry moved there a year later and started a settlement. It could be from that time. First settlers' bones. That'd be four shades of awesome, wouldn't it? Like something you'd watch on the History Channel. A first settler killed in a gunfight."

"Looking for a front page story again, the sheriff is." Sylvia D.

The voices became a confusing susurrus that swirled around her, and she could only pick out "bones," "coins," "big mystery," "gun," and several mentions of "Paul Blackwell." Maybe the old farts thought her dad would do a better job working the cold case. He'd apparently keep them apprised of what was going on, regulations or no.

She nearly walked out, but instead took charge. "Maybe your club could help me." Piper more closely scanned the room. There were roughly two dozen computers—a mix of desktops and laptops, the latter probably belonging to the senior citizens sitting in front of them, the desktops likely the library's. People sans computers had iPads and tablets. Only a few were going old school with just books and notebooks in front of them.

"How could we help?" Gary Frank.

"I'd do anything to help." Zeke the Geek.

"I'm in," said Cassidy.

"Me, too." Man in the Navy cap.

Spencer County covered a shade more than four hundred square miles. Four hundred and ten, actually, but roughly a dozen was water. There were seven hundred and thirty-eight miles of county roads and one hundred and forty-seven highway miles. And, somehow, despite the place being a rural as Hooterville, Piper realized that news traveled like quicksilver from one edge to the other. She figured since the old farts club was likely to learn everything she did about the bones anyway, maybe they could help.

"We believe the bones belong to a boy roughly nine years old, who was right handed. He might not be from around here. It's possible he was originally from Arizona. We have a piece of evidence with an Arizona link."

"The belt buckle," Sylvia D said. "Your dad told us about the Arizona belt buckle."

"Yeah, there was a belt buckle. The boy might have come from Arizona. If instead the boy was from around here, he likely knew someone from Arizona, had been given the buckle."

"I'll help you, Sheriff!" Sylvia D chirped.

"I'll lend a hand," said a jug-faced man wearing a Colts cap. "I've been doing genealogy for twenty years. I know every family in the county."

Mark the Shark grumbled and sat again, bending down to retrieve his canes.

The whispered conversations that ensued sounded like a strong breeze cutting through a gap in a doorway. But they ended when Piper nodded to NOSOCIALLIFE.

"What would you like us to do?" Zeke the Geek asked. He'd had his hand raised. "You want us to use our genealogy resources, right?"

"Right. Look through your own family's backgrounds. You're already researching ancestors because of this club. See if anyone was missing, say forty to sixty years ago. That range, roughly. A boy. You come across something like that, a missing relative, please contact the department." She reached into her pocket, where she kept business cards. "I don't have quite enough to go around." Piper handed them to Cassidy, who started passing them out. "We also have a webpage, and you can email us there if you come up with any suggestions. That's all I have on the bones right now. Honest."

Mark tugged on her sleeve. With the conversations buzzing again, she had to strain to hear him. "Why'd you have to come here looking for me? Now these folks are all gonna wonder what I've got going on and—"

"They're not all gonna wonder anything about you, Mr. Thresher."

"Mark."

"Mark."

"Mark the Shark."

"They're not going to think anything about you because all they're interested in right now are the old bones and some gun that I don't know a damn thing about." That was all she was interested in, too. She should have gone back to the office rather than coming here.

"I 'spose." He stood again, holding his canes rather than using them. "Let's go outside. Got something to show you. In private."

She asked for Sylvia D's contact information then followed him to the library parking lot, and Zeke the Geek followed her.

"Hey, Sheriff. Got a minute?" Zeke wasn't just broad-shouldered, he was muscular, and the NOSOCIALLIFE t-shirt was tight across his chest. He had dark brown hair that was cut military short and a soul patch under his lip. "I'm—"

"Zeke," Piper said, nodding at his nametag.

"Ezekiel, actually. Ezekiel Whitman."

She waited for him to go on.

"I'm a senior, graduate in less than two weeks, and I don't want to go to college. I'm eighteen. Well, eighteen the day after tomorrow. I put in an application for that deputy position you have open. I've been to the Law Enforcement Adventure Camp in Raleigh—twice. I can shoot. I'm good with computers, self-taught. *Real* good with computers. President of the computer club, and I set up these sessions for the genealogy club two years ago, got school approval for our last hour of the day to be here once a week—except when there are pep rallies. I thought maybe you might overlook my application because of my age. Or because I don't have a college degree." He stuck his hands in his pockets. "I don't want you to overlook me. I'd make a great deputy."

"I don't have a college degree," Piper admitted. But she did have four years of MP military experience. "I don't discriminate based on age."

"Great. So..." Ezekiel tapped the toe of his tennis shoe against the pavement. "Okay. I just wanted to put my face to my application. That's all." He turned and jogged back into the building.

Mark shook his head. "Good kid. He's worked with our club a lot. Smart and patient. Set up my home computer for me, handled the wireless connection. Said he'd give me his old laptop when he gets a new one for graduation. But I don't need his charity. Just don't want to hurt his feelings by turning down his gift. Good kid, I say."

"Seems like it."

"Isn't he too young for your department? I thought deputies had to be twenty-one."

"They do. But I might have an opening for something else." Piper stared across the lot and saw a Chevy—a glossy black model that looked seriously old and beautiful. After seeing the vintage car in his garage, she knew this was his. But she asked for confirmation. "That yours?"

"My baby, a 1935 three-window coup. Belonged to my dad, and he let it go to hell. Gave it to me when I retired from the Navy. Restoring it was a hobby—when I wasn't in the field plowing. It's mint. I keep it up."

Piper figured the old man would like Nang. They could talk about fixing cars.

"Got me another old one at home, too. Old men like old cars. The new ones are pieces of shit designed to be disposable."

"Did you mention to anyone that I was looking into the bank money thing?"

He shook his head. "I keep my business to myself. I talk to Marmalade about it, though."

"Marma—"

"My cat. Camaro, too. My dog. The dog's a better listener. I've named all my dogs through the years after classy cars. In fact, I had one big terrier I named after my favorite car, a—"

Piper feared he would start into a rambling story about vintage autos. "You said you had something to show me."

"I printed off my bank statement." He reached into his pants pocket and pulled out several sheets of paper that had been folded over and over. It was heavy paper, linen, like someone would use for resumes and correspondence, rather than for printouts. He glanced around. "Gotta make sure no one's watching. Printed them this morning, figuring you'd be over then."

"No one's watching," Piper said. Except the small-eyed librarian who was looking out the front window.

"See? Look at it. This line and this line and this one. And here. Here. Those are transactions from the past three weeks. Look at it. I only noticed a couple of days ago 'cause I wasn't checking my finances all that often. Hadn't thought I'd needed to. I called you right away 'cause the damn bank wasn't helpful. I didn't think you quite believed me last night in the park. I think God was scolding you for doubting me. That was God's scolding finger—that bone—poking up through the ground and tripping you. God was telling you to pay attention to me."

"I do believe you. God didn't need to get my attention. You did that." Piper studied the printouts. The pages detailed checks he'd written, deposits, and withdrawals for the past sixty days. There was a string of fifty dollar checks to the kennel club, garden club, American Legion, Friends of Lincoln, Lion's Club, Kiwanis, Optimists Club, Masons, Hazardous Waste Taskforce, Hatfield Recreational Committee, and the First Baptist Church.

"I belong to all of those," Mark said, pointing at the fifty dollar string. "Hard for me to keep up with all the meetings, though."

There were five sizeable withdrawals and they totaled—she

quickly did the math—$174,950. Nearly fifteen thousand higher than Mark had mentioned yesterday, but she noted that the latest withdrawal was for $14,950, and it was from early this morning.

"See? I didn't make those withdrawals."

"According to this printout, you made the withdrawals."

"I didn't make any of them. Well, all those fifty dollar checks, I wrote those. Like I said, I belong to them clubs and like to give 'em a little money now and then. All the same amount so I don't show favoritism. And the electric bill—I pay that online, phone bill, too. But those big ones. I didn't make those withdrawals. So see why I don't trust the bank? The bank's in on it. I tried to do my own sleuthing, but I came up with crap. Some damn Democrat at the bank. So that's why I called you, met you last night. So I gotta go to the bank. I'm gonna get my money out this afternoon—what's left of it—all the rest of the money this afternoon. I just want you to go with me and—"

"It's nearly four, Mr. Thresher." And Piper doubted the bank was prepared to fork over all his money with no advance notice.

"Mark."

"Don't have much time left this afternoon, Mark the Shark. And the bank—"

"Then we better hurry."

"I'll follow you over there, and we'll clear this up."

He frowned, all the wrinkles on his face deepening so his skin looked like a piece of bark from an ancient oak.

"I'll follow you," she repeated. "Let's take care of this now."

*Let's get this over with so I can get a look at the gun and where it was found at the park.*

"Yeah, all right. I want you to get my missing money back, too, like you promised. And I hope nobody follows the both of us over there." Softer, "Some damn Democrat spy. I just know it. A damn Democrat in cahoots with a Democrat at my bank is spying on me, probably getting a cut of my money. You trail after me a bit, make sure no one is shadowing."

## ELEVEN

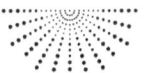

The gun was a Hubley Texan Jr., nickel-plated cast iron. "From 1940-something," JJ had printed a note in the detested Comic Sans font. "They pulled up the trees and found the gun, badge, and rope. Those were canoe birch, or white birch, planted forty-two years ago according to old parks department records. The gun was tangled in the roots. No hits yet on a missing boy from Arizona or Kentucky or Ohio—I tried there, too. Nothing from Indiana either. But it's early. And now for me it's late. See you in the morning."

The toy gun was a little more than eight inches long and weighed about a pound. The cracked plastic inset in the handle was of a horse in a circle. There was a coat of rust on it, but thin enough the details showed. Iron needed oxygen to rust, and being buried in the dirt had helped protect it.

The badge was shield shaped, made of tin and bent, but Piper made out "Lone Ranger Deputy" and a seven-digit number stamped under it. JJ's note said the badge also dated to the 1940s, but she hadn't pinned down the exact year.

*A toy badge. A toy gun.*

The coil of rotting rope was partly nylon, filthy and stinky and knotted to form a loop. A lasso, likely made from clothesline. *The murdered boy was playing sheriff*, Piper thought. That curl of leather with two punched holes she'd looked at this morning? She realized that was a hatband. The hat had likely disintegrated with the flesh and clothes. Maybe it had been straw. But shoes? Wouldn't there have been some trace of shoes? Or cowboy boots? They wouldn't have disintegrated, not entirely. Maybe he'd been barefoot. Maybe it had been summer. And what did the piece of barbed wire have to do with it?

She shuffled into her office, typed up another job description, and posted it to the local paper, the department Facebook page, and a Spencer County website. She noticed there were already some email applications for the detective job she'd posted this morning. There was also an email with the message WARNING in the header. She clicked it:

BACK OFF AND KEEP BREATHING.

The sender's email address was a string of numbers, different than the address of the previous note, and ended with two letters—FU.

She glanced at some of the other email messages, confirming that all applicants were for the detective opening—plus one page of coupons for laundry detergent. Nothing yet from any genealogy club members. She deleted the coupon page, and nearly did the WARNING note. But she decided to keep it, see if someone in the department could track the sender. She tried, but her attempt bounced, as if the sender's address did not exist.

"*Mañana*," Piper decided. She'd look through the applications tomorrow and see if there was anyone worth bringing in for an interview. Or maybe she'd ask Oren to pare the list down. She had four interviews scheduled after lunch for the open deputy slot—two to mollify the local politicians, and two she'd selected from candidates living outside the county and looked promising. She wanted to fill the position soon. Probably should have had Oren look through that stack and do the initial weeding. He might have found a more promising soul that she'd passed over.

A call to Sylvia D who'd she met at the genealogy club. Then quick calls to Nang and her father to tell them she might be late for dinner.

───────

I t was 5:30 and she should be on her way home. Piper was hungry, having skipped lunch because she'd been so busy, but eating a handful of chocolate-covered raisins before she stopped here. She couldn't pronounce what Nang was going to fix, but she knew it would be delicious. She loved everything on the menu at his quick mart in Fulda.

*Should* be on her way home, but instead she was walking the bluff park again, making a circle of the ground staked out by her deputies and partially covered by Teegan's tent. She kept glancing over her shoulder. It felt like someone was watching her. Several times she'd looked in her rearview mirror on the drive here, the sensation of being followed niggling at her.

"Pay attention to those impressions," a drill sergeant once told her. They'd served her well during downrange assignments in Iraq. Here? There were two teenage girls sitting on a bench near the sidewalk. One had a big cup of coffee and was reading something on a small tablet; the other had a stack of books on her lap and was texting on a cell phone. People and electronic devices. Why didn't they just sit and talk to each other?

The girls weren't watching her, didn't appear to notice her walk by. Piper didn't see anyone sitting in the few cars along the curb, but the sensation of being watched persisted. It being the dinner hour, most folks were home eating, and so she had the bluff to herself. Maybe someone in a house at the far edge of the park was watching. The feeling would not go away and sent shivers down her arms.

*Stop letting Mark the Shark get to me. Have I caught his paranoia bug?*

Back off and keep breathing. She shook the email loose from her memory.

*The bones. Focus on the bones.*

Piper remembered picnicking under those clump birches—once with a sophomore classmate named Thomas, never Tommy, Breck. He'd had his driver's license and use of his father's car, and after lunch one sunny day they'd driven to the waterpark in Santa Claus where he kissed her in the deep end of the wave pool. She thought she was in love. Had they eaten on the boy's grave? How many children had played atop it? The bluff was popular in the summer. The bluff and the landing below because there wasn't a lot to do in Rockport. Or at least she hadn't thought there was when she was growing up.

The boy didn't get a chance to grow up. Someone had stolen all the summers he might have enjoyed. Had he been from Arizona? Had he been visiting here? Had he been discarded along some killer's cross-country drive?

Piper made a slow circle of the park, smelling the river, looking up to see the sky full of birds and high tissue paper clouds. The air tasted clean and was laced with early wildflowers. She held the scent deep. Spring could be beautiful in Spencer County. But such an ugly thing had happened in this picturesque place.

*What if I hadn't come out here last night to meet Mark the Shark? What if it hadn't rained so damn much the past few weeks? Record rains. What if I hadn't slipped?*

Would the bones have ever been found? Would continued rains have washed them over the edge and into the river? Would animals have carried them all away?

What if she'd never run for sheriff?

What if she had stayed in the Army?

Peering in the hole left from pulling the trees, it was an empty grave she stared into. Who would strangle a nine-year-old and bury him in the park? What sort of soul could have done such a thing? Nine years—dogs lived longer than that. Fourth grade likely.

Despite Piper's determination to work this case, she knew there'd be no real justice for the boy—all these decades gone, his killer gone with them. No one to pay for a horrible crime. But maybe the boy's spirit would find a measure of peace if she could solve the mystery. Put a name to him. Get him buried in a proper place.

Had he been playing sheriff?

Was she merely playing sheriff herself?

Piper's chief deputy had decades more experience. *Everyone* in her department had more experience. Not that she didn't have any. Four years as an MP; that counted for something. But Spencer County was a world away from Iraq. And her sheriff's department was far removed from the cruisers she patrolled in at Fort Campbell.

Four months on this job.

Could she really tackle a cold case?

"Who were you, boy?" she asked, staring at the hole. "And why were you killed? And how did you end up buried on the bluff?"

"I'll try to help you with the 'who.' The why and the how—that's for you to answer." The speaker had come up to her side so silently Piper jumped. No wonder she thought someone had been watching her. "Maybe the 'why' can't be answered. Ever. A lot of years have passed." He waited a beat and extended a hand. "Dr. Ulysses Abernathy. I'm a forensic anthropologist with USI. I specialize in bones. Osteology. Your coroner asked me to consult."

Piper shook his hand, finding his fingers lightly calloused and the grip firm. He had a youthful aspect, but a serious expression. He quickly recounted the report he'd given to Oren.

"Sixty years," Abernathy said. "The coins and the buckle are the real tell. The cement to my bone analysis. Sixty to sixty-five years. That's how long the boy was in the ground. It's a firm range, though it will be weeks before some test results come back. They'll just back up that range, maybe pin it down a little tighter. I've never given an incorrect estimate. That's why I'm brought in to consult on cold cases. I'm always right."

Piper thought his tone coupled with his posture made him come across like a pompous ass. Still, Oren had radioed her that he'd been impressed with Dr. Abernathy's work.

"Your coroner has dentals, uppers only, emailed them to various agencies. But no test results to report yet. Tests always take longer than you'd like," he continued. "The results will let me create a more detailed biological profile for you. They will reveal any diseases that might have compromised the bone. Nutritional disorders, vitamin deficiencies that might have impacted bone mineralogy, lesions. It is possible something like tuberculosis had been in the history, polio, measles—diseases prevalent in children in those years." He came up for air and then went on. "I detected a healed fracture in his ulna. From an injury three or four years before his death. My biological profile will be useful in helping to find an identity."

"Can you tell if he died in the summer?" Piper was still thinking about the lack of shoes.

"Possibly," he returned. He pointed at a dark red sports car at the edge of the park. "I have a testing kit. I want to take my own samples of the soil, plants in the immediate area, gather some roots and insect husks. Possibly I can give you a season. The likely cause of death, like I told your chief deputy, I'm listing as strangulation."

Piper shuddered. The serial killer who'd plagued the county during the holidays had strangled his victims.

"Thank you for assisting, Dr. Abernathy." Piper wondered if her department or the coroner would be paying his bill. Her budget was pretty tight, and would have to include repairs to her Ford, though insurance might cover most of that. The forensic anthropologist wasn't going to be cheap.

"I'm staying tonight," he announced. "I've a room at the hotel near the bridge. I don't have classes tomorrow, so I'm going to take a close look at the birch roots that were pulled. Take some cuttings, maybe a wedge from the trunk. Stop at Monkey Hollow Winery since it is so enticingly close, get a case of something semi-sweet." He gave a half smile. "But that's for my indulgence. As for the bones, I'll finish my write-up and pass it along to your coroner. I can copy you if you'd like."

"Please," Piper replied.

"We could share dinner this evening," he suggested. "Talk some more about the skeleton, other cases I have consulted on."

"I have dinner plans. And I'm going to be late for them," Piper returned. Had he asked her out? "But, I would share breakfast with you if you're an early riser."

"Very early."

"Six?"

"A good time. Breakfast, then. And perhaps dinner another time."

Yeah, he had asked her out. She told him where Rockport's small restaurant was.

He gave her a perfunctory nod, circled the area, and took pictures with his cell phone while she watched. "I'll be collecting some soil samples now. There is still good light. We'll talk more at breakfast. I hope your little restaurant serves a passable Eggs Florentine and a good *cafetière*."

*Biscuits and gravy. Eggs over-easy is about as complicated as it gets. Coffee, yes, but no French press cafetière.*

The breakfast, lunch, and dinner menus were simple and all fit on one double-sided laminated sheet.

"I'll see you at six." Piper took another long look in the hole, raised her gaze to the edge of the bluff, and turned toward the sidewalk, noticing the two girls were gone. She headed to her car, her stomach growling with each step.

Her heart stopped a beat when she reached for the driver's side door handle. "What the hell?" There was a deep scratch down the length of the vehicle, an angry mark from front fender to the back bumper. And on the driver's door was an equally deep X. The marks weren't from her run-in with the drunk on the tractor, and they'd not been there when she drove from her office to the bluff.

The nearby cars had no such scratches. Hers had been singled out.

The two girls on the bench? No. As soon as that notion surfaced, she squashed it.

Someone else.

Someone had been following her.

"Pay attention to those impressions," her drill sergeant had said.

"Who?" she asked, staring at the scratches. "And why?"

The latest email came back, looming. BACK OFF AND KEEP BREATHING.

# TWELVE

"This is delicious," Piper pronounced. "What's in it?"

She'd arrived a half hour late to the May Day dinner in her father's kitchen. But Nang had also been delayed because of a problem with the diesel pump at his quick mart, and so they didn't sit down to eat until nearly seven.

"Chả Lụa is a traditional dish," he explained. "Pork, very lean, potato starch, garlic, black pepper, and fish sauce. I pound the pork until it is like paste. You never grind it. The preferred way to cook it is by wrapping it in banana leaves and boiling it. You have to wrap it tight so no water gets inside. But I use aluminum foil. Can't seem to find banana leaves around here, not even at the Asian grocers in Owensboro." He winked at that. "Gà Nướng Xã, this dish is simple enough that it is often on my menu at the store. It is the marinade that makes the chicken delicious. I use soy sauce and lemongrass in equal amounts. Also garlic, papaya paste, chili powder, pepper, mushroom and kosher salt, lime juice, shredded lettuce and cucumber, shallots, green onion, peanuts, a few jalapenos, and palm sugar and mint leaves."

"A simple dish?" Piper laughed. "Oh my, Nang! That's more

complicated than anything I'll ever attempt. A simple dish is a frozen entrée I stick in the microwave."

"Drew shouldn't have called me," Paul Blackwell said, abruptly changing the direction of the conversation. "Shouldn't have told me everything going on. And I shouldn't have listened, shouldn't have asked him questions, and got him to tell me even more. But I could tell he was dying to talk about it." He speared a forkful of Chả Lụa and wagged it. "And I certainly shouldn't have mentioned the gun—any of it—to the people at the library. I don't know what I was thinking. I certainly wouldn't have done that if I was still with the department."

Nang looked back and forth between the two, eyebrows raised.

"I'm going to talk to Drew about it in the morning," Piper said. "I certainly don't want to talk about it now."

"So, the skeleton really is from a boy?" Paul ate the sausage and cut off another piece. "This is delicious, Nang. Buried in the park a long time? Would have had to been buried at night for no one to notice."

Nang poured glasses of wine and sat. "A dead boy?"

"Skeleton of a boy," Paul said.

Piper swallowed a bite of chicken and licked her lips. "This is soooooo good. And you are sooooo the only soul in this county not to have heard about the bones, Nang. By now I'm sure the old fart's club has spread it everywhere. It's probably made its way across the river and into Owensboro." She gave them a brief description of her day, leaving out the scratches on the Ford and the sensation she was being followed. She almost mentioned the troubling email messages, but stopped herself on that count, too.

"The drunk on a tractor and the woman slaying mailboxes are better things to deal with than a nameless dead boy," Nang decided. "And they would make good lyrics for a country song." He passed the Chả Lụa around for seconds. "I like country music."

"What about Mark the Shark? Mr. Conspiracy?" Paul asked.

Again Nang's eyebrows went up.

"I went to the bank with him this afternoon. He thinks someone is withdrawing money from his account. At first I thought he was maybe moving money around and got confused. But the bank manager took him seriously and filled out a fraud report. She said she'd contact the main office and get the fraud department to investigate, and that it could take a few days to 'follow the money' and see what's going on. Then work to get his money back. I think there really could be something unusual going on. I believe him."

"Mark always has unusual things going on," Paul said, tapping his head. "His wife died of dementia. After the crop circle incident I was pretty sure Mark had it, too, dementia. He was convinced it was aliens that cut the patterns. Couldn't prove it, but I'm certain it was local kids messing with him. That was three years ago, and right after that he put the rest of his farmland up for sale. He'd built this new house in Hatfield, settled into it. He was ninety at the time if I remember right, didn't need to be farming at his age anyway. He's had a good run. Crop circles and all."

"Crop circles?" Nang shook his head.

"For another dinner conversation," Paul said. "Crop circles and Democrats. Wait'll Mr. Conspiracy talks to you about Democrats."

Piper noticed Nang slip a piece of chicken to Wrinkles under the table. Wrinkles was her father's pug, who'd previously been owned by a victim of the county's serial killer. The dog had quite a bit of age to him, and a fondness for table scraps. She refused to participate in the dog's overfeeding.

And to prevent her own overfeeding, she declined a slice of the amazing looking red velvet cake. "Don't offer it a second time," she told Nang, "or I won't turn you down." She'd noticed that Oren had dropped some pounds and was looking almost svelte. She should lose a half dozen to get back to her Army weight. Piper attributed the gain to over-indulging on Nang's cooking with her frequent stops at his quick mart, combined with her morning donut binge. The latter was going to stop. The former—she was becoming increasingly fond of the chef. She'd start jogging again to help make up for it.

After dinner Piper stood with him outside at his pickup, a 1966 Chevrolet stepside he'd restored in his spare time and painted burgundy with antique gold metallic trim. Nang had an automotive technician degree from Owensboro Community College, and was

89

building a three-bay service-station garage next to his quick mart so he could repair cars. Piper found him delightfully ambitious for a twenty-seven-year-old who'd purchased his business from the proceeds of a scratch-off lottery ticket.

"Not inviting me up tonight." Nang gestured with his head to her apartment above her father's garage.

"I'm working."

"Ah, the cardboard box."

"The skeleton." She leaned into him. "I'm digging through old case files, looking for missing person reports. I can't allow the distraction right now. I'm obsessed."

"I'm obsessed, too."

She grinned. "You could be obsessed *after* I solve my case."

He hugged her. "You shine, Piper Blackwell. You are a most excellent sheriff and I am glad I voted for you."

"Thank you for dinner. And for making so much of it my father will have leftovers." She tipped her chin up. "And thank you for the May Day basket. It was a nice surprise. Everything was—"

He kissed her, and she thought he tasted like Chả Lụa and Gà Nướng Xã, red velvet cake, and bliss.

His truck was gone by the time she hauled the box upstairs to her big two-room apartment.

Her dad used to rent it out a long while ago. It had sat empty for more than a few years until Piper claimed it when she left the Army to come home and shepherd him through chemo. The place was complete with orange shag carpet and avocado colored appliances. She'd hung a couple of photos on the wall, of young people in battle dress uniforms, herself in one of them. A large matted photo in a wood-pitted frame hung above a gray futon couch—a Christmas tree in the background, Paul Blackwell and his ex-wife, Piper and her sister when they were little girls, were seated in front of them.

The kitchen connected, with a table for two with a Formica top and padded straight-backed chairs covered in vinyl. Her dad didn't want rent; said he was just happy she was here and had won the sheriff's post. Piper paid him anyway, and had to nag him to cash the checks. She thought she might fix the apartment—a fresh layer of paint, rip up the carpet and put down a shade of Berber that would complement the old appliances. It would make it easier for her father to rent it to someone else later.

A nice apartment, really, it shouldn't go vacant.

Piper was thinking of moving elsewhere—nearby so she could easily keep tabs, but put a little distance. Her father cancer free again, she could afford to be a handful of miles away—maybe still in the same tiny town or one close. Maybe what she was really looking for was to put some distance between her and Paul Blackwell's shadow.

Piper heard a *thump* outside, loud and odd enough that she padded to the window. She moved the drape aside and looked down at the street, seeing a small car parked directly across from the driveway, the door closing like someone had just gotten in it. A Honda or Toyota with some age to it, the dome light on but looking ghostly because the windows were tinted. There was one person in the car. Not enough light to make out anything more than a shape. Then the dome light went out.

Something...

Piper stared. When she'd drove to the bluff late this afternoon, there was a gray car along the curb near where she parked. Maybe it was silver. There were a lot of silvery gray cars on the road, a popular color. Could be a coincidence. Could be she'd caught more than a touch of paranoia from Mark the Shark.

BACK OFF AND KEEP BREATHING.

Piper intended to go downstairs and take an up-close look at the car, maybe talk to the driver. But the headlights came on and it pulled away.

She returned to the case files box, placed it on the table, and started to read.

In the morning she'd discovered what had made the *thump*. A brick had been slammed into the hood of her Ford, seriously denting it.

The gesture had made the email tame in comparison.

# THIRTEEN

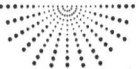

## WEDNESDAY, MAY 2ND

Oren stood at the edge of the bluff, peering down at the river.

Sixty to sixty-five years ago the boy had been killed—dead as long as Oren had been breathing.

The cold case dominating his thoughts, he'd been restless yesterday evening, tossing and wondering if chatting with people older than himself might prove more useful than searching moldy department records. When he'd radioed Piper and she'd mentioned her trip to the genealogy club he figured he could take a similar approach. After work today a drive across the river to Owensboro would be in order. He'd stop in to see his dad in the nursing home. Maybe go to Bee Bops downtown first for a sandwich, have them make up an extra-thick grilled cheese for his dad, who always griped about "the stuff here they try to pass off as food." Oren was overdue for a visit anyway. Maybe his dad would be lucid enough to remember the decades past. His dad had joined the Spencer County Sheriff's Department right after the Korean War, transferring to the Owensboro police department in the early 60s when he moved to Kentucky after the divorce. Law enforcement ran in Rosenberg blood. Maybe he'd remember a boy missing, a case he'd never been able to solve.

Rockport Police Chief Hugh had a clerk going through files in storage trying to find unsolved missing person reports. Oren would check in later with him this afternoon and see if any leads had surfaced. The police chief in Santa Claus was doing the same, but hinted he'd pass it along to someone else, as he was considering retirement. Henderson and Owensboro Police Departments also had been contacted.

JJ had video conferenced a lieutenant in Phoenix's cold case division before she went off-shift yesterday. She said they'd be searching records, too. Phoenix probably had everything on computer, he mused, big city like that. Probably wouldn't take long for them to get back.

A boy dead as long as Oren had been alive.

Even though there'd be no one to bring to justice, Oren still wanted to see this case all the way out. A point of pride and honor to close something like this, his duty. If he could solve it—at least get the boy identified—that might be a good note to leave on. His wife had mentioned retirement again at dinner last night. Talking to the Santa Claus police chief had stirred the notion, as well.

He growled from deep in his throat. Why was he so opposed to hanging it up? It'd make his wife happy if he walked away from the department. "More time together," she'd told him. He loved her, but how much "time together" did she need?

Oren turned back and fixed a stare on Teegan's canopy. A mist covered the ground, obscuring the grass. It had been knee-high when he got here, but the sun coming up was burning it off. He padded toward where the birches had been. It had rained again last night, a deluge; the ground was comfortable to walk on.

The canopy-covered hole, the wispy fog surrounding it, looked like the maw of some hungry beast. He was thankful the locals had left the area alone, respecting the yellow tape. The department hadn't needed to station anyone here. Metal detectors had come up with nothing else, so he suspected it would be filled in tomorrow before someone could fall into it and bring a lawsuit.

He headed back to the station, stopping at the convenience store for the largest cup of steaming coffee they served—the sludge in the office was a small step above awful. He almost picked out a couple of donuts, instead opting for a low-fat strawberry yogurt—had to consider his calorie-laden trip to Bee Bop's tonight.

It was nearly seven when he pulled into the lot. Piper's Ford wasn't there, but when he strolled in he noticed she was. Must have taken her ride in for repairs. She was at the dispatcher's desk. A doughy-faced older woman in a polyester pantsuit sat in a chair a half-dozen feet away from her. They chatted about genealogy. Oren thought it an odd hobby. Why spend so much time searching for dead relatives when you could spend that time with your living ones?

Oren hung back behind the doorway, curious what Piper was up to. She had a stack of papers in front of her. Drew came in and brushed by him, stopped at the desk.

"Morning, Sheriff," Drew said. "Where's Lucy? She had to leave early?" He glanced up at the clock. Oren looked at his watch and saw it was five minutes past seven. "Ooops. I'm a tad late. I was walking Merry and hadn't realized the time, I guess."

Piper stood and stuck her hands in her pockets. "Drew, I need to see you in my office. Now." She nodded to the doughy woman, who got up and took the post at the dispatcher's desk.

"What's this about?" Suddenly Drew seemed nervous to Oren.

"In my office." She started down the hall. "Oren, I'd like you to sit in on this."

Oren followed the pair. He had a feeling where this was going—an unfortunate start to the work day.

She pointed to the pair of chairs opposite her desk. Oren let Drew sit first.

"I'm letting you go, Drew. Today. Now." There were twin stacks of cardboard file boxes up against the wall, dates scrawled on them, the old case files Oren knew she and JJ had been picking through. But there was an open empty box on the floor nearby.

She gestured to the empty file box. "Gather your things."

"What the hell?" Drew said, halfway coming out of the chair. "What did—"

"I warned you before, Drew, about calling my father—calling whoever—and talking about cases in progress. I can't—"

"Sorry. The skeleton, the buckle and everything. It was just so interesting. I'll try not to let it happen again. Your dad hired me, you know, after I was—"

Oren knew what he was going to say. Drew had lost a leg in an accident at the power plant. He used the settlement to buy a small house, and ignored the disability pay and instead took the dispatcher job. Drew contended he wasn't disabled. For the most part, he'd been an above-average dispatcher. He just had a mouth that wouldn't quit flexing.

"I can't risk the chance you'll continue the behavior," Piper said. "Talking about cases like you did, that's a violation of State Certification training and DCI standards. Your misconduct has liability issues. We risk losing the ability to run DCI checks for records, DMV, open wanted cases. We risk losing that capability for six months or a year if this behavior comes to light. It doesn't matter who you chatter to—my dad, your neighbor, the media, the postman. It's a violation. Pack up your stuff."

Oren hadn't thought Piper had the *chutzpah* to fire someone, let alone a handicapped and congenial soul like Drew. But she was right. The dispatcher's wagging tongue was a liability and violated codes. He'd heard her warn Drew twice before. *The third time that tongue wagged was the charm.* He would have fired Drew, too.

"So, what? I'm just supposed to leave?" The young man's normally pleasant tone was acid.

"After you gather your things from the desk and your locker."

Drew snorted. "So, what? You're gonna take my shift?"

"We'll manage. I can give you the option of resigning. Maybe that way you can collect unemployment. I wish you well, Drew, truly, and—"

"You're a bitch," Drew spat. That wasn't in Drew's character, Oren knew. Caught off guard by the firing, the man was verbally lashing out and would no doubt be sorry for his words later. "A stinking bitch."

Oren stood, thinking he'd intercede if this started to go bad, but Piper stopped him in mid-step with a narrowed glance.

"I understand that you're upset," Piper continued.

"Upset? No. Relieved. I'm relieved, actually. Your dad was a great sheriff. You're a joke. You've got no business being sheriff, and you know it. I'm relieved I don't have to work for a joke." Drew pushed out of the chair and grabbed the cardboard box, whacking it against the side of her desk. He stomped out of her office and headed up front. Piper followed.

"I'll be back," she told Oren. "We need to talk."

Oren heard a drawer open in the reception area, the clatter of a few things being dropped into the cardboard box. The drawer slammed shut.

"I can get a better job, working for someone I respect, someone's who's not such a bitch," Oren heard Drew say. "And I'm not resigning. I won't fucking give you that satisfaction. Too bad your dad got cancer. Too bad it wasn't you instead."

*Stupid, stupid, stupid move,* Oren thought. *Always resign if you've the chance.* Maybe he'd call Drew after lunch, give him some space to cool off, and suggest the man reconsider. Maybe get Drew to apologize to Piper for the knee-jerk, profanity-filled outburst. Resign and have a clear path to unemployment.

Then Drew, box in front of him, tromped past Piper's office and down into the room with the lockers. Piper walked a few steps behind. Oren moved into the doorway and watched down the hall, pried the lid off his coffee, taking a deep swallow. Across the hall was another doorway, to the all-purpose room. An errant helium balloon clung to the ceiling of it, the curl of green ribbon hanging down, a remnant of a happy birthday lunch for Drew.

He heard a locker door bang open, more things dropped into the box, mumbled words about how great Paul Blackwell was and that Oren should have won the election, a locker door slam.

"I need your key," Piper said.

A moment later Oren heard the back door swing open, then slam shut. He took another long pull on the delicious coffee and returned to the chair. He knew there'd be some shuffling, letting one of the veterans move up to the first shift. The department had four full-time and two part-time dispatchers that covered the phones 24/7. He wanted to be that proverbial fly on the wall when Piper told her dad over dinner that she'd fired one of his favorite hires—a man with a prosthetic leg and a blind, three-legged rescue dog. But Drew would probably call Paul and break the news himself, inadvertently sparing Piper the task.

Piper, cheeks red, came in, sat behind her desk, and let out a sigh.

"I want to talk about the skeleton and the detective opening," she said.

Oren had figured she'd want to talk about what just happened with Drew. He knew she'd had him witness the firing to protect both parties. He held the coffee in his hands. The warmth had faded a little, but it still felt good against his palms.

"I had breakfast with Dr. Abernathy this morning," she continued.

"Pompous ass," Oren said. "But a smart man. My granddaughter took some classes from him, calls him Doc Natty."

Piper gestured to the basket of goodies on her desk.

"No thanks. But the coffee in there looks gourmet."

"I thought I'd make some in a little while."

"I'd try some of that," Oren said.

A silence settled and Piper picked up the basket and sat it on the floor behind her desk.

"Doc Natty is indeed a pompous ass, but I'm glad the coroner called him. I asked him about how we'd go about doing a facial approximation on the boy. I thought if we had a picture to post and show around it might help stir some old memories, especially with the genealogy club."

Oren waited and drank some more of his coffee.

"Doc Natty says approximation, reconstruction—whatever you call it—is a last resort, and maybe in this situation not a good one. I guess I watched too much CSI when I was a kid. He said it would be especially tough because there is no bottom jaw. He talked about stuff like graphic design software, tissue depth, clay sculpts—all of it time consuming and quite expensive. Said he recommends against it in our case, told me stick to missing person records."

"So we dig. This is why I knew Chief Hugh wouldn't argue for this, would let us have it. Cold cases are rough."

"We don't have any hits yet from in or out of state. You're thinking we might not solve it."

Oren shook his head. "Not saying that. Damn well not saying that. It's solvable. Just won't be easy. Time consuming as all hell, something like this. Not that I've ever worked one, not a cold case murder. But I read the state newsletters, watch *Cold Case Files* on television now and again. It's one of those long hauls unless we get lucky."

"Lucky."

"And luck's not likely." Oren finished the coffee and thought about those fancy Italian coffee packages in Piper's basket. "Like I said, this could take a while."

Piper let out another sigh, the hair hanging down in her eyes fluttering. "I need a haircut," she said idly. "I know. I know, no wonder we don't have a hit yet. It's only been, what?" She glanced at the vintage clock on the wall. "Not even thirty-six hours since I tripped on the boy."

*What was left of the boy.* Oren wondered where they'd bury the bones when this was through.

"Not two whole days yet," she went on. "Not a single lead. I didn't expect to solve it this fast, two days. But I thought we'd at least have a lead. I thought we'd get, I dunno, something. Just something. A hint."

"Young people are always in a hurry." He wished he could have taken that back. But it was true. Cell phones with Google to get them an answer to anything immediately. Can't take the time for old-fashioned, thorough research. Gotta have it now, and gotta have it displayed on a teeny screen in your hand, the print so small you needed a magnifying glass to read it. Or twenty-three-year-old eyes.

"Sometimes," Piper admitted. "Sometimes I'm in a rush. It will be weeks before we get some of those test results back that Doc Natty and the coroner ordered. Zeropatience. That was the password I put into my first laptop. I picked that login because my dad said I had zero patience."

"Patience," Oren said softly, "is a virtue."

She reached down to her side and retrieved a package of Eight O'clock Dark Italian Coffee. "I have four interviews this afternoon for the open deputy position. I'm looking at Sampson's nephew and Ayer's son-in-law."

"Important to mollify the local politicians. Especially if you want to ask for an increase in the budget." Oren had received a few calls from Ayer, touting the virtues of his deputy-candidate—an out-of-work son-in-law. "Who knows? Maybe one of them might actually be good."

"Deck is stacked against them." Oren was taken aback by Piper's frankness. Maybe the two of them were finally falling into a better working relationship. He shuddered at that. He didn't want to like Piper. "I need to play politics, I know. Sampson's nephew. Ayer's son-in-law. But I'd like another woman in the department, what with JJ leaving. My other two interviews are both women. Got a couple more women applicants in the stack, but none with the right qualifications. So I'm hoping one of these two women this afternoon will look good. I'd pick one of them over Ayer's son-in-law or Sampson's nephew. Deck stacked."

"Do you have backups? Going to advertise again?"

"I should have had you look through the applicants. I'll have you do that for the detective inquiries." She shook her head. "I do have four more candidates picked out, my second choices, all men though. I'd like to fill it soon. As soon as possible 'cause we'll be down a detective after the high school graduates. JJ and her husband are moving to those greener pastures. And I have a feeling we'll have one more deputy opening in the next few weeks."

"Because Vanderburgh posted."

"Yeah, Evansville is attractive. I know three of our guys applied for the open deputy spot there. A little more money. More opportunities to move up. A lot bigger county. Even if they don't get it, that means we have three 'looking' for a bigger venue."

*Because maybe they don't like working for a twenty-three-year old with only a high school diploma,* Oren thought. *Maybe the venue has nothing to do with it.*

"The detective slot..." Piper had told him she wanted to talk about that.

"I just posted the ad online yesterday morning, you know. It hasn't been in the local weekly yet, and already there's two dozen resumes sitting in the queue. Maybe more. I haven't looked since last night. Two of them are from in-house. Jake and Diego." Piper shifted the coffee package from one hand to the other. "I expect we'll get four or five more from in-house. They're probably polishing their resumes. More money. Better hours." She frowned. "But I don't want to promote from within this time."

Oren was surprised she admitted that. If he was hiring a detective, he'd look outside, too. He thought her moving JJ up so fast had been a mistake, should have taken a more open approach. It had left some rough feelings, other deputies thinking they'd been overlooked because they didn't wear a bra.

"I want someone with drug experience."

"Because of the county's meth problem." Oren was well aware that drug producers were difficult to catch and operated in Spencer County because it was so rural. Manufacture it here, drive it over to Owensboro and Evansville and other points south where the markets were bigger.

"Can you take a look at the detective applications? See if there are any standouts in this first batch? Anyone worth bringing in? I should have had you do that with these deputy resumes. We'll talk about your picks—if you find any you like—decide who to interview, videoconference if they're more than a state away because of our budget. Wait a few days and look at more applications coming in. Can't spring for a plane ticket unless it's someone stellar, someone we got to have and want to meet face-to-face. I want you in on the interviews."

*Someone stellar?* Oren swallowed his chuckle. Spencer County wouldn't be luring anyone wanting to make a real mark in law enforcement. If you weren't a lifelong southern Indiana resident, this was only a stepping stone to somewhere else—like to Vanderburgh or up Indianapolis way, though Oren had never wanted to step elsewhere because he liked it here. And now he was too old to do any stepping. Maybe someone with experience and a handful of years away from retiring, looking for a more leisurely workload. Spencer County, population twenty-one thousand, could offer a slower pace.

"I'd be happy to take a pass through them. Women? Minorities? Are you looking to—"

"Just someone with drug experience. Get some references for anybody who pops out as your favorites. I'd like some diversity, but our county isn't really built that way. We're pretty damn white. Experience matters. Not skin color or whether they buy boxers or lingerie. But if I find that one of these two women this afternoon would be good for our regular deputy opening—"

Oren stood and rolled his shoulders. "JJ leaving. Be nice to have another woman. Different perspective and all. JJ's going to be missed."

And maybe there'd be a few women in the detective application queue deserving of a look. Oren had never considered himself sexist. Ageist? He could well be that. Oren was staring at a sheriff who was only twenty-three, and he couldn't get that to sit right with him.

"Good. I'll make us some coffee."

At least she hadn't asked him to do that. Oren's stomach growled. The yogurt hadn't been enough. He focused on the notion of a double-cheeseburger at Bee Bop's tonight, maybe with some fries, and hoped that thought would hold him over.

# FOURTEEN

Stefan Sampson, the county commissioner's nephew, was actually a reasonable candidate. Piper had received twenty-eight applications for the open deputy position. Oren had told her that was a record, that usually eight to ten came in, with a handful not meeting the minimum requirements. Piper had easily pruned half of the stack before she picked the candidates for interviews, rejecting people who'd had DUIs in the past several years, those lacking a high school diploma or GED, and a few had so many typos in their resumes she cringed. If a person could not spell correctly on a resume, what would their filed arrest reports look like?

Stefan was thirty years old, worked security for the power plant, and hadn't been able to get off the night shift despite three years trying. As a deputy he'd have nights, but the shifts occasionally rotated, and he said he looked forward to "getting up sometimes when roosters are still crowing." He lived in a trailer on a farm his father owned, but anticipated moving into an apartment in Rockport if Piper hired him.

She was startled that she liked him, had originally discounted him because his uncle had been pestering her. But while Commissioner Sampson had been the most annoying, he certainly hadn't been the only local politician or businessman pushing for consideration of a relative. Oren had explained that the pressure wasn't unique to Spencer County. Deputy postings had reasonable salaries, benefits, and were therefore desirable. He told her to expect prodding on the detective position once the locals noticed the vacancy. Politicians would always "throw their weight around" as the saying went, if given the chance. Piper could easily see Stefan as a deputy, but she had three more interviews to go before the afternoon ended.

Ayer's son-in-law had looked fine on paper, had landed very near the top of her stack. A four-year degree in computer science, President's List, impressive credentials. But where Piper had spent nearly an hour talking to Stefan Sampson—and had budgeted an hour for each interview—she had Jeffrey Coombs out the door in less than fifteen minutes. He'd arrived in blue jeans, a faded Hillary Clinton for President t-shirt, and a leather vest with a Harley Davidson stick pin on it. There was a reason he was out of work, she decided, and after a few questions he admitted he'd applied just to get his father-in-law off his back. "I think I would rather go back to school and pick up a master's in something," he said.

That gave Piper forty-five minutes before the next interview. She retrieved a box and started going through the old files. The box indicated cases from 1955-1958, but there was a folder from 1985 that had been misfiled. She pulled it out and tossed it on her desk, intending to file it correctly later. She rifled through the rest of the contents, looking for unsolved cases and missing persons.

"That was great coffee," Oren said as he stood in the doorway. He knocked on the frame and entered, placed several printed sheets on her desk and tapped on them. "These guys. I'd bring in these three. Required to have at least three interviews. And the one on the bottom, I'd bring him in first. You mentioned finding someone stellar." He tapped the sheets again. "The bottom guy—the best for last. He could be stellar. Might not have to bother with any of the others after that interview. Might be able to pull down your advertisement now, in fact. Of course, once you get him down for an interview and he takes a look at the county, he could tuck his tail and go back to the big city."

He made a move to leave.

"Hold up." Piper turned away from the file box and gestured for Oren to sit. She picked up the sheets and looked at him. "Kevan Melkan, fifty-two, retired after twenty years with the Indiana State Police in West Lafayette. Lots of solid experience. Probably bored with retirement."

"No doubt," Oren said.

"Sheriff Jefferson Polanger, forty-eight, twenty years with the Keweenaw County Sheriff's Department, two stints as sheriff. Where's Keweenaw?"

"I Googled it," Oren replied. "Northernmost county in Michigan's Upper Peninsula. Least populated county in the state. Real tiny. Twenty-one hundred folks in the entire county. They deal with drunk snowmobilers and handle crazy people hunting moose. I pulled his application because a small-town guy like him would fit here." He laughed. "Hell, this would be big from his point of view. I suspect he's looking for a change—and a warmer climate."

"Kevan we can bring in for an interview. Earliest convenience, but the sooner the better. By Monday I hope. Sheriff Polanger, we can video conference him, see if he's worth a closer look."

"That'd count for two interviews." Oren gestured at the final application he'd pulled. "I went through all thirty-two nibbles that have come in so far." He brushed at a spot on his shirt. "That 'fill as soon as possible' tag you put on it got a quick response." It looked to Piper like he'd spilled a big drop of that "great coffee." Then Oren smoothed a wrinkle out of his sleeve and adjusted his belt. She knew he always had to have the uniform as perfect as possible. "Always expect a lot of applications for a detective job, more than for a standard deputy. More money, friendly hours. The jobs don't come open as often, so they're like that flashing blue light at Kmart. Attractive. I figure if you don't pull the ad down you might get upwards of sixty or seventy queries." He paused. "Even with it being Spencer County."

She skimmed the next sheet and whistled. "Thirty-two years old. Four years Navy. Top of his class in the police academy. Four and a half years as a patrolman. Five years as a detective, one with Major Accident Investigation Section, four with Gang and Narcotics."

"Hence the drug experience you asked for," Oren put in.

"Commendations. Decorations. Why the hell would this man want to come here? Gotta be something off. He's gotta be in trouble, dodging discipline, or—"

"Next page. I emailed him one question—why Spencer County? While I waited for his answer, which he sent over lunch, I called his captain and had some of his records faxed. Clean background. No complaints. He's headed toward a promotion, in fact. The captain doesn't want him to go, but knows he's looking. Anyway, next page. That's the answer he sent. He's not dodging discipline. But he's clearly dodging something."

Piper read the email reply.

Chief Deputy Oren Rosenberg:

You ask why I'm interested in the Spencer County Sheriff Detective opening. I have three reasons—

• Esme Meredith, my wife.

• Shaya Meredith, my five-year-old daughter.

• Jelani Meredith, my three-year-old son.

I googled Spencer County after I saw the advertisement. Small. Rural. Comfortable driving distance to some bigger cities for weekend getaways. My wife enjoys weekend getaways. You have a town named Santa Claus. My kids would like that. You don't have as much snow or as many days below 0. I would appreciate that. You have a few murders. But you didn't have 762 homicides in 2016—more than LA and NYC combined. You didn't have pregnant mothers and their toddlers killed by stray bullets in gang fights. You didn't have 4,368 shooting victims. You don't have a flood of illegal guns...our department confiscated well more than 8,000 illegal guns last year.

My work here is exciting and interesting. There is never a dull day. Chicago has wonderful museums, professional football, hockey, basketball, and baseball teams. But you have a waterpark, and the Evansville Otters minor league team is only an hour away. My wife's parents live in Nashville. You're closer to Nashville than Chicago is. Most important, you have playgrounds where Shaya and Jelani will be safe, schools they can walk to without fear of stray bullets.

I would prefer to provide a two-week notice.

I look forward to hearing from you,

Basil Meredith

Piper quickly glanced again at the other two Oren had selected. Her chief deputy—with his decades of experience—knew better the type of qualifications needed for a detective position. He'd weakly protested her promoting JJ—and he'd been right, though she wouldn't admit it. That decision had caused a lot of hard feelings among the others in-house who'd also applied. And there were already too many hard feelings because the deputies were working for her—someone who'd won the sheriff's badge without previously spending a single day in the department.

Piper'd also had the notion to look through all the emailed detective applications, just to see if her tastes matched her chief deputy's. But she pushed that idea away. Oren had three solid candidates, Meredith standing out. She was going to lean on Oren for this posting, and wished she would have for the open deputy slot.

"Basil. Good name for a detective," Oren mused.

"Huh?"

"Basil. Basil Rathbone. Basil Meredith."

Piper rubbed her chin. "Who's Basil Rathbone?"

"*Gornisht helfn*," Oren whispered. "Basil Rathbone played Sherlock Holmes."

"Never heard of him. Jonny Lee Miller, Benedict Cumberbatch. I've watched them play Sherlock. Never heard—"

"Before your time," Oren growled softly. "Late thirties, into the forties. Black and white."

"Basil Rathbone, huh. Isn't that before your time, too?"

"Reruns. Forever in reruns. Sorry I mentioned it."

"I'll keep the ad up for another few days. Just in case," she said. "But email Basil Meredith and see how soon he can come down for a face-to-face. Chicago's a drive, but doable. We wouldn't have to fly him." *Besides*, she thought, *if they flew him to Indianapolis or Evansville and had him rent a car to drive here it wouldn't cut down much on his travel time.* "Six-hour drive, thereabout. Tell him we'll put him up in a hotel for a night." She unsuccessfully forced down the grin. "He could be good here."

"He could be bored here," Oren returned, standing and stepping to the doorway. "But, yeah, he could be very good."

"Basil and Kevan, we'll bring in, and we'll do Jefferson with a video conference." Piper returned to pawing through the files, pulling a few folders out for more scrutiny, until Sylvia D called with the next interview.

This one took a half hour and made Piper's heart sink. She wanted another woman in the department, but this one had eight years of deputy experience with four different Indiana counties. This candidate could well be a "gypsy cop," switching places either because she was an oddball not fitting in or she was close to being fired each time and jumped before that could happen. Piper preferred someone without such itchy feet, someone to keep around for a while. But she'd brought her in because she met all the requirements. The sinker was when Piper had asked her why she moved around so much.

The woman replied, "I'm just looking for a good place to settle, I guess. That might be here. Right now that certainly isn't Lagrange County. We're a little bigger than Spencer, and a whole lot dumber. Almost forty percent of the adult population lacks a high school diploma. I need to be around smarter people."

Piper wished her well in her search.

Amelia Isaakovitch—Piper had saved what she'd hoped to be the best for last, wanting to end the day on an up note. Amelia was graduating from a university this weekend, had certificates of completed firearms training in basic and advanced handgun, point shooting, and rifle/carbine, and she looked physically fit.

"I intend to pursue a doctorate degree in criminal law," Amelia said. "I'll do that online in my spare time. Through Concord or Keiser. It'll take me a while. I don't know if I'll ever actually be an attorney, but I want the degree and the option. I know that I need to do this, law enforcement. A deputy position here? Pretty much perfect for me."

"Because—" Piper prompted.

"Because my grandfather helped me with college, taught me to love the law. He's why I don't have any college loans. Pops helped me with everything. I'd like to start paying him back. And I'd like to live in the area. I've found an old house to rent here in Rockport." She laughed. Piper thought her voice sounded like crystal clinking. "Provided they get the electricity and plumbing working."

"So your grandfather—"

Amelia nodded. "Yes. My grandfather is your chief deputy. And, I didn't tell him that I applied." She sucked in her lower lip.

"Complicates things," Piper said, "relatives in the same department." But she knew law enforcement—being a cop or sheriff's deputy —ran in families. Blue in the blood, some called it. She knew Oren's father had been a deputy here and later was with the Owensboro police. Her own grandfather had been with the state police, and her father had been a fixture in this department. Piper came from very blue blood.

Piper hadn't thought that she'd offer anyone the job right on the spot, but she wanted this young woman, suspected she'd make a fine deputy.

"I can work the schedule so you wouldn't be on the same shift." Piper noticed Amelia scoot forward in the chair. "You graduate Saturday, right?"

"Yes."

"I'd like you to start a week from Monday. Can you do that?"

"Yes!"

Piper stood and extended a hand. "Welcome to the Spencer County Sheriff's Department, Amelia. See Teegan at the desk. She'll give you some papers to fill out, work out sizes and get uniforms ordered. They should be in by the time you start."

"Thanks, Sheriff." Amelia returned the handshake. "I go by Millie."

Stefan Sampson. If Piper did get that other opening she and Oren had mused about, she'd call him back in and have him fill out paper-work, too. Or maybe he might be the ticket to adding an extra deputy slot. Her department was understaffed given the size of the county, and Piper'd put in a request for added funding for another deputy. Maybe she could play politics with Commissioner Sampson, the nephew a pawn on the board that would let them both get something they wanted.

Oren had left her a note on Teegan's desk, said he didn't want to interrupt her interviews. Piper figured he certainly would have inter-rupted if he'd known Amelia was here. "Basil Meredith is available to come in Monday. Going to Owensboro to visit my dad. If you need me, call the cell. Oren."

"Monday. Teegan, call this Basil Meredith and tell him Monday is good with us. Morning if he drives down Sunday, say nine or ten, his choice, and I'll slot an hour."

"You heading home, Sheriff?" Teegan asked. "You've been working some long hours."

"Soon," Piper returned. "A few things to go through first."

"Like finding a replacement for Drew? Do you need to talk about it? Firing him?"

"No. I'm good." Piper had wondered when Teegan would bring that up. The Goth woman was friends with Drew Farrar. No doubt he'd called her and vented. "I've already posted the vacancy. We have Sylvia D until it fills. You interested in moving up to first shift?"

Teegan shook her head. "I'm married to the middle shift, Sheriff. Do not, do not, do not move me."

Piper nodded. "Just checking."

"Uh, Sheriff—" Teegan's face pulled together curiously. "I'm worried about him. Is Drew going to, I dunno, be all right?"

"I hope so." Piper retreated into her office and picked up the 1985 folder that had been misfiled. Eight separate incident reports were inside, dates ranging from May to October of that year, all on the same stretch of road in Fulda. Three mailboxes torn off their bases in the first report, the investigating deputy believing a baseball bat was involved as the posts remained undamaged, and the boxes had big dents in them. Mail scattered in the ditch. Apparently that had been a pastime of bored youths, the recording deputy had noted—counting coup on mailboxes. Another report indicated a mailbox had been blasted by a shotgun, the package inside ruined. A third report had more mailboxes knocked off their posts. The fourth, another shotgun blast. The other reports were similar. The last sheet in the file listed the names of teenage boys that had been brought in for questioning, as the two deputies who investigated the claims were convinced it was young people joyriding, rolling down a car window and seeing how many mailboxes they could destroy. A barely legible note mentioned mailboxes damaged along the same road the previous year. There was no pattern to the day of the week, time of the month, morning, night, middle of the afternoon. The incidents were seemingly random. No witnesses, no confessions—no arrests were made.

On a hunch, Piper went to the records room and pulled out an old county directory, thumbed through the residential listings for Fulda and found Gretchen Brown's name. The woman lived in Gentryville now. But in the early to mid-1980s she had a Fulda address.

"Really? The Mailbox Mauler's been pulling this shit for thirty years?" Just how far back did the woman's nefarious exploits run? Piper brought the directory back to her office, dropped it on the middle of her desk, and growled. The misfiled folder contained a cold case—eight cases, actually, and in a dozen minutes she'd managed to solve them. At least the "who" behind them. Gretchen apparently had graduated from baseball bats and a shotgun to using her car. An old woman, maybe she didn't have the strength to heft a baseball bat or shotgun anymore. To get to the "why" of it, Piper would send JJ out in the morning to talk to Gretchen, who'd been released yesterday right after posting bail. Gretchen needed some serious help, and maybe JJ could track down a relative and make that happen. She'd also have JJ search the computer files for additional unsolved mailbox maulings. If her detective was leaving for those greener pastures of North Carolina, let her deal with the rural pastures of Spencer County for the next day or two.

Pull JJ off the bones and leave that case to her and Oren.

Piper did a quick look through law files in her laptop. The statute of limitations was two years for the Criminal Mischief Gretchen had practiced in 1985. Apparently mailboxes were not worth enough to warrant longer attention. And that two-year deadline applied to when a prosecutor filed the charges in a case. But if Gretchen had bashed more boxes in the past two years that she hadn't been charged with, they might be able to find some things to stick within the boundaries of the statute. And each offense could technically be a separate count, an individual case. The whole notion of a woman with a history of destroying other people's property had thoroughly pissed Piper off.

She didn't care that Gretchen was now into her eighties. Age was no excuse for rotten behavior, especially since it had apparently been going on for decades.

Piper glanced at the clock—5:25. "I'm heading out," she told Teegan, as she grabbed another sixty-year-old file box and started walking to the garage. The mechanic said if the Ford's repairs weren't finished, he'd have a loaner ready. She figured walking the dozen or so blocks to the garage would justify dinner and dessert tomorrow with Nang. And it might help her burn off some of the ire Gretchen had stoked.

The sheriff's department sat near the downtown, but there wasn't much operating along the main street that stretched away from it and into what amounted to the business district. She passed the courthouse, a few taverns, Harlan Cook's law office, and an antique shop that opened when the aging owner had the whim. She paused and looked in the window, seeing a vintage China doll at the forefront, seated with legs splayed and petticoat showing at the bottom of a sun-faded red dress. Gray velvet shoes had probably once been black. There were faint spider web cracks on the beautiful angelic face, and the hair was a long side-braid that looked perfect, tied with a faded red ribbon. *The childhood treasure should be on a shelf,* she thought, *back where the sunlight couldn't reach it and suck out the rest of the color that remained.* Rising behind it was an off-white dress from the 1920s, trimmed with fringe and lace, and rich with beads along the neck and the shoulders. It was pretty, and maybe had been a pastel shade that had been leeched because of its prominent spot in the window.

Other items on display, all faded and thereby looking older than they likely were, included a rack of Matchbox cars, a tricycle made mostly of wood that perhaps should be in a museum, a stack of books that by their angle she couldn't read the titles of, and a massive vase made of carnival glass. The display hadn't changed since Piper had window shopped when she moved back to town a little more than a year ago. Maybe she'd call the owner, see when the place would be open, and actually take a look inside. Would there be something from the years the unknown boy had lived? Something that might give her clues to a boy's life that many decades past?

Had he been playing sheriff?

A car reflected in the window and she whirled in time to see a silvery-gray Honda or something similar directly across the street. It had been parked and now pulled away too quickly for her to get a look at the driver, the windows being tinted. The rear panels and trunk were coated with dirt, like the car had been mudding, the license plate so obscured she couldn't even tell the state.

Coincidence?

She couldn't do a search on it because she couldn't read the license plate and wasn't sure of the make or model.

Was it the same car she'd spotted from her apartment window last night?

Had the driver rammed the brick into her Ford's hood?

Was someone really watching her?

BACK OFF AND KEEP BREATHING.

Coincidence?

Or was she letting Mark the Shark's paranoia burrow deeply into her brain?

# FIFTEEN

## THURSDAY, MAY 3RD

Piper had found three "open" cases in the file box she'd taken home yesterday. One, the robbery of a liquor store in 1962—a quick search showed the store had closed a decade later, and the woman who'd owned it died in a nursing home in 2012 at the age of one hundred. The second, from 1963, reported that three cows were shot dead at a farm outside of Dale. The third was from the same year. Bertram Thresher—a look at the records revealed that was Mark the Shark's father—had reported a break-in at his house. He'd stated that nothing appeared to have been stolen, but furniture had been subtly rearranged in every room. The report included a separate written statement from Thresher.

"The changes were small. An armchair turned near the window, and the lamp moved by a few inches. When I cast an eyeball around in the bedroom I saw that my sweet Mae's toilet water bottles had been repositioned. In the kitchen, a plate was in the wrong cabinet. A no-good greaser or a fream, for certain. I don't have no smog in my noggin. Someone's been in my house playing games."

The deputy who'd filed the case noted that he'd checked with the neighbors, and none of them had evidence of a break-in. It said he would investigate further, but there were no additional notes.

Suspicion ran thick with the Threshers, Piper mused.

She marked the cases "closed-unsolved," and knew that there wouldn't be—and didn't need to be—a resolution to them. The skeleton from the bluff? That absolutely had to be resolved. She'd been having trouble sleeping because of it. And there'd been no overnight messages from Kentucky or Arizona. Nada. Zilch. Piper realized a cold case could take a long while, but this was festering.

Who would kill a nine-year-old boy?

And had it happened in the summer?

She still thought about the lack of shoes.

"Hey, Sylvia D," Piper hollered. "What's a fream?"

Sylvia laughed. "It's an old word, Sheriff, and you're too young. It means someone who doesn't fit in."

*Maybe I'm a fream.*

Piper wondered if she'd ever fit in here. Despite being gone from the military for more than a year and a half, she missed that life. It was active, rigorous, filled with an important purpose. Sometimes it had been dangerous, but that satisfied her adrenalin addiction. There'd been something she enjoyed about "life on the edge," as her first drill sergeant called it. Would she run for sheriff again? Her father had asked her that shortly before she took the Plainfield Sheriff's Academy test. It had taken her a while to realize it was because he was feeling good, was cancer free, and was looking for something to do. Piper was pretty certain that Paul Blackwell wanted to be the sheriff of Spencer County again.

He'd win if he ran, she knew. He was beloved in the county. And it was because of his last name and reputation that she had clinched the election in the fall. He'd even hinted at applying for her detective vacancy. She wouldn't hire him, obviously, even though she'd just hired Oren's granddaughter. It was a different situation. Somehow it was different.

*Dear God, let me find someone fast—before Dad applies and before I'd have to disappoint him.*

Would she return to the Army after her term as sheriff was up? Maybe. It was an option she wanted to keep open. She missed the life.

Would she run for sheriff again? Absolutely not. Let her dad have the office. Or Oren, even though he'd be sixty-nine. Piper would vote for either one of them.

"Oren should have won this time," she said. Not that she would ever admit that to another soul. "He's way the hell better at this than—"

"Sheriff, Mr. Thresher is on line two," Sylvia D chirped.

Piper stared at the lit button, grimaced, and punched it.

His voice sounded weak coming through the speaker.

"Morning Sheriff Blackwell. I need to talk to you. In person. Same spot. Have to risk being seen, daylight and all. I don't need you coming out to my place and getting slowed by another drunk on a tractor. It's urgent. I'll meet you there in an hour." The line disconnected.

"Really?" Piper said. She glanced at the clock. 8 a.m. "Really?"

After a moment. *I'll send someone else.* Another moment. "Shit."

The threatening email, the damage to her car—that was connected to Thresher's case, wasn't it?

She had an hour before Mark's meeting, and she assumed he meant the bench in the park. But it couldn't be all that urgent if he was waiting an hour. Had he been threatened, too? Had someone damaged his vintage Chevy?

A skim through email she'd received from the department's website and she'd be on her way to meet Mark, then from there to Jasper, the closest State Police district office. She had a consult set up with their lead criminologist to talk about missing children. Piper would rather spend that time working on Mark's case, especially since the threats. But she'd asked for the appointment and wouldn't cancel. Jasper and back—and then back to the bank issue.

She quickly deleted notices about refinancing her mortgage, which she didn't have; enlarging an organ, which she didn't have; and various advertisements for ebooks and magazines. How did this stuff get sent to her sheriff's department personal email address? The address was public—listed on the department webpage, but still...

Piper decided to poke through the email options later, beef-up the spam filter. Next came a polite note from Stefan Sampson, thanking her for the interview.

Piper dashed off an email to him, letting him know the job had been filled, but that he'd be considered for other openings. Then she sent a similar email to the other two she'd passed on. She was about to send an email to Oren, telling him she'd hired his granddaughter.

"That's a chicken shit move," she whispered.

*Maybe he already knows. Maybe Millie called him yesterday. But maybe not.*

Piper punched in Oren's cell phone number and delivered the news. "I would've told you face-to-face," she admitted, though she thought that might have been uncomfortable. "But you'd already left yesterday. And you're not in the office now." She knew he was pursuing a lead on the bones. "Your granddaughter was the best applicant. We'll make sure the shifts don't match. I'm heading out in a while to Jasper. Missing children specialist there, a criminologist. I'll let you know if something shakes on our boy. You do the same."

The bones case belonged to Oren and her, and she suspected they were in a race to see who could solve it first—despite the chief deputy telling her cold cases could take a long while. Why else was she going to Jasper in a little while? To hurry the cold case.

One last email in the queue. It had come in early yesterday evening.

*Like the detailing I did on your car, Sheriff Blackwell?*
*I will do that 2 your face*
*If you want 2 keep breathing, leave the cheddar alone*
*Walk away*

The email was unsigned, and the sender was not a string of numbers this time. The sender was listed as herself, the personal email account that she'd had since high school. Piper grabbed up her cell phone and checked that personal account's "sent" folder. There was no evidence that such an email had been composed.

"What the hell?"

Someone had hacked or spoofed her account and sent her a threatening note. Probably the same sender from the previous threats. And to what case did it refer? Mark the Shark? Had to be, right?

Or could it be the bones? Gretchen the Mailbox Mauler? Maybe even Sandy Schmidt, who was still enjoying the hospitality of the Spencer County Jail. There were a plethora of DUI cases, all on the surface routine. Maybe one of the DUIs was a computer nerd and made the threat to get the charges dropped. And what did cheese have to do with it?

No. It had to be about Mark Thresher.

"What the flaming hell?"

"Something wrong, Sheriff?"

Piper had raised her voice so loud that hard-of-hearing Sylvia D had heard her.

"Yeah, something's wrong." Piper came out of her office and in a half-dozen long steps was even with the dispatcher's desk. "Someone hacked my email."

"I've had my Facebook hacked before." Sylvia D had a matter-of-fact expression. "Twice. Both times some idiot was trying to sell sunglasses to all my Facebook friends. I have a lot of Facebook friends. I had to reset my password and everything." She paused and took a quick call about the upcoming Sheriff's Sale of unclaimed property. "Pain in the butt it was. They didn't even look like quality sunglasses."

Piper didn't mention the threatening email messages. "I've got some things to do today, gotta go out, Jasper in a little while. I'll be back around lunch. JJ's here for a while, then she's going to deal with Gretchen Brown and her penchant for destroying mailboxes. Diego's in a car, his last week on first shift for a while. He's coming back within the hour to write up a few reports. So there'll be someone in the office."

"Yeah, I heard. Diego took the car fire in Dale. Thinks its arson for insurance. Did you know that Florence Henderson of the Brady

Bunch was born in Dale? In 1934. Sang in the choir in the Catholic Church in Rockport before she moved out and became a big deal. Somebody in the genealogy club told us that, some shirttail relation of Henderson's."

"Didn't know that," Piper admitted. *Didn't need to know that.* "When the first shift is making radio checks, ask if anyone is a computer whiz. Ask Teegan to do the same for the second shift when she comes in. I want someone to look into the hacking."

"You want to find out *who* hacked you? That it?"

"That's it," Piper said. She was relatively computer savvy, but didn't know the first thing about tracking a hacker. The email threats, coupled with seeing the silvery-gray car a few times, had put Piper on alert. "I want to trace the hacker."

"Okay, boss. I'll put the word out. But, really, you should talk to the Geek."

Piper turned to go back to her office, but stopped. "The Geek?"

"Zeke the Geek. He helps with the genealogy club. You met him Tuesday at the library. I suspect no one in the whole county knows more about computers than the Geek. He's a bloomin' genius with computers."

Ezekiel Whitman, Piper remembered. She had his resume on her desk. It wouldn't be prudent to let an outsider deal with the department's email addresses. But her home email address? That was the one perhaps compromised. She was going to call him in anyway, talk about the dispatcher opening.

"That's a good idea, Sylvia D." Piper scratched the back of her hand. "He's in school now. But—"

"I have his email address," Sylvia D cut in. "Everybody in our club shares addresses. I can send him a note, say you want to talk to him."

She really did want to talk to him, make the meeting both a job interview and a chat about her hacked email. Piper had advertised the dispatcher job yesterday. She was required to do that, and to have at least three interviews for any position. But she wanted to talk to Ezekiel, see if he was interested. He was too young to be a deputy. But a dispatcher, that was a distinct possibility.

"Yeah, see if he can come in after he gets done with class. Let's say four. If today's bad, ask about tomorrow."

"Okay, boss." Sylvia D grinned, clearly pleased that she'd been useful.

Piper noticed that the blue-tint of the temporary dispatcher's hair perfectly matched the shade of her blouse.

# 16

## SIXTEEN

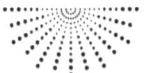

"I picked the Navy because I didn't want to walk a lot. I knew the Army would make you walk a lot. You can only walk so far on a ship." Mark the Shark was on the same bench, same jacket with the hood pulled up over his head despite the clear sky. The twin canes were between his knees, and he leaned forward, resting his chin on the curved handles. It looked awkward and uncomfortable to Piper. "The Navy made us walk some, too, but it wasn't that bad. I've always had a little trouble with my dogs, you know. Most of my farming I did sitting on a tractor. They're hurting me pretty bad right now, my dogs. Old men lie if they tell you their feet do not ache."

She sat next to him and put her hat in her lap. Her curls hung down over her forehead, again reminding her that she needed a haircut. Several yards away, near the edge of the bluff, two park employees worked to fill in the hole from the birch trees that had been pulled.

"I was a wog until we crossed the equator, then I was a shellback—after I passed the initiation. It wasn't brutal, not like the hazing that goes on in colleges today and you read about in the paper. Nobody died from it. We had to crawl on our bellies across the deck, slide down a tube of chicken fat and get hosed off, kiss Poseidon's belly. I got a tattoo one time when we were in Pearl. I'd had a beer or two. Maybe three. Maybe even four. I don't drink anymore, can't mix alcohol with my pills. Did you get a tattoo?"

Piper nodded. "Yeah, on my left shoulder. Screaming Eagle. I'd had a beer first, too."

"My name above an anchor, on that tattoo," he continued. "The anchor meant I'd sailed across the Atlantic. There was a gold and red dragon coiled around it, green eyes, and it meant I'd served along the coast in Asia. The gold because I'd crossed the International Date Line. All of the red is gone, just blue left, the anchor, and it's real faint, hard to tell what it is. Looks like an odd-shaped bruise."

Piper wished he'd get to the point of this meeting, something to do with his missing money, certainly. She'd rather talk about that than listen to his Navy tales. It was making her miss the Army life.

He rose up and squared his shoulders. Pride crept into his voice. "I was gunner's mate first, loaded two big guns. *USS Bremerton*. Out of Seattle. Bunks three high. I had a top one. I'd spend four hours in a turret—with the *Bremerton* and then with another one I was on later, the *Duluth*. I was on more than a few ships in all the years I served. The *Bremerton* was a Baltimore Class Heavy Cruiser, built in Camden, New Jersey. I liked riding the waves, the feel of that ship. I didn't like some of the midshipmen who'd went to officer school, thought they were pretty smart, but they didn't know shit. Served for a time under Captain Mallard, and he was okay. More than a thousand men on the ship that took us to the Philippines, the *Bremerton*. Displaced thirteen thousand, six hundred tons, six hundred and seventy-three feet long— and five inches. Could take her up to thirty-three knots when we needed to. One thousand and forty-two officers and enlisted on board. I was one of the enlisted. My dad had signed the papers 'cause I'd been seventeen."

*I know, you told me that the other night, about your dad signing permission.*

Piper waited and felt the breeze, inhaled the scent of the river and the dirt from the hole, and the warring fragrances of Mark's liniments. He'd said this was urgent, when he'd called an hour ago. All that money missing? That really was urgent, but she knew it could take the bank some time to look into the matter.

*Urgent must mean something different to old men.*

"I remember Guantanamo Bay in Cuba. That was 1945 for me. Went in there to repair typhoon damage to our bow. I recall Tokyo Bay from that year, too. We joined the seventh fleet for the Korean War. I worked the eight-inch guns and the five-inch guns. When I wasn't in a turret, I was a line server in the mess hall." He paused to take a few deep breaths.

Piper wanted to ask him what was so burning that he had to see her now, if something had changed overnight with the lost money, if it had somehow mysteriously reappeared in his account. If he'd been threatened, watched. But she held back, figuring he would get to it eventually. She might as well enjoy the sunshine.

*Patience,* she told herself. *Patience. Patience. Patience.*

"I had the best time during liberty. We'd go ashore, go to bars. Some of the guys, they'd take their peters out in those bars, and the girls would play with them, get the guys to go into the back rooms, get them to spend money. The girls didn't know English. I wanted no part of that. I'd seen pictures of wieners with sores on them. I wanted no part. Some of us took a rickshaw once to a cathouse. There were a dozen girls on a bench. A guy clapped his hands and the girls jumped up. He said, 'Take your pick.' But I didn't. I just wanted the rickshaw ride. I'd seen them pictures of bad wieners, you know."

She scanned the cars parked near the sidewalk, her loaner from the garage—a blue Hyundai Tucson because her Ford wasn't close to being repaired. Piper was looking for silvery-gray foreign cars. Nothing.

"The best liberty was in Australia. There was a red-haired girl there in a pretty green dress. I spent the afternoon with her in Kings Cross. She gave me a tour, and I bought her coffee and a cupcake, and that was all we did, walk and talk and eat. In Melbourne three girls came on the ship during a visitor day. They weren't allowed to go below deck, but somebody let 'em go below. No one would admit who'd done it. The girls were found out and we dropped them off in

Sydney. One liberty on the Island of Truk some hotdogs and beer fell off a food truck, so we grabbed as much as we could and ran. Ate a lot that day for free, and I haven't had a hotdog since. I saw a woman on that island, nursing a baby. She had the longest tits I'd ever seen. I saw a lot of things during the liberties."

"Mark—" Piper's patience dissolved with his mention of sailors getting the clap, deciding she'd had enough of his rambling. "What did you need to—"

"In 1964 I was on the *Maddox*, and we sailed out of Long Beach to Vietnam. We skirmished with some North Vietnamese torpedo boats. In history class it's called the *Maddox Incident*, and it upped the United States' involvement in the war. And it was a war, Sheriff Blackwell. It was no police action." He turned his head and looked at her. "I'd been drinking before I got the stones to go get that tattoo way back on Pearl. But I wasn't so drunk I didn't remember how much it cost me. Four dollars and eighteen cents, same price as I paid for a Stetson on an earlier liberty. I suspect I'd gotten taken, the beers in me, you know. But it was a good tattoo. Real good work. Four dollars and eighteen cents. Numbers? Money? I could always remember stuff like that. I remember that the *Bremerton* displaced thirteen thousand, six hundred tons. Numbers, I'm good. The years haven't numbed my brain, Sheriff, not to numbers. I know someone's siphoned money out of my bank account, now my money market, too. I signed into my money market this morning while the coffee was brewing. I'm bled dry. None of it because I'm misremembering numbers. None of it because I made a mistake. Someone's robbed me. Someone's just about took everything. Some damn Democrat most like. You have to believe me."

*Patience. Patience. Patience.*

When he stopped talking, Piper listened to the shushing sound the shovels made as the workers finished filling the hole. One of them started tamping dirt down. Cars drove by on the street, a silvery one, but not the same style as the one she'd seen a few times.

"I believe you, Mr. Thresher."

"Mark."

"I believe you, Mark the Shark." She touched his shoulder. "Have you gotten any threatening phone calls or email?"

He nodded. "Email. Damnedest thing, email. You can't tell who's sending you notes, just a damn string of numbers that are always different. Those damn nasty emails started the first time I called the bank and emailed my complaint to their manager. 'Put it in writing,' one of them tellers had told me. 'Send it in an email.' Damnedest thing, electronic communication. Got more of them after I called you. Told you I was being spied on."

"I believe you. I've gotten some threatening email, too," she admitted. Maybe someone had connected to Mark's computer and was privy to his note to the bank. "Did they mention cheddar?"

"Yeah, said I didn't need cheese."

"I'm going to fix this. I'm going to find out who is doing this, threatening you, taking your money."

"Going over to the bank again, in just a little while. I put a hold on that savings-checking account yesterday when we were there, when I filled out that fraud paperwork. You watched me. Should've thought to close that money market, too. I wished I would have. I wish I'd never put it all in a bank, should have diversified, stocks and such. But I trusted the bank more. Should've done that, closed that money market. If wishes were fishes, eh? I know them bank folks said they'd put some fraud specialist on it, but that's a fellow in Indianapolis, I'm sure. Maybe New York or Chicago, someplace big where the main office sits. No one from around here."

"Probably." Piper watched a hawk circling. It dropped over the edge of the bluff, maybe seeing something down along the bank to pursue.

"But the thief. The thief's from around here."

Piper nodded. "Someone who knows you, where you do banking, how you do banking, how much money you have." *Who knows I'm investigating this.*

"Had." Mark spat at the ground between his feet. "How much money I had."

"Someone who is good with computers."

"I should've never signed up for that online banking shit. Online anything. Should've never bought a damn computer. I worked for that money, Sheriff Blackwell. Farmed a lot of years for that money. Sold a lot of land for a lot of money. Sold my dad's farm. Sold all but two of my old cars. Not right that someone would take it from me. Not right. Now maybe I'll have to sell my motorcycles. Didn't want to do that. They were my safety net, them bikes. You believe me."

"Absolutely." She actually did believe him about the stolen money, the spies—or spy—the one driving a silvery-gray foreign car. Maybe it was the precise story about the cost of the tattoo or the conviction in his voice. Maybe he was indeed missing a few fries from his Happy Meal, like her Goth dispatcher claimed, but he seemed to have retained most of them. And though she discounted his conspiracy theory of Democrats, he was no doubt right about being followed. The image of the silvery-gray car flashed behind her eyes again, the scratches on her Ford, the dented hood from when she'd parked it at her apartment, the threatening email. Piper shuddered.

"How much was taken this time? From your money market?"

"Three hundred and ninety-one thousand, four hundred and thirty-eight dollars from my money market. Left me four dollars in that account, just enough to cover the breakfast special I usually order at the restaurant. The thief hadn't messed with that account before, the money market. That's why I didn't think to tell the bank to shut that down. I just hadn't thought about it. Crap."

"Dear God. That's a lot of money." Piper realized she spoke too softly for Mark to hear her.

"You promised you'd fix it."

"I will."

*Why, why, why did I say that?*

"I'll fix it somehow. I promise." She put her hat on.

"You know, I don't have a lot of time left, Sheriff. I'm an old, old coot, past my expiration date you might say. No one is promised tomorrow. Don't none of us know how many tomorrows, how much time we have, though I suspect my future years are a single digit. Just hope I don't have to spend them in some damn nursing home. But time's the one thing we all have in common. And it's the most valuable possession, don't you think? I learned a long while back that time's worth more if it's well-spent, if you do good with it, make a difference, don't squander it. Don't waste it. I hope I'm not wasting yours, this hunt for my money."

"You're not wasting my time, Mark the Shark."

"Until this happened, I thought I was well off. Almost rich. Don't want to be on the county dole. Gonna have to sell my old bikes. Money market emptied, I won't have enough for one of them nice nursing homes, that's for sure. Not if I'm in there for any big amount of time. I still got some money buried, and I got those bikes. But, oh, hell. I shouldn't never have signed up for that online banking shit. Should've never bought a computer. My sweet Mae went through money like a faucet gushing when I had to put her in one of them nursing homes. Wished she would have had longer. Wished I would've had to keep spending the money on her. Better spent on her than the damn thief that got it. If wishes, eh?"

"Have you seen a Honda near your house?" Piper needed to change the subject.

"A gray one?"

"Looked kinda silver to me."

"It's not a Honda. I know cars. It's a Toyota, a Celica, at least ten years old, probably closer to fourteen. Someone's kept the body in pretty good shape, but the mileage has to be way, way, way up there, that old of a car. The paint job is a redo, metallic. I can tell. I know cars, I say. That Celica was in my neighborhood yesterday morning, about the time you were supposed to show up. Had gotten real muddy. When I'd seen it before, it was nice and clean. Is it following you, too?"

"Yeah."

"I couldn't get a look at the driver. The windows have a tint. That's not original, the tint."

"I didn't see the driver either."

"Some damn Democrat," Mark said. "Told you someone was following me. Told you I had a spy on my heels."

Piper knew the threatening email had been sent to scare her off. But rather than scare her, the email—and the suspicious car—were making her more determined, had thrown fuel on her ire.

"Did you get a look at the license plate?"

Mark shook his head. "Had mud on it. Didn't pay attention to the plate when I saw the car at the library."

"The library? The genealogy club?" Piper would call Diego on her way to Jasper, have him do a search on Toyota Celicas registered to drivers in Indiana and Kentucky. Maybe get lucky right away and find one in the county. If Diego got an address, she'd stop there on her way back from the State Police. If the driver was the thief, it would be quick to wrap it up. Getting the money back? Hopefully that would be quick, too.

"Yeah, at that little library. Saw the Celica a few other places in town, too. Once at the grocery store, that I recall. Can't be that many Celicas around. That's why I noticed it. Toyotas now are sleeker. That one, maybe the only Celica in the county," Mark said, mirroring her thoughts. "Democrats drive foreign cars, you know."

"That old of a Celica," Piper mused. "Yeah, hopefully just one around here."

"You fix—"

"Yeah, I'm gonna fix it. I told you I would. I promised."

*Somehow I'm gonna fix it.*

"I voted for you."

Piper studied the cars around the park again.

"Maybe meeting in daylight was a good idea," he said. "I can see the street better, see if someone's taking undue interest in me. If your department had one of them drones—"

"They cost seven thousand, the drone I want. A drone's a handy thing for a department, especially with everything so rural."

"Had a drone, you could send it off looking for that Celica."

She thought a drone might come in handy looking for meth manu-facturers. "It's not in the budget. A lot of things aren't in the budget." She hadn't needed to add that last part. She had no business venting to Mark. He had his own awful problems. "Don't have a drone to fly over your property or off looking for an old Toyota. But we'll be searching for the car with a computer."

"Damned computers." Mark pushed up on his canes. "I parked real close this time, dogs bothering me and all. You watch me leave, see if anyone follows."

"Sure."

"I'm going back to my attorney, let him know about my siphoned money market. Then I'm going to the bank. Get that last four dollars and buy breakfast with it. Fill out another one of those damn fraud reports. Push 'em. I'm gonna push 'em. But their fraud department—them people aren't here. And the thief—"

"Is," she finished. "The thief is right here in Spencer County."

"Damn straight. You meet me here tomorrow. Same time. You tell me if you find that Celica driver. You tell me if that's the thief twirling his fingers in my bank business and bleeding me. Maybe I'm not his only victim. You tell me if you arrest him and he's behind bars and is gonna rot until he's bones like that boy on the bluff you found. Make him give me my money back. Every penny. You fix this. I voted for you. I believe in you, Sheriff Blackwell. I ain't got anybody else to believe in."

She opened her mouth to tell him it wouldn't be that simple, but stopped. "I'll meet you at this bench tomorrow, Mr. Thresher."

"Mark the Shark."

# SEVENTEEN

"You're not missing if nobody's looking for you." That's what Oren's dad had said last night when they talked about the bones.

And if the boy had never been listed as missing, Oren inferred, he would be impossible to identify. It would be a cold case forever frozen.

But his father had half-remembered something from sixty years or so past. The old man had dementia, but there were gaps in the clouds when long-ago memories surfaced crystal clear. Last night, the clouds had big gaps in them.

Oren's ears were warm. He touched the back of his hand to his cheek and felt the heat there, too. The flush wasn't due to some bug he'd picked up; it was because he was pissed.

At the nursing home for not being more attentive to his father—who had been sitting in soiled pants when he'd arrived—and clearly had been that way for a while.

At twenty-three-year-old Piper Blackwell for hiring his grand-daughter.

At his granddaughter for applying for the deputy opening without telling him.

So that's why Millie hadn't wanted to talk about law school, and was her reason behind renting a house in Rockport. His grand-daughter was hoping to get hired by Piper. Oren figured that with her degrees she'd been the standout among the applicants. No one could have touched that high-bar. Plus, Piper would've been looking for the opportunity to add a woman to the department. A smart, young one with blue in her blood. Millie'd been a magnet, and Piper hadn't been able to resist the pull.

"Shit and back again," he grumbled.

He would have tried to talk Millie out of applying—and she probably knew that, was probably the reason she hadn't told him, probably didn't want to get in an argument with Pops.

Oren hadn't helped pay her way through college just so she could end up in the same sheriff's department in a sparsely populated county, working for the same twenty-three-year-old boss who only had a high school diploma. Millie'd been going to pick up some doctorate degree in law or some such, be a big-time attorney. Really make something of herself.

But a part of him was proud that Millie wanted a taste of law enforcement—keeping it in the Rosenberg line. He'd bragged to his dad about that during the nursing home visit. From great-grandfather to grandfather to granddaughter. Only skipping one generation because Millie's parents were—were what? Not together and not close. Her dad was a crab fisherman way the hell up in Alaska, and her mom worked in the accounting department of an Indianapolis hospital and had run afoul of the law because she'd killed a boy.

Maybe down the road Millie wearing a badge for a little while would make her a better attorney. Maybe he shouldn't be pissed. Maybe instead he should be pleased.

Nope. He couldn't let himself go all the way to being happy about it. He'd been too blindsided by the whole thing to smile.

"Shit and back again."

---

"You're not missing if nobody's looking for you."

He sat in an uncomfortable chair in a back room of Rockport's library.

"We rarely get anyone wanting to use this machine," the librarian said. She was young, but not *that* young. Oren guessed she was in her mid-thirties, and she was wearing way too much perfume and jewelry—three necklaces, one with a seashell fob that hung down to her waist. He'd not seen her at the library before. But then he rarely came here, usually only on an occasional weekend when he was out with his wife and she wanted to stop in and check out a few mysteries and romances. He'd sit in a chair and wait for her. "I hope it still works."

The machine was bulky and big, and the plastic that had covered it was cracked and yellowed and made a crunching noise when she took it off.

"So much is on computers, they're easier and don't take up as much space. We've had no call to scan in these old newspapers you want to look at. No one asks for them. I'm surprised we've kept this machine, actually, and all the microfiche slips. But then we really don't throw out much. Just worn-out books we toss at the summer sale." She stepped back and retrieved a gray box that Oren suspected had been white decades ago. "What years did you say you were looking for?"

"I'll start with five. 1952 to 1956."

She whistled. "This covers 1950 to 1960. Long time ago."

Oren frowned. In that overall scheme of things it was a heartbeat. He was no older than the films he'd requested. He figured the librarian considered him an antique. Again retirement thoughts flickered. But he didn't want to leave yet, especially with his granddaughter joining the department. He'd stick around in case she needed help. Oren grinned. He'd found an excuse to stay on the job that his wife would accept. He wasn't so pissed off at Piper and his granddaughter after all.

"Yeah, ancient history," he said dryly. "Practically stone age time."

"Be careful with the films," the librarian cautioned. A pause. "You know how to use the machine, right?"

Oren detected a hint of worry in her voice. Maybe she didn't know how to use it. Maybe she was afraid he'd ask her to demonstrate. He almost did. He was in that sort of a mood this morning.

"Sure. I know how to use it. I'll put the box back when I'm done." He waited until she left. It really didn't matter if she watched him, he wasn't doing anything secretive. He just wanted to page through history by his lonesome and not be forced to inhale all that flowery perfume.

Oren opened the box. Inside were pocket pages labeled *Rockport Weekly Democrat*, each holding a four-by-six-inch piece of film. He inserted one into the viewer. Newspapers in Spencer County stretched back to 1855, and there used to be more than one. Oren remembered that sometime in the late seventies the *Rockport Democrat* and the *Rockport Journal* merged. It was the *Journal-Democrat* now.

Oren skimmed the headlines, a mix of international, national, and local—the latter always on the front page, though not always above what would have been the fold. He had to admit that he liked searching news articles on the computer. The screen brighter and it was easier to adjust the type size.

1956.

February: Nikita Khrushchev denounced Stalin's excesses.

March: Morocco gained independence from France. He skipped ahead a month and noted Morocco also gained its independence from Spain.

"Bully for Morocco," he said.

The summer of that year saw a worker's uprising against communism in Poland; Egypt took control of the Suez Canal; and the British and French invaded Egypt at Port Said.

Oren noticed the national news was diverse. The first black student at the University of Alabama was suspended from classes after riots. A hydrogen bomb was tested over Bikini Atoll with the force of ten million tons of TNT. The Yankees beat the Dodgers in the World Series. *Marty* won Best Picture at the Oscars. Oren had seen *Marty* a couple of times. Good picture, worthy of an award, he mused. Needles won the Kentucky Derby. Federal spending topped seventy billion dollars. The cost of a first-class stamp was three cents. *Peyton Place* became a steamy bestseller. Tommy Dorsey died.

"And some damn fine music died with him."

In local news *Our First One Hundred Years* was published by the Free and Accepted Masons of Grandview, Indiana, Grandview Lodge. Oren's father was a Mason. He laughed softly, recalling how his dad had tried to get him to join. *An Archaeological Survey of Spencer County* by James H. Kellar of the Indiana Historical Bureau was published in the same month.

Finding nothing else of particular note, Oren carefully put the film back into its envelope and pulled out a year earlier. His dad had suggested this, after he ate the last bite of double-thick grilled cheese sandwich.

"Sometimes people go missing and it doesn't show up in any police report. Sometimes you got to read the papers. You go read the old papers, Oren. I remember something about a nine-year-old boy. Maybe two of them. Maybe three. Maybe your dead boy was never missing. You're not missing if nobody's looking for you."

So that's what Oren had decided to do, read the old papers.

The weeklies in 1955 covered multiple films. He looked through two sheets, then got up to stretch. The third sheet was more interesting. The world population sat at two point seven billion; Churchill resigned; the Federal Republic of West Germany became a sovereign state; the Warsaw Pact was signed; Argentina ousted Juan Perón; and the United States spent more than two million to aid Vietnam.

"Fat lot of good that did," Oren mused. "Then we went to war in Vietnam for too damn long."

Rosa Parks refused to sit in the back of the bus, defying Alabama's segregated seating law. The AFL and the CIO merged into the AFL-CIO. The cost of a first-class stamp was three cents. The Brooklyn

Dodgers won the World Series, and Detroit grabbed the Stanley Cup. *On the Waterfront* won Best Picture. Oren never liked Marlon Brando, never saw the movie. Lee Meriwether won Miss America. *She'd been a real looker*, Oren thought, recalling that in the sixties she'd played Catwoman in a Batman movie. *Gunsmoke* debuted on CBS. Albert Einstein died at age seventy-six. James Dean died at age twenty-six in a car accident.

"Too young to go," Oren said of Dean. "But seventeen more years than the boy got."

In Indiana news the Crispus Attucks was the first all-black basketball team to win a state championship. Spencer County seemed pretty boring that year, and nothing stood out. After skimming the last film in the folder, Oren went on to 1954.

Racial segregation was banned in public schools, the cost of a first-class stamp still sat at three cents, and the federal debt was a paltry two hundred and seventy billion. The New York Giants won the World Series. Detroit got another Stanley Cup. Best Picture was *From Here to Eternity*. Oren thought that movie had been as boring as staring at clothes dryer lint. J.R.R. Tolkien published *The Fellowship of the Ring*. And locally Albert Kleber published the one hundred year *History of the St. Meinrad Archabbey*. The abbey was still in operation, one of Spencer County's crown jewels. Lionel Barrymore died.

In 1953 Joseph Stalin died; Moscow announced that it exploded a hydrogen bomb; Charlie Chaplin was labeled a Communist and left the U.S.; first-class postage was three cents; the Yankees topped the Dodgers in the World Series; Montreal claimed the Stanley Cup; a horse named Dark Star won the Kentucky Derby; and Ernest Hemingway won the Pulitzer Prize for fiction for *The Old Man and the Sea*. Oren loved that book and had read it several times.

"And now I am *The Old Man*," he said, rubbing the back of his neck. He was getting stiff from sitting in one position so long. "An old man with a better boat than Hemmingway gave his character."

Cecil B. DeMille's *The Greatest Show on Earth* took home the Best Picture Oscar; Sir Winston Churchill was handed the Nobel Prize for Literature; Lucille Ball gave birth to Desi Arnaz Jr; *Playboy* appeared on newsstands with a nude Marilyn Monroe on the cover; Queen Mary died—and so did three nine-year-old boys, drowned in the Ohio River near Rockport.

"Rescue crews from Owensboro and Rockport searched for three boys still missing after their raft broke apart on a windy Halloween," Oren read. "The boys had just finished supper and on a dare from a classmate tried to recreate Abraham Lincoln's cast off on a raft from a point near the bluff. The fourth grade was studying Abraham Lincoln's time in Spencer County. A searcher found an Abe Lincoln-style hat and a pillowcase with candy in it tangled in fallen branches near the remains of a raft. The searcher said the boys must have gone trick-or-treating first. A spokesman for one of the search teams said the raft broke apart and spilled the boys into the river. It had been a heavily-overcast night, and though temperatures were unseasonably warm, the river would have been cold, the spokesman said. It was unknown if the boys were good swimmers."

That must have been the incident Oren's dad remembered—about a missing nine-year-old boy. Except it had been three of them, not one. And they weren't exactly missing.

"Maybe your dead boy was never missing," Oren's dad had said. "You're not missing if nobody's looking for you."

*Or gave up looking for you because they thought the river took you under.*

Oren sat back in the chair. The drownings, the newspaper article, might not be connected to the bones on the bluff. But the age of the boys fit, and the year fit—at least within the parameters Doc Natty presented. The bones might not belong to one of those three. They might be from another boy entirely—one from Kentucky or Arizona, one that hadn't been listed as drowned, one that might be named through dental records or flagged in another agency's computer.

But the age fit, and the year could fit.

Oren pulled out a notebook and recorded the three boys' names.

Edgar Killian.

Neal Huffman.

Rory Martin.

He read a follow-up article from the next week. One body had been recovered, Edgar Killian, found by a woman walking her dog along the bank. The boy had his father's Brownie on a strap around his neck, apparently intending to document their raft trip. Funerals for all three were scheduled. Two burials would be empty caskets.

That article went on to quote one of the Spencer County deputies who'd been involved in the recovery. "Drownings in Indiana are unfortunate and continue to happen every year. Nearly half of the victims are children and teenagers. They don't understand all the dangers attached to water. It's up to parents and the community to teach young people to respect the water, especially our river."

"Maybe your dead boy was never missing." The words played through Oren's mind. "You're not missing if nobody's looking for you."

He crossed Edgar Killian's name off his list.

That left Neal Huffman and Rory Martin.

Oren would have a sit-down with Piper when she got back from Jasper.

She might find a lead through the State Police.

But he doubted it would be more interesting than this one.

# EIGHTEEN

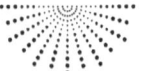

"There's a website keyed to our state." The State Police officer looked a lot like Oren, big, quite a bit of age to him, immaculately dressed. "It's called—"

"Missing in dot org." Piper took the seat closest to his desk. "Missing and unsolved dot com is another one. Been over every pixel of both of them. Been through a lot of websites, actually. And like I mentioned, we've sent our preliminary coroner's report to Arizona, Kentucky, and—"

"I have a copy."

She'd also brought print copies, which she handed over—just in case he didn't have everything.

"NAMUS is a good one," he said.

Piper cocked her head. That was one she hadn't tried.

"National Missing and Unidentified Persons System." He wrapped a meaty hand around a mug of coffee and took a long drink. "You've been Spencer County Sheriff, what—"

"Four months, three days," she glanced at the clock on the wall; it was 10:40 a.m., "ten hours and forty... forty-one minutes."

"I read about you, back in January, catching a serial killer, one week on the job." He took another drink of coffee. "I know your dad. He was sheriff a lot of years. How's he doing?"

"Cancer free again." Piper crossed her arms. She didn't come here to talk about her lack of experience.

"Good." He drained the coffee and pushed the mug aside. He looked down at a sheet of paper. "MP, a sheriff only a few months, let me give you a little perspective. I printed this out yesterday after you called. The missing person tally for NAMUS this year," he waved the piece of paper, "was six hundred and sixty-one thousand. A lot of people reported missing, right? Well, six hundred and fifty-nine thousand of those reports were canceled. People came back, were found, dead or alive, but most were never really missing. About two thousand remain unsolved. Sometimes people go missing 'cause they don't want to be found."

Piper started to say something, but he kept going.

"At any given time, there are about ninety thousand people estimated as missing in the US. Each day? About twenty-three hundred are reported missing. In Indiana right now—" He looked at his paper again. "A little more than a thousand people are listed as missing. That's five hundred and thirty-three adults and four hundred and ninety-six children. You've got an old missing persons case, but not the oldest-unsolved. I read about a four-year-old, Marjorie West, last seen picking a bouquet of flowers in a field near where a Mother's Day picnic was going on. That was in—"

"April, 1938," Piper supplied. "There's an older one, twenty-five years before that, Ambrose Bierce, a journalist in his seventies who went missing in Mexico while covering a story. I said I've been digging through the Internet."

He leaned back in the chair and gave her a small smile. "Paul's daughter is all grown up and is the Spencer County Sheriff. I like your dad. I like you. I really want to help you. But there is nothing in any of our files—and we have most of it on computer now—that matches your bones. In fact, I dug through some national law enforcement sites you might not know about and came up with nothing. Oh, stuff is close, and I printed those close ones out for you." He stretched an arm out and grabbed a thin manila folder, tossed it on the front of his desk where she could reach it. "Those are close. A couple of ten year olds, a couple of eight year olds, an eleven year old, a twelve year old, and a nine-year-old girl in case your coroner ruled wrong on the sex. A few more that might fit. All from the Midwest, except the girl. She's from Florida. But the years don't match your sixty to sixty-five range. Oldest case in that folder goes back to 1960. The eleven year old. But that's close. Spitting distance. A mix of races in that folder. You say Caucasian, right handed. Those files don't list right or left. But they're worth you taking a looksee at."

He shifted in his seat and stared at a picture on the wall. Piper suspected he was looking at something far removed from his office. "Missing kids? Ninety-nine percent of kids who go missing today come home alive. The recovery rate is amazing, in part because of social media. Amber alerts, Facebook, Twitter, what-have-you. Pictures of the missing kids are bounced across the country. But if the kids have been abducted? Not simply missing? More than half come home, the rest are killed—and a lot of those stay open cases."

"My chief deputy says a cold case like this could take some time." She picked up the folder, but did not open it.

"Could. Sometimes bones, with dentals, you could get a match right off. You might not ever solve yours. Especially if the parents were poor and didn't take the kid to a dentist. No dental records, that's possible. Don't beat yourself up over this one. Put it on a side burner, work it on and off."

Piper couldn't do that, the bones were festering. "I appreciate this." She indicated the folder. "But I really wanted to chat about motives. Sure, I could poke around on the Internet, the state database, about motives. But I learn more talking to people." That was true. She learned much more as an MP by talking to her drill sergeant than she ever got from reading the manuals. "Our coroner, and a forensic anthropologist, say the boy was murdered."

He nodded. "Killed sixty to sixty-five years ago is the guess, right?"

"Yeah."

"So your doer is dead, too."

But that didn't mean she couldn't find justice. Put a name to the boy, find out what happened. The mystery coupled with Mark the Shark was keeping her Fort Campbell thoughts at bay.

"I want to talk motive. What motivates someone to kill a kid?" As an MP with the Screaming Eagles she'd covered some domestic disturbances off base, husband and wife spats, but nothing that had involved children.

"Murder's always ugly," he said. "Murder of a child. That goes beyond ugly. A few years back I read about a South Carolina man, a young father, who'd led police to the bodies of his five kids. In Georgia, I read about another father who intentionally left his son to die in a hot SUV, had strapped him in the back seat for the whole time he was at work, Googled how long it took kids to die in hot cars. In Utah, a woman who kept giving birth during a ten-year stretch strangled her newborns. Hid the bodies in a garage in plastic totes." He picked up his coffee mug and regarded it a moment, put it back down. "I look at the FBI reports that come along with the state newsletters. More than four hundred kids are killed yearly by their parents. Most of the kids are under five, and most die of injuries from beatings. Fathers are more likely to kill, whether by beating or shooting. The average age of the father is thirty, and they tend to plan the murder in advance, sometimes kill the entire family. Excuse my sexism, Sheriff Blackwell, but violence is a male pursuit."

"I won't disagree."

"When mothers kill, those kids are usually babies, not even a year old. Postpartum depression, mental illness, stress they can't cope with. The mothers tend to be young, early twenties."

"Why? I want to know *why* someone would kill a nine-year-old boy. You're a criminologist. That's why I wanted to talk to you. I appreciate these missing children reports you've given me, truly, but I'm looking for a why. I want to understand this."

"Funny. I've been trying to understand violence against kids for decades." He steepled his fingers. "People who kill children are shuffled into five categories, for the most part. A parent who has some sort of a psychotic break. The killing isn't something they would do if their mind was right. They could be an altruist, killing because they don't want the child to grow up without them—and they're not going to be in the picture because of divorce, or because they're going away to prison, for example. Then you have the nutcase who kills kids for revenge against a spouse or boyfriend or girlfriend. The significant other has the kids or does something to piss the doer off. The murdered kids are the revenge—makes the target of the hate suffer."

Piper probably could have gotten this stuff from a book or the Internet, but it likely would have taken her longer to ferret it out than it did to drive the forty-six minutes to this office.

"Sometimes the kids aren't wanted, are inconvenient, getting in the way of the life a parent wants. Maybe the kids cost too much—doctors, clothes, babysitter—and suffocating them with a pillow is better for the budget." He took a deep breath. "Sometimes it is an accident. The parent neglected the kid, looked away, or was reckless, honestly didn't mean to take a life. And sometimes a parent kills for some of those reasons stirred together in a sick, mental pot. There are scattered incidents of kids killing other kids. In the nineties there was a three-year-old killed by two ten-year-olds in England. They stoned him and left his unconscious body on train tracks to hide their crime. I read about a case in the US where a little boy wanted to see the neighbor girl's puppy. She said no, so he got his dad's gun and shot her. Those cases are rare. Kids are better people than adults, don't do the real evil shit. I got three kids, all grown and away. And they got kids. No matter how many cases and statistics I've studied, I've never been able to wholly wrap my head around child murder."

"So the person who killed the boy on the bluff—"

"Was likely his father, who certainly wouldn't have reported him missing, was in the neighborhood of thirty years old, and so would be dead or in a nursing home." He stood and extended a hand, signaling the meeting was over. Piper stood and shook it. "Your cold case might stay frosty forever, Sheriff Blackwell. Not only do you have a missing person case—where the kid was probably never reported missing—you have a murder case. A cold one. You might never get an identity. Or justice for your victim."

"But I might," Piper said. "I just might."

"I like you, Sheriff Blackwell. Give my regards to your dad."

She'd wanted to add a topic—email and hacking—but she'd take that up with the Geek. She checked her phone as she slid into her loaned Hyundai and saw Sylvia D had left a message that Ezekiel Whitman would be in at four. Nothing yet from Diego on the Celica. A message from Nang, asking about dinner tonight. She smiled and replied: Frozen pizza, my place, 6:30. Was she enjoying his company too much?

There was another message:

*You don't listen*
*Still chasing the cheddar?*
*going 2 the state police?*
*That's not backing off, bitch*
*Don't expect 2 suck air much longer*

# NINETEEN

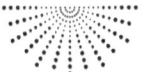

Piper was on 62 when Sylvia D radioed.

"Sheriff Blackwell, where are you?"

"A few miles past Dale." The time read 11:44, and she was thinking about stopping down the road at a little café in Chrisney to look at the threatening email again.

"Then you're real near Gentryville."

"Yeah."

"Better get over there, Sheriff. JJ just called. Just. Like a half-minute ago. She's at the Mailbox Mauler's place. Gretchen has a gun, and JJ's looking for backup. You shouldn't've let Gretchen out of jail the other day."

"She made bail." The words came out flat. Piper remembered that Sylvia D had criticized her at the old fart's club for having Gretchen arrested. The tune had changed apparently.

Piper called JJ on the cell, not wanting the chatter over the radio.

"Five minutes," Piper told JJ. "I'll be there in five." She resisted the notion to call for additional backup. The department's two women could more than handle Gretchen. She didn't need one of her men shooting the crazy octogenarian.

"Excuse my sexism, Sheriff Blackwell," the State Police officer had said, "but violence is a male pursuit."

"Unless you're an old woman with a vendetta against mailboxes," Piper muttered.

Gretchen's place was on a blacktop road where the houses were spaced far apart, the yards each covering an acre or a little more. On the approach she saw three mailboxes on their sides, posts broken. One of the yards had a new post, but hadn't yet put on a box. The destruction was from Gretchen's latest spree. A few houses later Piper spotted two more postal fatalities, a stout middle-aged man at one of the busted posts waving frantically to get her to stop. He was holding a mailbox that had been bent to resemble a Chinese fortune cookie.

She rolled down the window and pulled over. He had a t-shirt with a big wolf on it stretched tight across his middle. His face was pale, sweat beaded up on it, his hair straggly and hanging to his jawline. He looked ill.

"Damned old woman. Second time this year. Look at the box? I'm gonna have to replace all of this again. Again! Can't you keep her locked up? I'm home sick with the flu and I gotta deal with this crap. And why? Just 'cause the mailman accidentally put my package on her stoop yesterday. This is her retaliation! Somebody misdelivers something and she goes on the warpath. She should take it out on the post office not me." He slammed the mailbox down and kicked it. "Hell, I ain't gonna replace this. I'm gonna leave it this way and mow around it and get a P.O. Box. Then she can't ram my property again." He coughed and waved dismissively, turned and headed toward his house, kicking the mailbox one more time.

Piper cruised farther and saw JJ standing by her Ford, which was parked off the side of the road across from Gretchen's. Piper edged in behind her.

"This is nuts," JJ said as Piper got out. "I will so not miss this effin' backwater county."

"I'm sure North Carolina has people like—"

"No. Nowhere else in the world has someone like that... like that... like that effin' old woman." JJ pointed to her Ford and Piper counted eight holes, plus assorted dents, all from shotgun pellets. "She's in her house, watching us from that window. If I make a move toward the driveway, she shoots. She's got a shotgun, I'm thinking ten gauge. How the hell can she lift it? She's little. And old. Almost hit me. Look what she did to her own mailbox. Shot it, and I damn well know that was an accident. Hell, she probably can't see well enough to aim right."

But with a shotgun, Piper knew the pellets spread, and you didn't have to be all that great of a marksman to hit something.

"Old doesn't necessarily mean weak," Piper said.

"I came out here, just to talk, just like you told me to." JJ made a huffing sound. "Except I saw two more busted mailboxes, and Cooper Henderson—he's the big guy in the wolf shirt you were talking to down there—stopped me and said she'd just zoomed past and deliberately took out his. So I figured I'd arrest her. Do more than talk."

"When did she start shooting? After you said you were arresting her?" Piper peered at the kitchen window. Gretchen's face was half-hidden by a gauzy curtain.

"I didn't get that far. Didn't say a word, didn't get a chance. I pulled in her driveway, got out, and she opened the front door and hollered 'you're not taking my babies.' Then she blasted the passenger side. I jumped in, backed it out here, and used the PA. I told her to come out and drop the gun. Hell, Piper, she shot again. We're out of her range here, I'm pretty sure. I called Sylvia D, and you got over here a lot faster than I expected."

"I was nearby."

"Thank God for that. I'm surprised she's not stormed out here to shoot us."

"Maybe she's out of ammunition."

"Fat chance." JJ glared at the house and ground the ball of her foot against the road. "We can't shoot her. We can't. She's eighty-two. It'd be like offing my grandma. And with that gun, I can't get close enough to taze her. I'm pretty sure no one else is in there with her. Henderson told me she lives alone."

"How'd Diego arrest her the other day?" Piper hadn't read his report yet. She'd been too obsessed with the old case files.

JJ snorted. "He saw her pulling weeds around those big tires. She came over to him half-friendly. He cuffed her and brought her in, said she screamed the whole way. Diego told me the story twice, said he's gonna put it in a book he's writing. I had no clue she had a shotgun. We should have kept her locked up."

"Couldn't. She made bail." Piper studied the house. It was an older brick ranch, small, probably two bedrooms, a single attached garage, the door down. A deep flowerbed stretched all across the front and around the side to meet a row of hedges. Three more flowerbeds were close to the road, in massive truck tires. The place looked pretty and well-maintained.

"She won't be able to make bail after this, I'm betting. That's assault with a deadly weapon," JJ fumed.

There was a big picture window, but the curtains were drawn. The only open curtain was the one Gretchen stared out of. No window wells that Piper could see, so maybe it didn't have a basement, maybe there was a crawlspace. There were no neighborhood gawkers out, probably all at work—*hopefully at work*, Piper thought. Or perhaps they were afraid of Gretchen and were all inside with their doors locked.

"How do you want this handled, boss?"

"Peacefully," Piper said. "Stay here." She went to the back of the Hyundai, popped the hatch and reached for her vest and strapped it on. "And put your vest on, JJ. I shouldn't have to tell you that." Piper recalled a domestic disturbance she'd handled at Fort Campbell, an armed soldier holding his wife hostage. She and her partner talked the man down and he got the psychiatric help he needed. She figured Gretchen needed help, too.

Piper edged away from the car, hands out to her sides, and slowly crossed the road and stood at the end of the driveway. She saw that JJ was fastening her vest and grumbling about it.

"So far, so good. Let's see how close I can get."

Piper took a few more steps and noticed Gretchen had the window open several inches, the gun barrel propped on the sill. It would give her a steady aim. "Gretchen! I'm Sheriff Blackwell. I just want to talk to you. Can we do that? Just talk?" A few more steps. The driveway was short, and she was halfway to the house now, close enough to smell the flowers in the beds—daffodils, tulips, pansies, and petunias—a riot of color that stood out against the blonde brick. The rains had brought a profusion of flowers early to Spencer County. There was a hint of something foul, too, like a dead animal was rotting in one of the beds. "Can I come in and—"

"Noooooooooo!" the woman shrieked in a voice that Piper thought might shatter glass. "Noooooooooooo!" Then Gretchen fired, barely missing Piper, but striking so close her sheriff's hat sailed away with the shotgun pellets. Piper hurriedly backed up.

"Gretchen! You need to put the gun down!" Piper called. "Put the gun down now!"

"Noooooooooo!" Another blast, this time at Piper's feet, the pellets striking the concrete and chipping it. She made it back to JJ, pretty sure that her detective was right and they were out of the gun's effective range.

"So how do you want this handled, boss?" JJ repeated. "Should I call for more backup?"

Piper shook her head, her obduracy holding. "I'll take the road north of this and go on foot, cut through the neighbor's, get to Gretchen's backyard." She pointed to the radio on JJ's belt. "I'll call if I need a distraction, if I need you to make some noise. I'm hoping I can get in the back without her seeing me. Maybe if she's got a crawlspace, I can get in that way. Or maybe through a garage door. I want to check it out."

"I am not going to miss this effin' county," JJ hissed. "But I will miss you."

Piper got in her Hyundai and drove away.

# TWENTY

A handful of minutes later Piper was parked on the street behind Gretchen's property. She called Sylvia D. "Check county records. See if Gretchen has any kids or grandkids in the area. Get a list with phone numbers." Then she called JJ. "She still at the window? Good. Hold tight until I radio you again."

Piper worked her way around a pale green saltbox with a six-foot high wood fence in its backyard. She skirted the fence and kept to the corner, studying the back of Gretchen's. Where the front had looked like it could appear in *Better Homes & Gardens*, everything seeming immaculate, the back was a mess. The grass was cut, likely courtesy of the riding lawnmower under a metal canopy.

No wonder the people behind Gretchen had built a six-foot fence to block the view. There were crooked stacks of plastic milk crates of various colors, all bleached by the sun, rusted wire cages the size for rabbits, mounds of tires and hubcaps, coils of discarded rubber hoses that looked split from seasons of freezing and thawing, broken bird-baths, and piles of *things* that amounted to garbage in her estimation. All of this was directly in the back of Gretchen's house and so likely not visible from the road in front, a big garden shed blocking the view from one side, and a hedge blocking the view from the other.

"She needs help," Piper whispered. "Lots of help." No sane person would keep all this junk—and destroy the neighbors' mailboxes. Fortunately, the detritus provided hiding spots as she scurried closer, pausing behind a stack of milk crates to radio JJ.

"She's still at the window, boss."

"I don't see any window wells." But Piper thought they could be concealed by the assortment of debris. Stacks of milk crates blocked the backdoor to the garage. She moved closer and perched next to a mound of tires of various sizes, the tread looking bare. "No. No basement. Can't tell if there's a crawlspace, at least not one with an outside access. I'm going to try the backdoor, probably opens to a kitchen. Give me a little distraction, wave at her or something."

Piper heard a shotgun blast and raced to the backdoor, plastering herself up against the wall next to it. The screen door hung crooked, but the wood door beyond, though the paint was chipped so badly it looked like dried fish scales, appeared solid. Something smelled awful and sour, and she couldn't identify the reek, maybe just the jumbles of refuse in the backyard. But when she eased open the screen, stood on the step and reached for the knob of the wood door, the stench seemed to intensify.

Something *inside* the house smelled dreadful, the odor seeping out under a crack at the bottom of the door. Was there a corpse rotting inside? Maybe a couple of them?

"You get!" Piper heard Gretchen screech, the thin voice carrying around to the back. "I'll put holes in you!"

Piper tested the knob—it turned. The backdoor wasn't locked.

When another shotgun blast sounded, Piper twisted the knob, nudged open the door, slipped inside, and doubled over. The stink was overwhelming, and her eyes teared. She fought against the nausea and stood, holding the door for support. She left it open, hoping fresh air might filter in and help. But after a moment, she wasn't sure anything would improve things.

She padded into a kitchen, shadowed because the shades were drawn, diffuse light filtering in through the material. The kitchen table was stacked with cat food boxes and cans and litter sacks, more under the table. The counters were covered with dishes, some of which cats were eating out of. There were more cats on the floor, kittens playing. Some of them looked ill and malnourished; some were missing patches of fur. There were litter boxes against a wall, but they were overflowing, and feces was scattered across a laminate floor that was stained, the planks bowed from being soaked with too much urine—that odor strongly identified itself. Piper felt the coffee she'd downed earlier rising in her throat. A green garbage bag in the corner had a couple of dead cats in it. She could tell by the outlines.

Gretchen needed a lot of help.

How could this situation have gone undetected? Hadn't the neighbors noticed something wrong? Clearly Diego hadn't gotten a look inside. Hadn't anybody seen this? Piper immediately tamped that thought down. Of course *someone* knew something was wrong—she was running over mailboxes every few months, and the victims were howling about it. Why hadn't someone done something?

*None of that mattered*, she thought. She was going to do something about it. Fix it.

A skinny white cat rubbed against her leg, a fat gray striped one with matted eyes followed. Not all of them were underfed. She counted two dozen cats, in addition to a moving mass of kittens of all colors, but she knew there were more. Piper could hear them meowing from another room.

Some of the cats were agitated. One spit and hissed, ears down. Another's ears were flat, pointing backwards. One with no hair—Piper hoped it was one of the hairless varieties, like a sphinx—arched its back, and she swore it was growling. A fluffy charcoal gray on the kitchen table had puffed itself and the tail was sticking straight up.

Not only was Gretchen a Mailbox Mauler, she was a cat hoarder. Maybe a hoarder of a lot of things. Vases in the window held flowers that had dried a long time ago.

Piper breathed as shallowly as possible, but that didn't cut the pong. As she crept forward, she clung to the stove, then the refrigerator—a massive double-door one that maybe held a massive amount of milk. She was careful not to brush against the plethora of refrigerator magnets that held coupons that at a glance she saw had expired a few years prior. On top of the fridge were two open boxes that had envelopes and cards piled inside and reaching to the ceiling. A cat peered out between them. Across from her the sink was filled with clean dishes on one side, dirty on the other, with two cats busy licking at the latter. The floor creaked as she went, and she feared Gretchen might hear her. Piper knew she should have some sort of mask. The air was toxic and making her sick to her stomach, her eyes watering worse now. But she wasn't going to leave and come back with the proper gear. She was going to take Gretchen out of here now.

"I told you to get!" Piper guessed Gretchen was in the room just beyond this doorway. "I'll put holes in you! I'm warning you!" It sounded like she was getting hoarse. "First they send the spic, and then they send a skinny shit woman. I'll shoot you! Get on outta here!"

Piper stretched her fingers down to her hip, felt the gun, and almost unsnapped the holster to pull it. She sucked in her lower lip. Her MP training dictated she draw her gun. Everything she'd ever studied screamed that she should draw her gun. But if she did that, she had to be prepared to use it—and that wasn't going to happen. No way in hell would she shoot this old woman.

Tackle her? That was the plan. Carefully tackle so as not to break her bones.

She glided forward until she reached the doorway, feeling a cat snake around her calves to rub its head. She looked down and saw bugs scurrying across the floor. Another step and she was beyond the kitchen. Gretchen was at the dining room window, a dozen feet away, the shotgun cocked and barrel resting on the pane. She was small, the floral housedress ballooning around her and making her seem even tinier. Gray hair as fine as spider webs stirred in the faint breeze coming in through the open window. A scrawny black cat sat on the sill and looked out.

Tears spilled down Piper's face and she blinked. Her eyes burned terribly, and she felt her throat go dry. How could Gretchen survive in this place?

A massive table was between Piper and Gretchen. Chairs were

pulled out all around it and newspapers and magazines were stacked on them. Watchful cats crowned the piles. Plastic bowls of different colors and sizes were on the tabletop. An orange striped cat worked at something congealed in one of them.

The carpet was stained and dotted with feces and dried hairballs. Litter boxes against the wall overflowed. She spied a desiccated cat corpse in the gap under a hutch. She felt dizzy.

Piper moved closer, nudging a lazing Siamese out of her way. To her left she saw a long couch with cats on it, an easy chair with more cats. The front of the house was one big room that served as both dining and living areas. There were more overflowing litter boxes. A doorway next to the easy chair probably led to the bedrooms and likely more cats. Another step and a cat emitted a high-pitched yowl.

*Shit.* Piper had stepped on a tail.

Everything seemed to happen at once.

Gretchen turned, bringing the gun around with her and firing, eyes widening, and screaming, "Noooooooo!"

Piper leaped for the dining table as the pellets sprayed and chewed into the wall behind her and into left arm, shoulder, and vest. It felt like she'd been punched and the air rushed out in one great *whoosh*. Her momentum made her slide on her stomach across the tabletop, knocking bowls out of the way. Cats hissed. She registered first a burning sensation and pressure where she'd been hit, then the pain slammed her, like someone had repeatedly jabbed a screwdriver into her flesh.

Her course took her straight into Gretchen, who without the support of the windowsill was having a tough time bringing the barrel back up. Piper reached out with her right hand, grabbed the end of the barrel, and yanked with all the strength she could summon. But Gretchen was stronger than she appeared and kept hold of the gun.

Piper was lightheaded, from the fire racing down her arm and the awful smell of this place, from gulping in the reeking air. The tears were so thick she looked at the old woman through a film that rendered everything blurry. Her left arm and shoulder were nearly impossible to move.

"Nooooooooooo!" Gretchen continued to scream. The old woman tried to pull the gun out of Piper's grip. But as Piper spilled over the other side of the table, she kept her hold on the barrel and heaved the gun free, landing sprawled on top of it and adding to her misery. Her left arm throbbed in an agonizing pulsing sensation. The carpet was wet with cat urine and Piper could taste it. Gretchen starting kicking Piper and hissed, sounding like some of the cats who'd come in the room to protest the sheriff's intrusion.

Piper tried to get up, but Gretchen kept kicking, and then toppled a stack of magazines on her.

"Nooooooooooooooo!"

Piper heard the front door slam open. Somehow Gretchen screamed even louder. Piper felt like she was swimming in sludge as she pushed herself to her hands and knees, magazines falling away, managing to keep her good hand on the shotgun so the old woman couldn't regain it. The room spun in colors like looking through a child's kaleidoscope.

"Don't shoot her," Piper gasped, knowing it was JJ who'd come in. "I've got her gun." Then she gave up what had been breakfast, the stench so powerful against the floor it overcame her. She felt like she was going to pass out. The colors swirled sluggishly and darkened.

"Oh God," JJ said. "Oh God. Oh God. You're hit."

"Get her out of here," Piper said.

JJ rushed into the dining room and pushed Gretchen back, spun her around and grabbed her right arm with one hand and pulled out the handcuffs with the other.

Piper thought she heard JJ start to read Gretchen her rights.

"Don't hurt her," Piper said, getting to her knees. "Oh, crap. I hurt. I really—"

## TWENTY-ONE

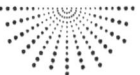

Piper heard voices, men she didn't know, JJ in there. Someone screamed, "Noooooooooo!" That must be Gretchen. "Noooooooooooooo!" The howl muted now, traveling away from her.

"Gotta be a hundred cats in there." Piper had no clue who said that.

"Need Hazmat suits." Another stranger.

The floor made creaking sounds.

Cats hissed.

"I'm calling Oren." That was JJ again.

Piper wanted to say something, check on Gretchen, issue orders, tell JJ that Oren's presence wasn't necessary, she didn't need to call him. The Mailbox Mauler was in custody. She was, wasn't she? Piper remembered JJ handcuffing the old woman.

"This place should be quarantined. Nuked from effin' orbit." Sounded like JJ.

"She's in shock." A stranger. "Definitely shock."

Were they talking about the Mailbox Mauler? Or were they talking about her?

More cats hissed, the sounds blending and seeming like a nest of serpents that someone had stirred.

The swirl of colors thickened and turned gray like clay. The air felt like clay, too, wet, and it was heavy, pressing down on her. Piper tried to get up, but she felt fuzzy. The air pushed her down with more force.

A soft meow, something pleasant against her hand, maybe a fluffy cat rubbing against her? She couldn't see the cat for the clay.

She was on her knees, right? She needed to get up, walk this off. Or had she already gotten out of the house? The air smelled a little better. She could take it to the bottom of her lungs. Was this a dream?

Oh, God, her arm burned like it was on fire.

---

"Where am I?" Suddenly Piper didn't hurt as much, the aches dull and pulsing, but no longer burdensome. She still felt fuzzy, imagining cats rubbing against her. Was she still in that awful house that should be nuked from orbit?

"Rest." Another strange voice, this one matronly. "Don't try to get up."

Piper focused and discovered she was on an uncomfortable gurney, raised so she reclined, her head on an uncomfortable pillow that made a crinkly noise when she moved.

"Where—"

"You're in the emergency room at St. Mary's in Boonville, Punkin. It's where the ambulance took you." Paul Blackwell stood on one side of the bed; a nurse was on the other, checking an IV. Something clear dripped from it down a tube and into Piper's good arm.

Her left arm and shoulder were wholly bandaged and tied against her.

"What's this—"

"It's called a sling and swathe," the nurse explained. Hers had been the matronly voice. "You have hairline fractures in your humerus and clavicle. The pellets hit your bones, but didn't penetrate. You were lucky. Couldn't put a cast on the shoulder, so they used a sling. It will keep your arm immobilized, give your shoulder support, help everything heal. You're going to have to wear it for a week or two." She stepped back and crossed her arms. "They used a local, Lidocaine, and you have a few stitches. Ortho's looked at your x-rays, said you can leave after the antibiotics are done." A nod to the IV drip. "Pharmacy has a couple of prescriptions. You'll need to take it easy. Nothing strenuous. Don't use the arm. The doctor will be back in just a little while to go over everything. But I've probably covered it all." She walked to the door, her pant legs making a swishing sound. "Like I said, you'll need to take it easy."

"But I can go," Piper said.

Her father nodded. "When the IV's done, and after the doctor's come back. They said I can get the prescriptions for you. What were you thinking, Punkin? You could have been—" He stopped. "Doc says you were unconscious when they brought you in, that you were in shock. They took eight pellets out of your arm, and two out of your shoulder. Cleaned you up."

"Thinking? I was thinking there was no way in hell I was gonna shoot that crazy old woman." Piper turned her head to look out the window. It was still light. "What time is it?"

"Half past five."

"Shit."

"Punkin—"

"I had a meeting at four with a kid I was looking at for the dispatcher job, who I was gonna ask about hacking and—"

"Sylvia rescheduled him for tomorrow. And I can talk to him if you're going to stay home." Oren had stepped into the room. "You should stay home, Sheriff Blackwell."

"She is staying home," Paul said.

Piper couldn't. She had Mark the Shark at nine. The bones. The old case files. Gretchen to resolve. She needed to see if Diego had come up with anything on the Celica. Her routine was no longer dull, and she refused to miss any of the current goings on.

"I'll take it easy," she compromised. "But I'm going in. Gretchen? The Mailbox Mauler. What happened?"

Paul stepped back, mumbling about letting them talk business. But she noticed he didn't leave. *Nosey*, she thought. But she couldn't blame him.

"She's been arrested on charges of littering." He laughed when her eyes widened. "Just kidding, but we could. I met with DA Scales an hour ago. We got her on assault with a deadly weapon inflicting serious bodily injury, assaulting an officer—those are thirty to fifty-year felonies, but she doesn't have that much time left on her ticket. There's damage to property, resisting arrest, hoarding, and seven or eight more charges." He shifted his weight from one foot to the next. "Nothing will stick in the end, you understand, no judge around here will send an eighty-some-year-old woman to jail for decades. Dementia, they'll say, mental illness. But it'll hang over her as a threat, force her to get help, maybe force her to be institutionalized. She's nuts, that's obvious. DA Scales says it's tough to prove Guilty By Reason of Insanity, because it's pretty clear that while Gretchen is missing all the fries out of her Happy Meal she knows right from wrong. But the intent is to get her off the street and get her some help, put her in a safe place that'll treat her."

"Any kids? Grandkids?"

"Sylvia came up with a daughter and a grandson in Paducah. We called them, and they'll be here Saturday."

"The cats?"

He laughed again. "I took cats from a crime scene back in January, remember? I'm up to three now. Wife won't let me take anymore. The kittens were cute, though, almost caved on a white fluff ball. And there was a shitload of 'em, kittens. Four shelters are removing them —*still* removing them, going to get them vetted. Last I heard on the radio, they were up to one hundred and thirty-five cats and kittens, and two ferrets. Found quite a few dead cats, too." He backed up and stood in the doorframe. "Just thought I'd stop by and check on you. Really, you should stay home a day or two." Another step back. "But I figure I'll see you tomorrow morning anyway. If you've got more of that Dark Italian, I'll brew some and we'll talk about the bones."

"That sounds delicious," she said.

Then Oren was gone and the doctor came in, giving her a once over and noting the drip was done.

"Let's get you home, Punkin."

"What time is it?"

"Fifteen minutes since the last time you asked."

"I'll make it back in time for Nang. I invited him over for pizza."

He scowled. "They said take it easy."

"I'll let Nang do the cooking."

## 22

# TWENTY-TWO

"I sell these in my quick mart." Nang stared at the pizza he'd taken out of Piper's freezer. It looked like he was scrutinizing the ingredients.

Piper laughed. She stopped. Laughing hurt. A glance at the clock—seven. She was due for a pain pill, but she'd wait and get some pizza on her stomach. She'd had nothing to eat since the donuts and coffee at breakfast. "Where do you think I bought it? When I stopped to get gas last week."

"This pizza might give you gas."

"Not funny."

"I have never baked one of these."

"You were born here, Nang, and you've never baked a frozen pizza? I find that impossible to—"

He grinned. "Not one of *these*. I usually make my own pizza or bake a DiGiorno Supreme. I carried DiGiorno once, but they didn't sell. My customers wanted cheaper pizzas. I ended up eventually buying all of them. I had stocked so many that I had pizza for months. Always been curious what one of these tasted like."

He ripped the cellophane off and slid it onto the rack, then stepped to the refrigerator and opened it. "You don't have juice. You should have juice. It would be good for you, healthy. You have a bottle of soda and energy drinks."

*I could use an energy drink right now.*

"In the freezer," Piper answered. "I have juice in the freezer. Grape, orange. Do orange."

He continued looking in the refrigerator. "You don't have much in here. I'm going grocery shopping for you tomorrow."

"I can shop for myself, Nang. I can—"

"Your dad said you're supposed to take it easy. Shopping would be difficult with one arm."

"Nang, I'm—"

"Not going to argue with me." He closed the refrigerator and opened the freezer, plucking out a frozen can of orange juice and eyeing the rest of the stock. "Not much in here, either. These little dinners you have—"

"Are convenient. Easy to microwave. I like them. And, look, there's vegetables in them."

"Frozen."

"I bought them at your quick mart. And I don't eat here all that often because—"

"You are so busy." He shut the door and put the frozen concentrate can of orange juice in the sink and ran hot water on it, then found a carafe on the counter to mix it in. "Tomorrow I will shop for you and make a big batch of *Canh Chua*."

"What's that?"

"Hot and sour soup, my own recipe. Pineapple, mushrooms, tomatoes, basil, bean sprouts, okra. I'll make a big batch so your father has some, too. And a pot of *Banh Nuoc*—noodle soup. You will have plenty of soup, and soup is good for mending. It keeps well."

"Thanks, Nang. I really appreciate it, but—"

He turned and stared at her. "Please don't argue. I like to cook, and I like you. Let me do these things. We'll both feel better for it."

"Okay." Piper watched him turn back to the sink and fix the orange juice.

She liked him, too, maybe too much. He was smart, kind, industrious, good looking. She enjoyed his company and his cooking, looked forward to their get-togethers, thought about him in quiet times at work, and wondered if this would go farther than casual dating. But she also thought about the life she'd left behind. She truly loved the military; it fit her better than being sheriff of Spencer County. If her dad hadn't gotten so ill with the Non-Hodgkin's she'd still be with the 101st, would have never come back to take care of him and then indulge his suggestion she run for sheriff. A hot-runner, she'd be advancing in rank and responsibility in the Army.

But she had the top rank and responsibilities in the sheriff's department. And as the weeks passed, she liked the job more and more—despite being shot by a crazy octogenarian during what should have been her lunch hour. Piper realized she could have been killed today. But there'd been plenty of lunch hours in Iraq where that could have happened, too.

A part of her was not happy that she was liking all of this.

This small county and its residents and being so near to her father —even though she was planning to move a little farther away. She needed more distance.

Whatever she had with Nang, liking him maybe too much. Probably too much. If she let her emotions get thicker they'd weigh her down like an anchor, cement her to this small county.

Working with Oren Rosenberg, who should have won, who'd wanted it more than she had, who would have been better in the lead role. She couldn't say she *liked* him, but she enjoyed working with him, respected him, and relished the competition in trying to solve a case first, like the boy's bones. There'd been a competition involved with the serial killer, too, back in January, her winning—but not by much.

Being in charge of something, having the power to hire and fire, even though she felt bad about the Drew thing.

Facing two very different cases, a child's bones and the theft of an old man's life earnings. Both of them sad and interesting and dominating her dreams.

"Your father says I don't cook enough beef dishes," Nang said.

He'd been saying something else, but she'd lost it in her musings. "I like chicken dishes, the way the ingredients go together, and so I serve a lot more chicken in my quick mart. The profit margin is better, too. But I will make some *Com Bo Nuong* tomorrow. And before you ask what it is, *Com Bo Nuong* is basically grilled beef, better than what the country club in town serves. Beef, I slice it thin, scallions, carrots that I usually shred, mushrooms, bok choy—which is Chinese, not Vietnamese, but I like to use it—and crushed peanuts. That adds texture, makes it interesting. I will make a great deal of it tomorrow so I can serve it at the store, bring some here. I'll use *nuoc mam* sauce."

"Don't you use *nuoc mam* sauce on that roast chicken you make?"

"*Com Ga Quay Dzon* roast chicken. You shine, Piper. Yes, I do."

"I think that's my favorite, that *Dzon* chicken."

"Then I will make some of that, too. All day I'll be busy for you."

She blushed. "I don't need—"

"Of course you do. We'll both feel better for it," he repeated.

They ate the pizza on the couch, which is where Nang said pizza is properly eaten, and he pronounced it passable, that he'd continue to offer it in his store. Piper pronounced it delicious, and she ate more than half of it, could have eaten the whole thing she was so hungry.

"Your dad wants you to stay out of your office for a few days."

Piper shook her head and finished the last of the pizza, washed it down with a glass of orange juice. "I can't. And I can drive with one hand. I've got these cases. I've got to meet the old man in the park in the morning."

"You have so much to do. I know. Your dad should know that, too."

"He does. He probably wishes he was the one working the cases." She couldn't hold the smile in. "You know, it's awful, the things I'm investigating. Bones of a boy murdered a long time ago, an old man being swindled by a savvy computer hacker—these are awful things. It's awful that someone has stolen almost everything from him, a war veteran, a charitable guy who'd been giving bits of money to a lot of local organizations. Doesn't matter that he's ninety-four I think, that he doesn't have much time left. Doesn't matter that he's had a great life and really didn't need the money that was stolen. It's not right. It's unconscionable and evil and—"

"And yet—"

"Yeah, and yet it's a little exciting, too. In a way. Not for him. For Mark it's wholly rotten. But for me, it's something I need to fix, something I need to—"

"Keep you busy. You are a very good sheriff, Piper Blackwell."

She held out her glass for more orange juice. "I have pills on the counter, would you—"

He was quick to bring both.

"And the bones. They're opposite ends of life, you know. That little boy had nine years on the earth, Mark ten times that amount. Wrong was done to each of them, and I can't help the boy. Dead, dead, dead, dead. Nothing can help the boy. But I can help Mark, he's still breathing. I can get his money back. *Try* to get his money back. Settle his mind and get him some peace. I want justice for both of them."

"A very good sheriff. You are passionate." Nang turned to tidying up Piper's kitchen. "Your dad must be very proud of you."

"I think he wouldn't mind if I went back to Fort Campbell after my term. He misses being sheriff."

"I would miss you," Nang said, "if you went back to Fort Campbell."

Piper yawned, feeling a wash of fatigue spread through her. The pill couldn't be working that quickly. Maybe the entirety of the day was crashing down.

"I need to check on Gretchen, the crazy cat lady, the Mailbox Mauler. The Celica. I need to check on that, too, find it. That old car might be the key to helping Mark. I should be doing that now. Diego might have found something on the registration. Oren might have something on the bones. And—"

"Tomorrow," Nang suggested. "It's not that many hours away."

Less than a dozen hours until when she would be at her desk.

Piper finished the second glass of orange juice and stood. She was a little off balance and didn't move for a few moments. She padded to the window and looked out, seeing her loaner Hyundai in the driveway. Someone had brought it from Gretchen's. Her dad was in the front lawn walking Wrinkles. He started down the sidewalk. They never walked far. The elderly pug didn't have a lot of stamina, but he sure liked to hike his leg on any vertical surface. A shadowy-colored car was parked on the street across from her dad's house. It edged away and turned on its lights.

Was it the Celica?

She hadn't gotten a good enough look. *Paranoid, I am. Not every car is a decade-old Celica.*

"I really should go back to the office." Piper said it to herself, not Nang.

"Tomorrow," he repeated.

Nang carefully put her to bed. "I'll be on your couch if you need anything."

She started to protest his staying, but a dream of a thousand cats overtook her and pushed away the boy's bones and Mark the Shark, and like a huge, toothy thresher it swallowed her.

# TWENTY-THREE

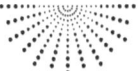

## FRIDAY, MAY 4TH

"Neal? My grandfather's youngest brother? Yeah, Neal Robert Huffman, my great uncle. Well, he *would've* been my great uncle. Sixty-five years dead now. Neal Robert would've been, oh, seventy-four if he hadn't drowned that day."

"Too young to die, nine years old." Oren felt like he should say something.

"My grandfather only lived to be forty, so I never met him either. Brain tumor."

Oren spotted two city cops come in and slide into a nearby booth.

"Forty's too young to die, too, but he got a lot more years than poor Neal Robert did. My grandfather, Julian Joseph Huffman was—" The young man tipped his head back, lips working as if he figured a math problem. "Sixteen then, yeah. Sixteen when Neal Robert died. Seven years older. My grandfather was the oldest kid in the family. I'm a little bit into the genealogy stuff. Not by choice. My wife really likes that shit. She's doing a whole family tree thing."

They were in a Denny's on Fredricka in Owensboro. It wouldn't have been Oren's choice for breakfast, but it was near the landscaper where James Harrison Huffman worked, and James—the young man he was interviewing—had picked the spot. Oren had searched county records for Huffmans, Killians, and Martins—the last names of the boys who drowned sixty-five years ago. There were a few Huffmans and Martins left in Spencer County, but those Huffmans said they were no relation. Only one Martin said he was connected to the dead boy. Oren had an appointment to meet with him early tonight. It would be a long day.

There might be female relatives who'd married, changed their last names, and so would be more difficult to find. But Oren was patient. Maybe he'd turn to the old fart's club for help. Piper had mentioned talking to the group a few days ago.

He'd also made some calls to Huffmans and Martins outside of the county, connecting with this young man—James Harrison Huffman, age twenty-five, of Owensboro. There was a Killian down in Bowling Green that looked promising, but he told Oren to call back after the weekend.

The waitress set their orders down, refilled Oren's coffee cup, and twirled away.

James Harrison said this was the only time he was available, as he and his family were leaving for Nashville tomorrow for an extended weekend. But he'd seemed eager to talk.

"My wife says our family is the Twenty Club. Grandpa Julian Joseph—a thing in my family for the men to use both names—was twenty when he got married and had my dad. My dad, Buddy Dean, was twenty when he got married—had to 'cause he got the neighbor girl pregnant with me. I got married at twenty, but not because I had to. We have a two-year-old boy, Ridley Thomas." He reached in his back pocket and pulled out his wallet, opened it, and proudly showed Oren a picture of the toddler. "My wife says she's doing this family tree thing for Ridley Thomas." He shrugged. "I think she's doing it 'cause she got tired of scrapbooking. Good, eh? Scrapbooking is an expensive hobby. She was buying shit all the time. Genealogy is a hell of a lot cheaper."

"Nice looking little boy," Oren said politely. He stirred the eggs, took a bite, then set the fork down and reached for his coffee. When he got back to the office he'd see if there was more of that Dark Italian. Hell, he might call Nang and ask where he got it, buy some for himself.

"Sixty-five years. That's a long time ago," James Harrison said.

*Depends on your perspective*, Oren thought.

"Why are you interested in a drowning from sixty-five years back?" He replaced his wallet and dug into his stack of pancakes. "I mean, you got me all curious. That boy was a relative of mine."

"It's connected to a cold case. Maybe." Oren decided to be honest. He wouldn't be revealing anything that hadn't gone out over the scanner. "We found some bones on the bluff, of a nine-year-old boy. We're trying to identify him."

"And it might be related to my great uncle and the other boys who drowned? Maybe a friend of theirs? From the same class? 'Cause they were all nine?"

"Maybe." Oren drained the coffee. "Right now I'm just gathering information. Those boys drowned likely the same year the boy on the bluff was killed."

"Interesting. Nine years old? All of them?" James Harrison shuddered and continued to shovel the pancakes. He said something that was garbled because his mouth was full. "Sorry. Wife says I eat too fast. I can't tell you much about my great uncle, Neal Robert, or my grandfather, Julian Joseph."

Oren scribbled in his notebook, trying to keep the names straight.

James Harrison stopped to take a drink of apple juice. "Like I said, never knew either one of them. But I know they were both born in Rockport. My grandmother is still kicking, Julian Joseph's widow. She lives in Evansville. Never remarried. She could probably help you. She's pretty big into the genealogy stuff, too. Or at least she used to be. Must be a woman-thing, huh?"

Oren immediately thought another trip to the Taj Mahal lunch buffet was in order. Certainly more appetizing than these eggs.

"Are you going to eat that bacon?"

Oren shook his head. "Help yourself." He was strict about not eating pork, hadn't thought to ask the waitress to leave it off when he'd ordered the "special" that wasn't very special.

"Grandma Huffman still works. Seventy-seven, I think, maybe seventy-eight. She runs an antique store down on Bellemeade, The Treasured Past. My parents are co-owners, but it's basically hers. They just helped her buy it a while back. She lives upstairs. They'll probably sell it when she croaks. Hell, maybe I'll buy it from them. Landscaping? My back aches every night."

"Are your parents around here, then? Evansville?" Oren thought there might be quite a few Huffmans in the area for him to interview after all. Maybe they were unlisted. He hadn't found a Buddy Dean Huffman in any Indiana or Kentucky directory.

James Harrison shook his head and spooned up the leftover syrup, not leaving a drop to waste. Then he grabbed Oren's bacon strips. "No. They live in Nashville. My dad works backstage at the Grand Ole Opry. Mom manages one of the small hotels down there. She gets me great deals when we want to get away for a weekend, like tomorrow. Dad gets us tickets to the Opry. Vacations on the cheap, you know. Tomorrow night we're seeing Rascal Flatts."

"Maybe your grandmother—"

"Oh, she'll be happy to talk to you. Once you get her started, she won't quit talking." He pulled a napkin from the holder and wrote an address on it. "This is her shop, on Bellemeade like I said. I can't recall the phone number, but it's in the book. She's in the book—Virginia Huffman."

"No middle name?"

James Harrison shrugged. He pulled a jump drive out of his front pocket and slid it over.

"Grams'll talk to you, but she wouldn't have known Neal Robert. Don't thinks so, anyway. She would've been—" Again he tipped his head back and counted. "Twelve, thirteen. Okay, I suppose she might have known him. She was from Rockport, same as my grandfather was. Childhood sweethearts I was told. So, maybe she did. That drive there is a copy of my wife's genealogy stuff. Maybe it'll help you."

"Thanks." Oren grabbed the bill and the jump drive. "I'll mail this back to you when—"

"Don't worry about it, those things are cheap. Four bucks at

Walmart." James Harrison slid out of the booth. "Listen, nice to meet you, Sheriff. I have to run. Can't be late for work. If you need anything else, or want to talk to my wife about those files, call us next week. We get back late Monday." He headed for the door and looked over his shoulder. "Thanks for breakfast."

Oren pushed his plate away, decided he'd save his calories for the Taj Mahal. Maybe Millie was available for lunch again. The Taj twice in the same week. Yeah, he could handle that.

It was a few minutes past eight when he pointed the Ford west toward Evansville. He called into the office, but Piper wasn't in yet.

"Coming in late," Sylvia D reported. "I'd imagine she's hurting bad, getting shot yesterday by Gretchen. Surprised she's coming in at all. She's meeting Mr. Thresher at nine in the park, and then she'll be in. Do you need me to call her—"

"Nope. Just let her know I'm going to Evansville to—"

"You're digging into the bones, aren't you? A lead?"

Oren let out a breath. "Digging," he said. "I'll be back after lunch."

"Hope you find something," Sylvia D said. "The boy needs a name."

"And so does his killer," Oren returned.

He'd be in Evansville by nine, figured he'd spend an hour at the antique store, find a reason to kill another hour in the city—he could spend the time dallying, he'd be working late today—and then scoot over to the buffet. See if Millie wanted to join him. He hit his hand on the steering wheel.

"Millie."

His only granddaughter—and soon to be fellow deputy—was graduating tomorrow and he hadn't bought her a gift. He and his wife had talked about it, but hadn't come to a consensus. They'd been going to toss her money for law school, but that wasn't happening now. Maybe dishes, pots and pans. She'd need all that for her place. Maybe she already had that stuff. Maybe he'd get her a necklace. He'd call his wife for ideas and then spend the hour shopping.

"Shit and back again," he grumbled. Good thing he had a credit card.

# TWENTY-FOUR

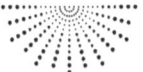

Piper sat on the designated bench in the park. Someone tap danced inside her head—a whole chorus line of tap dancers that aspirin wouldn't silence. Her morning had gotten off to an ugly start.

When she went to get in the loaner Hyundai this morning she stared at the spot where the driver side mirror should be. It could have happened at Gretchen's, or when someone brought the car back yesterday, but the BITCH in dayglow yellow spray paint spaced out across the doors had come courtesy of whoever was intimidating her. Probably had torn off the mirror, too. The random blobs of color on Nang's classic pickup had made matters worse. Fortunately, her and her father's personal cars were in the garage.

But the double garage door had been tagged, too, and Paul Blackwell was furious—and concerned when she mentioned the previous damage to her Ford and finally talked about the email threats.

Paul said he was going to report the vandalism to the Rockport police on his way back from a big box store in Owensboro, where he would buy paint, motion sensor lights, and a home video surveillance system. He squealed away before she could present an effective argument.

The spray paint was nasty, but harmless, just another notice, done late last night. The neighbors said they didn't see anyone or hear anything.

Harmless, yes, but it was an escalation. What was next? Serious damage? Maybe burning the place? A half-full gas can—that didn't belong to her father—had sat in front of the garage. It had only made her more angry and determined.

Her dad had taken the gas can with him, said he'd give it to the police, said he'd mention the threats, too. They wouldn't find fingerprints on the can. Piper knew her foe was too careful to leave prints.

---

She looked at her watch. At 8:55, she was five minutes early to the park, but actually late to work. She'd intended to be in the office by six-thirty so she could see if Diego had come up with anything on the Celica. If he'd found an owner and address, she had planned to pay the soul a visit and hopefully make an arrest. Have something good to report to Mark the Shark. But none of that happened. She'd have to attend to that after this meeting.

Her head pounded.

Piper passed the time waiting for Mark by using her phone to scroll local classified ads, see the apartment listings. It wasn't the spray paint that fueled the fingers of her good hand; it was the desire for a little distance from her father. His raised eyebrows at Nang's early-morning presence hadn't been lost on her. Piper's life. Piper's business. Nothing happened, but her dad didn't need to know that. And her dad's garage hadn't needed to be targeted by the vile soul pestering her and Mark the Shark.

*I really need to get my own place.*

Not that her apartment wasn't *her own place.* But above her father's garage, it was less than twenty feet from his house. The proximity had been great when he was ill. It felt smothering now. Maybe she could find something furnished because she didn't want to acquire...things. "Stuff" was an anchor. The more you had, the more it weighed you down—cementing you to a town, a county. Her future was too murky for...things.

Not a single listing looked appealing. Was that why Millie was going to rent a one hundred and thirty-year-old house that currently had no working plumbing or electricity?

She tipped her head back and let the slight breeze drift across her face, ruffle her too-long bangs. Damn, she still needed a haircut. Just ought to whack it off herself. She could do that one-handed, right? Maybe she'd pass Sylvia D a pair of scissors when she got back into the office and say, "Have at it, please, before I go get the damn Celica and end this."

The sky was Chicago Blues by Benjamin Moore. Piper had color samples in her desk drawer at home, had been entertaining the thought of painting her living room. Chicago Blues, or the lighter and gray-tinged Bracing Blue by Sherwin-Williams. She'd not yet decided. Then the carpet would get replaced because otherwise it would clash horribly. But if she moved, she didn't have to worry about painting—and wouldn't have to walk across old orange shag.

Not a cloud in the sky, one solid swipe of color. Definitely Chicago Blues.

The day warm, it felt like full-blown summer. Smelled like summer, too, a touch of the river, flowers, and still she could pick up the heady scent of the earth from where the park employees had filled in the hole. They'd seeded, straw thrown down. They'd tossed seeds in most of the bare spots across the entire bluff. The straw wasn't doing a good job of keeping the birds from feasting.

9:05.

Mark was late. Maybe he was parking a block or so over because of the spies. He'd been right on that, hadn't he? Someone in a metallic gray Celica had been keeping tabs on them—and probably was responsible for the spray paint. Had Mark's place been vandalized, too?

She looked at the few cars nosed in at the edge of the park, stared at her loaned Hyundai, which had been a little tough maneuvering with one hand.

*Wonder what the garage will think of that lovely spray paint?*

No Celica. She wanted to get back to the office to see about that registration search, cursed herself for not getting up earlier.

Piper ticked off the items on her to-do list.

• Meet with Mark the Shark

• Check on the Celica registration

• Get an update on the Gretchen charges

• Call Nang and thank him for shopping and breakfast...because she hadn't earlier, apologize for the paint on his truck

• Talk to Oren, learn what he had going with the bones

• Interview Zeke the Geek

• Wish that she could get a do-over on the past couple of days

Piper had been interested in seeing if Ezekiel Whitman would be a good fit for the dispatcher position—even though she was required to interview three candidates. But if he was as computer savvy as others claimed, she'd interview him about more than just the job opening and the threatening email she'd received. Ezekiel Whitman was connected to Mark the Shark through the old fart's club and accompanying computer tutoring. Did he drive a Celica?

Was it possible Zeke the Geek had siphoned Mark's accounts?

Could he be the one who sent her the threatening email? Spray painted last night?

Piper pulled out her phone and checked her texts and email. She'd had three texts from her dad, which she flipped through. He was still fuming about the vandalism and worried about her. She would call him when she got to the office.

She called Mark. He didn't have a cell phone, but she thought maybe he was still at home. If he'd heard about the Gretchen incident, and that she'd been shot, he might have figured this meeting was off. No answer. If he'd been vandalized, Piper was certain he would have called her. She'd wait just a little longer to see if he showed up.

She tipped her head back again and closed her eyes.

*Must've dozed off there.*

Had to be the pain pills that warned "may cause drowsiness." She'd stop taking them and suck it up.

9:40.

*Definitely had dozed.*

She called Mark again. Still no answer.

Called Sylvia D.

Oren was in Evansville, the bone case, and would be back after lunch. She wondered if he was meeting with Doc Natty. Maybe some test results had come back much earlier than expected.

JJ was in the office going through old case files.

Diego had not left any notes about his Celica search. And at the moment he was fielding a situation in Fulda involving Chris Hagee. Hagee's neighbor had been a victim of January's serial killer, and Chris had been jumpy ever since, calling the department frequently.

Mark Thresher hadn't called in.

"I'm going to Hatfield, out to Thresher's," Piper said.

With no traffic, and no sign of a Celica, it took her only fourteen minutes to reach Mark's long gravel driveway. She parked the Hyundai even with his house, got out, and approached the front door, passing the motion-sensor lights, the ADT post by the walk, and the BEWARE OF DOG sign at the stoop.

When she pushed the doorbell, there was no thunderous "woof" this time. Piper waited, tapped her foot, and knocked.

Concerned and curious, she went to the garage, rose up on her toes, and peered in through a side window. The motorcycles and the vintage Franklin convertible in one double-bay, his Chevy in the other. He hadn't driven anywhere.

Piper stopped at the side of the house, stood on the cement block planter, and looked in between the bars of a window and into the den. The old recliner she'd noticed from her previous trip—Mark sat slumped in it, an orange tabby curled in his lap, the old golden retriever lying across his feet. The dog picked up its head when Piper tapped on the window, but it didn't budge. She tapped louder and looked closer.

It didn't appear that the old man was breathing.

Piper called Sylvia D and hurried to the front door, gritted her teeth, and rammed her good shoulder at it. The door was oak and strong and held. She raised her leg and kicked just below the door-knob. One more kick and she forced it open. The ADT alarm went off. Ignoring it, she turned right down a short hallway, passed by a spare bedroom, and found the den.

"Do I need to send an ambulance?" Sylvia D asked.

"No." Piper stepped into the den and stared at the old man, who had on his jacket despite the warmth of the day. His right hand looked like a claw that had grabbed at his shirt and froze that way. His car keys dangled from the fingers of his left hand. "No, I don't need an ambulance. And ADT will be notifying you."

"Just did. Told 'em you had to break in." She rattled off a code so Piper could turn off the shrill sound.

"Thanks. Call the coroner, please. Ask Dr. Neufeld to come here as soon as she's able."

The cat turned its head and looked up at her.

The old dog kept its position.

Piper sat at the desk, stared at the threesome, and sobbed as the alarm continued to keen.

# TWENTY-FIVE

It took Oren fifty-two minutes to reach Evansville, another ten to find The Treasured Past. Next to a shiny new pharmacy and across from some stripe of dollar store with a bright yellow facade, the two-story building looked like an antique, and out of place in the block. Interesting, eclectic, but not ugly. Definitely didn't fit with its neighbors.

Weathered siding, old-time shutters, wagon wheels leaning under the front window, and an assortment of milk jugs, rocking chairs, and large crocks spread across the front. Everything had a little white price tag on a string that flipped in the breeze.

He looked at his watch. 9:30. The sign on the window listed the hours. Tues-Fri 10-6, Sat 10-2, Sun closed for God.

Oren peered through the window, seeing lights on and a woman dusting shelves. He rapped on the window, and after she finished with an aisle, she came to the door and opened it a crack.

"I open at ten." Her voice was musical.

"I'd like to speak with you, Mrs. Huffman."

Her eyes widened. "You caught the shoplifter! Come in! Come in, Sheriff." She opened the door and gestured Oren inside.

Virginia Huffman was stunning.

Old, sure, older than Oren by more than ten years according to her grandson. But she was stunning. *Nothing wrong with applying that word to someone elderly*, he thought, especially when the word fit so well. Stunning shouldn't be a word relegated to the young.

Her hair was a pale gray that shimmered like spun silver, short and swept around her head in lazy curls. She wore makeup, but not a lot, and likely had tinted contacts because her eyes were a vivid shade of blue that matched her sapphire drop earrings. Certainly she had wrinkles, but they were tiny, at the edges of her eyes and her lips, insignificant lines on her forehead. She wore navy pants with a slight crease down the front, a black blazer, and an off-white blouse with pearl buttons. She stood with shoulders square, no rounding to her back like a lot of old women exhibited. He picked up a hint of lilacs, probably her perfume.

"I'm not here about a shoplifter, though I hope the local department catches the thief. I'm Oren Rosenberg, chief deputy with the Spencer County Sheriff's Department.

"Rockport," she said. "I lived there back in the day. Miss it. But I like Evansville better. There's a lot more to do. And I can gamble on the riverboat."

He followed her to the counter. She stepped behind it and sat, rested her elbows on it and looked up at him.

Yep, stunning.

Oren recalled that on one Saturday library jaunt, his wife pointed to the cover of a fashion magazine—she always liked to ogle them, but never subscribed to any. Carmen Dell'Orefice's face stared back, an eighty-four-year-old glamorous runway model.

He thought Virginia Huffman could give her that proverbial run for the money.

"So what brings the handsome chief deputy sheriff of Spencer County to my antique store?"

Oren told her about the bones on the bluff, that the age matched the three boys who drowned.

She closed her eyes and let out a long breath. In the silence Oren heard a ceiling fan slowly turn. He looked up. It was huge, polished brass with blades made out of wicker. He thought it could have been a prop in a movie like *Casablanca*.

"I was thirteen years old," she said. "Rory Martin, he's the one who built that raft, though that Killian boy said it was his. Rory was nine. They all were nine. I wasn't about to bother with *boys* back then." To Oren, the emphasis she put on the word meant nine-year-old boys like Rory Martin. "But Rory Martin and his friends, they were always following me and Julie around town."

"Julie? Julian Joseph?"

She winked. "Julie was sixteen. *He* was someone to bother with."

"They only recovered one boy's body from the river." Oren wished he'd have printed out the old news article and brought it with him to show her. But apparently he didn't need it. Her memory was sharp.

"That Killian boy, Eddie. That was a sad day. When they found Eddie's body, before they'd identified him, Julie wanted it to be his brother. Closure, you know. No closure for Neal and Rory and their families. The river kept them boys. I'd imagine it has kept a lot of souls down the decades."

"I was thinking, maybe, that the bones we found buried on the bluff might be Neal's or Rory's. The age is right. Nine, according to the forensic anthropologist."

"You mean maybe another body had washed up? Neal or Rory? And someone buried it in the park? That doesn't make sense. That's just cruel. Why not let the families know their boy had washed up? *The Courier* carried a story—Wednesday, I think—about those child's bones turning up in Rockport, just like you say. Only two or three inches of type, the paper didn't give it much. But it had a Rockport dateline, and so I read it. Sixty-five years ago. That's when those boys drowned." She shook her head, her eyes and the sapphire earrings sparkling under the fluorescent lights. "Someone might have meant well to bury the drowned boy up on the bluff. All the boys played on the bluff, but where's the closure? My Julie died still wondering about his baby brother."

"I'm just gathering information," Oren said. He wanted to tell her that the boy buried on the bluff had been strangled, not drowned. "I talked to your grandson this morning."

"James Harrison," she said.

"Yes, ma'am. He pointed me here, said you might remember the boys, what they were like."

She smiled, her teeth white and even. The magazine cover of the elderly model came to mind again.

"Those boys were rascals, always shadowing us. Gave them something to do, I guess," she said. Then she laughed. "Back in my young years, boys were always following me. And Julie was always jealous. There wasn't a lot to do in Rockport, in the county. We made our own fun, fishing, swimming, running—things kids today don't do enough of, I think. Sometimes we'd just sit and read comic books and talk about what we wanted to be when we grew up. I wanted to be a movie star."

*She could've been*, Oren thought.

"But I liked Julie a little too much for my own good. Pregnant at sixteen. It would have been a scandal if our parents hadn't covered it up. Momma put me in baggy clothes, and me and Julie got married on my seventeenth birthday. I never finished high school. Julie had just turned twenty, and we moved into an apartment above a laundromat —helluva place to live, hot and noisy. I think if the neighbors did the math, they'd've known we had to marry, that the baby came four months after the wedding, not nine. God, I loved Julie. He was an auto mechanic working days. I waitressed at night. We didn't have the money for a babysitter."

She chattered on for a long while, and Oren listened, not minding being tangled in her memories. When she came up for air, he jumped in.

"What do you recall about those boys, Neal and Rory?"

"You're not asking about Eddie Killian because they found his body, right?"

Oren didn't answer.

"Neal was a pistol, I remember that. Since he was baby of the Huffman family, he got away with everything. The other kids would get paddled, but never Neal. Rory Martin was the quiet one of their little gang. And it wasn't just the three of them. There were a half-dozen. Otto Benson, Chuck Schleevogt, and Trigger Holms were in the mix. My memory is still crystal, Sheriff. Trigger, that wasn't his real name, but everybody called him Trigger. Red hair, freckles, picked his nose and ate the boogers. I couldn't tell you what his real name was. As I mentioned, I didn't much bother with *boys*."

"I understand."

Oren glanced around. The shop was well organized. Carnival glass and Rosewood pottery—ugly bowls and vases and such that his wife found "beautiful"—were against the far wall. Another aisle was devoted to vintage toys. A Mr. Magoo car caught his eye. He'd had one when he was a boy. One aisle was reserved for dolls, most looking like they had china faces. Tall glass cases in the center displayed pocket watches, jewelry, Meerschaum pipes, coins, stamps. He suspected the real valuable stuff was in the cases.

"Did the boys have trouble with anyone that you remember? You said they were rascals. Did they steal or do something that would make someone mad enough to," he paused, "hurt them? Hurt one of them?"

Virginia's face became unreadable. She sat back and dropped her hands to her lap. Oren noticed she wore large rings and had a few gold bangle bracelets.

"You think someone drowned the boys? On purpose? Did something to that little raft to make it break up? It was such a small raft, really only one boy should've been on it. And it certainly shouldn't have been taken out on the river. But Eddie was into Abe Lincoln, reciting the Gettysburg Address and all. He wanted to recreate young Abe casting off from the shore. I remember that. Folks in the neighborhood thought Eddie would grow up to be the president when he was old enough. Pity to not get that chance, don't you think? I wasn't around the bluff that awful day. It was a Saturday in October, Halloween, if I remember right. Later I heard Eddie had dressed up as Abe."

She made humming sound and closed her eyes, and Oren

suspected she was snarled in those long-past days. "They were hooligans, but all *boys* were then. I can't think of anyone they wronged enough to do them harm. I just can't. No, those boys drowning, that was an accident. We all knew it then, and I still know it now." She stood. "I wish I could have been more help, Chief Deputy Rosenberg."

He looked at the large clock hanging on the back wall behind her counter. Its yellowed face displayed Roman numerals, all of it framed in a dark wood that was pitted in places. It read 10:15. They'd been talking for roughly fifty-five minutes.

"That clock's from a railway station that used to operate here in the city," she said, catching his gaze. "I have to use an extender tool to wind it. Worth the effort."

On either side of it were smatterings of old framed sepia and black and white photographs. The largest was an oval roughly two feet long by half that wide. The boy had hair that fell in curls to his jawline. He was scowling.

"1918," she said, pointing to the oval. "That's Alan Earl Mooney, one year old there. He grew up to be a military photographer. Had a college scholarship for football, was a big-armed quarterback and everyone figured he'd be drafted by the Green Bay Packers or the Chicago Bears. But he was drafted by the Army instead. Didn't have a chance at the pros. Injured his knee on some reconnaissance mission."

"Photographs." Oren's eyes popped wide. "Would you happen to have any photographs from Rockport, ones that might have those boys in them?"

"Oh! I just might! I should've thought of that right off. I have Julie's keepsakes, most of them, anyway. They're upstairs. There are a few old photo albums I've been telling myself I should give to James Harrison. His wife is into genealogy. I tried my hand at it, but found it too time consuming. I spend my free time down at the riverboat. Wait here, Sheriff. Mind my store if anyone comes in. Stall them, you understand. I don't want to miss a sale." She excused herself and disappeared into a back room. Oren heard the creak of stairs.

It was 10:30. He recalled what James Harrison said about his grandmother. "Oh, she'll be happy to talk to you. Once you get her started, she won't quit talking."

The buffet opened at 11. He made a quick call to Millie, who said she could meet him at the restaurant in an hour.

He took a look at the Mr. Magoo car. Mustard-yellow tin, black cloth top, rubber Magoo in the driver seat. The tag read Vintage, 1961, with box, $422. Oren whistled. "Wish I would've kept mine."

In the jewelry counter an old cameo pin caught his eye. He guessed it to be an inch and a half in diameter and circled with gold filigree. The centerpiece was a carved lady justice, the woman with a blindfold and in flowing robes, sword in one hand, scales in the other. He whistled again. He tried to read the price, but the little tag was flipped over. *It would make a nice graduation gift for Millie*, he thought. Wouldn't take up any room, and she loved jewelry, and justice—Millie was all about justice. "Perfect," he said.

He looked at the other pieces, but kept coming back to that cameo. Probably expensive. Probably why the price tags in this counter were all facedown, so as not to scare the customer.

Two women came in as he continued to study the jewelry. He guessed they were in their fifties, wearing baggy jeans, one in a long-sleeve polo, the other wearing a black t-shirt with a Boston terrier's face on it. They went straight to the doll aisle.

A few minutes later, Virginia came back with two dingy-looking photo albums tucked under her arm. She set them on the counter, tended to the women searching through the dolls, and sold the Boston terrier woman a Madame Alexander doll that looked like a Disney princess.

"A good sale," she told Oren after the women left. "That was the Jo doll from the Little Women collection. One hundred dollars. Used to go for twice that. Antiques are a funny thing, values always changing based on what people are fancying in any given year."

Oren pointed to the cameo.

"Do you know much about cameos, Sheriff?"

"Nope."

"They date back to ancient Rome, third century Greece. Fascinating, really. The old ones are made of agate, and other stones that have layered colors. They carve the stone right where the colors meet, cutting away all of a particular shade except for the raised part. Like lady justice there." She reached into her pocket and pulled out a ring of keys, used one to open the case. Taking out the piece, with her free hand she took Oren's and placed it in his palm. "It feels a little warm, doesn't it?"

He nodded.

"Stones have a natural warmth. How you can tell the difference between real things and clever plastic. Anyway, they carve all of a layer away except for the thing they want illustrated, and when they carve that part, it's real intricate. Lots of cameos are of women's faces, or maybe of Diana with a skinny hound, sometimes flowers. This is the only lady justice I've seen. Iustitia, the Roman goddess of justice. She got the blindfold sometime in the sixteenth century. This particular piece, turn it over, stamped by the jeweler, is one hundred and twenty to one hundred and twenty-five years old."

Oren noticed the price when he'd moved it. $370.

"Ouch," he said softly.

Virginia laughed. "You're forgetting what I said about antiques. It's been here quite a while. Make me an offer."

*It really would be perfect for Millie*, Oren thought, and he knew his wife would more than approve. "I don't want to insult you—" he started.

"Make me an offer," she repeated.

"Two hundred and seventy."

She shook her head. "Sorry. I can't do that. But I can do two hundred."

"Really?"

"Really. They're not quite as popular now as a decade ago when I put that in the case. Besides, I've enjoyed talking to you. Two hundred."

"Sold." Oren grinned. "Do you have a box for it? A little box? I'm going to give it to my granddaughter for her college graduation."

"Certainly."

He followed her back to the counter and pulled out his wallet, handed over his credit card. Then he pointed to the photo albums. "I can look at these?"

"Certainly." Virginia put the cameo in a little box with tissue in it. "She'll love this. Antique jewelry is a more thoughtful gift than something you buy new in a shiny store."

Oren opened one of the albums. The first few pages held black and white pictures, no names, nothing to indicate who the adults and kids were.

Virginia loomed over it and pointed. "That picture there is all of the Huffies. That's what the family was called back then. Seems everyone used nicknames. My maiden name was Oakley, and the kids called us the Okie-dokies. That's Neal, Gary, Sandy, and my Julie. Wasn't right, him getting a brain tumor. Awful thing, cancer. Here's Julie and his dad working on an old Chevy. Julie and Ambrose Smith —they were the same age—and little Rory Martin in this one."

Oren focused on that picture, as Rory fit with his "possibilities."

"Here's a color picture of Rory." She turned a few more pages. "And here are all the scoundrels lined up at the Catholic Church picnic. Otto Benson, Rory Martin." She pointed at each one with a manicured nail. "Chuck Schleevogt, Neal Robert, Eddie Killian—Killy Dilly they used to call him—and Trigger 'boogie eater' Holms." She touched a photo on the opposite page, Julian with a beautiful young girl.

"That you?" Oren asked.

"I was thirteen then. I'd go back to thirteen again," she said wistfully. "I was thirty-seven when Julie died. Buddy Dean, our boy, was twenty and away at college. I moved to Henderson and got a job at the racetrack. Bet the ponies on my days off and did pretty well. Never married again. Never found anyone I liked as much as my Julie. If there really is a God and heaven, I'll be with Julie again."

She reached under the counter and retrieved a small paper bag that had The Treasured Past printed on it. Oren noticed that the logo incorporated a horseshoe and flowers. She caught his stare.

"I bought this store with winnings from the track," she said. "That's why I picked a horseshoe. Flowers for the win. Buddy and his wife paid half, said they wanted an investment. I could've footed the whole bill, but I let them share. Maybe they'll want to run it when they retire. Or maybe James Harrison will. My grandson can't carry trees and rocks around forever. He and his family could live upstairs. There are three bedrooms."

"Do you have a copier? Can I get a copy of this photograph?" Oren indicated the group shot of all the boys. He looked up at the clock again; he'd have to hurry to make lunch with Millie.

She shook her head. "I do, but just take the book. Both of the books. Look through them. You'll understand the *boys* better. But I want them back, you understand."

"Yes, ma'am." He took the albums and she placed the little sack with the cameo in it on top. "I'll be careful with them. And I'll try to get to know the boys better."

"They were rascals," she said. "All *boys* are."

# TWENTY-SIX

The coroner said she'd be a half hour.

Piper said she'd wait for her. Couldn't leave the house, she knew, disrespectful to Mark, and the door was open because she'd broken it. Couldn't have people wander in and steal something. Would have to get the door nailed shut or repaired, maybe replaced. *Something*, she thought, something needed to be done. What was the protocol for this?

She'd had enough of the alarm, so she retraced her steps to the front door and put in the code Sylvia D had supplied. Blessedly, it stopped.

Piper took a look around, anything to pass the time until Dr. Annie Neufeld arrived—anything other than sitting and staring at a dead man who'd expected her to "fix this." She knew not to touch anything, not until she got a search warrant.

The entryway was boxy and the walls were painted slate gray over a stomp-knockdown texture. It was striking, and Piper thought if she really was going to repaint her apartment—put off moving— she might try something similar. To her left was a dining room dominated by an oval walnut table that gleamed in the light coming in through the front window. It was an antique, made to look like its carved thick center post was a tree trunk, four roots spreading away to give it balance. Five straight-backed padded chairs sat around it. The china cabinet was also walnut and no doubt equally old, with beveled glass doors behind which gold-accented dishes and cups with pale flowers were displayed. She suspected no one had eaten off those plates in more than a few years. The walls had more knockdown, but a different pattern, and were a caramel-brown. A massive grandfather clock was near the china cabinet, and the wall across from the window was filled with pictures of various sizes.

Most of them were old black and whites, of ships and Navy men. Piper looked close and saw Mark Thresher in a few, as a young man, and later in his thirties and forties in color and with medals on his uniform. He'd mentioned serving thirty years, getting out at age forty-seven and buying a farm. There were photographs of Mark on a tractor, a white dog in his lap; she guessed he was in his mid- to late fifties. Another photograph showed him and a stocky woman with a heart-shaped face in wedding clothes. The woman was in a few other pictures, too. No children in any of the pictures.

Mark had said he'd no family left, but Piper would look through his computer after she got that warrant. He was in the genealogy club, so his spreadsheet might reveal some living relatives somewhere down the line.

She padded through another doorway into a living room painted off-white and speckled like sand. *Pretty*, she thought. No antiques here, not much furniture. There was a brown L-shaped leather couch with a black throw on half of it—lots of golden dog hair showing on the throw, and a big matching ottoman that was roughly two and a half feet square. Two remotes were on the center of it. A flat screen television hung on the wall, had to be sixty-five or seventy inches wide. On a long cabinet beneath it were DVD and VHS players and stereo speakers. She suspected the movies were inside the cabinet.

The tour was telling her quite a bit about Mark. That when he sold his farm, despite his advanced age he opted for a *nice* house with *nice* things, that he didn't like clutter, and that either he cleaned often or he had a maid come in. She didn't see dust anywhere, just traces of golden retriever hair.

There was a fireplace behind the couch, free-standing and double-sided so it could heat the living room and the kitchen. Gas burning. He probably didn't want the mess of wood and ashes. Beyond it was the kitchen, painted the same caramel as the dining room, the walls smooth and interrupted by a big dog door that led to the backyard.

Piper continued her tour and looked at a clock above the sink. She had another fifteen minutes before the coroner was expected.

The appliances were stainless steel and included a double-refrigerator and a six-burner gas stove she thought Nang would envy. The center island had only one stool against it, and next to that was a rug with dishes for the dog and cat and one of those automatic water bowls with a two-liter bottle on top. A small acrylic table with two chairs was in an alcove ringed by narrow windows. Fresh flowers—daffodils, iris, tulips—were in a vase in the middle of the table. She saw a sprawling flowerbed out the windows filled with tulips and daffodils. Mark must have recently picked some for the vase.

A doorway off the kitchen led to a laundry room with a matching Samsung washer and dryer in bright red enamel.

Everything spotless.

Retracing her steps to the living room, Piper saw a stairway leading down, a chairlift at the top so Mark could ride and not deal with the steps.

"C'mon, Annie," Piper whispered, trying to will the coroner to appear. She headed back to the hallway and looked in the spare bedroom. It had a daybed with dog toys scattered on it. And there was a carpet-covered cat gymnasium—for lack of any other word to describe it. There were scratching posts and perches at four levels, ropes hanging down with bells and rings on them, a box-like thing at the top with a hole in it. Cat toys were stowed in a wooden bin against the base, Marmalade painted on the side. Dog toys overflowed a larger bin that read Camaro. He'd spared no expense on his clearly beloved pets and had given them their own room.

What would happen to them now, she wondered. The dog looked

old, and old dogs didn't always find their way out of animal shelters. Maybe she'd get her dad to take Camaro, give Wrinkles a little company. The cat? Oren had taken in cats from a crime scene a couple of months ago, but he'd said he was at his limit with three.

"I'll take you, Marmalade," Piper said. "For as long as I stay in Spencer County." A cat could do well in her above-the-garage apartment.

She passed by the den, noting the dog and cat hadn't moved. At the end of the hall was a bathroom done in a gray-blue like one of the shades she was considering for her apartment. No tub, but a narrow shower. Only a hand towel at the sink. He probably didn't use this bathroom.

Next to it was a door that opened into Mark's bedroom. It appeared huge because there was only a single bed and a small straight-backed chair that looked like it went with the dining room table. The walls were a knockdown gray like the entryway, a few large photographs on them—all of the same kind of shark, a species with a tail about as long as its body.

"Thresher for a Thresher," Piper said.

A shelf near another door held a model of a ship, USS Bremerton in small letters on the side, a photograph of an old woman in a wheelchair with stuffed monkeys on her lap, and next to it a large stuffed orangutan. She remembered Mark talking to his tutor at the old fart's club.

"They called her the monkey woman," Mark had told the girl. His long index finger had tapped a name on the screen. "Because she had this box of stuffed animals, most of them monkeys. She had a big stuffed orangutan, her favorite, called it Clementine."

"Hello, Clementine," Piper said to the toy.

The woman in the wheelchair was an aged version of the woman in the pictures in the dining room. Mark's wife, the monkey woman. Piper cried again and went through a doorway to find a big closet lined in cedar. It was only a third of the way filled with clothes, though there were quite a few boxes. Across from it was an impressive bathroom with a walk-in whirlpool tub, like in those commercials for seniors who want to "live independently." Near it was a spa-like shower, and double sinks.

*At least he got to live in an amazing house for a few years*, she thought. She brushed the tears off her cheeks. "And he didn't have to go in a damn nursing home." She padded back to the den, sat at the desk, and looked at the old man.

"I am going to fix this," she said. "I am going to find who robbed you. I promise. And I'll throw them in jail for a long while."

The dog looked up and wagged its tail.

# TWENTY-SEVEN

"**S**heriff Blackwell!"

"Finally," Piper said. "In here, Dr. Neufeld."

"Shit," the coroner said when she saw the body. "I knew him."

"I think a lot of people did."

"Did you call the shelter?"

Piper shook her head and reached for her cell phone, punched her dad's number. He picked up on the first ring. "Back from Owensboro?" She listened as he rattled off what he'd bought and about his quick visit with Chief Hugh of the Rockport police.

"Dad, can you come out to Mr. Thresher's? In Hatfield? I'll help you paint the garage later. I need you to take his dog and cat. They're going to be staying with us. At least for a while. Mark Thresher died, Dad."

Maybe Mark the Shark had a will that specified who should take the pets. She wasn't going to let them go to the animal shelter. To Dr. Neufeld, "He'll probably speed to get here. He's bored in retirement. And he's pissed off because we had a little vandalism."

The coroner stood in front of the dead man. "I suspect your father won't be retired long. Santa Claus' police chief announced his retirement, and they posted an advertisement yesterday afternoon. It was on the radio. They might promote from within, but—"

"Shit," Piper said. If her dad applied, they'd hand him the job. No one in the county—except Oren and maybe the Rockport police chief —had more law enforcement experience than Paul Blackwell. "Shit and two is four and four is eight."

"Yep, he won't be retired long," Dr. Neufeld repeated.

Piper figured she should be happy that he'd have something to do. But if he went after the Santa Claus post and got it, he wouldn't be interested in the Spencer County Sheriff's office when her term ended. He'd stay in Santa Claus until he retired, and he'd be near his beloved Christmas store. Paul Blackwell had been a great sheriff; it fit him. Maybe the police chief job would fit him just as well. Fifty-five? Healthy again? He needed to do something, she realized.

She picked up the cat with her good arm and carried it to the spare bedroom. The dog followed unbidden. She shut them inside and returned to the den. Piper called JJ and told her to go to court, find a judge, and get a search warrant for Thresher's home so they could look for a will and a list of relatives.

"Get one for the safety deposit box, too," the coroner cut in. "Get 'em both at the same time."

"Good idea." She amended her request. "And do it quick, JJ. I don't want to sit here all day. Call me when you have it." To the coroner, "Sorry to bring you out for this, ninety-four years old, natural causes. But I didn't have an option. It's required."

Thresher's police scanner crackled behind her, something about a three-car accident near Lake Rudolf Campground.

"Car keys in his hand like that, he'd been getting ready to go meet me in the park this morning."

"Hand clenched and fingers snagged in the neckline of his shirt, probably a heart attack. See, his index fingers caught here behind the fabric. That's why his hand held, it's not rigor. Sudden cardiac death, but I won't know until I autopsy him. A good run, he had," Dr. Neufeld said. "He had a damn good run."

"I wish he could have run a little while longer," Piper said.

"Someone had been draining his bank accounts, and I'd promised to fix it, to catch the thief. If he'd only run just a little while longer—" Long enough to see her arrest his villain. "Autopsy? Aren't you going to take him straight to a funeral home? I had to call you, but do you really have to cut him up?"

"Wish I didn't have to, Sheriff." She took out her phone and took some pictures, touched his forehead, bent over, and looked into his eyes. "Like I said, no signs of rigor yet, still feels warm. He's been dead less than three hours. He's an unattended death, not in a hospital or nursing home, so an autopsy is required. Hate to cut him open, but that's the way of Indiana law."

"I understand." Piper did understand, having studied way the hell too much of the state's laws for the Plainfield Sheriff's Exam. Still, she thought that because of his age it might not apply. "I'm going outside to wait for my dad."

"I'll go with you and get the gurney. You can help me take him out of here. I'll do the lifting." Dr. Neufeld paused. "Heard you got shot. Oren said it was the Mailbox Mauler."

"Yeah."

"Good thing she didn't kill you. I'd be cutting you open, too."

When they were finished with the old man, Piper and Dr. Neufeld returned to the den, the latter with a clipboard. She talked to herself as she filled out an initial report.

"Scene of death: Mark Thresher's residence in Hatfield, Spencer County." Her voice was flat. Piper looked over the coroner's shoulder and read:

—Deceased: Mark Thresher, 94

—Found: sitting in an easy chair in his study, car keys in hand, wearing jacket, likely ready to leave the house

—COD: to be determined, presents as sudden cardiac incident

—No obvious signs of a crime, front door was locked, Sheriff had to break in

—No sign of a struggle, no sign of foul play

—Alerted by: Spencer County Sheriff Piper Blackwell

—Taken to: Morgue, Evansville, Vanderburgh County, IN

—NOK: to be determined

NOK? Piper wondered. Ah, Next of kin.

"I should probably call Oren," Piper mused, more to herself than to the coroner. "He'd know the protocol here and—"

"I wouldn't," Dr. Neufeld said. "Oren's a good man, and I love him dearly, my best friend. And he'd be happy as a clam at high water if you called and asked him what to do. You don't need him. And you don't need to let him know you want advice. I can give you that advice. Listen, my wife—"

"Bebe," Piper had met her once at a county board meeting.

"Bebe's an attorney, and she's come on a couple of calls with me. Here's the deal. You'll want to send a deputy around to the neighbors, see if they know any next of kin. If they do, great, call those relatives and get one to come mind this house. If you don't find one, once you get that search warrant, you can hunt for bills and bank statements. The bank might know next of kin. Because until you get a relative shepherding the house you'll want to send a deputy past here several times a day. A house? Once people know it's vacant, well, there are a handful of ne'er-do-wells in the county who'd come poking around, ADT or no."

"A will might name any relatives. He told me he didn't have any relatives left, but he might have meant he had none around here. The warrant will let me look for a will." Piper figured the genealogy file would be better on tracking down any relatives.

"Yep, either here or in his safety deposit box. You should be able to get the name of an attorney who prepared it. Then you call that attorney. If you don't find a will, you might find an attorney's business card in his desk or something."

"I know he had an attorney. He talked about going to meet with one."

"Good, so you'll find a name on a business card, in his address book, circled in the Yellow Pages. Something."

"Something," Piper said. She was still numb.

Dr. Neufeld continued, "If there's a will, the attorney needs to know that his client has passed away. Hell, word spreads in this county. The attorney will likely hear about it anyway. Any creditors will have to be dealt with, confirm any debts from the estate, resolve any balance. I'll post a public notice of death. That usually brings the creditors in. But you won't need to worry about any of that. Me? I'll worry about Mr. Thresher. I'll conduct an autopsy, keep him in storage until someone claims him or his attorney tells us what to do. A will might specify Mr. Thresher's burial or cremation plan."

"He was a nice man," Piper said. "And I don't think he was as crazy as people thought."

"Weekend on us like this," Dr. Neufeld said, "and this not a suspicious death, I know I won't get a slot for the autopsy until Monday sometime."

Piper rocked back and forth on the balls of her feet. "Oren and I have a couple of interviews Monday for the detective position."

"Neither one of you need to attend this autopsy," the coroner said.

"I don't want to see Mark the Shark sliced open," Piper admitted.

"You'll get my report."

Dr. Neufeld tossed Piper the keys that had dangled from Mark's fingers. She caught them with her good hand.

"In case you need to get in and out of here once that door's fixed."

"Thanks."

"You good here until your dad comes for the animals?"

"Yeah, and until I get that search warrant. I'm good." Piper was doubting she'd wait for that warrant.

After the coroner pulled away, Piper went back to the den and starting going through Mark's desk, the crackle of the scanner keeping her company. Yes, she *should* have a search warrant in hand, but it would be coming and she needed to do something. She couldn't just sit.

She should wait, but...

The attorney's card was the first one in the rolodex. Harlan Cook. She cringed. He had a bad reputation in the department, barely adequate in the courtroom, an ambulance chaser who represented a lot of drunks. Harlan *Crook*, some called him.

Piper called and got his secretary.

Yes, Harlan was Mark Thresher's attorney.

Yes, there was a will, recently updated and filed.

But Harlan was out of town today and would not be back until Monday. The secretary assured Piper that Harlan would produce the will and "set things in motion."

"Harlan Crook," Piper grumbled.

Thresher's address book was filled with the names of businesses, organizations, and their phone numbers, no names of people. It also listed website addresses and his passwords to Amazon, Barnes & Noble, BookBub, Facebook, Edward Jones, eBay, his online bank account—that set her stomach to churning—Outlook, LOTRO, whatever that was, Scott's Fantasy Football Pick'em League, and some she couldn't make out because the ink had run. Most of the passwords were similar—Clementine47, Marmalade47, Camaro47, 47Clementine, 47Camaro, 47Marmalade, and for the sites that apparently required a symbol, Clementine#47, Camaro#47. Forty-seven. He'd been that old when he left the Navy. Anyone who knew about him— the names of his pets, the name of the stuffed monkey his wife had treasured—with a dose of patience and persistence could have been able to figure out the passwords.

Tucked inside the back cover was a list of members of the genealogy club, lines through three names—maybe old farts who had died or quit and went on to another hobby. A second sheet was the latest bill from his veterinarian. Camaro had his shots and nails trimmed four days ago. According to the paper, the golden retriever was ten. Same age as her dad's pug Wrinkles, she noted.

He had a laptop in the side drawer, probably the one he had at the library. Piper decided she'd take it back to her apartment. The search warrant would cover computers. A deep drawer was full of hanging files—bills, tax returns, more veterinarian records, some military records, his wife's death certificate, information on this house, photocopies from the sale of his farm parcels.

"I can fix this door, Punkin. Hey, you here?"

Piper met him in the entryway.

"Beautiful house, Mr. Conspiracy had."

He was dressed in a suit and was wearing a navy pinstripe tie she'd given him several Christmases ago. She raised her eyebrows.

"I have an interview at two."

"For the Santa Claus job."

"Chief announced his retirement yesterday, and I called in this morning, just curious. They want to talk to me right away." He grinned. "I'll ditch this jacket and fix this door. Easy fix. You don't want people breaking in. Sad about Mr. Thresher."

"Yes, sad."

"He had a good run."

That's what Dr. Neufeld had said. Again, she wished he would have run a tad longer.

"Thanks, Dad. Okay you take the dog, at least for a while?"

His shoulders dropped a little in resignation. "Sure. There's a cat, too, right? Maybe Oren—"

"I'm taking the cat. At least for a little while."

"Let me get to work here. When I'm done I'll take the critters home and get over to my interview. I don't want to be late."

"Santa Claus would be fortunate to have you."

"It would, wouldn't it? A short drive from Rockport, and there's that Christmas store I love. A dozen different varieties of fudge in the candy counter." Paul Blackwell retreated to his car for his tools. "Too bad about Mark."

"Mark the Shark," Piper quietly corrected.

# TWENTY-EIGHT

Diego reported that a fourteen-year-old Toyota Celica was registered to Melanie Taylor.

It was the only Celica registered to someone in Spencer County. VIN—Vehicle Identification Numbers—showed up in the system until said vehicle was processed as destroyed or sold for salvage parts. Every owner of a vehicle could be tracked from date of manufacture.

Melanie Taylor was listed as the only owner, bought it shiny new.

But she'd let the tags on the car expire in April.

Piper drove to Melanie's house in Fulda and discovered the place had a For Sale sign in the front yard. Neighbors said Melanie had died in early February. *Explained the expired tags*, Piper thought, but not where the car was.

The neighbors had no clue about the car, said they'd seen a middle-aged couple bringing out boxes shortly after the funeral, figured it was relatives who were picking out the choice pieces.

Piper headed back to the office, determined to track down Melanie's relatives and learn who the car had been gifted to. There's been no transfer of registration, which should have happened if the car had been properly willed to someone.

She gritted her teeth as pain lanced down her arm. Piper had a prescription to help, but the bottle said, "May cause drowsiness. This drug may impair the ability to drive or operate machinery. Use care until you become familiar with its effects." She'd wait until she got home.

Diego had come with the search warrant for Thresher's and would be going through the house to find anything else relevant. Then he'd make sure it was secure and the ADT Alarm working again. They'd found an extra set of keys, and Piper was keeping one of them in case she needed to get inside again. She'd arranged for deputies to patrol by the house several times during their shifts.

---

It was two and she was starving, so on her way out of Fulda she stopped at Nang's quick mart and ordered a late lunch. Linner, he called it, lunch-dinner. Like brunch, but later. She ordered the fried rice "house special" with chicken, shrimp, eggs, and carrots.

"So friggin' good," she pronounced it. "So sorry about the paint on your truck."

"Not your fault." Nang sat across from her, sipping tea.

Piper had her customary big mug of coffee.

"You are hurting," he observed.

"Oh hell yes," she admitted, knowing she winced every time she moved. "But I'm gonna take my medicine when I get home, put my feet up, and pet my newly-acquired or perhaps-temporary cat named Marmalade." She told him about Mark the Shark and fought to keep from crying.

"I'm interviewing a young man in a little while for my dispatcher opening. But I'm thinking it might be an interrogation."

"Someone who applied for a job is a suspect? In your bones on the bluff?"

"No, suspected of stealing from Mr. Thresher. Maybe responsible for the spray paint, too. It's a long story, and I can't talk about it. Open investigation."

"Sure." He sipped at his tea and smiled at her.

God, he was good-looking. Why did he have to be good-looking and smart, industrious? Why did she have to be smitten with him? Why the hell had she stopped at his quick mart in January looking for clues to the county's serial killer? She'd been stopping at the quick mart ever since.

"I'm taking tomorrow off, I think." She finished the fried rice. Piper had eaten quickly; she'd been famished and in a hurry to get back to the office. "Unless in the next two hours I figure out what happened to an old Celica."

"You need a day off. It will help you heal."

"I know. I'll be better for taking it easy for a day. I have an interview Monday."

"You are very busy."

She smiled back. "I like being busy."

"You shine."

"You always say that, Nang."

"Because you always shine." He got up and waited on a customer who purchased gas and three lottery tickets. He worked behind the counter a few minutes. When he came back, she was just finishing the coffee. He was carrying a small take-out bag.

Piper raided an eyebrow.

"Four Saigon egg rolls," he said. "And shrimp sausage wrapped in bean curd. I know that despite all the groceries, you won't cook tonight."

"I won't need to the way I pigged out just now. But I'll take them anyway. How much do I owe?"

He shook his head.

"I'm taking tomorrow off," she repeated. Though she intended to do some work at home. She had two boxes of the old cases sitting under her kitchen table, and she had Mark's laptop. "I won't be going into the office," she corrected herself. "Because fate will not smile on me and deliver that Celica today. I won't be so lucky. Both the people I'm wanting to help are dead—some nine-year-old boy and Mark Thresher. I will stay out of the office tomorrow, Sunday if I need it.

Two days away might do me good. Give me a fresh brain. All the groceries you bought—"

"I will cook some of them, teach you a recipe or two," Nang interrupted. "Sunday afternoon I am busy with a wedding reception I am catering. But Saturday? I will take Saturday off. I had already planned on it, scheduled three employees to cover the day. There'll be too much noise around here to suit me."

He referred to construction of the garage next to the quick mart. The building had been going up fast, and Piper had noted a well where a hydraulic lift would be installed so a car could be raised for work on the undercarriage. She suspected the lift—and the rest of the mechanic equipment—would be expensive. But Nang was shrewd with money. Twenty-seven, and he'd made a thriving business with his gas station/grocery store/Vietnamese restaurant—and occasional catering concern.

"Maybe we can watch a DVD. My dad's got some," she said.

"So do I." Nang pointed to the Red Box against the wall. "Something that blows up? A new release that blows up real good?"

"Definitely."

He stared at her. "You're going to work this weekend anyway, aren't you?"

"I'm not going into the office. I've some things at home, files and stuff. A good way to spend Sunday."

"You remind me of my mom's old dog, a pit-mix. Once it had a hold of a bone or one of those supposedly-indestructible chew toys, it would not let go. And the toys, well they never lasted long."

"I look better than a pit bull."

"You shine, Sheriff Blackwell."

B ack in the office, she searched through old death notices, discovered that Melanie Taylor died of congestive heart failure and that her designated memorial was the American Heart Association. She found a listing for Melanie's daughter, Madeline Schwartz, and after some Internet searching came up with a phone number. Madeline and her husband lived in Bloomington.

"Didn't see mom's car anywhere when we came back and went through her things. We figured she'd sold it. Don't think I have any paper on that—got a box of her papers. But I'll look through it this weekend and call you if I come up with something," she'd told Piper.

Piper growled softly. Who the hell was driving Melanie's metallic gray Celica? Someone in that car had shadowed her and Mark Thresher.

"Shit," she said as Oren came in her office. "Shit and two is four—"

"And four is eight," he said, finishing the old cribbage phrase. "What's up?"

"Melanie Taylor—"

"Retired archaeologist from Fulda," Oren said. "Smoked two packs a day. What about her? She died a couple months back. Probably because she smoked two packs a day. Born here, moved to Evansville and worked the Indian mounds. Made headlines with some of her finds in the early seventies. Wrote a book that was a bestseller, made a bundle. Retired back here about ten years ago. What about her?"

That was the thing with small counties, Piper was discovering. Everyone seemed to know everyone else, and Oren was a wealth of information.

"You're not applying for the Santa Claus chief's job are you?"

He shook his head.

"Thank God." Had she just admitted to Oren that she didn't want him to leave? She groaned at that.

"So what about Taylor?"

"I dunno. I dunno." Piper tapped her good hand on her desk. "She had a car."

Oren sat in the chair across from her desk and looked up at the clock. She'd told him they had an interview coming in at four. It was almost four now.

"She had a car that had been seen around Mark Thresher's place. But she couldn't have been driving it because she was dead."

"Sorry to hear about Mr. Conspiracy," Oren said. "Real sorry."

"Maybe it's connected."

"What's connected?"

"Melanie Taylor and Mark Thresher. The car." Piper remembered Melanie's name crossed off the old fart's club list. "But just how is it connected?"

"Your interview is here," Teegan announced. "He's a kid. Still in high school." She ushered Ezekiel Whitman in and pointed him to the empty chair next to Oren.

Zeke the Geek had dressed up for the occasion. Khaki pants, shirt and tie, sport coat. He carried a briefcase and set it on the floor next to him. He looked nervous.

Piper explained the requirements for deputy, that he didn't meet them, but that he could qualify for the dispatcher job. She wanted to get the interview out of the way first, get him relaxed, and then hit him with all manner of questions that had been simmering on the drive from Nang's.

"Sometimes dispatchers grow into deputy openings," Oren pointed out. "That's how JJ started here, and she's our investigator." Piper noticed he didn't add that JJ was also on her way out of the department.

Zeke looked disappointed. "Okay. Okay. I figured I was too young, but I was hoping. Dispatcher, yeah, I'm interested. Okay. Yes. Definitely. I want to work in law enforcement. And I really don't want to go to college. But I have to admit, I don't really know what a dispatcher does. Answer the phone?"

Oren chuckled. "A lot more to it than that."

Piper cradled her aching arm. "A dispatcher connects people in the county to the emergency services they need—deputies, ambulance, fire. They prioritize calls and decide in many cases who should respond. It's a massive responsibility, even though the county is small in population. You'd have to keep records, files, oversee the filing systems, handle case logs, accident logs, warrants, restraining and protective orders. And that includes maintaining and updating 911 computer information. You'd have to keep medical run and fire run sheets, VIN checks, towing logs, be familiar with GPS, maps, and the county."

"Wow. A lot more than answering the phone," Zeke said.

"And there's even more to it," Oren added. "Our dispatchers have to maintain the department's equipment, make sure everything's working. They attend training courses and they have to work with other departments, like Rockport and Santa Claus police."

Piper wondered how her father's interview had gone.

"I'd really be into all of that," Zeke said. "What do I have to do to apply?"

"You have to answer our questions," Piper began.

She called the interview over at five, and Oren excused himself.

"Following a lead on the bones," he said. "I'll tell you Monday what I come up with. Got Millie's graduation tomorrow."

"I have an appointment with my couch tomorrow," Piper said. "Enjoy the graduation. Basil Meredith comes in at nine. Meet me here at seven?"

"Sure."

"We'll compare notes. I have another package of Dark Italian." She detected a hint of a smile on Oren's face. "Nang carries it at his quick mart."

Oren waved and disappeared.

"Don't leave yet," she told Zeke. "I want to talk about something else. I need to ask you a few questions about computer hacking and email spoofing."

She noticed he started to look nervous again. Very.

# TWENTY-NINE

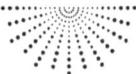

Piper had received one more message while she'd been eating linner at Nang's.

*Like the new paint job on your new car?*
*Heard you got shot bitch*
*Too bad U R still breathing*
*Go back 2 the Army B4 someone aims better*
*Leave the cheddar alone*

Because of the cheddar remark, Piper was sure it was the same vile soul who'd sent the others. Plus, it looked like Piper had sent the note to herself.

"There are apps out there, spoofing apps," Zeke said. He rubbed his palms on his thighs. "Some don't cost you anything. You can put them on your phone and call folks. The apps cover your real number. Telemarketers use them all the time. It's not illegal. Really, it's not illegal. Some apps are randomized, always assigning a different phone number when you call. Some apps let you plug in whatever phone number you want. You can make it look like somebody's mother is calling them."

Piper didn't have a phone problem.

"I'm talking email."

"Sure. Sure. Okay. It could be as simple as making up a similar email address. For instance, if yours is Blackwell@gmail, maybe the sender uses Blackwell@qmail. The q and g look a lot alike with certain fonts. It can look like the same email address."

"That's not it."

"Okay. Well, there are apps that let you send email, and your own account doesn't show. You can make up a fake email address if you want to."

"Or use someone else's email address."

"Yeah. Or make it look that way. The right term is email anonymizer. Most all of those are free. Most email addresses are free. Gmail, which has a good security level, Outlook, Yahoo, GMX. You have something like Lycos, and you can create aliases within your account. A great one is HMA. That's got a disposable email option. You can set an expiration date for the account, and you don't have to provide any personal information to sign up. I know one place where you can get an email address for two weeks, then it's destroyed. There are web-based services where you never have to create an account. Things like AnonEmail throws distance between you and your messages. The site relays it several times before it hits its intended target. There's a thing called 10 Minute Mail, at least I think it's still working. It sets up a disposable email account, and you've got ten minutes to send your messages before the account is erased. Silent Sender might do the same thing. Or you can just hack their account. That'd be just as easy. But if you're not a hacker, maybe you're a guesser, good at figuring out passwords. And there are browsers, too, TOR, that prevent snoopers from finding out where you are—*who* you are. I often use a VPN, especially when I'm someplace using a public wifi. I don't want people logging into my tablet. Most all of these tools are easy to find."

"Wow." Piper figured she should be up on this stuff. But she'd never been much for devices. A cell phone with an assortment bells and whistles, that's all she carried. She'd never been much into social media because she considered herself a private soul, didn't have a personal Facebook page.

"There's a reason they call me Zeke the Geek. I know how to use all this stuff, but I don't necessarily use it. I just like to know what's out there and what you can do with it. Curious, you understand."

"So you know how to spoof and hack." Piper didn't pose it as a question.

"Am I in trouble? Did the school call you?"

*The high school?*

"They had a hacker," Piper took a leap. "And they're pretty pissed about it."

"How'd they know it was me?" Zeke started tapping his feet. "How could they possibly know it was me? I went anonymous. No way in hell could they know."

"They know," Piper bluffed.

"Oh God. I didn't cover my tracks. I thought I'd covered everything. I screwed up. How the hell? President of the computer club and I screwed up. You didn't want to talk to me about the job, really, did you? You wanted me to come in so you could arrest me. Oh God." His words had come out machinegun fast.

"That depends," Piper said, leaping further. "It depends on whether you come clean to me about the high school. Come clean about everything. Then I'll make a decision."

"Oh God." Zeke sat back. "Oh God."

Piper wondered if the young man was going to cry.

"Only twice," he said. "I only hacked the school website twice. The other times. It was some other kids in the computer club. I swear to God only twice."

"And—"

"I rearranged the teachers' photographs back in November. At Christmas, I went in and changed the dates of graduation for every class for the next ten years. Oh God. I'm sorry. I wasn't hurting anyone. It was just for fun. Just to show that I could do it."

Piper believed him, but she decided to push it. "Those weren't the only hacks you're guilty of, Mr. Whitman. We know about the other sites you broke into."

"The Dark Web? Man, I only went there once, twice. Quick 'cause I was afraid of it. Just wanted to know if I could find it, you know. Grab a few tools."

"No, I'm talking about you hacking bank software."

"Jesus Christ! I'd never do that. You can give me a lie detector, Sheriff Blackwell. I didn't do anything else. And the high school? I did it just to see if I could hack into the school's system. I know. I know. I know. Stupid. President of the computer club, I thought I'd show off. Oh God. I'm sorry. I'm not going to graduate now, am I?"

Piper studied him. "I'll be back. Don't leave that chair."

She got up and went to the break room, noticed that the helium balloon from Drew's birthday lunch was still floating, but it had dropped down a few inches and was starting to deflate. She grabbed the ribbon and pulled it down, popped it against the doorframe, and put it in the trash. She poured a cup of coffee, added sugar and cream because it was Department Standard, not the good kind Nang had given her in that May Day basket. Her arm throbbed—one or two weeks in this sling. *Argh*, she thought. *Just argh.*

She stopped at Teegan's desk.

"Nothing much going on, Sheriff. Everything's pretty quiet. A guy named Basil confirmed a nine a.m. Monday interview. You have an eleven a.m. Skype interview with a Sheriff Polanger. Sounds like he has a Yooper accent—*ya hey dere*—like on that show *Fargo*. And a one o'clock here in the office with a Kevan Melkan. He sounded pretty nice, was real polite. You're gonna fill the detective opening fast, aren't you? I'll miss JJ." She set down a pen. She'd been scribbling jewelry designs in a sketchbook. "I'm sorry about Mr. Thresher. I'm going to miss him, too, really miss some of the weird calls from him. Aliens in the cornfield and such."

"Maybe the county will produce another Mr. Conspiracy," Piper said.

She returned to her office, sat at the desk, and stared at Ezekiel Whitman. Perspiration glistened on his forehead.

"Bank hacking. We'll get back to that. Let's talk email. I've been getting threatening notes sent to my department email address," she started. "And it looks like I emailed them to myself from my longtime personal account. But I wouldn't send myself nasty notes. So, maybe someone hacked into my email account, maybe someone just pretended to and used one of those anonymous things."

"I didn't hack you," Zeke said. "I'd never. I'd never spoof you. I wouldn't do it to anyone. Spoofing? It might not be illegal, but it probably should be. I didn't—"

She took a long swallow of the coffee. It wasn't even average. She set it down, and pushed her cell phone across the desk. "Read them."

His fingers twitched, but he opened the directory and started scrolling.

"What's cheddar?"

Zeke shrugged. "Cheese? Sharp cheese? I don't eat cheese, extra calories."

Piper didn't really have anything in her email messages that she didn't want read, nothing too personal.

"Oh, these aren't good. These are threats. Cheddar. The cheddar reference here is money, Sheriff Blackwell. It's a slang term, kinda old, but you still hear it. Wow, it does look like you sent them to yourself."

"So how can I tell who *really* sent them? How can I tell if I was hacked or spoofed, beat all this anonymous sender stuff you told me about? The Dark Web tools?"

"You can't." Zeke shook his head. "You probably can't tell. Not if the sender's any good. Not if he used one of those accounts I mentioned, especially if he used HMA."

"What?"

"Hide My Ass. Really, if he's any good, you just can't find him. It's impossible. Maybe if you've got the Department of Homeland Security next door. Maybe they know how to do it." A pause. "But I doubt it. HMA, some Dark Web stuff. Invisible."

*Shit.*

"Okay. Let's talk about hacking some more. Into bank accounts. Let's go back to that."

"I told you, I have never, ever, ever hacked a bank account. I've never done that. Oh God. Sheriff, just the school website. Twice. Only twice. Oh God. I am so screwed. Are you going to arrest me?"

She shook her head. "Since I believe you, since I believe that you didn't send me the email, I'm probably going to hire you. I have to interview two more candidates for the dispatcher job. That's required. I have to go through the motions at least. But I'm probably going to hire you, get someone with Internet savvy around here. And, no, I'm not going to arrest you. And, no, I'm not going to call the high school. No one from the school called me to report any problems with the website. Maybe they called the Rockport Police Department. Not my concern."

"Oh God." Zeke sat back, relieved, crossed himself, showing he was probably Catholic. He slid the phone back to her. "Thank you. Thank you. Hire me? Really?"

"And let's talk about the old fart's club," she said. "And Mark Thresher and Melanie Taylor." She paused. Their initials were the same. M. T. Another connection? "And a metallic gray Celica. Do you know anyone who drives a Celica?"

"No. I don't think so. I don't really pay attention to what people drive. Except Mr. Thresher from the old fart's club. He has a sweet old car. I have a motorcycle. He has a couple of old bikes. We talk about motorcycles sometimes."

"Do you drink coffee?"

"Yeah. Sometimes."

"I'll get you a cup. It's not very good, but if I hire you, then you'll have to get used to it. I want you to tell me everything you know about hacking, how you can hack a bank. And why someone would do it, other than 'because they can,' okay?"

Piper walked around the office, wishing she was on her couch with Marmalade the cat and a pain pill. She went through the break room, looked at the bulletin board, then got Zeke a cup of coffee. She'd wanted him to stew for a while, let his nerves play.

She came back and held out the coffee.

"What did you do to your arm?" She'd seen him stare at the sling. Apparently his curiosity was trumping his nerves.

"I was shot." She sat back behind her desk. "Now, hacking, banks and such."

"Anyone can hack if they have a computer and patience, half an ounce of intelligence, and are careful with the websites they go after. You want to hack government sites, FBI and shit, you're looking for trouble. Firewalls and security. Sure, you read about people who can hack that stuff. The really good hackers download stuff off the Dark Web, tools." Zeke took a sip of the coffee and grimaced. "People think Russia hacked into the DNC's email servers. I think it was, oh, two years back that somebody hacked into the Ukraine's power grid—probably the Russians behind it. More than two hundred thousand people were without power for a long time in the Ukraine."

He held the cup in both hands. Piper noticed he hadn't taken a second sip.

"Bank hacking," she prompted again.

"Well, they have firewalls. I'm sure they do. They'd have to."

"Individual accounts."

"I think you'd be better off hacking at the source. The person, not the bank. You'd hack into the person's online banking. Grab their passwords. Find their PayPal accounts, a lot of those are tied to bank accounts. Get their passwords. If you have access to a person's computer, well, most people save their passwords right in the computer. So if you get into their system, you can get the passwords that way."

"Yeah, I'm figuring that," she said. "I'm pretty certain someone either had access to his computer or hacked into his account remotely." There was a series of law enforcement courses coming up over the summer about digital crimes; she needed to sign up. She was woefully out of her league with this. "Who could do that? Hack into an account like that? A bank account? PayPal? 'Anyone with a computer and patience' as you said? Anyone?"

"Well, I could, probably. But I wouldn't. Anyone? Yeah. Any kid in their basement could do that if they really, really, really wanted to."

"How? The Dark Web tools?"

"Probably don't need that. If you don't have access to their computer—you find a weakness in people and exploit it. You take advantage of the people who don't know how to create strong passwords. A genealogy buff for example. I'm a little into genealogy now after helping with the old fart's club. You exploit the weakness of someone into genealogy, family, history. You can figure out passwords by playing around with their relatives' names, birthdates, wedding dates. That sort of stuff. Names and dates—a lot of people use those as passwords. Pet names. Fantasy football team names. Star Trek buffs use NCC-1701. A genealogy buff would use relatives, ancestors, birthdates."

"Mark Thresher from the genealogy club was hacked, his bank." Piper watched his reaction.

"Mr. Thresher? You think someone from our computer club did it?"

She pushed a legal pad toward him. "Give me the names of every student in your computer club." She already had the names of the old farts via Mark's address book. "Phone numbers or email if you know them. Real names, not nicknames."

Again the words came machinegun fast. "You think it's one of *my* guys? That's why you're asking me all these questions? I wouldn't," Zeke said. "I would never do that, hack someone, especially a friend. Geeze, he's a neat old man, a friend. I'm going to give Mr. Thresher my old laptop, which while old is a helluva lot better than his laptop. Gonna give him my old iPad, too. He doesn't have one. It's got the Kindle app on it. He can read books and pump up the font size. I'm getting new tech for high school graduation. I am going to graduate, right? You're not going to hang me up? You said you wouldn't. He's a little off, Mr. Thresher, but interesting. I'll have to ask him at the club Tuesday—"

"You can't ask him anything. Mr. Thresher's dead. And I don't want you alerting your club members that I'm investigating them." *Or will be after this weekend.*

"Dead?" Zeke looked shocked. "Mr. Thresher's counting worms? Piss. I liked him."

"So did I," Piper said softly.

Neither said anything for several minutes. Zeke stared into his coffee.

"I can still graduate, right? You said I was free and clear on that. You said you weren't gonna call the high school."

"I'm not calling the high school," she repeated.

It was quiet for a few more minutes. Piper heard Teegan take a call about an accident near Dale.

"Are you going to hire me? For that dispatcher job?"

"It might be the late shift. The eleven to seven. That might be the one opening. The current dispatcher there, I'll offer her the morning slot. Though I rotate sometimes."

"I can do the late shift." A pause. "So, are you going to hire me?"

"I have to interview two more people. That's required."

He nodded and looked around, clearly trying to figure out what to do with the coffee cup.

"But, yes, I'm going to hire you."

"I can start the Monday after graduation."

# 30
## THIRTY

N athaniel Martin lived just past Christmas Boulevard in Santa Claus, not far from Oren's neighborhood. The chief deputy figured he'd have a brief chat with Mr. Martin, get home in time for warm meatloaf and potatoes, and show his wife the cameo they'd be giving Millie tomorrow for her graduation.

Nathaniel was as tall as Oren, but would have had a few inches on him if his back wasn't curved. An old man, though he hadn't sounded old on the phone, the years had not been as kind to him as they had to Virginia Huffman. Nathaniel said he was eighty, and he'd been fifteen when his brother Rory drowned sixty-five years ago.

Oren sat on the couch, across from Nathaniel, who slowly rocked in an impressive high-backed glider he said he'd made in his workshop. The living room was filled with beautiful walnut furniture—a china cabinet displaying Depression glass, a narrow grandfather's clock, and a curio cabinet filled with Precious Moments figurines, which Oren suspected had belonged to Nathaniel's late wife. Two hanging lamps were carved walnut, as were end tables and a coffee table.

"I like to work with wood," Nathaniel proudly said. He talked about the pieces and offered to show Oren more, eating into the meatloaf time. Oren obliged him and hoped his wife would be under-standing.

Pictures on the wall were of people and dogs, and Oren recog-nized Rory from a photo that matched one in Virginia's book. There was also a large framed photo of Christ kneeling at a rock and pray-ing, sunbeams highlighting his upturned face. There were eight crosses of various sizes around the room, all but one made of walnut. It looked very Catholic to Oren. A rosary on an end table confirmed that.

Oren waited until Nathaniel was done talking about his wood-working. Then he explained about the bones in the park and his quest to put a name to them.

"You think they're Rory's?" Nathaniel shook his head. He had quite a mane, thick and snow-white to his shoulders, but the hairline had receded several inches, and age spots dotted the shiny scalp. More age spots were on the backs of his long hands, stains on the fingers prob-ably from woodworking, and likely permanent Oren thought.

"Maybe they're Rory's. I don't know, honestly. I'm fishing. Some bone specialist says the boy who was buried on the bluff was nine. Buried sixty-five years ago, it looks like. The nine-year-old thing—"

"Same age Rory had been when he drowned."

"Same age as the Huffman and Killian boys," Oren added.

"But they found Killian's body, washed up, a dog walker. I remember that. You know, I still miss Rory, find myself talking to him sometimes." Nathaniel stopped rocking. "I was fifteen when it happened, almost sixteen. Death didn't mean as much to me then. Rory's death was the first I had to deal with, and I don't think I mourned properly. I remember the service at the church lasting too long. Rory and Edgar and Neal. Three separate services, all lasting too long."

"All Catholic?"

Nathaniel nodded. "But they found Edgar Killian, that dog walker did. There was a casket at that service, closed. That was the first service. I mean, the town knew they'd drowned. But no bodies. I think the parents were hoping the boys would turn up in Kentucky, like they'd run away from home. But everyone knew that they'd not run anywhere, that they hadn't respected the river and the river took them. The Killians got to bury a body." He started rocking again. "What makes you think it might be Rory? Those bones you found?"

"The age," Oren said. "Nine years old. The bone expert believes it was a nine-year-old boy buried on the bluff, right-handed."

"Most folks are right-handed. Nine out of ten I read once."

"No nine-year-old boys were reported missing in the county that year." That Piper has uncovered in those old records, he added. None in the newspapers he'd looked through at the library either.

"Could've come from outside the county."

"Could've," Oren agreed. "But I don't think so. Bones on the bluff, I think it was someone who lived around here. The bluff means something to the locals."

"Picnics," Nathaniel said. "We used to picnic there."

"No boy of any age had been reported missing sixty-five years back. That points to Rory or Neal."

"Because if a boy drowns, he's not reported missing," Nathaniel said. "I get you. Makes sense. Rory and Neal—and Edgar until they found his body—were reported dead, not missing." A gray-muzzled German shepherd padded into the room, sniffed Oren's crotch, then laid in front of the grandfather clock, where he could watch both men.

"That's right," Oren said. "You're not missing if no one is looking for you."

"Rory's in the river. His bones are," Nathaniel said. He looked to the dog and smiled. "Duke's a good boy." The dog's tail wagged. "I know in my heart the river kept Rory. Those aren't his bones you found on the bluff. Rory died because he was stupid. But nine-year-old boys aren't the brightest of God's creations." He crossed himself and silently mouthed something.

"Why do you say Rory was stupid?" Oren's stomach growled. He looked at the grandfather clock. 6:15. He'd told his wife he'd be home by six. She'd probably called him. He'd turned his cell phone off—always turned it off during interviews to be polite.

"It was Edgar's raft, I remember that. Rory claimed he built it, but it was Edgar. His raft. Sixty-five years ago and I remember. You don't forget things like that, your only brother dying. If it hadn't been so warm, they wouldn't've been out on the river. But it was warm that day, God keeping fall from really taking hold." Nathaniel reached for his rosary and held it, ran his thumb across the beads. "Edgar's raft was built for one person. I told Rory not to get on it, not to go. But Rory wouldn't listen. Me and Julie—Julian Huffman, he was most of a year older than me—were up on the bluff, watching. We could see the boys shove off, head out onto the river. We turned away and went to the drug store for soda. Damn fool boys."

"So you saw Edgar and Neal and Rory on the raft."

"No. I said I saw Rory and Edgar on the raft. Neal wasn't there. Bad enough two of them were on the damn thing. Damn foolish of them to play Abraham Lincoln. Edgar was wearing a stovepipe hat. Damn stupid." He ran his thumb over the beads faster, and his lips worked. Oren figured he was apologizing to God for using profanity. "Just Rory and Edgar. It was Edgar's raft. They found Edgar, buried him. I think they found the damn hat, too. The river kept Rory. And my brother? Rory was left-handed."

"But Neal wasn't with them?"

"Nope."

"But the newspaper said the three boys drowned."

"Never read the paper back then, but I heard them say it was the three boys. Maybe Neal went swimming. Maybe he drowned that way. But he wasn't on the raft."

Oren sucked in a breath. He believed he'd just discovered who was buried on the bluff. Neal Robert Huffman. There were other possibilities—a kidnap victim from states away murdered and buried, the killer moving on. A local boy who'd died at the hands of an abusive father, and the body hid, never reported missing to conceal the crime. And the forensic anthropologist—Doc Natty—might have got it wrong. Maybe the bones had been buried forty years ago, or eighty, or a hundred. Maybe the time frame was off, the age of the bones off.

But he didn't think so. Oren believed Doc Natty was right; the bones belonged to a nine-year-old right-handed boy. And Oren was certain the bones had been Neal Robert Huffman. Cop's instinct. Now to prove it—and now to find out why Neal Robert Huffman didn't drown, but had died nonetheless. And by who's hand?

"So you were friends with the Huffmans, back then, Nathaniel? When you were fifteen?"

"Sure. Me and Julie were pretty thick, when he wasn't with Virginia. He was in love with her." Nathaniel stopped rubbing the beads, and put the rosary in his shirt pocket. "We were a year apart, me and Julie—though I turned sixteen before he hit seventeen. I was a sophomore in high school anyway at fifteen. I'd been bumped ahead a year when I was in the sixth grade. I was lightning with math."

"Do you remember if Neal had problems with anyone? His father maybe? Too rough with him? Did he fall in with the wrong crowd?"

"Wrong crowd? Nine years old is too young for a wrong crowd." Nathaniel shook his head. "Neal was a pistol. Ill-behaved. A scallywag, people used to call him. A troublemaker. But their whole gang had spirit. If you ever saw those old *Our Gang* comedies, with Alfalfa and all of them... That was just like those boys. Otto Something-or-other, Rory, Chuckie Schleevogt—Chuckie still lives in Dale, I've got his phone number—and Trigger 'boogie eater' Holms.' Boogie eater died a couple of years back. Cancer. Probably from all the boogers. They all hung together. Not much to do around here, so you made your own fun."

The dog got up and left the room. Oren heard lapping. The dog returned, sniffed Oren's crotch again, and then stretched out at Nathaniel's feet.

Nathaniel wrote down Schleevogt's phone number, and Oren put it in his shirt pocket. He pulled out a business card and passed it over. "In case you think of anything else."

"Have I been of any help?"

"A great deal of help, Mr. Martin." Oren glanced at the clock. His dinner was going to be cold, but he didn't care. He learned who'd been buried on the bluff. Now he had to figure out who put Neal Robert Huffman there.

# THIRTY-ONE

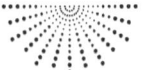

## MONDAY, MAY 7TH

"**N**eal Robert Huffman," Oren told her, laying out all his evidence.

Piper whistled. "Wow. Old school." She saw Oren cringe at the comment. "I meant, I'm impressed that you did it without computers. That you started with microfiche. I wouldn't have thought to go that route." She was also a little disappointed. Oren had won this race—at least in identifying the victim. Piper's time had been torn between the old case files, the Mailbox Mauler, and Mr. Thresher. Oren had been able to concentrate solely on the bones. "Impressive," she repeated, meaning it.

They drank Eight O'clock Dark Italian Coffee. Piper had laid in a supply, as Nang had given her a case at his cost. Now all she needed was a better coffeemaker for the department. *Small steps*, she thought.

"All those names you mentioned, the kids—"

"Neal Robert Huffman, Rory Martin, Edgar Killian."

"The three who were said to have drowned that day."

"Their buddies—Otto Benson, Chuck Schleevogt, and Trigger Holms. Chuck Schleevogt is in the county. I called him last night. He's a member of the genealogy club, said he saw you at the library last week. They meet tomorrow at the main branch in Rockport. I'll talk to him then. Trigger's dead. Haven't gone looking for Otto yet."

"The old fart's club," Piper mused. "I have to go tomorrow, too."

"Good, but I'll drive."

She shared her suspicions that Mark Thresher had been hacked by someone in the high school computer club, and that she needed to find out who was driving a dead woman's Celica. She mentioned her threatening email, figuring he already knew about it through her father.

"I haven't had any more email messages though, not the bad ones, not since yesterday's."

Oren scowled. "Electronics. People hide behind their gadgets."

"I'm going to find him," Piper said.

"Computer club members, narrow it, get some warrants and check bank accounts. See who among them has a windfall of cash." Oren frowned. "Kids. I hope you're wrong. That'd be a shame. But kids are connected to their electronics."

"The genealogy club's down three members in the past six months," she said. "Four counting Mr. Thresher. We better talk to the ones who're left before they die of old age." She saw Oren's eyes narrow. "I want to know if any of them are also missing money."

Before she could elaborate, Sylvia D popped in to announce, "Gretchen Brown has been moved to Owensboro Health Regional Hospital. Her daughter's got her in the psych unit, and they're gonna keep her until the trial. Phone. Gotta run. Basil's here. Early. Should I show him back? He's a tall drink of water."

Piper was going to miss Sylvia D, who had made it clear she didn't want to keep the dispatcher job, but would be happy to fill in for emergencies. Meeting her was one good thing to come out of the old fart's club.

B asil Meredith had a presence. He was six feet tall, lean, his skin a deep sienna and his eyes so dark she couldn't easily discern the pupils. His hairstyle was a slow fade, about an inch on top and down the back, shaved close on the sides, complimented with a trimmed Van Dyke. Small silver hoops in both ears. Wearing a double-breasted English-cut graphite suit, he looked like he could pose for GQ. Sylvia D was right—a tall drink of water.

Piper caught herself staring. Recovering, she took him to the break room with Oren and closed the door.

"Coffee?"

He shook his head. "I avoid caffeine." He had an orotund voice, and she detected no Chicago or Midwestern accent.

They started with friendly talk to learn more about him. Born in Puerto Rico, orphaned at sixteen, moved to Chicago to live with his aunt and uncle, joined the Navy right out of high school, and after serving four years became a Chicago patrolman. Went to school on the side and earned a two-year associate degree in criminal justice from City Colleges of Chicago, where he met his wife.

It was the five years as a detective, one with Major Accident Investigation Section, four with Gang and Narcotics, that iced all the cupcakes for Piper.

"You're seriously qualified," she admitted. "Commendations, recommendations. Your commander doesn't want you to leave. You could probably go to any big city of your choosing. And yet you're interested in Spencer County."

Basil held his hands out, palms up. He lowered the right, giving the impression of the scales of justice. "It's quite a bit less money than I make now." He brought the hand up even, then raised the left. "Blitzen Lane, Santa Claus, less than two hundred and fifty thousand dollars buys a brick house with four bedrooms, three bathrooms, and a two-car garage. Whirlpool, a deck, a half-acre. The kids could have a dog. We've looked at real estate, and drove around yesterday, stopping at For Sale signs. Chicago? Edison Park where we live, I'd have to pay a million for the same house. And there wouldn't be a big yard."

He went on with the balance. On the negative side. "Sleepy county." On the positive side. "Sleepy county." Negative. "I might be bored here." Positive. "I might be willing to be bored."

"We don't have a gang problem," Piper said. "Not really. And your commander says you shine dealing with gang crimes. But we have a meth problem. And I want to do something about it."

"More than eighty percent of meth in this country comes from what we call 'superlabs' in Mexico and California. The cartels use safe houses on reservations. But meth is all over. A rural county like yours? Easy to hide a small operation, easy to transport the product to the big cities, using country roads. The small labs—the difference with small labs is the variation in recipes, hundreds of different recipes, always experimenting, difficult to get a signature to trace it back to any one spot."

He scowled. "You know, it takes only a thousand dollars to make twenty thousand worth of meth. Manufacturing it has a huge financial upside. You can produce it in a kitchen, bathroom, shed, camping trailer, and the equipment would fit into a cooler. The price of a cocaine dose that would give you, say, a twenty-minute high? You could get buzzed for a couple of days spending the same on meth. Buying it is a cheaper rush for addicts, much more bang for the buck. Meth is the number one drug cops battle today. Burglaries and robberies have increased because of meth, domestic violence, assault. More than a million and half people are suspected of being regular users in this country, with twelve million having tried it. Okay, those are guesses, federal estimates, but I buy into the numbers. And the users—the repeated users—"

They talked for an hour and a half, Oren asking most the questions. Piper had wanted it that way; she wanted to sit back and listen. She was liking Basil Meredith a lot. But she wasn't sure he'd be comfortable here.

*Put it on the table.* Piper leaned forward.

"Roughly twenty-one thousand people in the county," she began. "Ninety-six, ninety-seven percent white. Blacks? Less than one percent. Maybe a hundred black people in the whole county."

"Maybe less than a hundred," Oren said.

"That bothers my wife," Basil said. "A lot. We talked about that yesterday when we drove around. It's a serious sticking point with her. She wanted me to call off this interview. She wants the kids to embrace their roots, and Chicago is diverse. But she also wants out of the city, and as much as I like my job, I promised her I'd look elsewhere. She says she worries every day I leave for work. I worry every day whether my daughter will make it home from school. Ten days ago, three blocks from our place, a two-year-old walking with his father was caught in the crossfire. Five o'clock. Broad daylight. His father, a teenager, was the gang member the rivals were after. But the shooters missed their target." He paused. "Or maybe they didn't."

He crossed his arms. "I've applications elsewhere, and nibbles. I've an appointment for an interview a week from today for an assistant chief slot in Murfreesboro, right outside of Nashville. Good house prices there, too. My in-laws live in Nashville, and Esme wants to be closer. You're about a two-hour drive from Nashville. I like my in-laws, but I don't want to live down the street from them." Another pause. "But we'll see where the interviews take me."

"We expect to make a decision soon," Piper said. "Our investigator is leaving and we don't want the job to sit open."

"Well, you think about me," Basil said. "And I'll think about you. And my wife will throw in more than her two cents." He glanced up at the clock. "She said she was coming by around eleven. I have an interview at one in Santa Claus."

Piper figured her dad had serious competition for the police chief post.

"Can you recommend a restaurant there? In Santa Claus? The kids will be crying for something to eat. Esme's been driving them around, said she wanted them to see the bluff."

Oren and Piper looked at each other. Neither mentioned the bones that had been found there.

"I'd go with Brick Oven Pizza. They have a lunch buffet. St. Nick's café is good, but a little slow for what you're probably looking for," Oren said. "We'd like to meet your wife."

They did that at the dispatcher's desk.

Esme Meredith was short and intense-looking, with waist-length hair in elaborate braids. Piper doubted she could get her hair styled like that in the county. Maybe it was a weave; she probably couldn't get that done here either. A little boy and girl, both with close-cropped curly hair sat in one chair and were intent on paging through an oversized Sesame Street book. They didn't even look up.

Sylvia D had been talking to Esme. She reached to her side and pulled up a cardboard box and started taking paperbacks out. The temporary dispatcher had apparently come to work prepared to meet Esme Meredith.

"I have all your books," Sylvia D said, acknowledging Piper and Oren with a curt nod, then turning back to Esme. "All of them. Every. Single. One. Under both your author names—Esme Meredith and Meredith Maguire. You sure have written a lot for being so young."

Esme beamed. "I write fast."

"Like lightning. How do you do it?"

"Well, I'm a full-time writer, and these romance books are only seventy to seventy-five thousand words. It takes about three months to write one, four with the rewrite and page proofs. So I put three a year on my schedule. If I didn't have the kids to manage, and him—" she pointed to Basil, "I could probably write more. I had to come up with a penname—Maguire is my maiden name—because the publisher wanted three books a year. He just didn't want all of them with Esme's name on the cover. So I started the cozy series."

Sylvia D smiled broadly. "I have these—*Born of Desire, The Love of a Stranger, The Heart's Embrace* in first-printings. Mint. I don't bend the spines when I read." She pushed each book forward as she named it. There were two copies of *The Heart's Embrace*. "*A Heart Can Dream,* and your Daisy Remington Western series *Love Takes a Holiday, Love Rides a Pale Horse, Rainy Days and Romance*—that was my favorite, and *Loving My Life Away.*"

Sylvia D took a pen out of the drawer and handed it to her. "I think your Western romances are so...real. *The Stranger and the Cowboy.* Where the heroine wakes up on a ranch with no memory of who she is or how she got there, and falls in love with the hero, who is struggling to make his ranch work. I cried at the end."

"Thank you. Do you want me to sign these, or may I inscribe them to you?"

"Oh. Oh. Oh. Make them out to 'my friend, Sylvia D,' if you don't mind. Except for one of *The Heart's Embrace*. I'm going to send that to my sister, Chantelle. Make that out to her C H A N T E L L E. I'm usually not much into period fiction, but your *Velvet Kisses*, set in 1700s England, I loved that. Innocent girl from a good family, rescued from thugs by a dashing mystery man called the Velvet Bandit because of his fine clothes and gentlemanly ways. I'm a third into *Harrington's Way*. Case Harrington has just hired a pet store owner to pose as his fiancée for an after-hours gala. He wants to throw off all the women who are trying to wed him. I bet he falls for the pet shop girl. Doesn't he?"

"That would be telling. I don't want to spoil it for you."

"I'm in a book club, Mrs. Meredith. Next month we're doing romances. I picked your *Love's Blistering Embrace* for a group read." She pushed that book forward. "The back here says its set in 1800s America, another period piece. 'A young woman of ill repute uses her charms to seduce her way into wealth. She learns along the way that if you dare to play with fire, you can get burned.'" Sylvia D looked up. "Do you write the cover copy, too?"

"Sometimes."

"Would you be willing to come to our book club next month? We could make a party out of it! I'll make sure it gets into the local paper. Oh, and sign these Meredith Maguire books, please. Everyone in my club will go nuts if you can come."

Piper noted the Maguire titles—*Love Me, Love Me Knot; Heart Strings; Threads of Love;* and *Knit Me Another Lover*. Definitely cozies, the Meredith Maguire tagline in script that looked like yarn.

"I hope Sheriff Blackwell offers your husband the job. It would be wonderful to have a famous author like you in Spencer County."

Piper and Oren looked at each other. Maybe Sylvia D was making Esme like Spencer County at least a little bit.

"We have that Skype interview," Piper said softly to Oren. Sylvia D and Esme continued to talk about books. "Would you show Basil and his wife around the department? See if they have any questions about the county. I'll take the interview solo."

Oren nodded, and whispered, "You should offer him the job."

"Yeah," she whispered back. "No question. But whether he'll say yes—"

Piper slipped into her office and opened the laptop. Time to interview Jefferson Polanger, see if Teegan was right about the Yooper accent. Jefferson probably would not be bored in Spencer County, and would fit in easier with the stark white population.

She fit in better in the Army; the life had suited her.

But maybe fitting in didn't have to be a requirement.

Maybe Spencer County could land that round peg from the big bad city.

32

## THIRTY-TWO

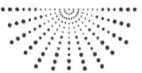

Jefferson Polanger hadn't impressed her. She liked Kevan Melkan though, and so did Oren. The retired state police officer would work as their second choice. The required three interviews finished and no one else in the application queue she wanted to bring in, Piper called Basil Meredith on his cell phone and discovered he'd just finished his interview in Santa Claus.

She offered him the job, crossing the fingers of her good hand. He said because she was in a hurry to fill the post, he'd let her know Wednesday or Thursday; Esme was warming to Spencer County. They'd talk it out on the drive back to Chicago.

*Thank you Sylvia D for bringing in that stack of romance novels.*

It was now 2:30. Piper would spend a few hours researching the members of the old fart's club and the high school students who helped them, get ready for tomorrow afternoon's genealogy meeting. Use the county records and newspapers, go "old school" maybe. And from there she'd figure out who to target for search warrants for computers and bank accounts—warrants were specific. Piper needed access to the students' computers to discover who had the software, the wherewithal, and who hopefully had left some digital tracks regarding hacking Mark Thresher and sending her the threatening email. She knew she'd need enough evidence to be granted the warrants, and she'd need to do it quietly and quickly so any stolen money didn't get transferred and the computers didn't get wiped. Could more than one student be involved? Could it be a club activity? Zeke the Geek had honestly been surprised by it all.

Sylvia D had packed up her signed books and was getting the desk ready for Teegan to come on shift at three.

"Sheriff Blackwell!" Sylvia D's shrill voice cut down the hallway. "Harlan Crook." A pause. "Attorney Harlan *Cook* called while you had that Melkan interview. Said he has time at three to talk to you about Mr. Thresher. Said you should come to him. That Mr. Melkan that you brought in seemed nice, Sheriff. But you should hire that Basil Meredith. Tall drink of water, that one. Get his wife to move here."

Piper decided to walk to Cook's office.

She'd never met Harlan Cook, but she'd heard a lot about him. Oren had told her the attorney was "as close to an ambulance chaser as you could get without being run over." His office was across from the courthouse, next to a tavern, which seemed fitting as he had a reputation for defending people charged with DUI.

He was slick, Teegan had said, explaining that he got a lot of the drunkards off without them losing their licenses—at least for the first or second offense. In that respect he'd forced both Rockport police officers and Spencer County sheriff deputies to take greater care when making DUI arrests, to not rely on an informal breathalyzer test given in the back of the car, to wait that required twenty-minute stretch where the offender was observed not drinking before a court-admissible test was administered.

Maybe the problem with Harlan Cook was that officers and deputies didn't like his clientele.

The building was old and well maintained, narrow with a reception area in the front manned by a doughy-faced woman with a mirthless smile, a conference table in the middle, and Harlan's office at the back. It was all paneled dark wood with darker wainscoting, brass coat hooks, and beveled glass-fronted bookcases.

Piper guessed Harlan to be in his mid- to late-forties. Clean-shaven, angular face, short black hair with flecks of gray at the temples. She thought he'd present well in a courtroom, but that obviously wasn't where he'd been today. He had on faded blue jeans, a forest green polo shirt, and a denim sport coat was draped over a spare chair.

He gestured her to sit across from his desk.

"Sheriff."

"Mr. Cook. Nice to meet you."

He smiled. It didn't make him look more handsome, it made him look smug and unfriendly.

"I want to talk about Mark Thresher," Piper started. "I found no living relatives looking through his genealogy notes and—"

"The Shark didn't have any relatives. He'd outlived them all." He touched a button on his phone even though his assistant was less than twenty feet away. "Emily, bring that file back please." To Piper, "Coffee?"

"I never refuse coffee."

Emily brought a pot and two cups and set a file in front of Cook. "You got a call from Hank Shepard," she told him. "About the DUI hearing tomorrow."

"I'll call him back."

Piper found the coffee good, but not close to the Dark Italian. "I was hoping to find a relative so we could get someone to go through the house, watch it, change the locks. Our deputies are patrolling but—"

"Not a single relative," Cook repeated. His voice was strong and each word separate like staccato music notes to be clearly understood. She figured he'd play well to a jury. "The Shark said it was just him, the last Thresher. But you never know, I guess. I'll be posting some public notices, some distant blood that he didn't know about might surface and put in a claim or contest it. But not likely. It's a solid will. Creditors have six months after publication of the legal notices to file a claim, though I doubt The Shark had any debts. He always paid me upfront. I never once had to send a bill. I'm administering the estate, and I think it will be simple, less than a year before everything is tied up with a big satin bow. But you never know if someone will challenge it, and disputes can drag it out."

"The coroner will be calling. Did Mr. Thresher specify what he wanted done—"

"I called Dr. Neufeld this morning and left a message. All of that is stipulated in The Shark's will. He'll be buried next to his wife. He'd even paid the funeral home for everything in advance several years ago." He took a drink of coffee and held the cup. "He'd been into my office a few times in the past seven or eight days, fine-tuning his will, complaining to me about his bank account. He told me he'd been robbed and that you were going to get his money back."

"My intention."

"That's good." Harlan took another sip. "Local organizations—including your department—will benefit from that money."

Piper sat up straighter. "He put the Sheriff's Department in his will?"

"Said you needed a couple of drones." Harlan smiled again, the expression a little warmer. "He liked you."

"Wow. Drones."

Holding the cup in one hand he flipped open the folder and pulled out a thin stack of legal-size papers. "Read this."

Piper saw a coaster on the edge of the desk and put her cup on it. The coaster was leather and imprinted with the scales of justice. HARLAN COOK ATTORNEY OF LAW in all caps beneath it.

The will started out with the usual,

"I, Mr. Mark Henry Thresher, residing in Hatfield, Spencer County, in the State of Indiana, United States of America, being of sound and disposing mind and memory, do hereby declare this to be my Final Will and Testament, revoking all prior Wills and Codicils." Then it went on to recite his marital status (widowed), descendants (none), predeceased family members (his spouse, Lucille), executor (Harlan Cook), and provisions for the payment of debt. Piper smiled at the language, "I do not have any debt. But Harlan says I need this language in here. Except for liens and encumbrances placed on property as security for the repayment of a loan or debt, I direct that all debts and expenses owed by my estate should be paid out in the manner provided for by the laws of the State of Indiana."

The legal text went on, and Piper quickly read it. She skimmed over most of the boilerplate about waiving any required bond for the executor, paying estate taxes, proper investments for the estate, incontestability of bequests, and the like. Finally, she came to specific gifts.

"I give, devise and bequeath my land, house, garage, and all the furnishings and contents, including my collection of vintage cars and motorcycles, to my friend, Piper Blackwell of Rockport, Indiana. Furthermore, I beseech her to care for Camaro and Marmalade, my beloved companions, until the time of their natural passing. They are to remain in their home."

"Oh." She sat back and felt her stomach rise into her throat. "Oh, God."

"The Shark apparently thought a great deal of you." The attorney appeared to study her. "I've been to his place. It's a very nice house."

"I— I don't know what to say. I don't know what to do about this. I don't—"

"Know what to do? Well, I understand that you've been living above a garage. I'd move into your new house, Sheriff Blackwood. The Shark was basically debt free, but I still have to wait those six months to discover if there are creditors, the extent of them, to close everything. And it is my responsibility as executor to sell property if necessary to cover those debts. That's just the law. But I knew The Shark. The house and all those fine vehicles are yours. You'll assume property taxes and all of that. I have a copy of his previous tax bills. Keep reading please."

"I give, devise and bequeath the sum of eighty thousand dollars to the

Spencer County Sheriff's Department to be spent precisely in the following manner:

• Twenty thousand dollars for the purchase, training, and equipping of a police dog, which should be named Thresher

• Fourteen thousand dollars for the purchase and operation of two or more drones

• Five thousand and five hundred dollars for the purchase and operation of fifteen or more body cameras for Spencer County Sheriff Deputies

• Four thousand dollars for video surveillance equipment for the exterior of the Spencer County Sheriff's Department

• One hundred dollars for the purchase of a Cuisinart DCC-3200 14-Cup Programmable Coffeemaker, available on Amazon, here is the link—

• Thirty-six thousand and four hundred dollars for a specially-designated fund to exclusively cover the upkeep, repairs, and replacement of the above-mentioned equipment, and for dog food."

Piper fought for breath. "I didn't ask him for this. I didn't want him to—"

"The Shark told me if his money and property outlived him, if he didn't end up 'in one of them damn nursing homes,' that he wanted everything put to good use, and with someone he respected. Like I said before, he thought a lot of you."

She read the last of it.

"I give, devise and bequeath the residuary of my estate in equal parts to the following organizations:
• Spencer County Kennel Club
• Spencer County Garden Club
• Santa Claus American Legion
• Friends of Lincoln
• Lion's Club of Spencer County
• Kiwanis, Optimists Club of Spencer County
• Spencer County Masons

• Spencer County Hazardous Waste Taskforce
• Hatfield Recreational Committee
• First Baptist Church of Rockport."

"I hope you can find who stole The Shark's money, Sheriff Blackwell, get it returned to the estate. It would certainly benefit those organizations."

"I promised him I would," she said numbly. "I'll fix it. I told him I'd fix it."

# THIRTY-THREE

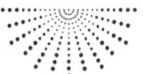

**P**iper didn't go directly back to the office. Her arm throbbed and she stepped in time with the pulse of pain. She walked to the park and sat on the bench where she'd met Mark Thresher seven days ago.

During those seven days she'd promised more than once to find the thief and return his money.

During those seven days he'd rewritten his will and gifted her that beautiful house.

And the vintage cars.

And the old motorcycles.

And an old golden retriever and an orange tabby cat.

Seven days.

She leaned back and tipped her head up, looking through gaps in the branches and noticing the sky had clouded over. The air smelled like rain was coming. *That would be fitting*, she thought. It had rained the day she met him.

It should rain right now, hide her tears.

The Sheriff of Spencer County shouldn't cry in public.

But she cried anyway, for Mark Thresher and the lost opportunity to know him better, mostly because she hadn't been able to "fix it" while he was breathing, that he wasn't able to see justice done. Last night she'd slept fitfully, wondering if she really could "fix it." Now she knew damn well that she could—and would. Piper hadn't backed down from anything, not at Fort Campbell, not during any of the deadly downrange assignments she'd fought through in Iraq, and certainly not here.

Piper had the bluff to herself. Kids in school, people working. An elderly couple was on the sidewalk, the man using two canes and reminding her of Mark. They kept going and crossed the street and Piper lost sight of them. She scanned the cars at the edges. No metallic gray Celica. No silver or gray anything. Where the hell was the car? And who the hell was driving it? She should get back to the office. Try to ferret out something on the car, the high school students, and the members of the old fart's club. The bones, too. There was that to consider. Or had she decided the bones were Oren's to solve?

She stayed rooted to the bench and let the breeze tease the hair she swore she'd get cut.

One week since she'd met Mark and tripped on the leg bone under the trees.

The bones of a nine-year-old boy that Oren was certain had been Neal Robert Huffman. Gut instinct, he'd told her.

Neal Robert Huffman's bones and a ten-inch section of rusted barbed wire; four marbles; two pieces of a thin black leather belt; a curl of brown leather with two punched holes that had been a hatband; five copper rivets from blue jeans; a handful of coins; seven small black buttons from a shirt; three slightly larger brown buttons from the jeans; a brass belt buckle that had been awarded to a paperboy in Arizona; a toy badge; a toy gun; and a coil of rotting rope that was partly nylon, filthy and stinky and knotted to form a loop. Neal Robert Huffman had been playing sheriff on Halloween.

So if he hadn't drowned on the raft, who killed him, strangled him, and buried his body in this park? And why?

And why hadn't Neal Robert Huffman been wearing shoes?

"Where were the damn shoes?"

Her phone chirped and she almost ignored it. Her father.

"Hey, Dad." She wanted to tell him about the house she'd just inherited. But that would be for a longer conversation, maybe over dinner tonight.

"I got the job, Punkin—you're talking to the soon-to-be Police Chief of Santa Claus. They called me this afternoon. Said they had to interview three candidates to meet their requirements. Just got the third out of the way apparently, and called me right after. And they met my terms."

"Terms?"

"That I could keep Wrinkles in my office. I can't leave him at home all day. He'll be a great police dog."

The Spencer County Sheriff's Department would be getting a police dog, a real one, not a ten-year-old pug more interested in sniffing for table scraps than sniffing for drugs. Still, she smiled at that. She was glad he could keep Wrinkles close at hand. The pug had become his constant shadow.

"Congratulations, Dad. I knew you'd get the job." Actually, she thought Basil might give him competition. And she was glad that wasn't the case. Maybe she could get the round peg after all. "We should celebrate."

"I bought three steaks. I'll grill them. Let me know what time you'll be done today."

Three steaks. Good thinking. She'd call Nang and—

"One steak for me. One steak for you. And one steak to split between Wrinkles and Camaro. The golden retriever's a good dog. I think I'll keep him in the office, too. They're both pretty sluggish, age to them."

"I'm keeping him, Camaro," she said. There was a big dog door at Thresher's house, and Camaro could go in and out as he pleased while she was at work. "And the cat. I'm keeping Marmalade."

"So you're staying," Paul Blackwell said. "In Spencer County. A dog, that means you're staying."

*And a house. I've a house, too.*

Had he realized she'd entertained returning to the Army? She'd never mentioned it to him. But he was good at reading people.

"It's an old dog, Dad." She wiped the tears off her face. The clouds overhead were thickening. "Listen, I'm not working at the office late. I'm going to bring some stuff home to go through. So an early dinner? Grill before it starts raining? I'll be there by five."

Piper hung up and made a move to get up. The phone again.

"Dr. Neufeld?"

"I just finished the autopsy on Mr. Thresher," the coroner said. Her voice sounded tinny, like she was using a soup can to speak through. "I want to meet with you tomorrow, bright and early. Talk about his autopsy, and one I did on Alfonso Lattimer. I almost hadn't caught that case. Alfonso was a nursing home resident, ninety-two, but he had been pretty mobile, had kept a car, drove to restaurants and his club meetings. He'd died in that car. Unattended death, I caught it."

"Alfonso who?" Something about that name played around in her thoughts.

"Lattimer. Alfonso Lattimer. He died November twentieth last year."

"Okay. Sure," Piper said. "What about—"

"I think Mr. Thresher was murdered. And maybe Lattimer was, too. Yeah, I think Lattimer, too. Probably."

"Murdered? I'll meet you now and—"

"I'm in Evansville. I'm finishing up, and I've got dinner plans tonight, some old college friends passing through here, and I'd hate to throw away the chance to reconnect. Mr. Thresher is going back in cold storage. Mr. Lattimer's been in the ground for many months. Besides, I want to go through my notes, lose some sleep over it. I'll come by your office. Eight okay? I'm not good much earlier."

"Eight's fine," Piper said. "Murdered?"

"Pretty sure," the coroner returned. "Pretty awful, huh? Let's keep this to ourselves until we talk it through. Until we see if I'm right."

"Yeah. Absolutely to ourselves." Piper felt like she'd been punched in the stomach. "Thanks, Dr. Neufeld. Have a good night with your friends."

She stood, unsteady. "Murdered," she said, the word feeling like rotten cabbage on her tongue.

Piper heard a whisper of thunder. It would be only fitting if it rained today.

The door had been locked at Mark's house; she'd had to break in. While she'd waited for the coroner she'd checked the place. Everything had been locked, except the dog door. There'd been no sign of foul play. No sign of a struggle. No blood. No sign of strangulation. But she hadn't checked the basement. Diego had probably done that. "Sudden cardiac something-or-other" the coroner had said at the time. But now she was saying murder.

He'd been ninety-four, a good run.

Maybe Dr. Neufeld was wrong. Ninety-four, that was a long life. Not many people made it that far. But Dr. Annie Neufeld was good.

Murder.

What had the coroner found? And who was Alfonso Lattimer? Someone to find in the county directory. Someone to…

"Wait." Piper visualized the list of the genealogy club members that had been in Mark's address book. Three names had been crossed off.

Melanie Taylor

Bruno Something-or-other

And Alfonso Lattimer

"Shit."

Someone was driving Melanie's car, had followed her and Mark the Shark, had been parked on the street outside her apartment one night, had been across from the antique shop she'd stopped at, mud so thick she couldn't read the license plate. Melanie to Mark to maybe Alfonso Lattimer.

Piper's head pounded.

There was something vile swirling, that had caught Alfonso Lattimer and Mark Thresher and maybe Melanie Taylor. They had all been members of the genealogy club, they were all elderly. Had Melanie been murdered as well?

"Who the hell?" Piper hushed. She walked back to the office.

Who the hell would kill Mark the Shark?

And why had the boy who'd been buried on the bluff not had shoes?

# THIRTY-FOUR

## TUESDAY, MAY 8TH

"**D**o you think he'll take it?" Piper was in her office, a quarter after seven, drinking coffee with Oren, who sat on the other side of her desk.

Oren shook his head. "Meredith would be bored here. Despite the bones on the bluff, our meth problem, he'd be bored. Big city cop, he's used to a different pace."

"He *might* be bored," Piper admitted.

Oren shook his head again. "He *would* be bored. And he'd be uncomfortable. Our county's white, that's just the way it is. He'd be out of place. *Feel* out of place." He held the coffee with his right hand. His left held a granola bar that he took a bite of. "But he'd also be excellent. I dunno, the blue-haired bat," at this he lowered his voice. "She helped by bringing in all those trashy books."

"I hadn't known Meredith's wife was an author. Never thought to ask much about his family. I was just interested in his experience."

"I just wanted the high points, his busts, conviction-rate follow through in the courts." He finished the granola bar and washed it down with more coffee. "Mentioned Esme Meredith to my wife last night. She got all excited and pointed to her bookshelf. Saw *Rainy Days and Romance* on the top shelf. Turns out she's a member of Sylvia

D's book club and is doing the group read on *Love's Blistering Embrace*." He gave a clipped laugh. "Hope he takes the job. My wife would be tickled."

"Yeah." Piper set down her coffee. "Your granddaughter apartment hunting?"

A nod. "Since that house she was going to rent has been declared uninhabitable. I have her boxes in my garage. Not that she's got all the much. It's probably all clothes. Had to move my boat out, though."

She went on before he might argue about her hiring Millie. "Dad— I haven't told him yet, but I'm moving out. I was going to anyway, need some space, you know. A little distance now that he's cancer free again. The apartment above his garage is furnished. Washer, dryer. A couple of big closets that would accommodate Millie's clothes. Do you know if she's a fan of *That 70s Show*? Orange shag, green appliances."

"I hated that show," Oren said. "Don't care for sit-coms, except I liked *Home Improvement*. I liked that one."

"Mention it to her. I suspect the rent would be reasonable, especially if Dad knows she's your granddaughter."

"Ha! I suspect she'll take it. I know she doesn't want to pay another week's rent at the hotel, and she won't stay with me. When are you moving?"

"This coming weekend, I think. I don't have all that much stuff."

He finished the coffee. "About you hiring her and—"

"Dr. Neufeld!" Sylvia D's high voice cut him off. "Should I—"

"I can show my own self back," the coroner said as she stepped into Piper's office. She was wearing a dress, a cornflower blue one with a full skirt that came to her knees, a patterned scarf around her waist as a sash. She had on jewelry and makeup. Piper hadn't seen the coroner with makeup—and in a dress—before. "Oh good, Oren's here, too. You both should hear this." She plopped her purse next to the empty chair. "Be right back. Coffee fresh?"

She came back with a cup and started talking as she sat. "Hunch, feeling, gut instinct, whatever you want to call it. I'm pretty sure Mark Thresher was murdered. I can't prove it yet. Maybe I won't be able to prove it and that'll be up to you. Yes, his heart stopped—sudden cardiac event was the first thing I listed in my report. And I'll stand by that, because that's what happened. But—"

"But what?" This from Oren.

"But Mark Thresher had a pacemaker. Not an unusual thing for a person to have, especially an elderly one with a history of heart issues. Alfonso Lattimer had a pacemaker, too. Again, not an unusual thing. Alfonso was ninety-two. And he died of a sudden cardiac incident. Not unusual for two old men with pacemakers to die of heart problems." She drained half the cup of coffee in one long gulp. "What did you do? Switch brands? This is actually pretty good."

"Piper bought—"

Again she charged forward. "Same brand of pacemaker." She finished the cup and set it on Piper's desk, missing the coaster. "An older model. I'd taken them both out, the pacemakers. Lattimer's was still in a box on the shelf in the morgue. Good thing. It let me send both off to the state. *Will* send. I'm going to the post office right after this. Look, honestly, it wasn't their age or the pacemakers or any of that. What got me looking was Sheriff Blackwell's comment Friday about Mr. Thresher having his bank account drained."

Piper started to ask a question, but the coroner kept going. "My wife, Bebe, she'd handled Lattimer's estate, was the executor of his will. She said that people thought all of his money went to pay the nursing home. He'd been in the home about six months before he died, but it was assisted living, not as expensive as full-blown nursing care. He'd still kept a car and drove to restaurants and his club meetings. Bebe said Lattimer had owned the used car lot in Chandler, and got a windfall when he sold it, redid his will then to include some nieces and nephews. He should have had plenty of money. But when the time came to dole it out to the relatives, Bebe discovered his money markets and bank accounts were essentially empty. A few dollars left in each one. She was basically a pro-bono executor, if there is such a thing. Bebe didn't make a cent. There wasn't even enough money to bury him. The family handled that, the burial, and the old fart's club chipped in and bought the gravestone." She looked at Piper. "Your dad would remember the collection taken for the gravestone. He's a member of the old fart's club, right?"

Piper nodded.

Dr. Neufeld came up for air, looked back and forth between Piper and Oren, and when neither one commented, she continued.

"So, it was Lattimer's squeezed bank accounts that did it, the sheriff here mentioning Thresher's money had been siphoned. Two old men with pacemakers, sudden cardiac incidents, money drained. Same model of pacemaker. Too many coincidences. I don't care if they were past their expiration dates." She leaned forward and tapped an index finger on the edge of Piper's desk. "So I hit Google right before I called you yesterday. A hunch, you know. I'd remembered reading something sometime back, needed to jog my brain. Google is my friend, cemented it. Found the big FDA warning. Certain brands of pacemakers are vulnerable to hacking. They have a transmitter that's part of a home monitor. The monitor connects the pacemaker to a wireless RF signal. The monitor can be hacked to send modified commands to a patient, shocking the patient, throwing off the heart-beat. I saw a monitor in Mark Thresher's den, on the hutch above his computer. There are patches for those pacemakers, the ones Thresher and Lattimer had. But you have to be online and connected to down-load the patches and prevent the hacking. If neither one of those men downloaded the patches—and I'll bet they didn't—then they could have been hacked. Like their money markets and bank accounts could have been hacked. A sophisticated crime for this county, wouldn't you think?"

"Murder," Piper said flatly.

"Yeah, I'll bet its murder. Both men," Dr. Neufeld said. "You're going to ask me about Melanie Taylor. She had a cardiac incident, too, but she didn't have a pacemaker. I don't know if she had a will. If she did, Bebe didn't handle it. I don't know if she was missing money when she died. You'll have to dig into that."

"Someone has her car, Melanie Taylor's," Piper said, looking at Oren. "I need to find the Celica."

Dr. Neufeld stood. "I don't know how long the state lab will take with the pacemakers. Gotta be a way to tell if they're hacked, right? I know pacemakers keep logs of what they do, the state lab could access that, find the hack that way. Honestly, I don't know all that much about stuff like that, but I'm crossing my fingers and toes that the state lab does. Two elderly men, same model of pacemaker, money drained. I wonder how many more old farts in that club have pacemakers. You better pray they're not models on the FDA's list." She reached into her purse and retrieved a printout, waved it, and then handed it to Piper. "Those are the models the FDA is worried about. Maybe you should show that around to the genealogy club. I gotta run. Post office and breakfast with Bebe and her son. He stopped here on his way to Indy."

She stood in the doorway. "Oren, congratulations on your grand-daughter being hired here. I'm sure she'll be a great deputy. The beginning of Shavuot, let's get your family to my place for dinner. Bebe and me will cook, and will make sure there's lots of dairy, finishing with ice cream and more ice cream—we'll stay up all night with the Torah."

Then she was gone and the only sound was the scanner squawking from another room.

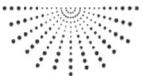

P iper read her notes.

"Mark Thresher, pacemaker, sudden cardiac incident.

"Alfonso Lattimer, pacemaker, sudden cardiac incident.

"Melanie Taylor, no pacemaker, heart failure—daughter said there was some 'very odd spending via her PayPal account to the tune of twelve thousand dollars,' but who'd otherwise left an estate valued at four hundred thousand.

"Bruno Gradicki, who died a year and a half ago of lung cancer at the age of seventy-one and left a comfortable estate."

"Gradicki. His parents owned the skating rink that burned thirty years back," Oren said. "Gradicki Skate and Date."

"Never heard of it."

"Thirty years back. You weren't breathing yet."

"Those four. Those are the deceased genealogy club members." She turned to the list and accompanying margin notes from Mark Thresher's address book. "The other club members—all still breathing." She pushed the list across to Oren.

- Paul Blackwell, longtime sheriff and Democrat
- Sylvia D
- Lamar Odon

- Gary Frank
- Billie Attkinson, named for William Frederick Attkinson who moved to Rockport with his family in 1849, got a good education, and bought 375 acres of farmland
- Megan Cappa
- Emily Johnson
- Kayla Clodfelder
- Stomp Barnett, descendant of William Wesley Barnett who was born in Spencer County in 1842, enlisted in the First Indiana Cavalry, came back to farm, operate a livery in Rockport, and father five children
- Anthony "Breemy" Breem
- Tina Steger, sometimes a Republican
- Janet Collins
- Chuck Schleevogt
- Biggie Hamilton, great-great-great-grandnephew of Bart P. Hamilton, one of eight children who honorably on June 29, 1865, mustered out of the Twenty-eighth Regiment Indiana Volunteer Infantry and went on to father twelve children because apparently they did not have birth control or self-control back then
- John Rasor, descendant of Spencer County Commissioner James Rasor, an exclusive Democrat who only advocated the principles of his party, and whose daughter Mary wed John H. Huffman and produced two offspring
- Steve Kaiser
- Janice Snoddy
- Carolyn Tibbetts
- Bruce Schrock
- Jake Bocce
- Missy Fable
- Paul Mooney, grandson of Ed Mooney who worked in a coalmine
- Sully Sullivan
- Steve R
- D.L. Stebo, prominent Republican and local folklorist

• Mercy Hershey

• Al Bingemer, barbershop quartet member from a very long line of distinguished barbershop quartet singers

"John Rasor," Oren said. "He has a Huffman connection. I want to talk to him, too. Him and Chuck Schleevogt."

"Dad says not all the members show up at every meeting, but hopefully we'll get lucky."

"At least Schleevogt said he'd be there."

Next, she pulled up the list of computer club members Zeke the Geek had provided.

• Ezekiel Whitman, president

• Mike Vola

• Gregg Hommer

• Chris Stiver

• Cassidy Keaton

• Neville Mooney—Piper wondered if he was related to Paul from the other list

• Gerald Roland

• Larry Pinscher

"JJ is at the high school. I gave her this list of names. She's talking to the principal, seeing if any of those kids have been in trouble—or are likely to do some computer hacking. Ezekiel wasn't much into ratting on his friends, but said he didn't believe any of them would do something like that."

Oren rubbed his chin. "School records, they're funny about that. Parents' permission, need warrants for records, all those things. I don't think you're going to learn—"

"I know, but JJ's husband is the athletic director, or still will be for a few more days. She thinks she has an 'in,' and volunteered to exploit that. Maybe get a finger pointed toward who we need to get warrants for. No way will a judge give us warrants on all eight students."

"Maybe JJ'll get lucky. It's often who you know in this world," Oren said. He tapped a name on the old fart's list. "And I hope Chuck Schleevogt there can tell me something about Neal Robert Huffman. Hope he remembers. John Rasor, too, maybe." He shook his head.

"You really think a high school kid swiped money from Thresher? Helluva lot of money."

"And from Lattimer, and maybe used Taylor's PayPal account. Sent me nasty email, spray painted the car. Yeah, I do. The kids in that computer club have access to those people, several of them bring their laptops, maybe share their passwords so the kids can help them with things. Yeah, I think it's one of the kids. Maybe more than one."

"So the question with most any crime is 'why,'" Oren mused. "With the kids, that's an easy one to answer. Money. Money is the 'why.' Always follow the money. Money buys dreams. So you just need the 'who' and the 'how,' Piper. The 'why' is the money. Everybody wants money—more money, and more money."

He'd called her Piper, a first. Always before it was Sheriff or Sheriff Blackwell, proper and impersonal, if he called her anything at all. Were they finally making a connection, over coffee and dead men and sixty-five-year-old bones?

"With the bones," Oren continued, "the 'who' and the 'how' are important. But not so interesting as they 'why.' Why would someone kill a nine-year-old boy—"

"Who was dressed up to play sheriff on Halloween?"

"Yep. I want Chuck Schleevogt and John Rasor to tell me something. Tell me why."

The "tell *me* something" wasn't lost on Piper. She knew Oren considered the bones his case, even though she'd been the one who literally stumbled onto it. If he was right about the identity, it really was his case. She hoped he could close it. She hoped she could find Mark the Shark's thief...and maybe murderer. Maybe it was the same person. That would be a win for her *and* Oren.

"Maybe all the answers will be waiting for us this afternoon at the library," she mused.

"Be nice if it was that easy. I'm driving."

Piper knew it was walking distance, but they'd want an Explorer in the event there was someone to arrest or bring in for questioning, and it had an evidence kit in the back. Besides, she preferred not driving the Bitch-tagged Hyundai.

*Please let me make an arrest for Mark the Shark.*

She lost the next several hours in researching pacemakers, hacking, calling up county obituaries—keying on heart problems—and finally reading through a lengthy email from the bank that said the fraud division detected a number of routing issues from Mark Thresher's account to accounts in other states that initially appeared to belong to relatives of his, but on closer scrutiny were fraudulent accounts.

"It's likely that money is in the Canary Islands," the banker told Piper when she called. "Or someplace where we can't reach. It was a very slick and professional hacking job."

Piper was further disappointed when JJ came back empty from the principal's office. He wouldn't discuss the students, citing privacy.

---

The community room at the Rockport library branch was far from empty, however. Senior citizens and computer club members mingled over genealogy projects. And there hadn't been any metallic gray Celicas—any Celicas—in the parking lot or on the street.

She did a head count—twenty-one genealogy club members out of the twenty-seven on her list; six out of eight computer club members. Naturally, Sylvia D wasn't present, as she had a half-hour left to go on her shift.

Oren filled up the doorway, told her he'd be the gate keeper so no one would leave.

"Good afternoon," Piper said loudly.

Immediately the chatter and key-clicking quieted. "I've a couple of announcements. Services for Mark Thresher will be held at the First Baptist Church at 11 a.m. Thursday, with a luncheon to follow. The private burial will be at Gentryville Memory Gardens."

Scattered conversations swelled.

"He had a good run." This from Gary Frank.

"It was his heart." Carolyn Tibbetts. "He'd been getting slower."

"Still, I figured he'd hit one hundred." Gary Frank.

"Aliens," Al Bingemer said. "He was worried about spies and aliens. Maybe he finally saw one. Gave him a heart attack."

"That's not nice," Carolyn shot back. "Mark the Shark was a good man."

*He was*, Piper thought, *and a very generous one*. She'd be going over to his house tonight—*her* house, taking Marmalade and Camaro home, giving Nang a tour, cooking a frozen pizza in that beautiful stove with six burners.

"Wonder who's getting his money? That nice house?" Piper didn't see who said that.

"No kids," Gary Frank said. "He married late. Not everyone has to have kids, don't you know."

"Maybe the Baptist Church," Carolyn suggested. "He was always putting a twenty in the plate when it was passed."

"Sheriff's got her arm in a sling because Gretchen shot her."

"Did you hear they took a hundred cats out of that house?" Gary Frank. "Who the hell would want even one of those critters? Shred your furniture and—"

"I have four cats." Al Bingemer.

"You can take your cats and—"

A shrill whistle cut through the clamor. Zeke the Geek stood on a chair. "Will you all be civil and let Sheriff Blackwell talk?"

"Thank you." Piper raised her free hand. "I have a few questions, and we'd like to speak with some of you."

"About what?" Stomp Barnett risked disturbing the silence.

"How many of you use online banking?"

Every hand went up except Paul Blackwell's. Piper knew damn well her father used online banking, managed all of his investments with the computer. She also knew he was crazy-curious what she was up to. He sat in front of his notebooks, arms crossed, and eyebrows raised.

"Have any of you noticed money missing from your accounts?"

Three hands stayed up—Al Bingemer, Stomp Barnett, and Janice Snoddy.

"My son told me I'm not managing the account right, not keeping track of my transactions," Stomp said. "I told him I didn't make no damn twelve thousand dollar error. I complained to the bank last week."

Piper wondered if it was the same bank Mark the Shark had used.

"Twenty thousand out of my money market," Janice said. "I'd convinced myself it was just the market slipping. But it didn't slip that much, did it? Something bad's happening."

"I ain't saying how much I'm missing." Al Bingemer scowled and made a fist. "But I got some fraud department on alert about it. I took the rest of my money out and put it in the credit union. And I changed all my passwords. Wrote 'em down in a book." He picked up a small notebook and held it so Piper could see it.

She also saw that five other club members had the same notebook, passwords printed on the cover.

Piper noticed that Oren was scribbling on a pad, probably recording the names and amounts Stomp and Janice said were missing.

"We'd like to speak with a few of you," Piper said. "Anyone who wants to talk to us, actually." She pointed to the only empty table, small and round near the room's entrance, three chairs. "One at a time, so the rest of you can keep working on your genealogy projects. She noted where Chuck Schleevogt was. John Rasor was one of the missing members.

"And—" It was a personal question that she'd not ask to a younger group. But she knew that older people overshared about their various medical maladies and so decided it was fair game. "How many of you have pacemakers?"

Only one hand—Chuck Schleevogt.

Oren tapped his pocket; he had a printout of the model numbers of the hackable pacemakers.

The room filled with conversations again, sounding like locusts had descended. Paul waived Piper over. Zeke the Geek got off the chair.

"What's going on Punkin?"

"On-going investigation," she said.

"Punkin, please don't give me that crap. I'm the Santa Claus Police Chief."

"*Next week* you'll be the Santa Claus Police Chief." She smiled. "Actually, I don't have time to talk about it right now. After this." She waved her free hand to indicate the room. "After I'm done with this I'll tell you about it. Pick your brain so to speak."

She stepped away and headed toward Zeke, noticed that Chuck Schleevogt had gotten up and stood in front of Oren, the pair deep in conversation, Schleevogt raising and lowering his arms and looking like a penguin trying to fly. Piper spotted Zeke the Geek and headed toward him, but a student cut her off.

"Sheriff Blackwell?" The boy wore a t-shirt with a lightning bolt down the middle, sarcasm is my super power printed across it. His name tag read Gregg Hommer.

Piper stopped.

"What did we do, Sheriff?"

"Excuse me?"

"Our club? The computer club. What did we do? Heard at school that your department is investigating all of us, that one of your deputies talked to the principal about us this morning."

"Don't worry about it," Piper returned. But she was suddenly worried. Two students were missing. She shot a look to Oren. He was still engrossed with Schleevogt. Were they absent because JJ's questions had tipped them off? "Don't worry."

She stepped around him and was nearly to Zeke the Geek when another student stopped her. His nametag read Larry Pinscher.

"The deputy at school today—" he prompted. "Does that have something to do about us working with these geezers? Do you think we're—"

"Don't worry," she told him.

Zeke the Geek stepped up to meet her. "We're all kinda concerned, Sheriff Blackwell. The sheriff's deputy at the school this morning and—"

"Yeah, well, I guess that was my mistake. I shouldn't've sent her."

"I didn't say anything to anyone," Zeke said. "I want you to know I kept my mouth shut and—"

Piper waved away the rest of his words. "Cassandra Keaton and Mike Vola." She looked at the student list. "They aren't here. Were they at school today? I'm curious why they're not here."

"Mike's a foreign exchange student from Finland. He got his diploma early, last week, went back home so he could graduate with his class."

"And Cassandra Keaton?"

"Sheriff, she was at school today. But she's not here."

"Obviously."

"She never misses our meetings with the genealogy club. Must've gotten sick or something."

"Or something." Piper frowned. "What do you know about her?"

"Cassidy? A geek. A nerd. Brilliant. She's got a scholarship to Caltech, full ride, I think. But she wouldn't hack anyone. She could. Piece of cake for her. In her sleep. But she wouldn't. She's sweet."

"Sweet, huh?"

"She even helps some of these people at home for a few bucks an hour."

"Probably gave them those password books," Piper mused.

"Oh God." Zeke the Geek looked a little paler. "Oh God. Oh God. Yeah, she did."

"Got Cassidy's home address?"

He shook his head.

Piper called Teegan, who was just coming on. "I need an address, ASAP. And I need a search warrant. Whoever's in the office—" She gave clipped instructions, not caring that Zeke the Geek, Larry Pinscher, Gary Frank, and Stomp Barnett hovered close enough to hear.

Finished, she looked at the quartet. "What kind of car does Cassidy Keaton drive?"

Zeke shook his head, so did Gary Frank.

Stomp stroked his white beard. "An older model silvery-gray thing. Used to belong to Melanie—"

Piper elbowed her way through the group, reached Oren, who was still talking to Schleevogt.

"The hacker is a student named Cassandra Keaton. I'm getting an address and a search warrant."

Oren handed her the keys. "I'll finish here," he said. "Then I'll walk back to the department, get another ride, and meet you. Radio me the address."

Piper rushed out to the parking lot—to discover the Ford had two slashed tires and BITCH scratched into the paint.

"She's sweet, eh?" Piper said. "Shit."

She returned the keys to Oren, cradled her bandaged arm, and jogged to the department.

# 36
## THIRTY-SIX

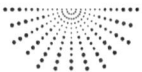

Diego Garcia Velazquez had come on shift and drove.

He was twenty-five, the youngest on the force next to Piper, as Oren's granddaughter didn't start until next week. Diego was half a head taller than the sheriff, and broad-chested from lifting weights. His uniform sleeves always looked tight. He'd taken second place last year in his weight class in the Indiana State Power-lifting Championships, and had gotten a few other deputies to try the sport. Diego had applied for the detective slot, and Piper thought he'd be good in the position—with a few more years' experience. She'd told him that before she brought in Basil and Kevan for interviews.

Piper wanted backup and was glad Diego was available. Dealing with a teenager, parents perhaps, and her with one useful arm—she was brave and headstrong, but not stupid. And Oren would be following soon. This wasn't a situation to step into alone.

The stop at the courthouse was quick, and the warrant granted with lightning speed because Spencer County was small. People knew each other. The seventy-something-year-old judge had been friends with Alfonso Lattimer, an acquaintance of Mark Thresher, golfed twice a month with Chuck Schleevogt—who had a pacemaker—and he didn't like the notion of elderly people being taken advantage of.

The warrant included the search of a Celica in the possession of Cassandra Keaton.

―――――――

"She's ain't home."

Piper guessed the boy was twelve. He stood in the doorway, dressed in blue jeans and a Star Wars t-shirt.

"My folks ain't home either. Working. You ain't coming in."

Diego held up the warrant.

Piper paused. The warrant, signed by the judge, let her enter the house—no matter who was or wasn't there. She hated to do this without an adult present, but she didn't want to wait. Finding Cassidy Keaton was urgent, and the girl's computer might be key to that.

"We are coming in," Piper said, squeezing by him and stepping into the living room. "Where is Cassidy? Do you know where she went?"

The boy shrugged. "I'm calling Dad."

"You do that. Please call him, ask him to come home." Piper was in too much of a hurry to be pleasant. "I'd like to talk to both of your parents." Maybe they knew where Cassidy was. "Point me to your sister's room."

"You can't mess with her stuff."

"The warrant is for her computers and all of her other electronic devices. I won't 'mess' with anything else."

He shook his head, crossed his arms, and stuck out his lower lip. She revised her estimate downward. Maybe he was ten, or nine, same age as the boy on the bluff had been.

"We'll find her room, then," she said. "And go call your dad." Piper barely registered the place, other than to note everything looked nice, clean, upper middle class, big flat screen television, thick carpet. She took the stairs. The girl's bedroom would be upstairs. Diego followed. Below, she heard the boy on the telephone, talking loud and angry.

First door on the right was the master bedroom; she passed it by. First door on the left had a sign on it. Tim's Domain: Keep Out. That must be Tim she'd met downstairs. She passed it. The next door was a bathroom, and across from it the door was closed. She knocked, thinking perhaps the girl was home after all and her brother had lied. No answer, so she swung it open.

Single bed, desk, lounge chair, everything flowery and pink. BLOSSOM in block craft letters on the wall. No sign of a computer.

Diego went to the closet and did a cursory look. "No computer." After a moment, he added, "No designer clothes or shoes. I got a sister, and she gets stuff like this at the Owensboro mall. If she has a lot of money, she's not spending it on clothes."

Piper opened the desk drawers, looking for a laptop or tablet. The search warrant was precise—computers and electronic devices. But there was nothing to stop them from eyeballing the place for obvious signs of excessive spending. No laptop, no iPad, no cell phone.

Diego looked under the bed. "Magazines. Computer magazines. Bedroom slippers."

"Nothing in the desk. Shit." *And two is four.* Piper was about to race back downstairs and find the boy. She didn't want to take the chance he might do something with a laptop or—

The boy stood in the doorway, cell phone held to his face. "Dad says he's coming home and you're in really big trouble. Dad says—"

"Where does your sister keep her computer? Laptop? Desktop?"

"She doesn't have any." Again he stuck out his lower lip. "Okay, Dad. Hurry up." He put the phone in his front pocket.

"Should I arrest him, Sheriff, for obstruction?" Diego gave the boy a serious look and touched his handcuffs.

"Downstairs, the basement. Her computer's too big to fit in her room." The boy backed into the hall, allowing Piper and Diego to pass. "Dad says you're in really, really, really big trouble. He's calling our attorney."

"Thanks, Tim," Piper said.

The basement stairs were off the kitchen. Piper took them two at a time, bumping her bandaged arm against the wall and biting her lip to keep from cursing. She flicked on the light at the bottom.

"Oh."

"Oh my," Diego said.

Against the opposite wall were two six-foot tables. Three desktop systems spread across them, and four large monitors hung from the wall behind. To Piper, it looked like a command center for a covert operation.

"Is this your sister's? Cassidy's?" Piper asked when she heard the boy tromp down the stairs a few beats behind them. "This isn't your dad's?" Her warrant covered the girl's computers. She mentally kicked herself, should have asked for *all* the computers in the residence.

"Dad's computer is in his office upstairs. He's got a laptop. Mom uses the laptop, too. This is all Cassidy's."

"How'd she afford this?" Diego was in obvious awe of the setup.

"She tutors geezers by the hour about computers and the Internet. She bought this with her tutoring money."

"I have a laptop," Piper said softly to Diego. "Never had a desktop. But I'm thinking this is expensive. Way the hell beyond an hourly tutor wage."

The basement was finished, but not fancy. Painted drywall, a drop ceiling, Berber carpet. At the far end was a treadmill, and next to that a weight bench. Another long table with shelves above it was set up for scrapbooking.

The warrant was specific. Piper took her cell phone out and started taking pictures of the computers. "You said this was all your sister's right?"

"You deaf?" the boy taunted.

"Why would you need more than one computer?"

"She likes computers," the boy answered. "She's gonna go to college for computers."

"It's a Genesis," Diego said, adding a low whistle. "This unit is." He turned the tower and started examining it. "Liquid cooling. ATX inverted mount. See the liquid cooling blocks? Steel frame chassis, vents at the front, top, bottom. It would have a spectacular LED display, probably has multiple graphics cards. Top mounted USB, microphone, headphone, easy to get at. I'm a gamer, Sheriff, and I couldn't afford this system. But I sure would love one."

"How much?"

"This Genesis?" He thumbed it on. "Password protected. Can't get into it easy."

"Figures."

"I'd say the Genesis ran her about six grand. Maybe more."

It was Piper's turn to whistle.

"The one in the middle. It doesn't look as fancy." She moved the mouse and a screen came on. "This one's on, was in sleep mode. Don't have to worry about a password." She sat in the chair. "Comfortable."

"Probably costs just as much." Diego stood behind her and pointed.

The computer's tower was a simple black box about nine inches wide, twenty-two inches high, and not quite that deep. It had a metal mesh front lit panel with neon blue lights, making it look eerie.

"You're the computer guru." Piper got up and gestured to Diego, who pulled three jump drives out of his pocket. They'd download information as a precaution, and then take the towers with them.

"I'll get the specifics first," he said. "I can get detailed part information if I run an application designed to do that. It might already have one installed, or we could potentially install one. I want to know the computer before I dig through it. I'd say she built this herself or had someone build it for her."

"She built it," the boy said. He'd crept up silently. "She bought the parts with her tutoring money and built it. She said she'd build me one for my birthday."

"Has a thousand watt power supply driving the processor." He rattled on about gigahertz and gigabytes. "Dual graphics cards, looks like a pair of GTX 1080 bridged together, solid state drives, Samsung Evos, those are some of the fastest. Check out the liquid cooling system on this one, too! And those fans are going and not even making a whisper. Looks like she got it hooked into all four of those big monitors at once! This baby would easily rock ArcheAge, Final Fantasy, EVE Online—"

"What?"

"Look, she's also got a virtual reality headset. And this little device, it's a programmable radio transmitter. No idea what she'd use that for. Here's full-surround sound system. And this chair. Your perp is one serious gamer. The chair is a Herman Miller Aeron. Expensive. This chair is over a grand. The self-built computer? She's probably got four or five grand in it. But this one?"

Diego rolled over to the third system.

"I didn't know computers were your specialty," Piper said, noticing there was also a police scanner wedged between the systems. "It's not in your file, the computers."

"I'm a gamer," he cut back. "Gamers don't list gaming on their resumes. I picked up weight-lifting to counteract the time I spend on my butt in front of a monitor. Yeah, I know some stuff about computers." He let out another whistle.

"That's my sister's favorite," the boy offered. "She got that one last month." He was not as defiant as when they'd first arrived. "I hear my dad upstairs."

"Would you please go get him?" Piper asked.

She heard him pound up the stairs hollering "Daaaaaaaaaaaaaad!"

"This is a Digital Storm, for someone with an unlimited budget. With all the options—and I'm guessing it has *all* of them. I can't log in, password protected. If it has all the options it'll run you between eleven and twelve thousand. It's a gaming system, but she might have other stuff on it. You can use it like a regular system." Softer, "But why would you want to?"

He pointed to the four monitors set up behind the systems. "Twenty-seven inch monitors like these, and this one a thirty-six, probably a grand each, maybe more depending."

"Go back to the one we got into." Piper paced behind him, heard an argument going on upstairs. "We're looking for things that tie her to members of the genealogy club, Mark Thresher, PayPal, eBay, see if she banks online, anything recent that might point to her location, though it is more likely her dad can supply that, and—"

Diego rolled to the middle computer and groaned as his fingers flew across the ergonomic keyboard. "The data files are wiped. It's there, I mean. Deleting stuff isn't getting rid of it, but eventually it'll become unrecoverable. The more recently they were deleted, the more likely it is that they can be recovered. A computer-smart person can make sure they can't be recovered by scrubbing it with random data, but that takes a little bit of time, and she was probably in too much of a hurry for that. It's gonna take work to revive the information. We'll need to take this to the office. And I've got skills, but probably not enough to—"

"What the hell do you think you're doing?"

# THIRTY-SEVEN

"What the bloody—"

"Mr. Keaton," Piper said. She gave him an abbreviated version of events, and her belief that his daughter, Cassandra Cassidy Blossom Keaton, had been stealing money from senior citizens. She left out the possible murder charges and damage to the department cars; she'd talk about all of that when Cassidy was in custody.

Andrew Keaton was pale. "I don't know where Cassidy is. I have to call my wife."

"I need to find Cassidy," Piper emphasized. "I need to find her *right now*." Because she was certain the girl was fleeing, tipped off at the high school by JJ's inquiries, and when she noticed the sheriff's vehicle in the library parking lot. Cassidy'd had enough time, either before or after flattening Oren's tires, to wipe data files on one computer, abscond with her laptop—because she most certainly had at least one laptop—and take to the road. A girl with that much money, and that sharp—she had the means to get out of the county. Maybe out of the country.

"Does Cassidy have a passport?"

He nodded.

"Does Cassidy have a car?" *Obviously*, Piper thought. *Stupid question.*

"A beater Celica. One of the women she tutored gave it to her."

Maybe, Piper thought. Or maybe she stole it after Melanie Taylor died.

"Please look for Cassidy's passport." Piper's warrant didn't include that. "Tell me if it's missing. And tell me where you think Cassidy might be."

"I don't know where she is. School? With the computer club maybe. These computers." Keaton stood rooted, watching Diego disconnect the towers. "I knew they were expensive, her computers. She told me those old people gave her a lot of money, for all the tutoring work."

"Mr. Keaton, they didn't *give* her this much money."

"Stole? My little girl stole?"

*Finally it's sinking in.*

"Stole. Sweet Jesus."

"Mr. Keaton? Where might Cassidy go?"

He blinked. "Wait! I have an app on my laptop. I can track Cassidy's and Tim's cell phones. Never told them about it. I trust them. I just, you know, a parent wants to know where their kids are. I don't use it. But I have it. I *can* use it. Should have put it on my phone. That'd be easier. But it's on my laptop and—"

Piper nudged him toward the stairs.

Diego had picked up the Genesis, cradled it against his chest. "I'll have to take these out one at a time." He walked around Keaton and started up.

"That app, Mr. Keaton. Will you help me? Help your daughter? We need to find her."

He nodded. "Sure. Yes. Oh sweet Jesus. I should've been paying more attention." He staggered like an extra in *The Walking Dead* climbing the stairs. He took Piper to his office and pulled up his laptop. He opened it and turned it on, called his wife with an earbud phone he put in. "I can't tell her everything," he said to Piper. "Not on the phone. She'll be hysterical, might have an accident and— Sweet

Jesus." He clicked some keys and a map appeared. He clicked some more keys, typing in a number.

Piper memorized the number, probably Cassidy's cell phone.

A blip appeared, moving.

"Oh sweet Jesus," he repeated.

Piper noticed a picture on his desk—Cassidy and Tim in front of a flocked white Christmas tree. More pictures of the kids and Mr. and Mrs. Keaton hung around the office. Everyone seemed happy.

"She's on sixty-six, near Hatfield. Should I call her?" He reached up to tap his earbud.

"Please don't, Mr. Keaton. I don't want her panicked. Bad things happen when people get panicked." Not that Cassidy already wasn't.

"All right." Keaton forced back a sob. "So what should I do? What do you want me to do?"

Piper thought fast. "Check her closet. See if she packed a suitcase, if stuff is missing. That passport, see if—"

He opened a desk drawer. "I keep all the passports here, and—" He retrieved a small leather folio, opened it, and spilled the contents on his desk. Three passports. "Oh sweet Jesus."

"We need to move, Mr. Keaton. Check the closet. See if she—"

"All right." He pushed away from the desk, nearly knocking her over. "Tim! Tim, come here." She heard Keaton and his son bounding up the steps, and when she went out into the hall she watched Diego taking another tower out.

"Oren's here!" he announced.

Piper hurried to the staircase.

The Keatons thundered down.

"Her backpack is gone, Sheriff, laptop, duffle. Some clothes. Her closet was stuffed with them, and there's room now. A lot of things are missing. Oh sweet Jesus, Mary, and Joseph. What can I—"

"Is your wife on her way?"

"Yes. But she works in Owensboro. It will take her—"

"Diego!"

"Yes, Sheriff Blackwell." He hurried back in. She noticed he wasn't sweating; carrying the heavy computer pieces was easy for him.

"Stay here with Tim Keaton. Mrs. Keaton will be here in twenty, thirty minutes. Don't alarm her, and don't tell her too much." She spun to Keaton. "Mr. Keaton, Oren and I are going to find Cassidy. I'm going to ask you to join us. Bring your laptop. Lead us to your daughter." She reached up and took the bud out of his ear. "And no phone calls. To anyone." She added, "Please." Then she put the earbud in his pocket. "Let's move! And pray she doesn't toss her cell phone."

Piper settled in the back seat next to Keaton so she could watch him and the laptop. The screen was difficult to read because potholes on the street made for a bumpy ride. He tethered the laptop to a hotspot from his phone.

Oren had commandeered JJ's Explorer. "Your kid did a helluva number on mine," he grumbled. "Punctured tires, bleach in the gas tank for good measure. One of the patrons saw her pour bleach in the tank, yelled, and she took off. Jumped into that Celica you've been obsessing over, Sheriff, and squealed away from the library. Someone had called the Rockport Police Department, and they got there as I was heading down the sidewalk. They gave me a ride to the department. I was in too damn much of a hurry to hoof it the whole way." Softer, "And too damn old."

"My Cassidy?" Keaton asked. "My Cassidy did that. Bleach? Tires? Sweet Jesus. She's a good girl, Sheriff. This can't be happening."

"Just tell us where she is, Mr. Keaton."

He turned the screen so Piper could watch better and asked a variety of questions, which Piper declined to answer.

Piper had a lot of questions tumbling in her head, too, about Cassidy's friends, spending habits, social life or lack of it, drugs, alcohol. All those questions would wait until after they had her. Get the girl first, then get all the answers. Find out if she acted alone.

The burning one was why steal from elderly people who trusted her? What sort of a girl could do that? Evil enough to hack pacemakers? She'd probably killed Mark because he was pushing the money issue, had contacted Piper and the bank, was making a little noise about it. Maybe Lattimer had, too. Killed them to shut them up. Bled them dry financially. Even with all the precautions Mark Thresher had taken, the secrecy, the night meeting in the park, the ADT system at his house, the six-foot chain link fence with barbed wire on top it. Small county. People knew things, especially a computer-savvy one like Cassidy—who probably had access to all Mark's passwords. He'd had one of those little books like she'd given to others in the genealogy club. She probably knew all his passwords.

"She's on six six two now," Piper told Oren. "Probably headed to Evansville."

"Catch up to her," Mr. Keaton urged. "Just don't hurt my baby girl. Whatever she's done. My fault. I didn't pay enough attention. My—"

"Not your fault," Piper corrected. "We'll catch her."

"It's that beater," Keaton breathed. "It chugs. Thank God it's on its last wheels. We'll catch her. She can't get far, not fast. She was going to wait until she got to California. She's going to Caltech."

*Was going to Caltech. Now she's going to prison for a very long time.*

"Wait and get a new car out there, something that meets California emissions. Cassidy is very ecologically minded. And she won't toss her cell phone. Kids—they're attached to cell phones. That's a six hundred dollar phone she has. Bad for the environment to toss electronics."

"Bought with tutoring money?" Piper regretted the question.

Keaton nodded. "Yeah."

Piper listened to him nervously chatter and continue asking questions she ignored. The passport thing bothered her. The girl was probably going to leave the country. She remembered the bank mentioning that the stolen money had likely been funneled to the Canary Islands or somewhere else safe. The girl was probably going there. How much had she amassed? How long had she been pilfering from the county's senior citizens?

"How long has she been tutoring, Mr. Keaton? How many people has she been working with?"

"Oh, various groups, down into Owensboro, too, at the big senior center there where my wife works as activity director. Cassidy's been going with her mom on Saturdays ever since her freshman year. Four years."

*Sweet Jesus*, Piper thought.

"So if her beater car won't get her far, she'll either pick up another one if she's got enough cash on her. Maybe in Evansville or Henderson. But Evansville has an airport."

"Jesus, Mary, and Joseph." Keaton's knuckles were white where his hands gripped the laptop.

Oren radioed Teegan to contact the Evansville Regional Airport, Vanderburgh County Sheriff, Evansville police. Piper gave a description of Cassidy, which Keaton improved on.

"I'm guessing airport because of the passport. If she gets to the airport before us," Piper said, "they'll stop her, Mr. Keaton. It will be all right." If she was headed to the Evansville airport it would only be to get a flight to a larger city where she could get something international. They needed to reach her before she got on a plane.

"She won't get to the airport first," Keaton said numbly. "We'll catch up. That old Celica. It really is a beater. I bet it doesn't go over sixty-five. Wait! She's stopped."

Piper leaned over. "Newburgh. Right on the river. Oren?"

"We're five minutes out from Newburgh, and I'm going seventy-five. You said no lights and siren."

"Why would she go to Newburgh?" Keaton mumbled. "Nothing's in Newburgh. She doesn't know anybody in Newburgh. Newburgh's a nothing burg."

"The river's there," Oren put in. "Right up against that itty bitty city is the big river."

Maybe Cassidy Keaton was going to take a boat.

# THIRTY-EIGHT

It had taken about fifteen minutes from Keaton's driveway to the edge of Newburgh, a town of about three thousand just east of Evansville. It was in Warrick County, and so Piper called their sheriff to let them know what she was doing; he'd already been on alert for the girl.

Piper had been here a few times when she was in high school, once doing research for a history paper on the Newburgh Raid. In the eighteen hundreds it was one of the largest river ports between Cincinnati and New Orleans, and had been the first town north of the Mason-Dixon Line that Confederate forces captured during the Civil War. Re-enactors gathered yearly to do battle.

It was a pretty place, with a charming downtown filled with specialty boutiques and antique shops. There were good restaurants along the riverfront. It was a place to live if you worked in Evansville and desired a slower pace when you came home.

And apparently it was where Cassidy Keaton intended to hop on a boat.

*But why not Evansville? The big city had better river traffic. Better chance to book a boat.*

"Why come here?" Oren mirrored Piper's thoughts. "Newburgh? What the hell?"

"She's at the Old Lock and Dam," Keaton said. "I don't understand why she'd—"

"Oren?"

"Almost there, Sheriff."

"Keep the siren off." She heard Oren growl, like she hadn't needed to tell him that.

In the distance they saw the Celica, trunk popped, driver's side door open, car empty, at the parking lot. The old Newburgh Lock and Dam was a recreation area now, complete with cement boat ramp that Cassidy Keaton was standing on.

Except she wasn't getting into a boat.

The sign nearby said JERRY W. HUMPHREY SEAPLANE BASE.

A single-engine white and blue floatplane, *Ohio Angel* on the side, had come in low and pulled up, the prop still turning. Cassidy tossed in a duffle and a backpack, and jumped in just as Piper and Oren got out of the Ford. Piper ran.

They'd told Keaton to stay in the car, but of course that didn't happen.

"Cassidy! Cass!" he hollered as he and Oren raced after Piper. "Casssssssssssssss!"

Piper hadn't expected a floatplane. But neither had she expected that a teenager was capable of killing two elderly men just for money. In a heartbeat she'd left Oren and Keaton behind, good arm swinging, feet pounding across the parking lot, over a strip of grass, and then onto the cement landing.

Cassidy had closed the door and was yelling something to the pilot. Piper couldn't make it all out, except for the, "Go, go, go!"

The plane moved away from the ramp, and Piper sprinted down the cement, feet touching the edge of the river as her leg muscles bunched. She leaped with every measure of her strength, right arm out and fingers grabbing a strut and Nikes landing hard against the pontoon. Slippery, she almost fell.

The plane rocked from the sudden impact, and she ducked under the single wing and grabbed the strut closer to the pilot's door. Looking in she saw it had four seats, but only two were occupied— Cassidy in the back, and the pilot in the front, big duffle on the seat next to him.

The spray soaked Piper and made gripping the strut difficult, and she knew she had made the plane unsteady, maybe was keeping it from taking off.

"Stop!" Piper hollered. She figured the pilot would be suicidal to take off with her hanging on the side, plane off balance. If she dropped into the water and managed to hang on, he'd have drag on top of that. But she didn't want to test that notion. "Stop you sono-fabitch!"

The pilot didn't. The propeller turned faster, the engine sounded louder, and the plane picked up speed, bouncing harder on the river's chop.

*Macho pilot*, Piper thought, gritting her teeth. *Suicidal, macho pilot.* Maybe he'd been promised a lot of money. Maybe he was good enough—or stupid enough—to lift off with someone hanging on the outside.

Maybe the pilot couldn't hear her; he had a headset on. But he had to have noticed her hitching a ride, unbalancing his attempt to take off. Perhaps Cassidy was promising him even more money.

It's always about money.

Oren was shouting on the ramp, Keaton screaming, "Cassssssssssssss!"

Piper steadied herself and leaned against the plane, released the strut and fumbled with her right hand on the fastening of her sling, yanked the tie lose and nearly fell in the river in the process. She recovered and grabbed the strut again. She praised the Army for putting her through rigorous training exercises. But this hadn't been something Fort Campbell had covered.

The plane picked up more speed, bounced harder, and angled toward the center of the river. That was the Jerry W. Humphrey Seaplane Base's runway—the Ohio River.

"Stop! Spencer County Sheriff! Stop!"

The pilot glanced at her, and then looked forward.

"Shit." She tugged at the sling again, finally wholly freeing her left arm. She had two hands now. Her left arm felt like she'd dipped it in fire. One to two weeks she was supposed to use the sling. Hell with that. Grabbing the strut once more with her right hand, she reached her left to the pilot's door, turned the handle, and flung it open. He'd tried to grab it, maybe hold it closed or lock it, but she was strong and fast and fueled by anger.

"Shut the damn thing off!" she howled. "Shut it down now!"

"Noooooooooooooooooo!" Cassidy keened. "I'll pay you more. Keep going!" The girl looked just like she had the day Piper met her in the library, cherubic face—no longer looking innocent—pierced eyebrow, wearing the same t-shirt, Music + Cats Make Life Worth Living.

"Shut it down!" Piper screamed. Her voice was going. Even if the pilot couldn't hear her—with his headset and the plane's engine, he could damn well get the intent. "Shut. It. Down."

It bounced a few more times, Cassidy continued to yell, and the pilot cursed and turned off the engine. He removed the headset. Cassidy opened the passenger door and flung her backpack into the river.

"Great. Your laptop, I'm guessing," Piper said. "Cassandra Keaton, you're under arrest for a shitload of things." To the pilot, "You're under arrest, too. For something. I'll figure it out."

Somehow Oren had commandeered a boat. Minutes later everyone was back on the shore, where cars from the Newburgh Police Department and the Vanderburgh County Sheriff's Department were arriving, lights flashing.

"They can have the pilot," Piper told Oren. "Sheriff, police. I don't care who takes him. Miss Cassandra Cassidy Blossom Keaton is ours."

On the ride back to Rockport, the Keatons shared the backseat.

Cassidy fumed and wiggled. "Handcuffs, really?"

"Protocol," Piper said. "You're a thief." She was about to add *and a murderer*, but stopped herself. They'd cover all of that when the girl was formally charged at the jail.

"It's not like those old farts needed the money," Cassidy spat. "All that money just sitting in their accounts. They were so stupid about computers. It was so easy to take their—"

"Don't say anything else, Cass," Keaton cautioned. "Nothing. Don't say another word until I call an attorney." He reached into his pocket, retrieved his earbud, and started making calls.

Piper was glad the girl was taking the advice. She wanted the miles to pass in as much silence as possible. It felt like the Mailbox Mauler had shot her all over again.

# THIRTY-NINE

## WEDNESDAY, MAY 9TH

Ezekiel missed his morning classes, on the okay of the principal and at Piper's request. The State Police had computer experts, but wouldn't send one until Thursday or Friday, and Piper didn't want to wait.

It took him almost to the lunch hour, but he was able to recover Cassidy's wiped files.

"Not easy," he told her. "A real challenge. I got websites, IP addresses. She had encryption software, but I had the right decryption protocols. I could tell she'd set up a proxy, pretending to be in Brazil rather than Rockport. She was slick. But really, she could have done a better job. I'm thinking she didn't expect anyone to go looking for her. A little county like this? I'm betting she thought she was invincible."

He found details on how much money she'd taken from each individual on Excel sheets—names, dates, amounts. Going back four years. If the records were accurate, she'd amassed a little more than nine million dollars, stashed in an account in the Cayman Islands. No taxes on income, capital gains, profits, or estates there, and secrecy laws were touted as being among the strictest in the world. But an expert with the State Police said there was a good chance the money was recoverable. They'd bargain with the murder charges if necessary so Piper could get the funds back to Cassidy's victims.

Ezekiel also found hacking software and several links to Dark Web sites. Evidence of the pacemaker hacks was among his discoveries. The transmitter they'd found in the Keaton basement had been key. That plus her software, and Ezekiel said she had the skills and tools to do it.

"She could hack right into his pacemaker. Get within twenty, thirty feet, probably stand right outside his house and do it. I just can't imagine, you know—I thought she was kinda sweet." Ezekiel's face drew forward like it was pinched. "But she wasn't sweet, she was a monster."

Cassidy Keaton was a monster who was going to prison for a very long time, Piper mused. She was eighteen, would automatically be tried as an adult—even though some of her crimes stretched back to her freshman year. But the murders hadn't. DA Scales said it looked like she'd hand over all the money in exchange for him taking the death penalty out of the equation. First degree murder, no death penalty, she'd be looking at forty-five to sixty-five years, eligible for parole after serving half of it. If the jury was generous and instead gave her life, she'd be eligible for parole after twenty.

"I'm taking Zeke to lunch," Piper announced. She poked her head in Oren's office. "Want to join us?"

He shook his head and pointed to a paper bag on his desk. "I'm following some Huffman leads," he said. "I'm going out to talk to John Rasor at two."

"He's the Huffman shirttail?"

"Yeah. I'm hoping he can give me more than Schleevogt did. He said he has some old photo albums to share."

Piper thought that sounded like nothing more than Oren had already gotten from his other sources.

"Mind giving me a lift home on your way to Rasor's?" They'd discovered that Rasor lived in Rockport and had missed yesterday's meeting because of a doctor's appointment. "I'm going to call it an early day, and take the spray painted Hyundai to the dealer." Her arm was in a sling again—for a prescribed additional two weeks, courtesy of a stop at a Rockport clinic.

"Sure."

"You can use my Ford, which they said is ready." Oren's was being repaired, the scratches, new tires, new fuel filter and lines, the gas tank removed and cleaned, the latter being the least expensive fix. "I'm going to use my 'suggestion of a car' tomorrow. Easier to drive."

---

P iper owned an apple red Smart Fortwo, a "suggestion of a car" her dad called it. It was a three-cylinder turbo-charged five-speed manual with an oatmeal hued interior, and it registered every dip and rocky patch in the road. It was not the smoothest of rides, but it averaged thirty-five miles a gallon and was effortless to steer one-handed. She loaded its tiny trunk with an overnight bag, Mark Thresher's laptop, and a frozen pizza she pulled out of her fridge. She called Nang and invited him to dinner at her house in Hatfield.

She put Marmalade in a cat carrier on the passenger side floorboard, coaxed Camaro onto the seat—apparently the dog loved car rides—and left a message for her father.

*Dad, I inherited a house, Mark Thresher's in Hatfield. I'm going to spend the night there. See if it fits me. I'll have my cell on. Hugs, Piper*

She had no trouble nesting her little car in the extra-deep garage, right in front of Thresher's vintage Chevy. She probably could have put a pair of Smart Fortwos there.

Piper let Nang see the garage first, used her cell phone to take a picture of his astonished expression.

"The Chevy's a 1935 three-window coup that Mark restored. The other," she'd looked it up on the Internet, "is a 1922 Franklin convertible. The wheels are hanging at the back of the garage." She'd been wrong about two vintage motorcycles. She'd only seen two looking in through the windows. There were four, and Nang visited a few websites on his phone to help identify them.

1953 Ariel Square 4

1951 Vincent Comet in showroom mint shape

1915 Indian 8-valve boardracer, that Nang estimated was worth more than eighty thousand

1928 Coventry Eagle

Piper felt like she might pass out.

"I can't keep all this," she said, waving her good arm. "*These*. I can't keep these, the cars, the motorcycles. And the house. Good God what was Mr. Thresher thinking? It wouldn't be right. All of this and I'd only known him a few days before he changed his will."

"Maybe his relatives—" Nang started to suggest.

"He didn't have any. He'd told me that, his attorney told me that. Last of the Threshers."

"Why would you refuse his gift? Why would you disrespect that?"

Piper stared at him, a thousand thoughts spinning.

"I need to think," she said.

"Think about this. You honored him by finding the thief, stopping that girl from stealing even more money. Discovered his murderer. How can you refuse his gift?" Nang appeared to study her. "I like country music. There is a song by Billy Currington about an old man who leaves his fortune to someone he meets in a bar."

"I know the song. I didn't meet Mr. Thresher in a bar. I met him on a park bench."

"Maybe someone will write a new country song."

---

Nang was impressed with the stove. He left the pizza in the freezer and used ingredients he found in the refrigerator and cabinets to make what he announced as Steak Asada, complete with fajita vegetables, pepian sauce, pico de gallo, black beans, and rice. It seemed that Mark Thresher had kept a lot of makings for Mexican meals. He'd also had a big stock of high-end dog and cat food.

While Nang cooked, she took a call from her flabbergasted father, who seemed a mix of happy and distressed. Next came a call from Basil Meredith. He said he'd take the job, that he'd start in two weeks, and that they'd return over the weekend and look at houses—particularly that brick one in Santa Claus.

*Maybe he won't be bored here after all,* she thought, reflecting on the activities of the past nine days.

A fter dinner they explored the basement. Clearly Diego hadn't come down here or he would have told her about the contents.

It was a half-finished basement, that part being a library. Hundreds of leather-bound books filled impressive oak cabinets, which she suspected were specially-made for the house. They were a mix of mysteries, horror novels, and biographies. Most were military books. She scanned some titles—*Brassey's Dictionary of Battles; Fighter Pilots of World War I; Legend, Memory, and the Great Air War; To Fly and Fight.* A section was devoted to various conspiracy works—*Unholy Trinity: the Vatican, the Nazis, and Soviet Intelligence; Puzzle Palace—National Security Agency; The Quiet Campaign to Rewrite the Constitution; Legend: the Secret of Lee Harvey Oswald; High Treason: the Assassination of President John F. Kennedy.* Piper smiled sadly. She didn't doubt that there weren't conspiracies in the world, but she didn't want to dive in. She would read some of the books, the mysteries especially—he seemed to have the entire Michael Connelly collection—but the conspiracy volumes...those she'd eventually hand over to the library.

There was a desk—a massive roll-top with a comfortable chair. Piper sat at it and opened the top while Nang continued to peruse the books. It looked like Mark had kept all of his genealogy notes here, paper copies of what she'd seen on his laptop. A note at the end of his family tree read, "Last of the Threshers." There was another printed copy of the genealogy club members, but it was older, stated 2014 Membership Roster at the top.

She stared at one of the names and pulled out her cell phone.

"Oren, sorry to bother you, but I found something. Remember the genealogy club members? Oh, nothing helpful from Rasor? Too bad. But this is interesting, what I found. That Gary Frank? I have a roster from some years' back that lists his name as Gary Frank Huffman."

"And two is four," Oren said. "Virginia Huffman, in Evansville. She loaned me photo albums. Wait a minute." Piper heard Oren set the phone down, heard pages rustling. "There's a photo she pointed to. Neal, Gary, Sandy, and Julian. The Huffmans, she said."

"Gary. Gotta be Gary Frank," Piper returned. "County's too small for it to be otherwise."

"I'll go out in the morning."

"I have an address." It was right there on the 2014 directory. "I'll go with you."

---

Marmalade was curled on the easy chair in the den. Camaro stretched out on a section of coach, his head on Nang's lap.

"I'm going to stay tonight," Piper said. "See what the house feels like."

"And?"

"And if it feels okay I'll take Mr. Thresher's thoughtful gift. The house, contents, garage. I will respect his wishes."

"And—" Nang let the word hang. "I would like to see how the couch feels tonight. I'd rather not leave you alone. I'd like to make sure you don't do anything that'll keep you in that sling for a lot more than two weeks."

She smiled at that. Maybe it would be all right to get attached to the quick stop owner. Maybe she was staying in Spencer County.

40

# FORTY

## THURSDAY, MAY 10TH

Piper used her good arm to carry the box of items recovered from the bluff. She thought showing them to Gary Frank Huffman might jog his memory about Neal Robert.

"If the bones really are Neal Robert's," Piper said.

"They are," Oren returned. "I can feel it."

He drove.

Gary Frank lived in a small Craftsman-style bungalow that likely dated to the thirties. It was in Evanston, an unincorporated village, fittingly in Huff Township. He was sitting on the porch, and after a little prodding invited them inside.

Piper sat back and watched. It really was Oren's case. She put the box on the floor and lifted the lid.

"We think the bones on the bluff belong to your brother, Neal Robert, who folks thought drowned sixty-five years ago," Oren said. "We'd like to prove that, and give him a proper burial."

"The raft," Gary Frank said. "Killian's raft. Or maybe it had been Martin's. One of them boys built the raft that sent them all into the river."

"It was a raft built for one," Oren said. "Not made for something like the Ohio."

Piper thought both men looked sad.

"Probably broke apart," Oren continued, "because two boys were on it. I've someone who said he saw two boys on the raft, Neal Robert was not one of them."

A black cat with a smattering of white on its head and front legs crept into the room and rubbed its head against Gary Frank's calves.

Piper pointed to the box.

"We found these things on the bluff, around the bones." She tipped the box so Gary Frank could better see them, then she rattled off the contents. "Cap gun, sheriff's badge, marbles, buttons, pieces of a belt, rivets from blue jeans, a buckle."

"Any idea why your brother would have an Arizona newspaper boy belt buckle?" Oren asked.

Gary Frank stared at the box. "We had a cousin. Him and his dad came through here at the end of that summer. Neal Robert took a shine to the buckle and Andy gave it to him. They traded buckles. That's why he had that newspaper boy buckle. Neal Robert was a newspaper boy, too. But you didn't get a belt buckle for delivering papers in Spencer County."

Oren shot Piper a look. It was the confirmation on who the bones had belonged to.

"What about the barbed wire?" Piper had wondered about that. It hadn't fit with the "playing sheriff" notion. "Do you know what that was about?"

Gary Frank sat back on his couch and closed his eyes. His expression clouded over with memory. "Neal Robert was dressed up as a sheriff that Halloween," he said. "I remember. He'd taken a twist of barbed wire and curled it around a boot, hooked a bottle cap to it and called it a spur, scratched the boot up. They were new boots. And they were too big for him."

"We didn't find boots, any evidence of shoes." That had bothered her.

"They weren't *his* boots. They were *my* boots. He shouldn't have taken them for his costume. He'd shoved newspaper in the toes because they were too big for him."

Oren's eyes grew dark and he mouthed something. He looked at Piper and then back at the old man.

Gary Frank opened his eyes.

"Is that why you killed him, Mr. Huffman?" Oren's voice was even. "Because he'd scratched your boots? Taken them?"

"Yep." Gary Frank started to cry. "Hadn't meant to. I was bigger than him, fourteen, had five years on him. Was a lot stronger. I grabbed his neck and squeezed. I was so angry. My folks gave me those boots for my birthday. Cowboy boots. Our family didn't have a whole lot of money. It was a significant present, and he'd treated them poorly. Did not respect me."

He reached down and scratched the cat. "I squeezed too hard. He kicked me, and I was so angry. And then he stopped kicking, his head lopped to one side. I realized what I'd done, and that if I told Ma she'd say I was going to Hell for it. I hid his body in the bushes. And I took my boots back."

The cat moved along to Oren's ankles.

"I didn't know what to do, and then everybody was hollering about Killian's raft breaking up. I told people Neal Robert had been on that raft with them, all the boys playing Abraham Lincoln. Everyone believed me."

"You buried him," Oren pressed.

"Yep. I went back that night with a shovel, after my family slept. Snuck out all quiet. We didn't live far from the bluff back then. I dug a hole. Thought I'd dug it so small and deep that no one ever would find him. Deep. Deep. Deep. My arms and fingers felt like they were going to fall off. I remember that, too, my aching fingers. I crammed him into the hole and covered him up. Picked a spot that didn't have no grass on it. Lots of places in the park that fall was missing grass. I stomped it down, and then I got all clever and dug at other places. Didn't want no one seeing the one spot I'd messed with. The rain helped. No one'd found Neal Robert."

"For sixty-five years," Piper said.

"Until you had to go and trip over him. Piss," Gary Frank said. "I suppose you're gonna arrest me."

"Yep," Oren said.

"What about my cat?"

"I like cats," Oren said.

---

The service for Mark Thresher at the First Baptist Church lasted about a half hour, the luncheon after three times that long. Piper estimated there were a hundred and twenty paying their respects and reminiscing over spaghetti and garlic bread.

The graveside affair was attended by ten, invitation only. Four men from the Mason's; an elderly man in a Navy uniform; Chuck Schleevogt, Paul Blackwell, and Sylvia D from the genealogy club; Ezekiel Whitman; and Piper stood at the grave.

The minister quoted from Corinthians. "Behold, I tell you a mystery: We shall not all sleep, but we shall all be changed in a moment, in the twinkling of an eye, at the last trumpet. For the trumpet will sound, and the dead will be raised incorruptible, and we shall be changed."

Piper listened and stared at the headstone. It was about the dash, her first commanding officer had told her after a service for a young man in her unit. It wasn't about the birth and death dates, but the dash between them, what you did with the dash.

Mark Thresher had done a lot, she knew.

"—and this mortal must don immortality," the minister continued. "Then this shall be brought to pass the saying that is written: 'Death is swallowed up in victory.' Until we meet again Mark Henry Thresher."

"Mark the Shark," Piper softly corrected.

# ACKNOWLEDGMENTS

Threads in this book were embroidered by people who either entered contests in my newsletters or reviewed technical sections to make sure I "got it right." I thank them for their help and inspiration: Carol Clarkson, nurse extraordinaire, for ensuring a gunshot victim was accurately treated; Derek White for sharing his Internet savvy; Vicki Steger for her eagle eyes; Mikael Arvola, Jim Butler, and Stephen Gabriel for building a computer platform in a character's basement; Donald J. Bingle for his knowledge on estates; Jerry Humphrey for the use of his perfect airport; and Laura Craig, Miya Kressin, Margaret Cutter, and Joe Cook for creating a wealth of romance titles that I nested with a character Jennifer Brozek named.

Spencer County, Indiana

It's a real place, about as far south in Indiana as you can go. The towns, roads, and some of the businesses I reference in this novel exist. There really is a Santa Claus—it is nestled between the Ohio River and Interstate 64; on my latest visit to the Christmas store there I picked up some walnut fudge and a Boston terrier ornament that I

had personalized. Rockport is about twenty miles away. I've fictional-
ized the county, taking considerable liberties. I used to live in Indiana
—Evansville, during my newspaper reporter days. Spencer County
isn't far from there. The place is a good home for Piper Blackwell and
company.

# AFTERWORD

I write ... a lot. Currently mysteries.

And I write with dogs wrapped around my feet. I get to wear sandals or bedroom slippers to work, and old, comfortable clothes.

When the weather is fine I get to write on my back porch. I love summer.

I started getting published when I was twelve, studied journalism at Northern Illinois University, and then went to work as a news reporter...eventually for Scripps Howard, where I managed their Western Kentucky Bureau. Getting itchy feet, I moved to Wisconsin and went to work for TSR, Inc., the then-producers of the Dungeons & Dragons game. I wrote Dragonlance novels for several years. I've been on the *USA Today* bestseller list, wrote a book about spousal homicide with F. Lee Bailey, picked up three Silver Falchion literary awards, and won a chili cook-off.

I've written thirty-eight novels, most of them fantasy and science fiction, more short stories than I care to count, and I've edited a lot of magazines and anthologies.

But now it's all about mysteries...thrillers, suspense, and uncozy-cozies. I had to change genres because my feet were itching again and I needed to do something different with my writing life.

I am a geek, a gamer, and a glass-fuser. I love dogs and museums and books, and I write about those things in my monthly newsletter.

Readers can sign up for the newsletter on my website: jeanrabe.-com. I have an active Facebook page, where I probably post too many pictures of my dogs.

www.ingramcontent.com/pod-product-compliance
Lightning Source LLC
Chambersburg PA
CBHW022137170626
46807CB00005B/1978